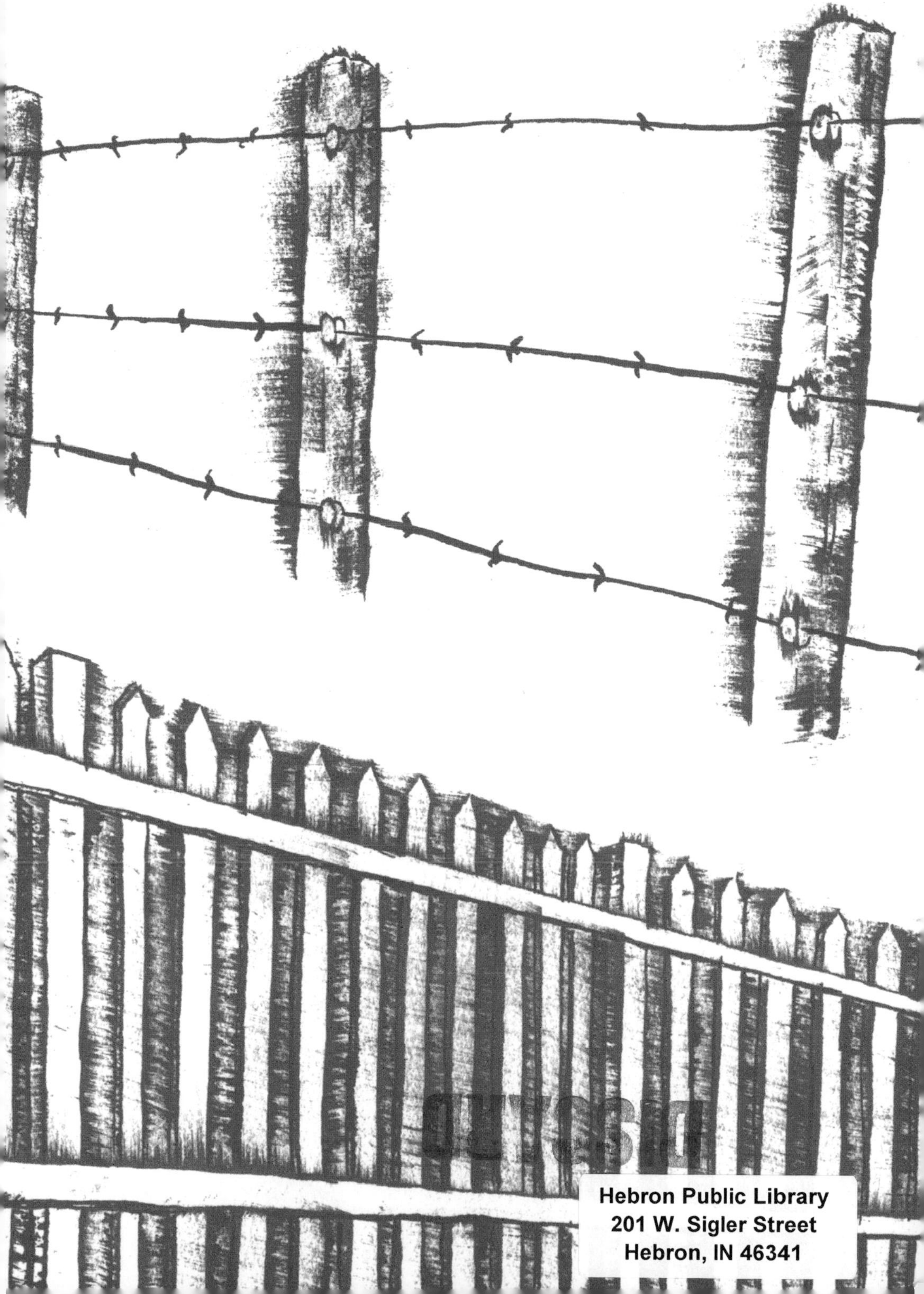

For the artists of the camps

Thanks to Melanie Comer, Scott Cunningham,
Calvin Pyle, and Roger Shimomura

The author wishes to acknowledge the photographers and artists
whose work he drew upon for inspiration:

Ansel Adams
Clem Albers
H. Ezaki
Himeko Fukuhara
William Shiro Hoshiyama
Mits Kaida
Masao Kondo
Dorothea Lange
Arao Matsuhiro
Captain Matsushita
Mineo Matoba
Kazuko Matsumoto

Suiko "Charles" Mikami
Toyo Miyatake
Michitaro "Henry" Mochizuki
Pat Morihata
Takizo Obata
Miné Okubo
Akira Oye
Seitaro Sasaki
Sadayuki Uno
Kamechi Yamaichi
Jack Yoshizuka

and the uncredited photographers
of the War Relocation Authority

Henry Holt and Company, LLC
Publishers since 1866
175 Fifth Avenue
New York, New York 10010
macteenbooks.com

Library of Congress Control Number: 2011924430

ISBN 978-0-8050-8286-9

First Edition—2012 / Designed by Kevin C. Pyle
Printed in China

1 3 5 7 9 10 8 6 4 2

Take What You Can Carry

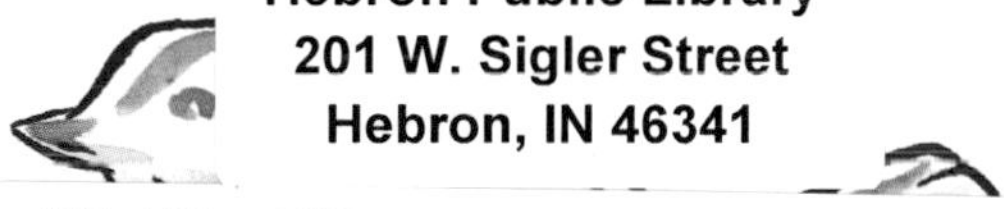

Kevin C. Pyle

Henry Holt and Company
New York

To Mercy, Pity, Peace, and Love
All pray in their distress;
And to these virtues of delight
Return their thankfulness.

—William Blake

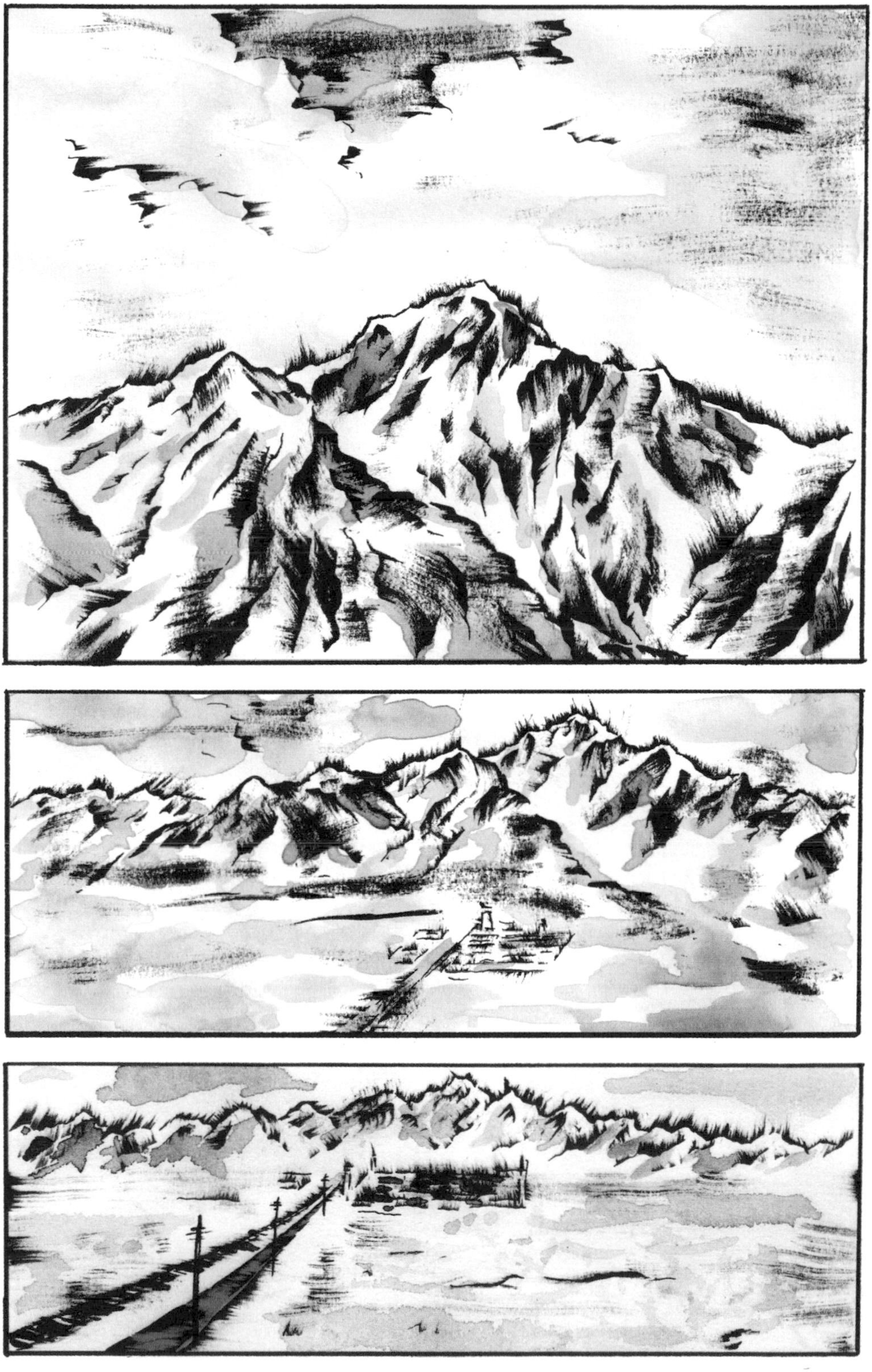

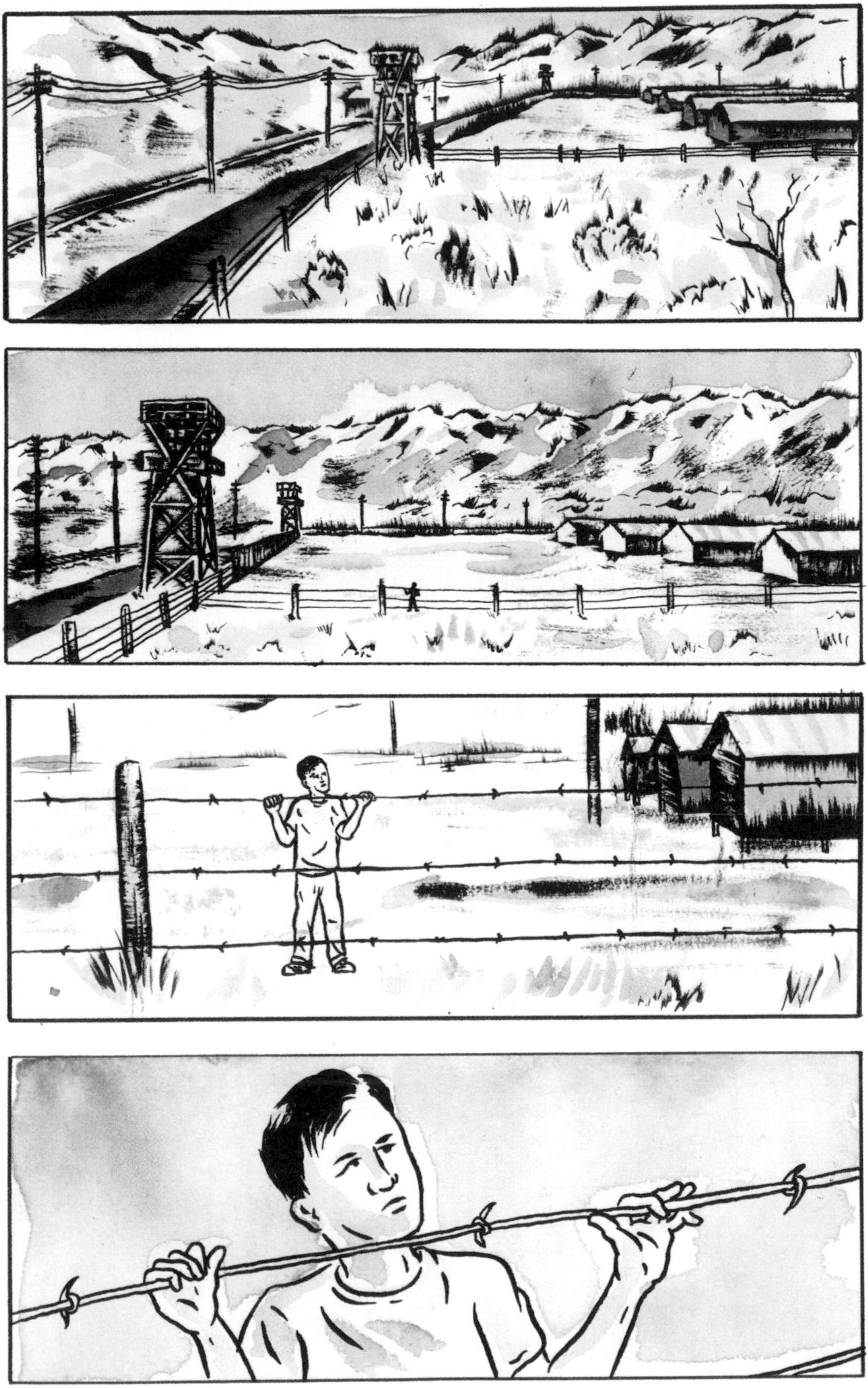

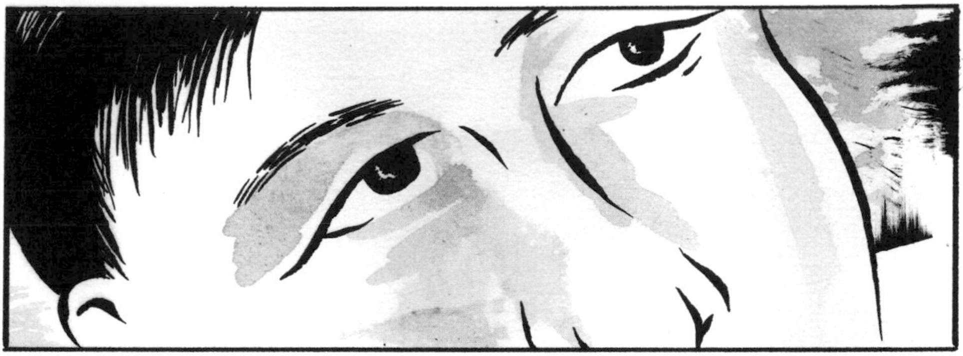
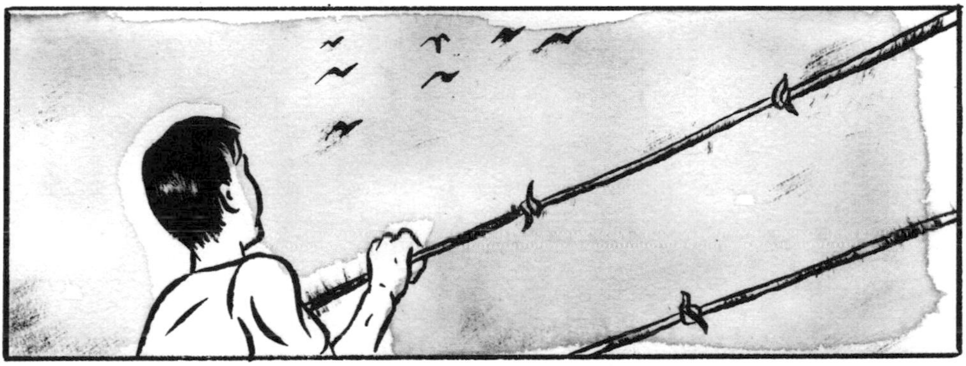
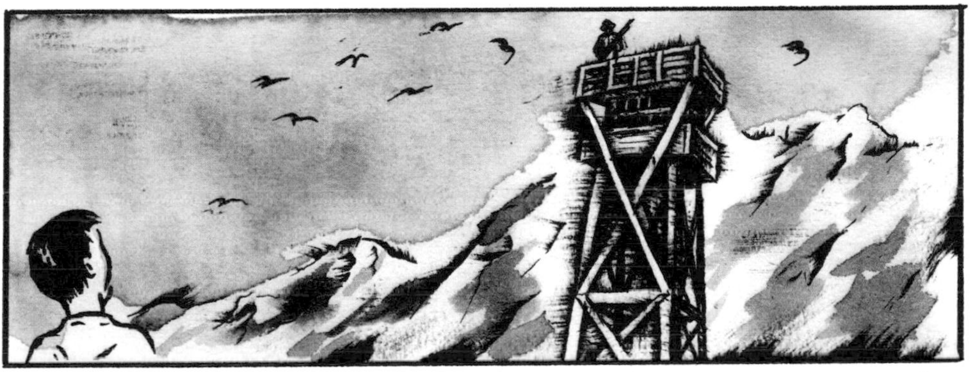
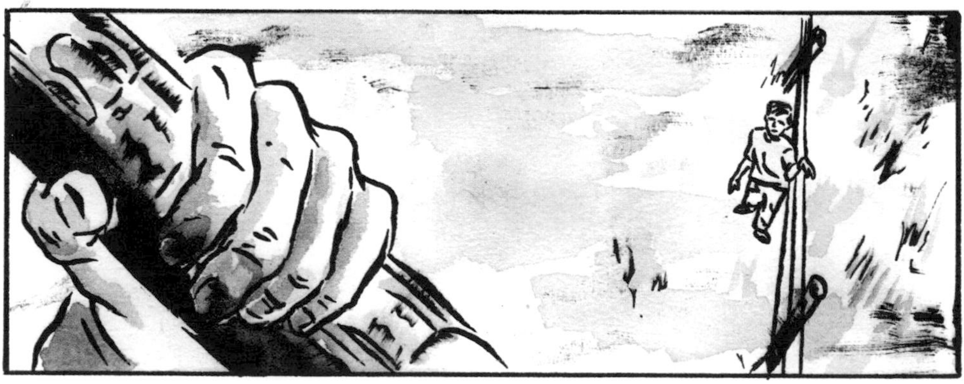

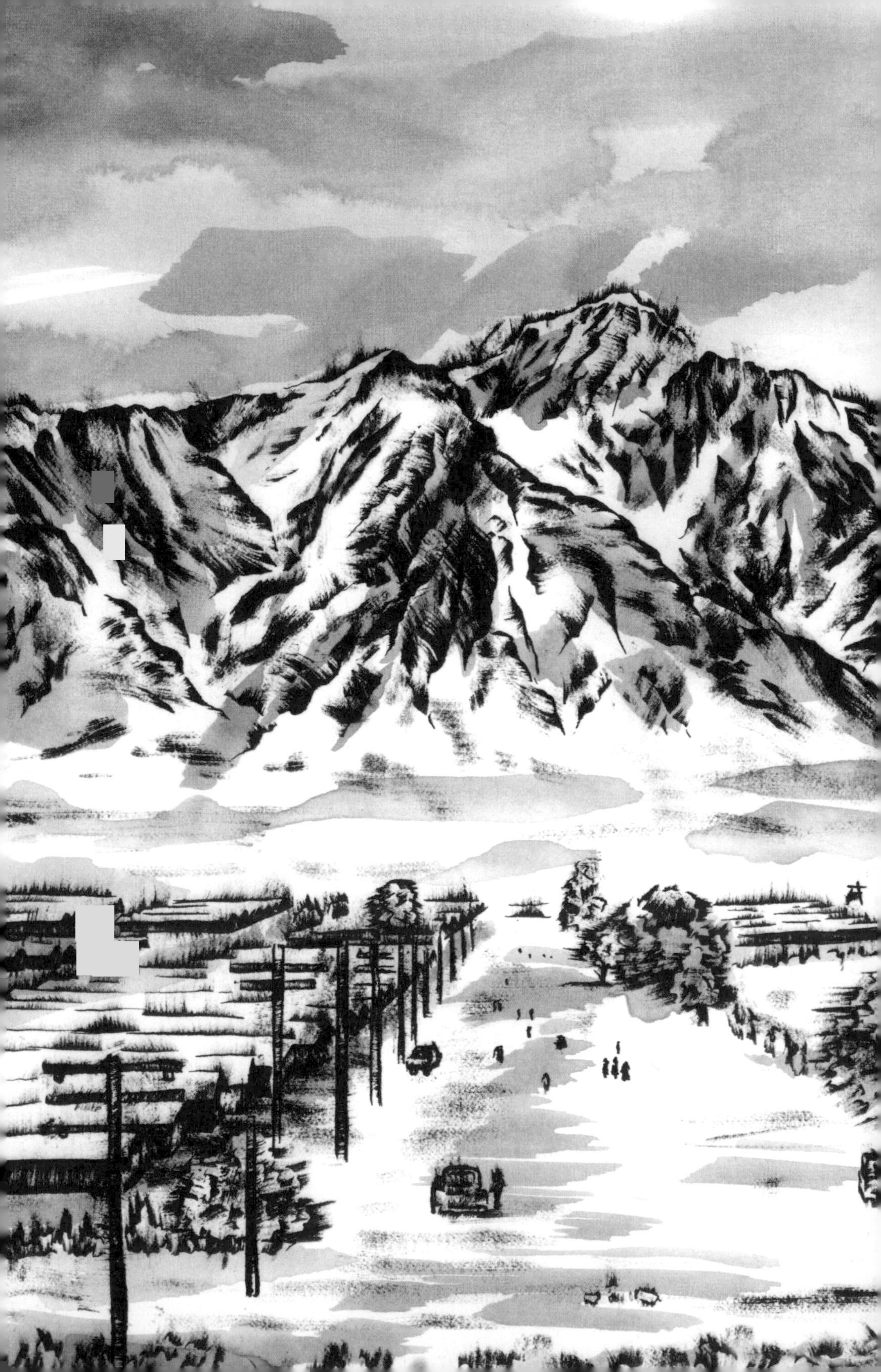

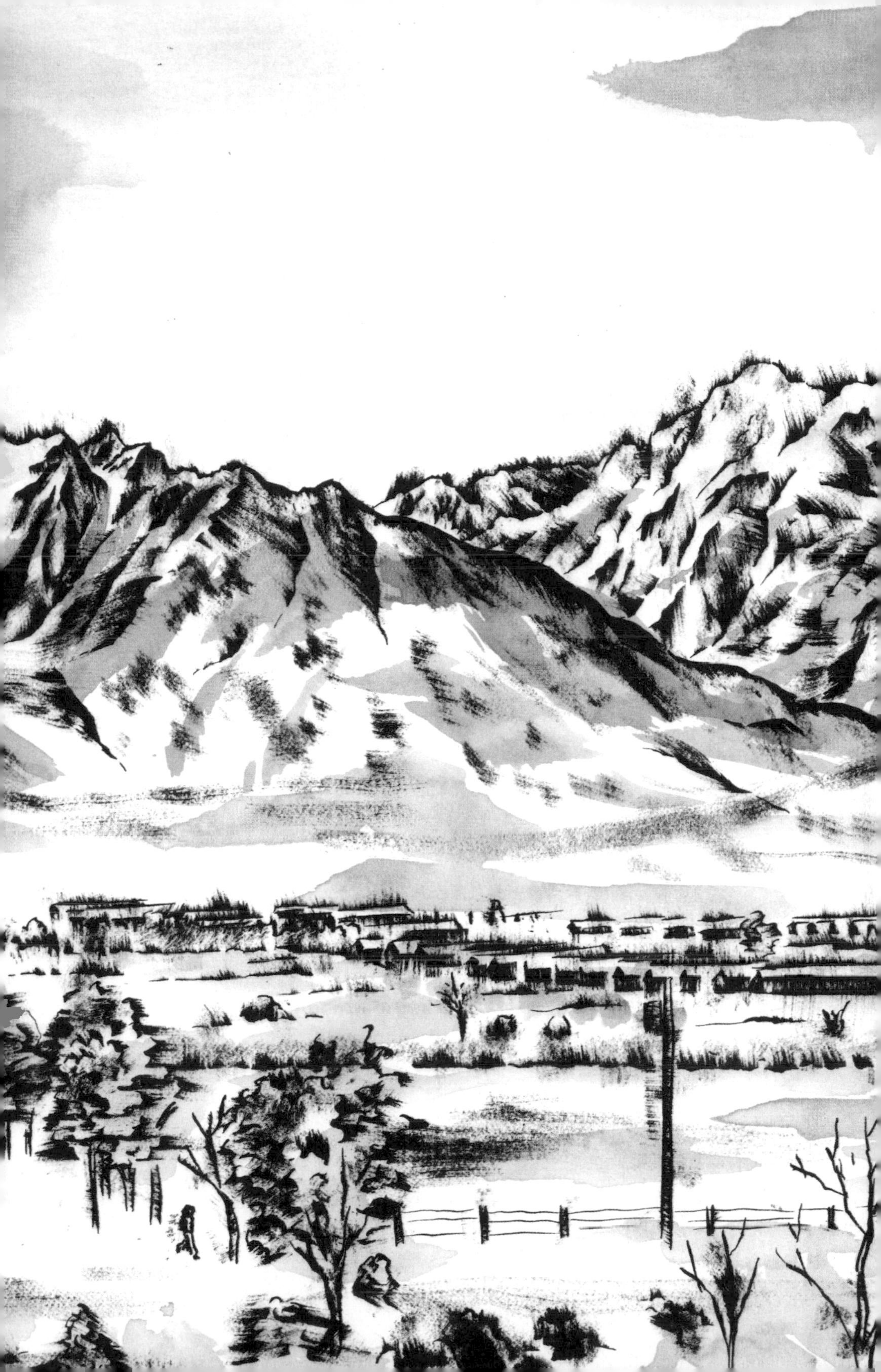

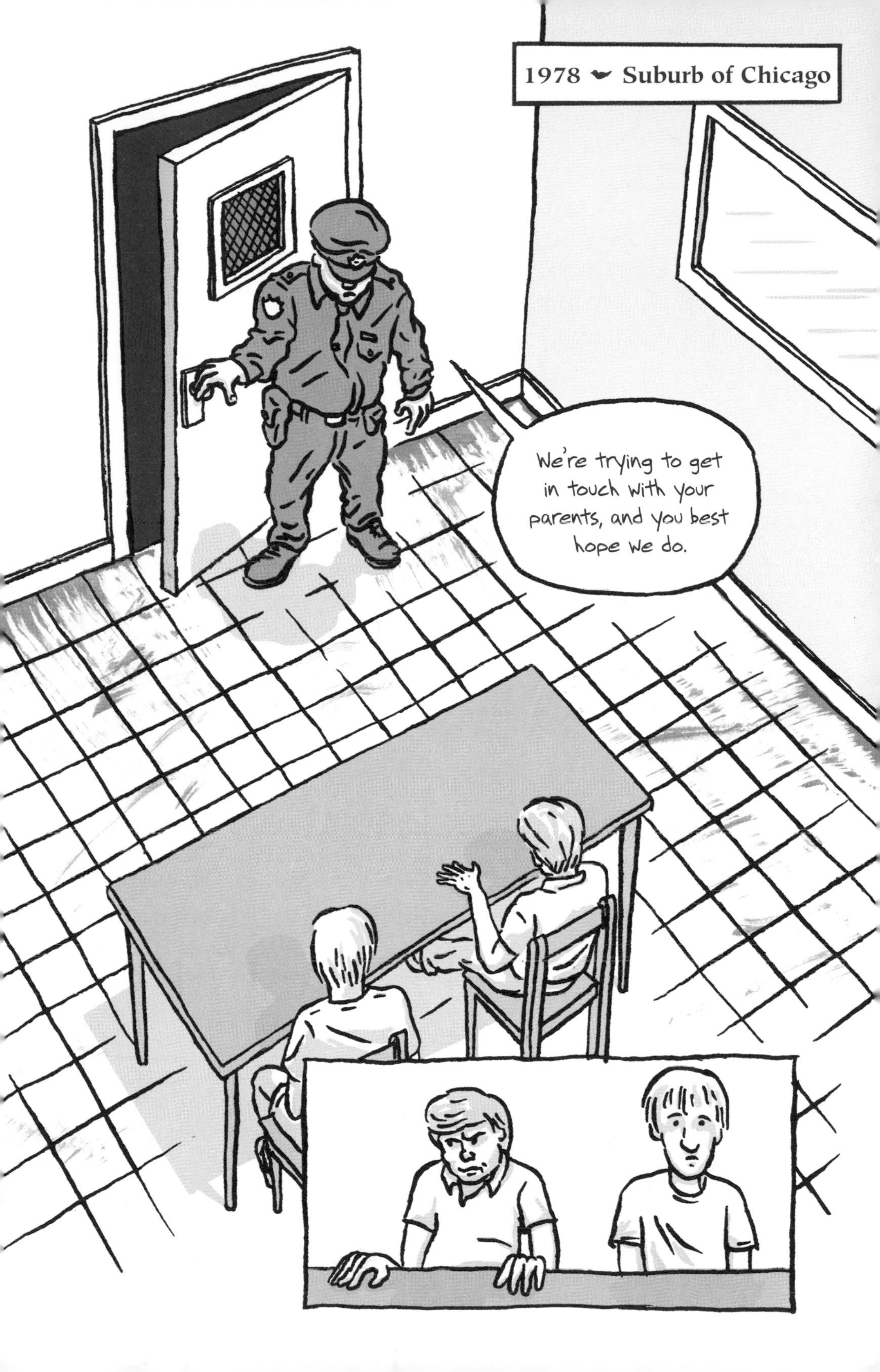
1978 Suburb of Chicago
We're trying to get in touch with your parents, and you best hope we do.

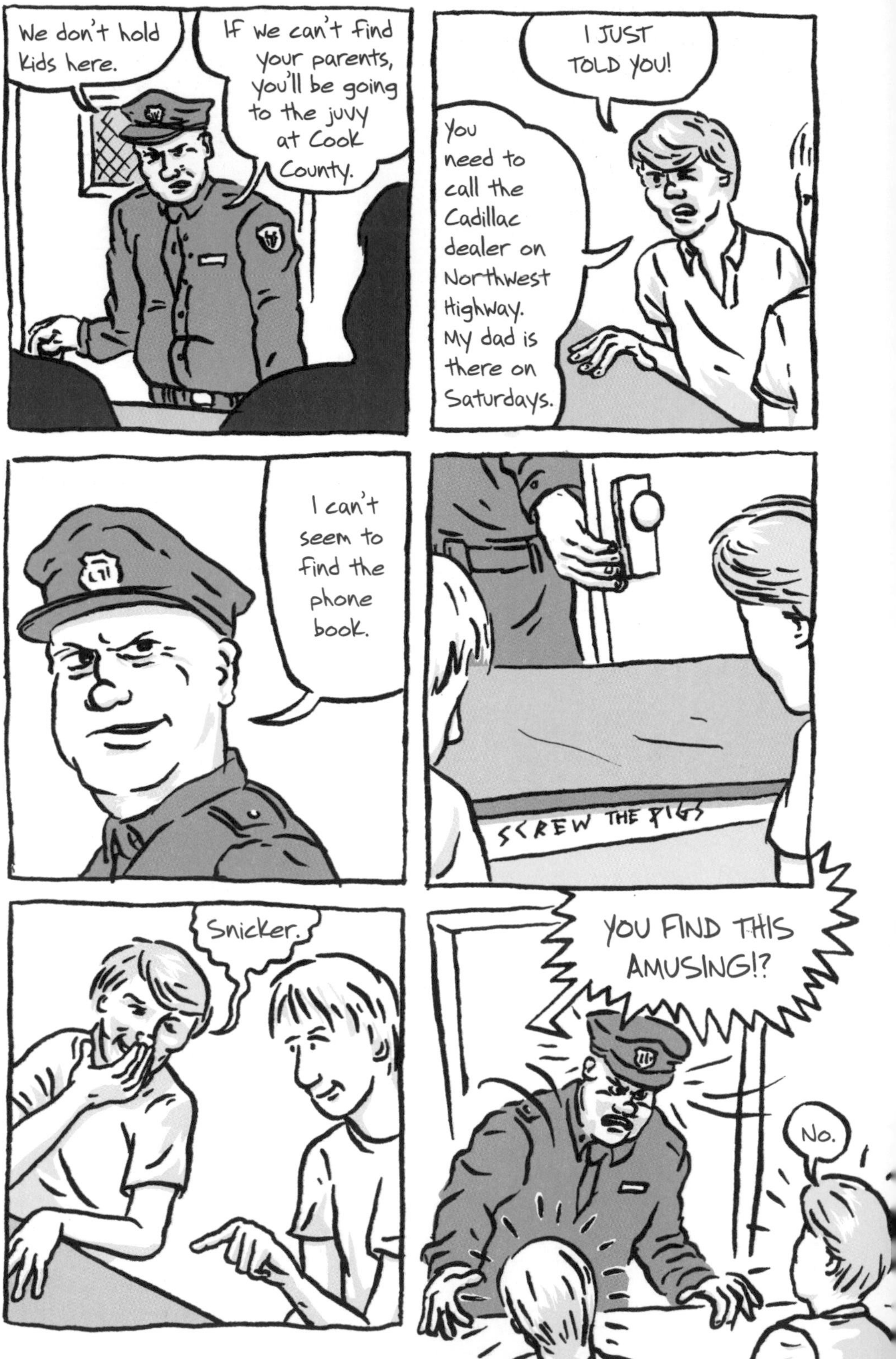
We don't hold kids here.
If we can't find your parents, you'll be going to the juvy at Cook County.
I JUST TOLD YOU!
You need to call the Cadillac dealer on Northwest Highway. My dad is there on Saturdays.
I can't seem to find the phone book.
SCREW THE PIGS
Snicker.
YOU FIND THIS AMUSING!?
No.

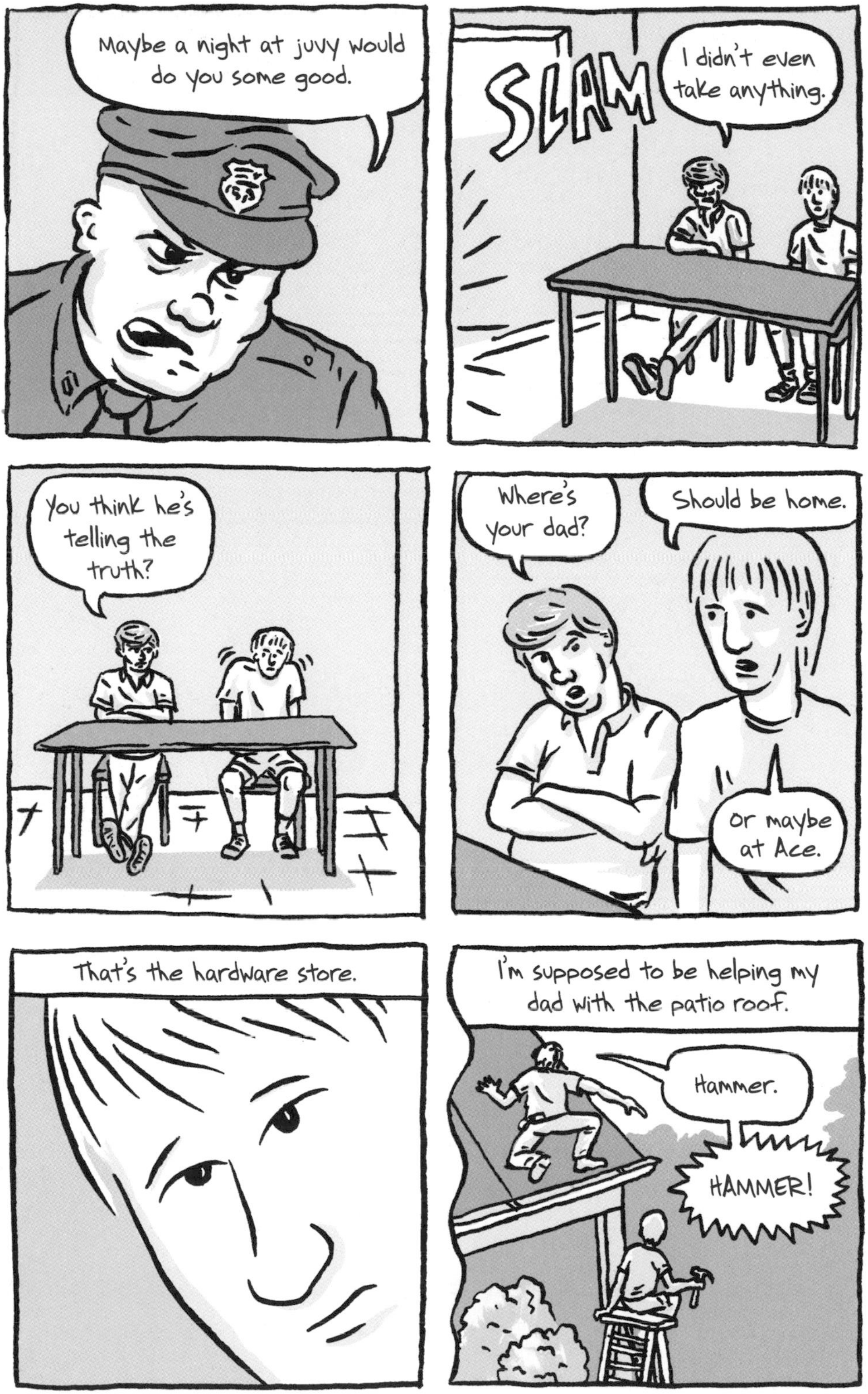
Maybe a night at juvy would do you some good.
SLAM
I didn't even take anything.
You think he's telling the truth?
Where's your dad?
Should be home.
Or maybe at Ace.
That's the hardware store.
I'm supposed to be helping my dad with the patio roof.
Hammer.
HAMMER!

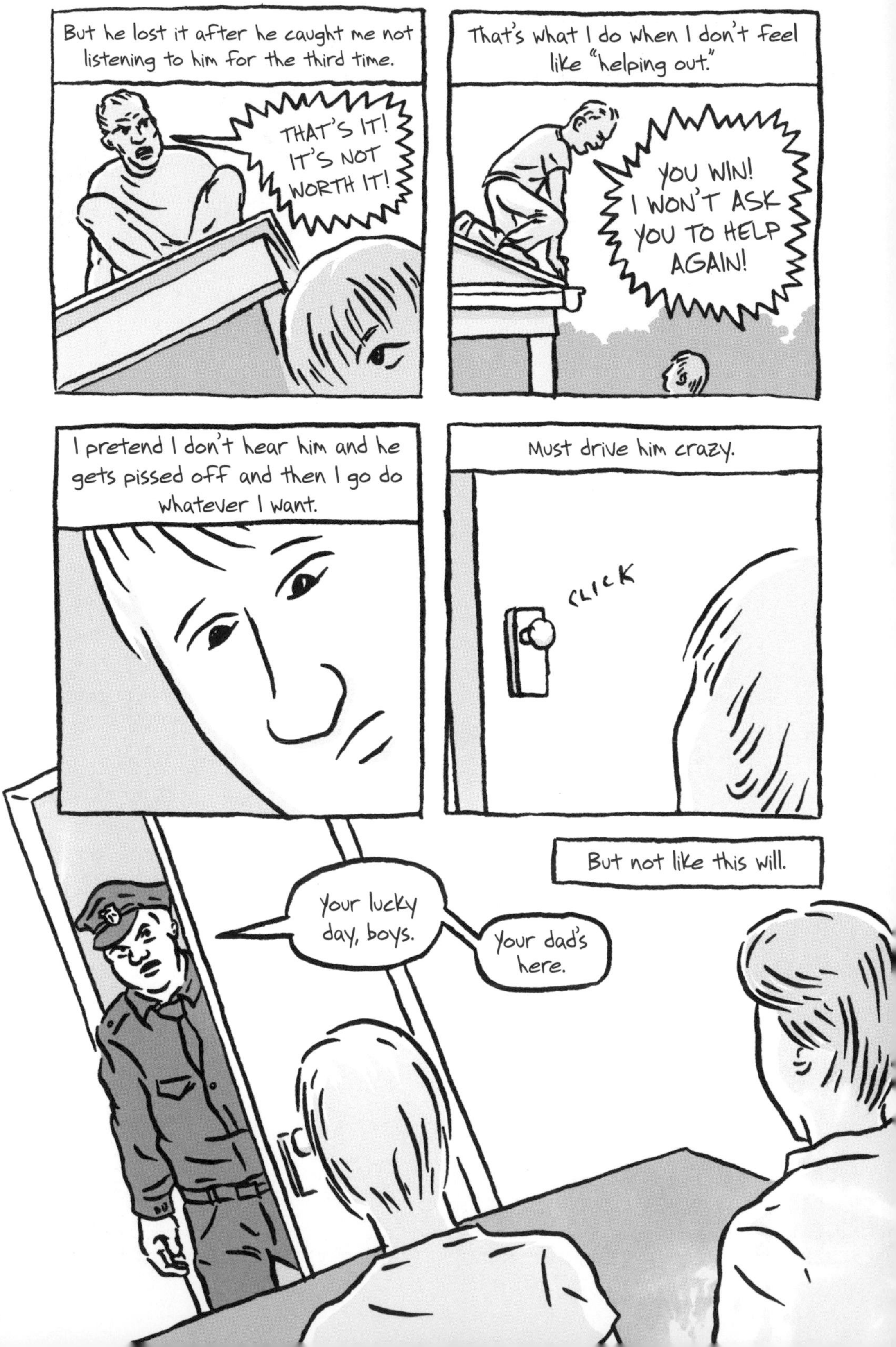

But he lost it after he caught me not listening to him for the third time.
THAT'S IT! IT'S NOT WORTH IT!
That's what I do when I don't feel like "helping out."
YOU WIN! I WON'T ASK YOU TO HELP AGAIN!
I pretend I don't hear him and he gets pissed off and then I go do whatever I want.
Must drive him crazy.
CLICK
But not like this will.
Your lucky day, boys.
Your dad's here.

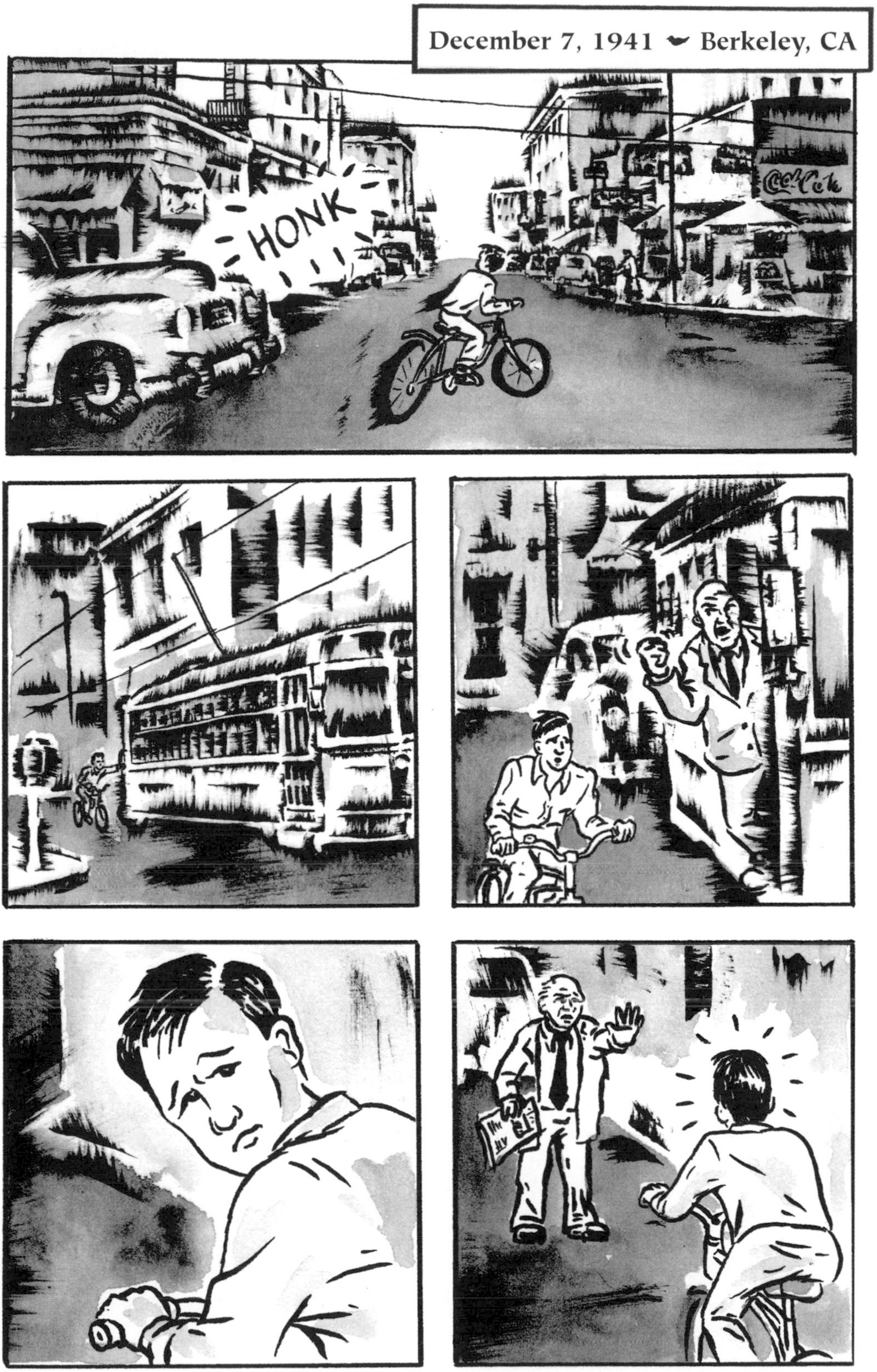
December 7, 1941 ❧ Berkeley, CA
HONK

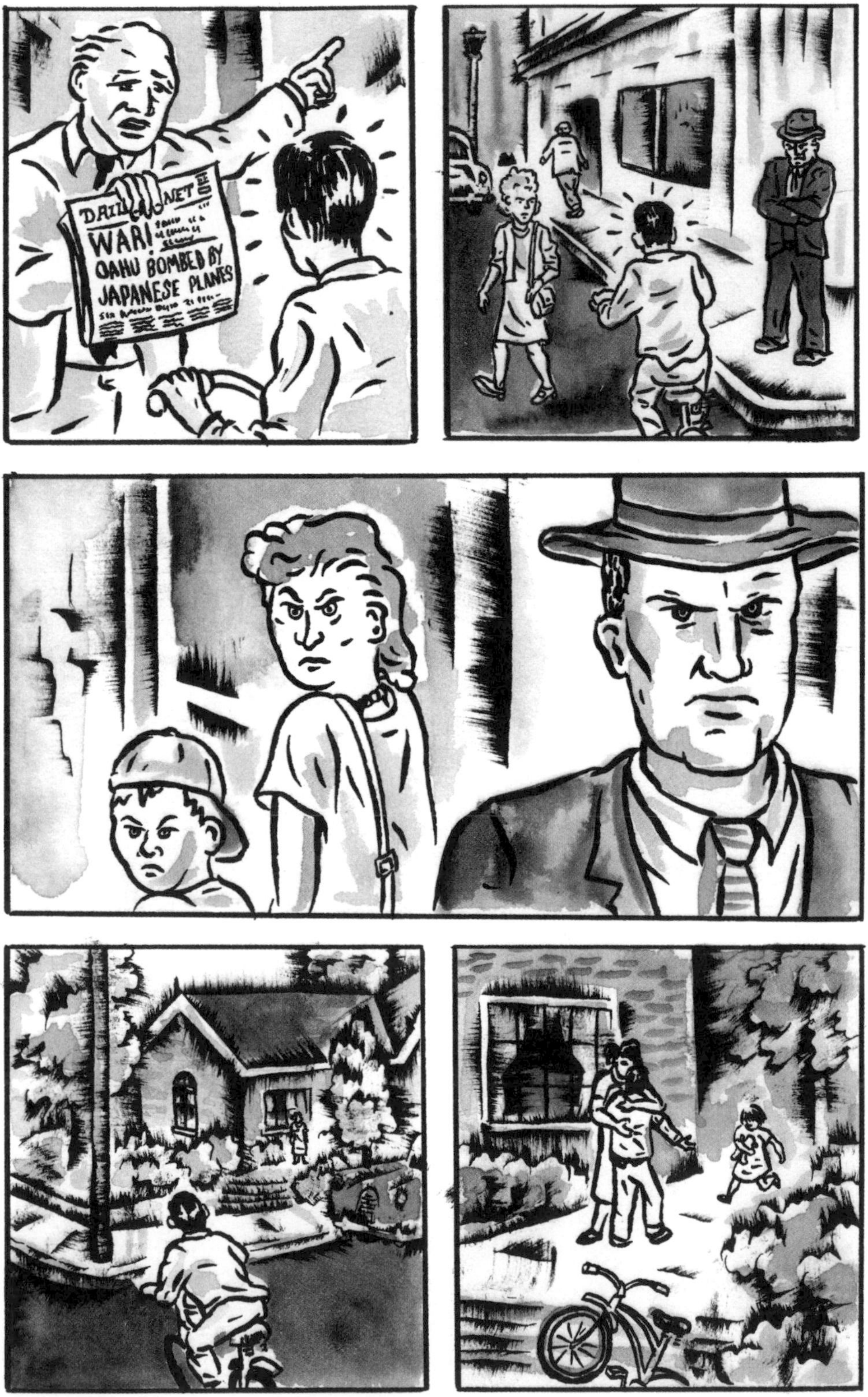
WAR!
OAHU BOMBED BY JAPANESE PLANES

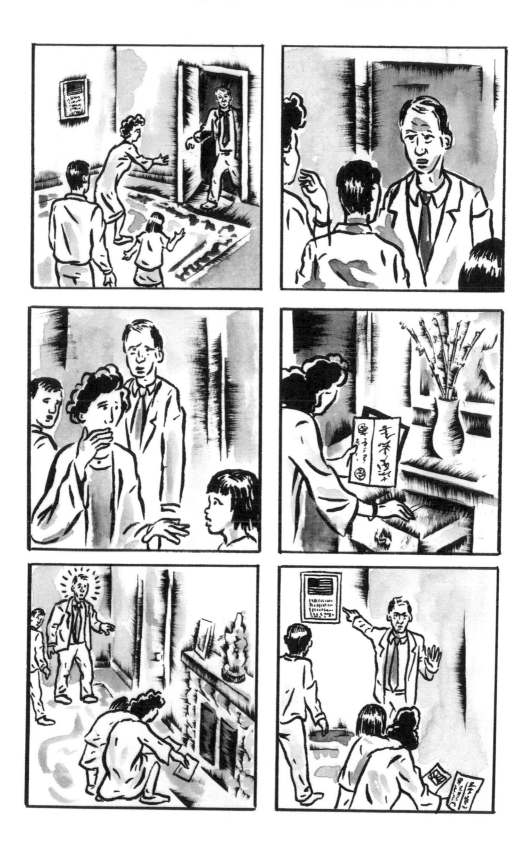

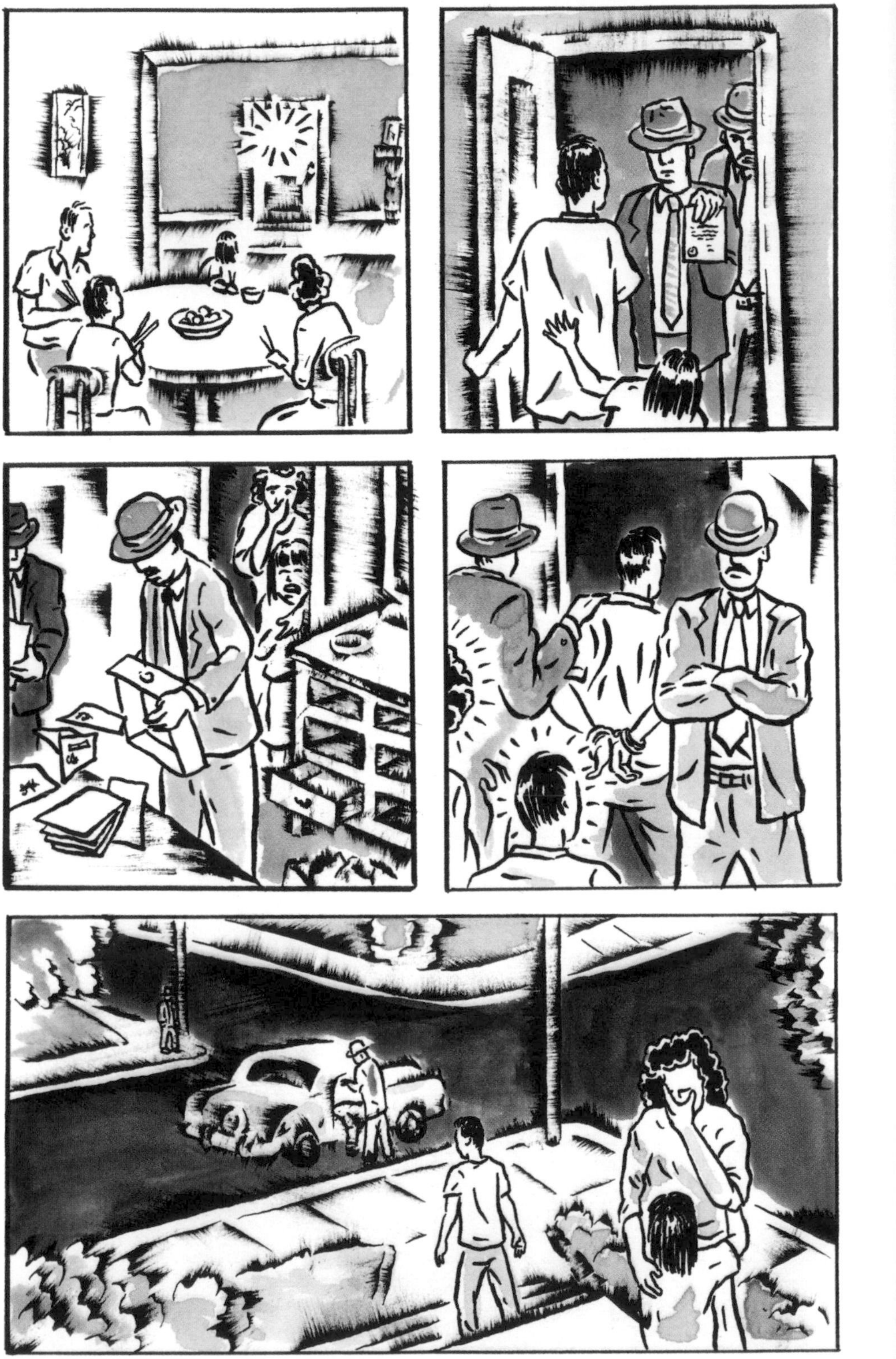

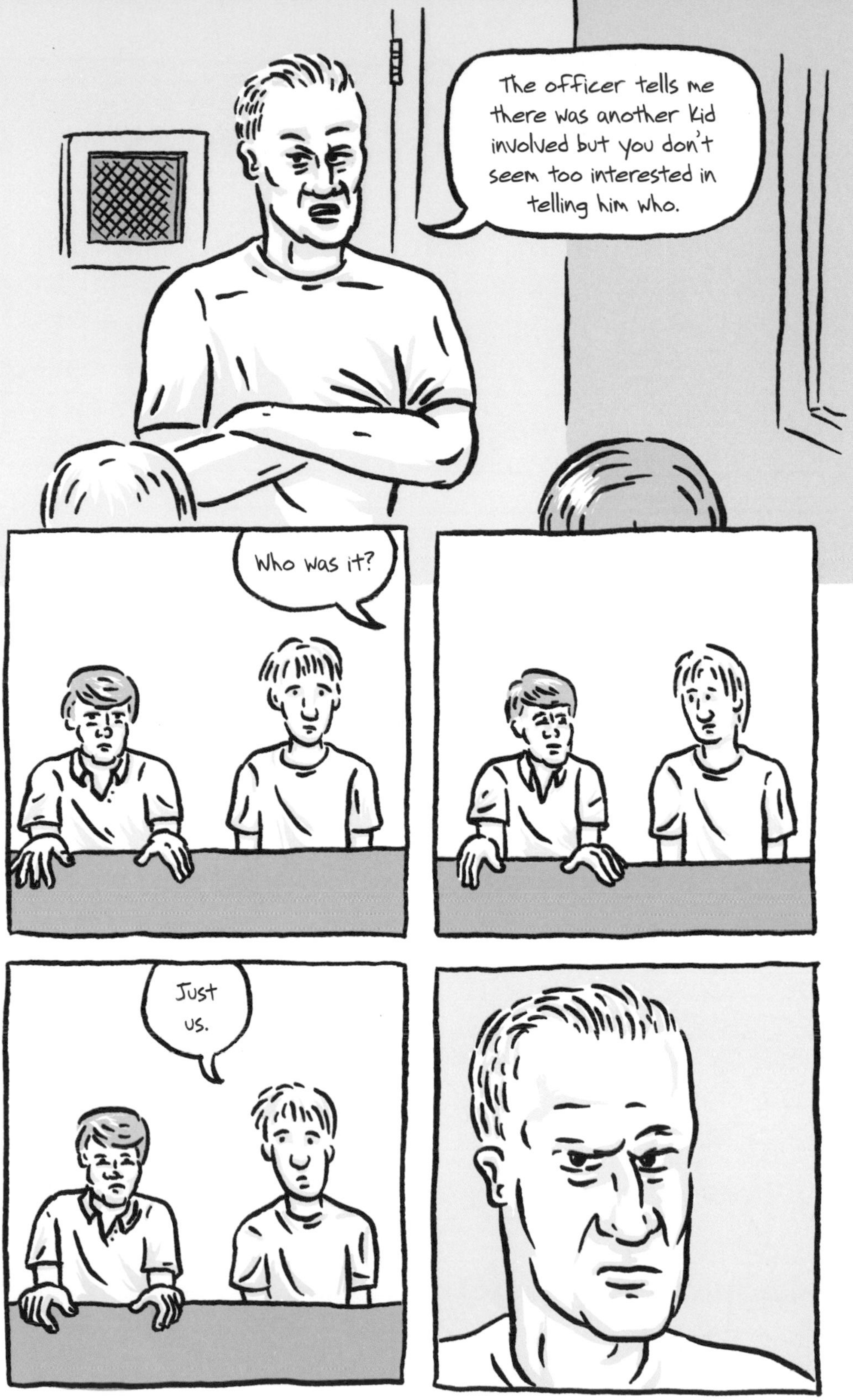
The officer tells me there was another kid involved but you don't seem too interested in telling him who.
Who was it?
Just us.

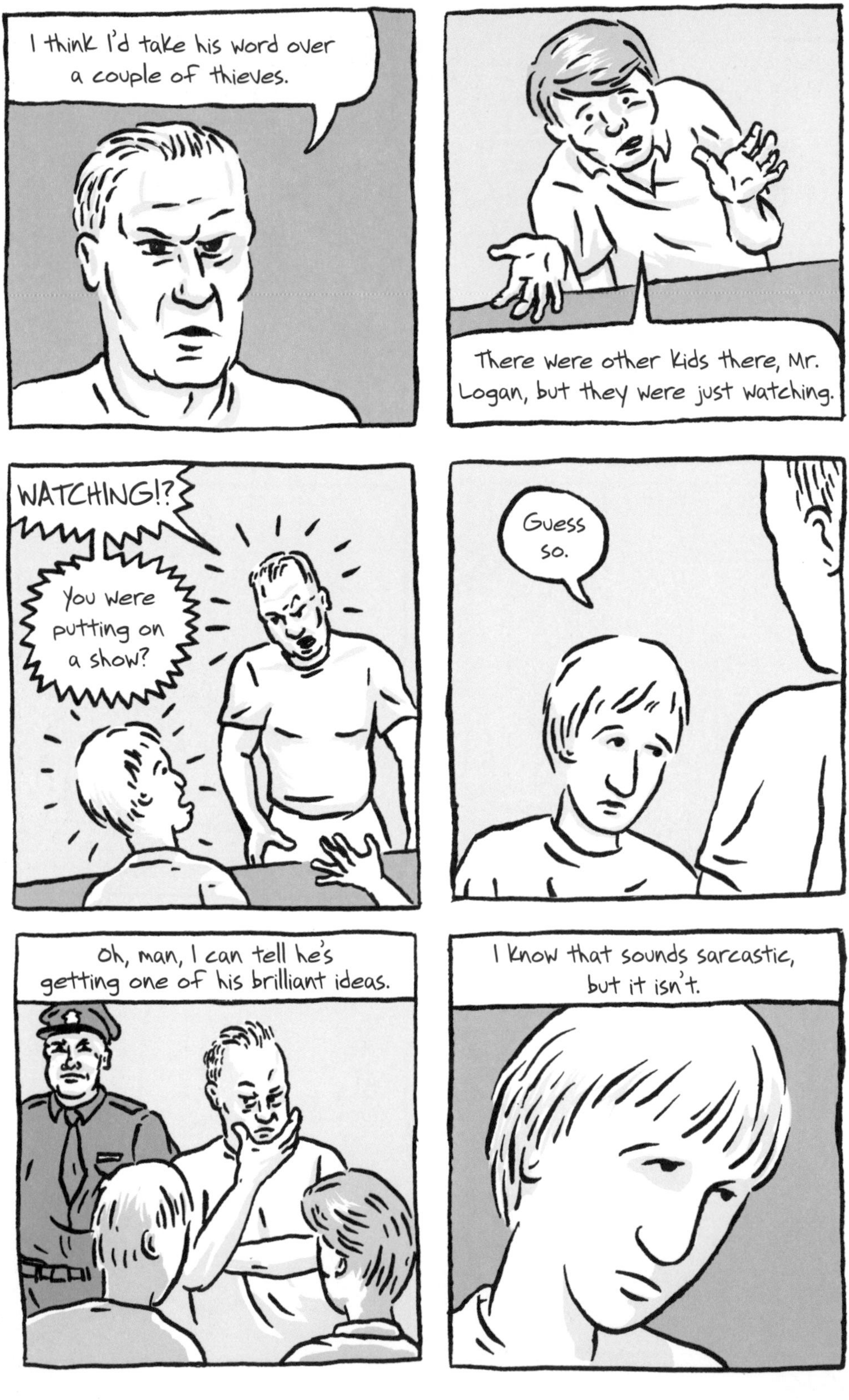
I think I'd take his word over a couple of thieves.
There were other kids there, Mr. Logan, but they were just watching.
WATCHING!?
You were putting on a show?
Guess so.
Oh, man, I can tell he's getting one of his brilliant ideas.
I know that sounds sarcastic, but it isn't.

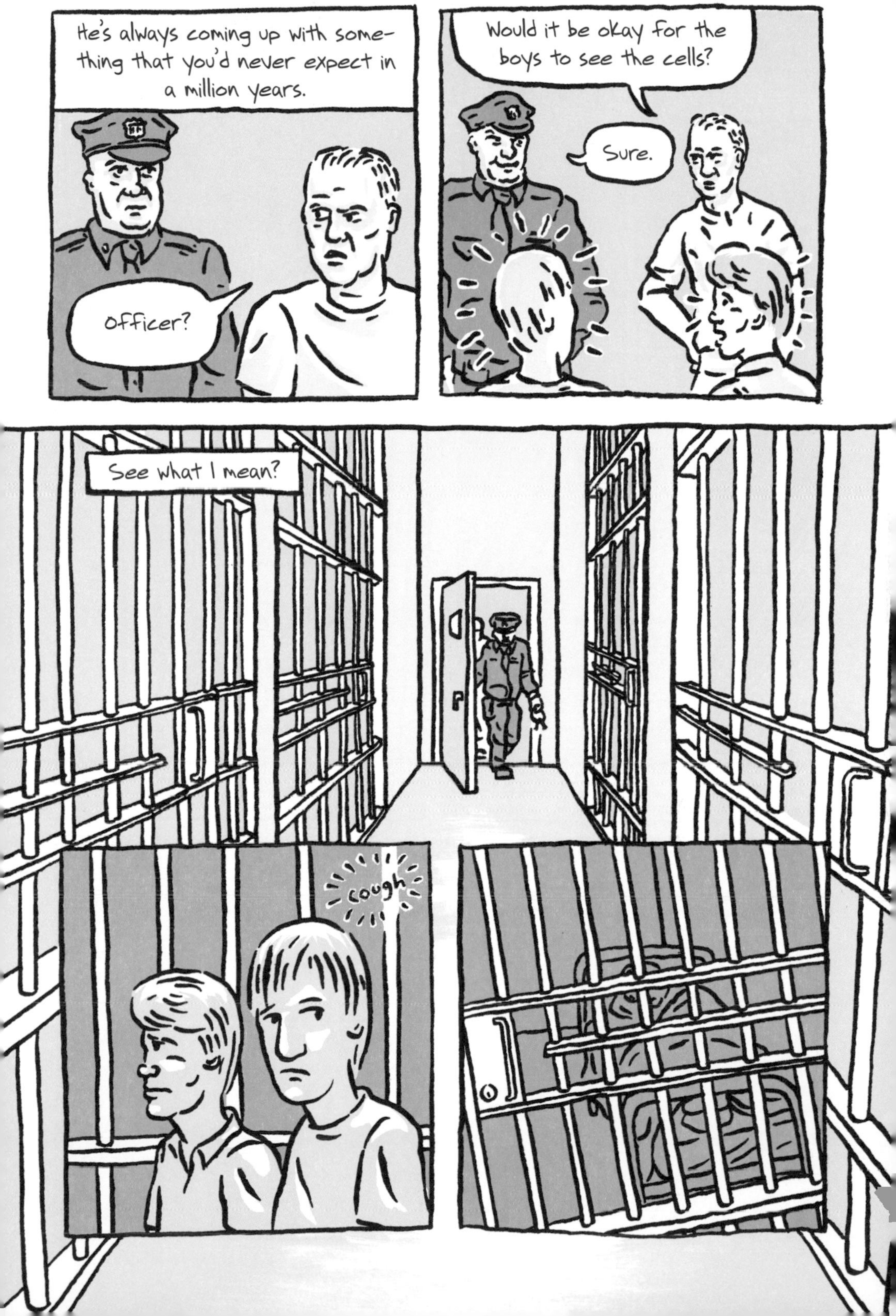
He's always coming up with something that you'd never expect in a million years.
Officer?
Would it be okay for the boys to see the cells?
Sure.
See what I mean?
cough

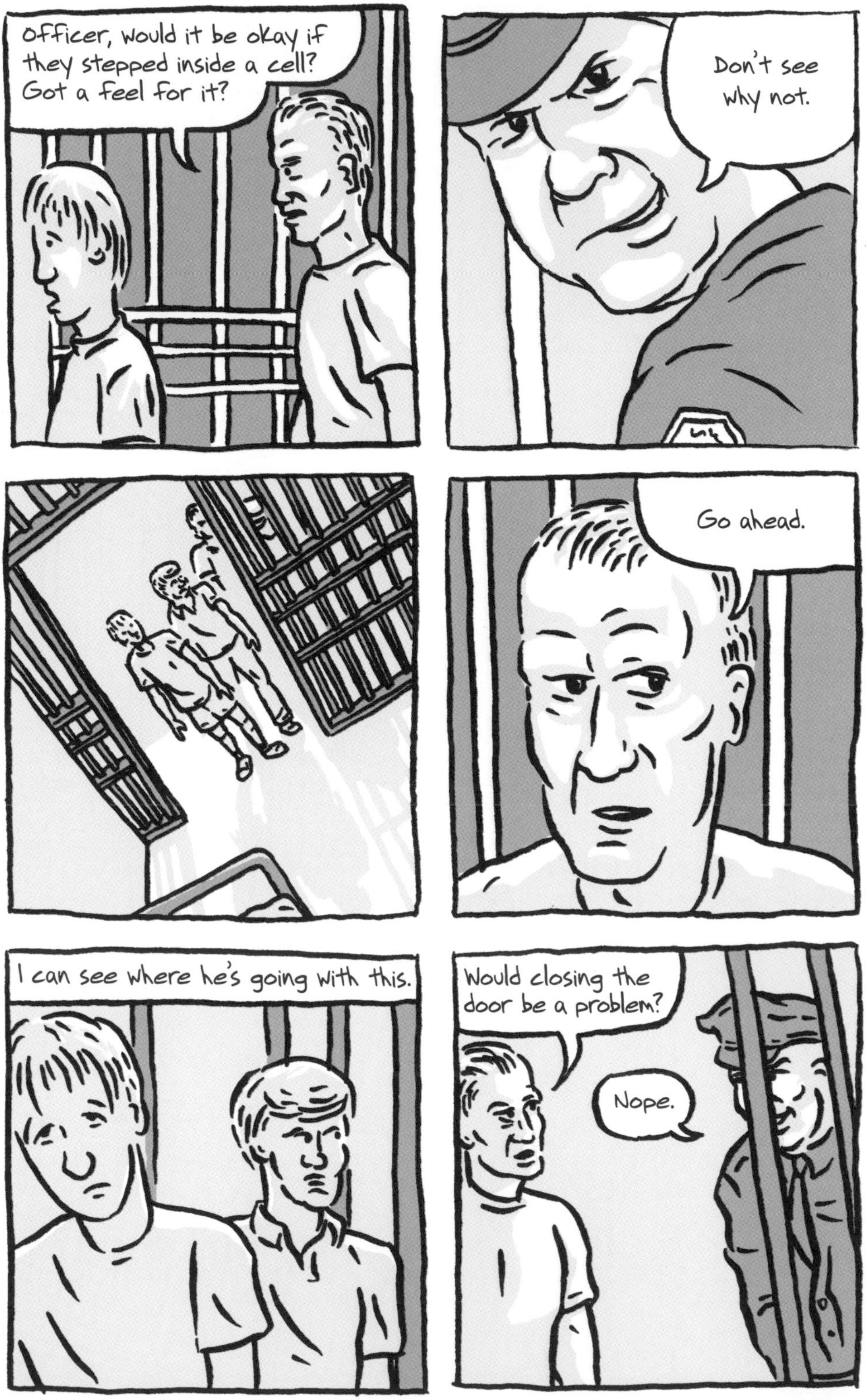
Officer, would it be okay if they stepped inside a cell? Got a feel for it?
Don't see why not.
Go ahead.
I can see where he's going with this.
Would closing the door be a problem?
Nope.

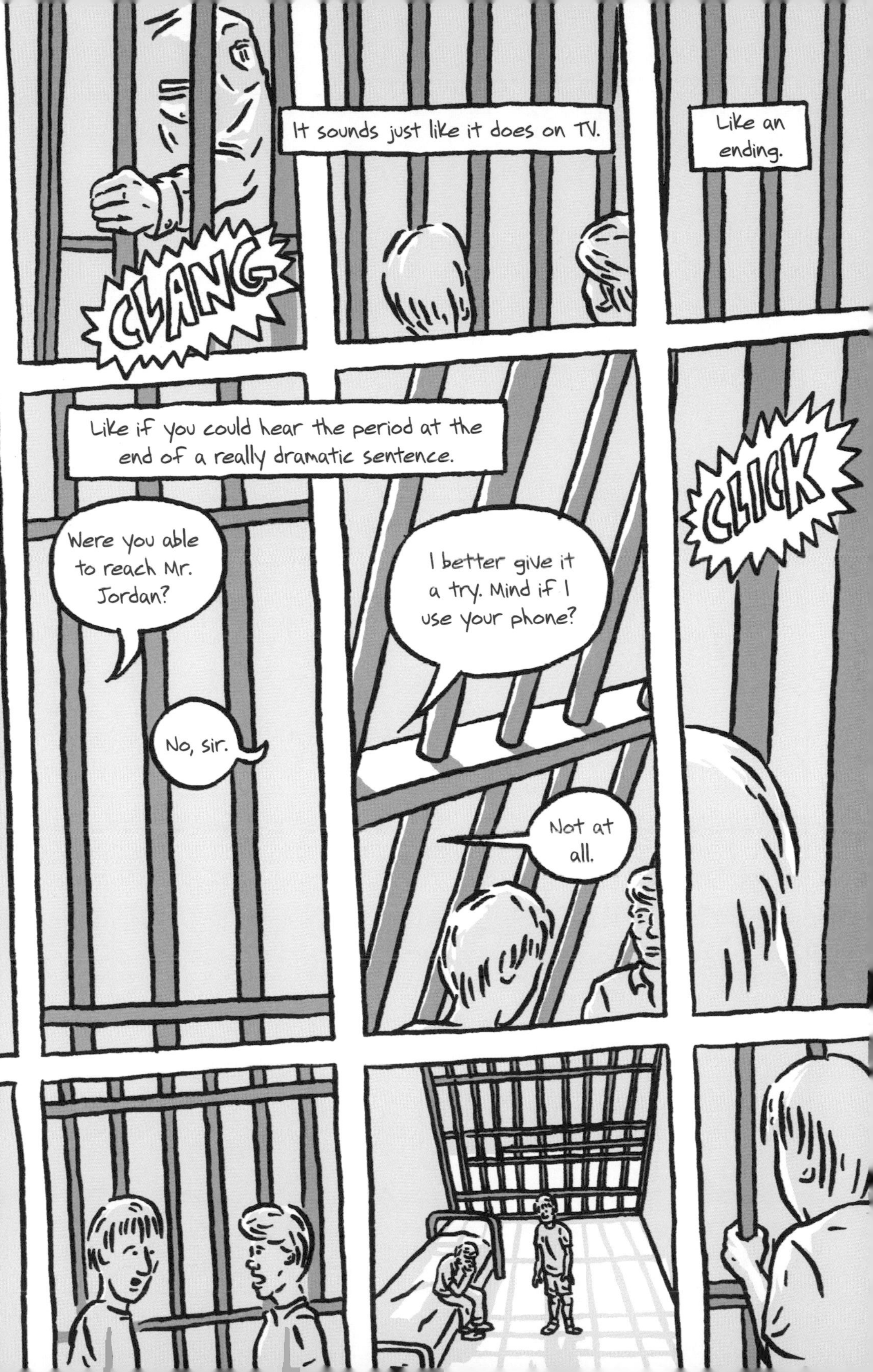
CLANG
It sounds just like it does on TV.
Like an ending.
Like if you could hear the period at the end of a really dramatic sentence.
Were you able to reach Mr. Jordan?
No, sir.
I better give it a try. Mind if I use your phone?
Not at all.
CLICK

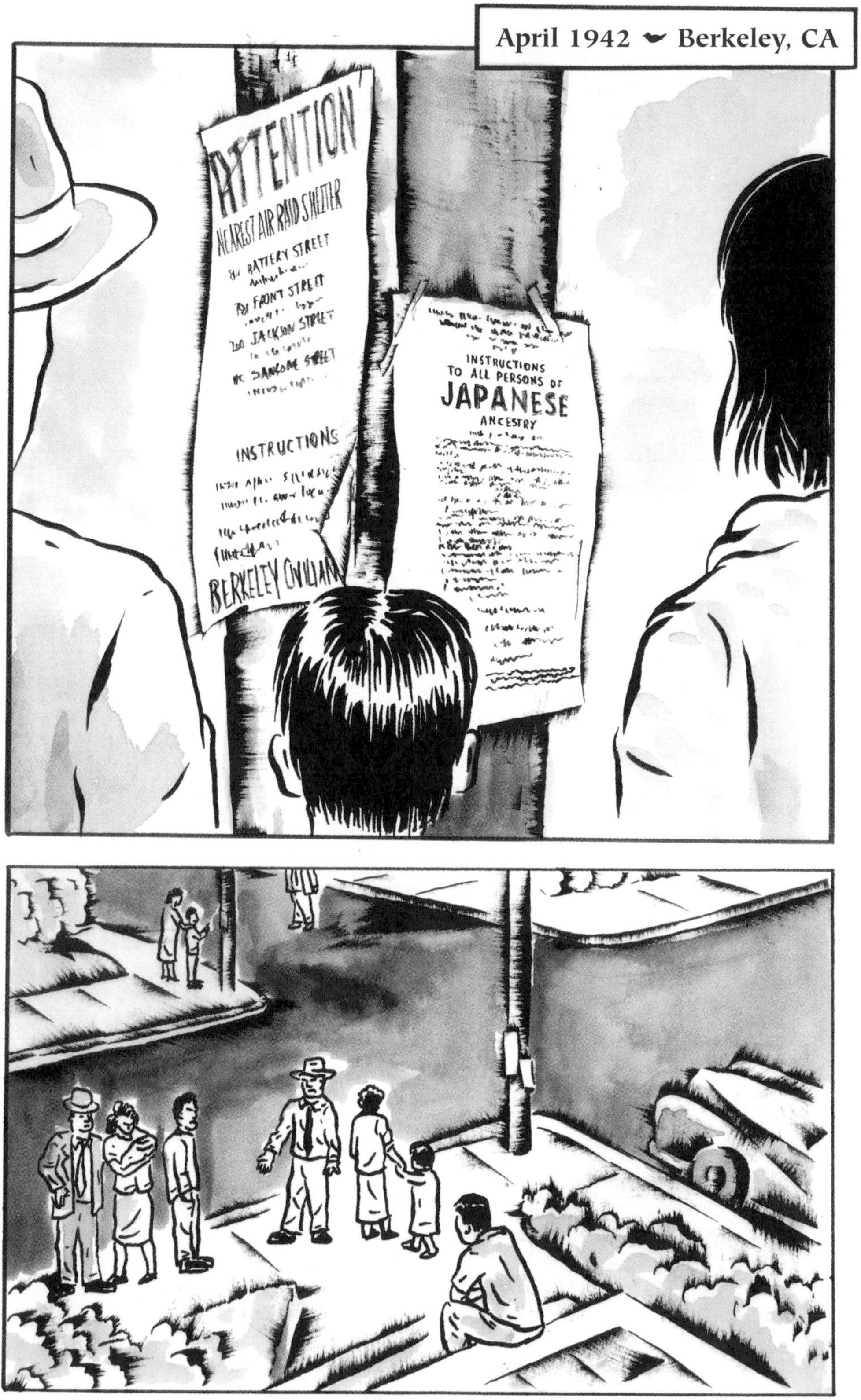
April 1942 ❧ Berkeley, CA
ATTENTION
NEAREST AIR RAID SHELTER
BATTERY STREET
FRONT STREET
JACKSON STREET
SANSOME STREET
INSTRUCTIONS
BERKELEY CIVILIAN
INSTRUCTIONS TO ALL PERSONS OF JAPANESE ANCESTRY

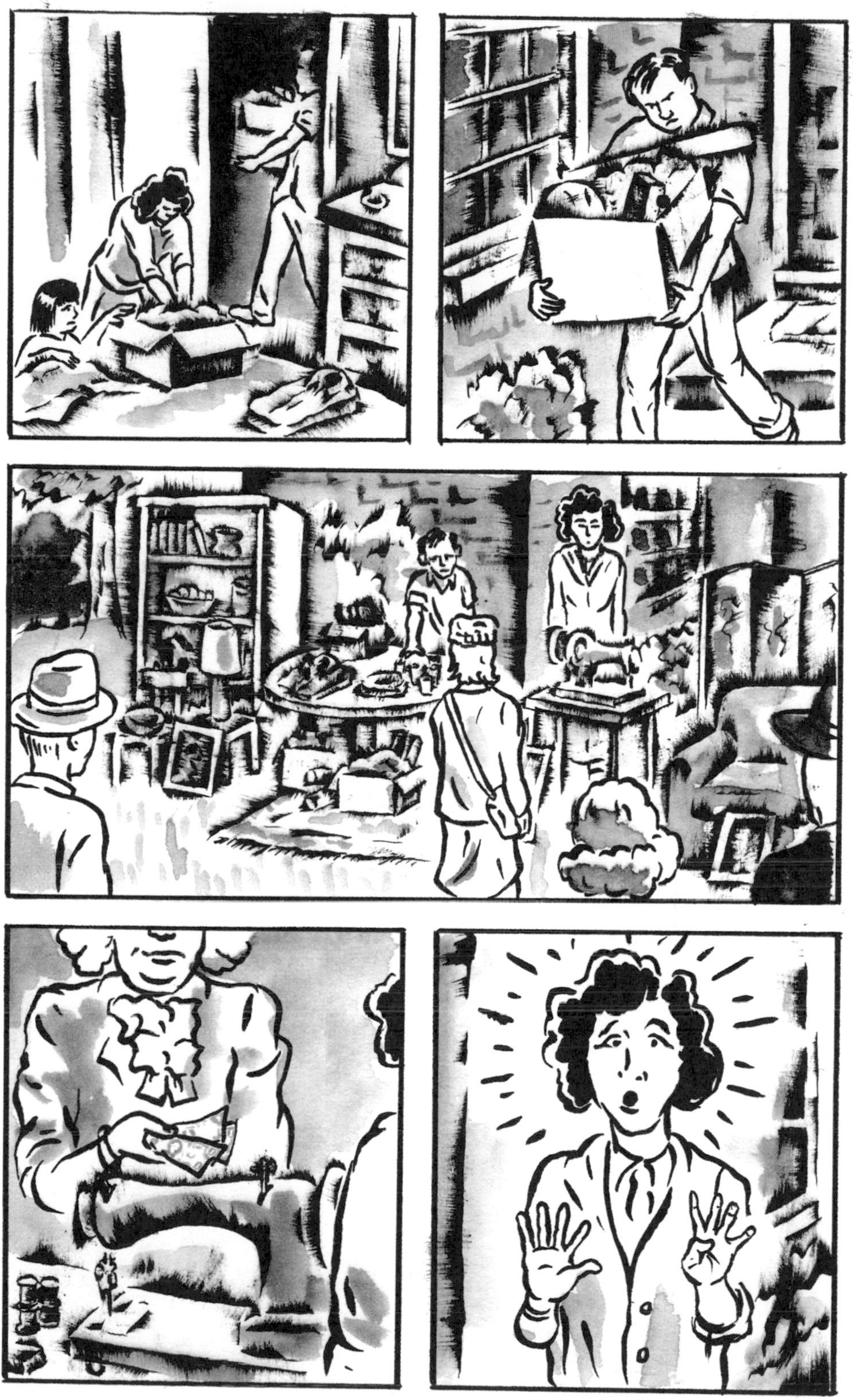

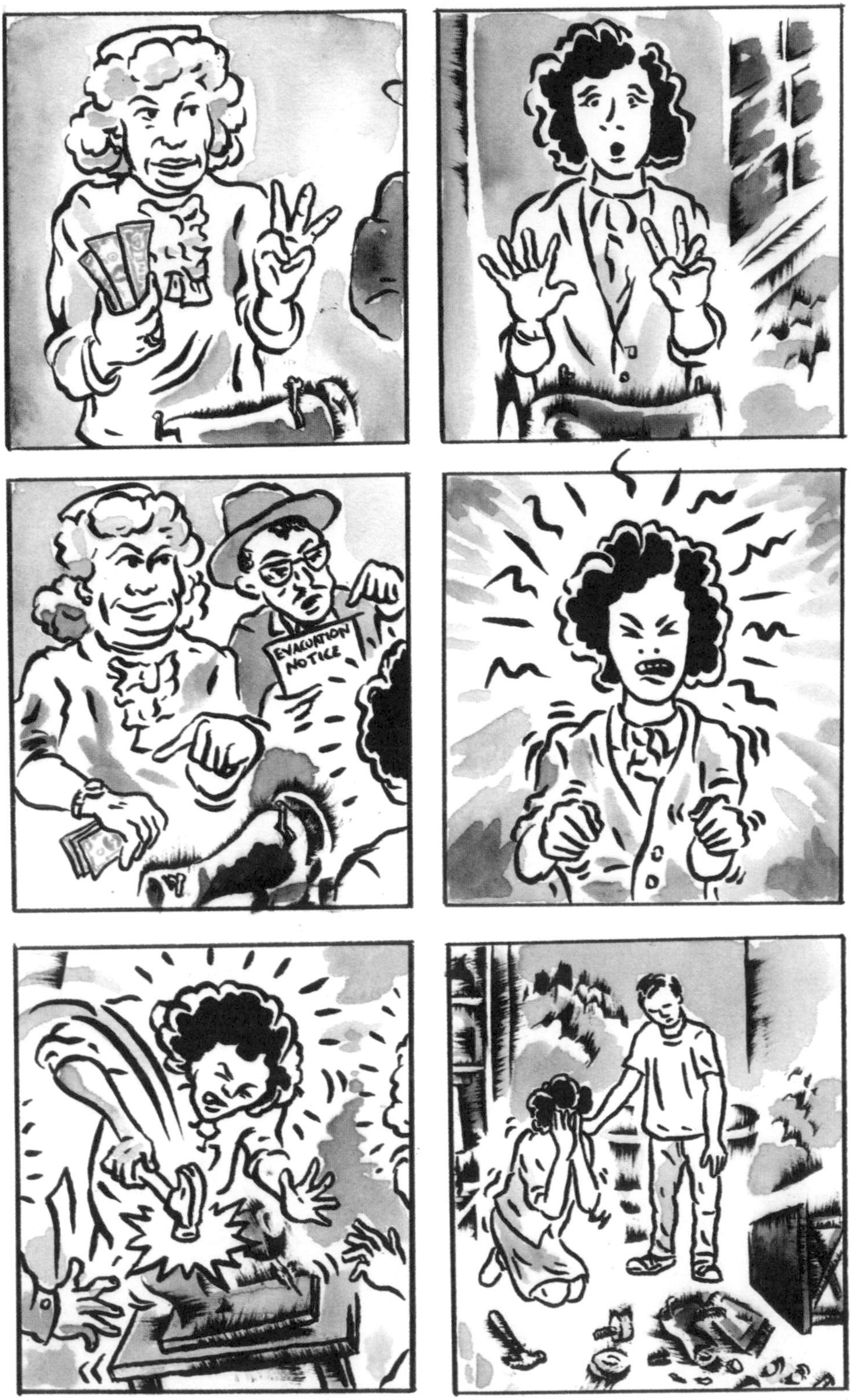
EVACUATION NOTICE

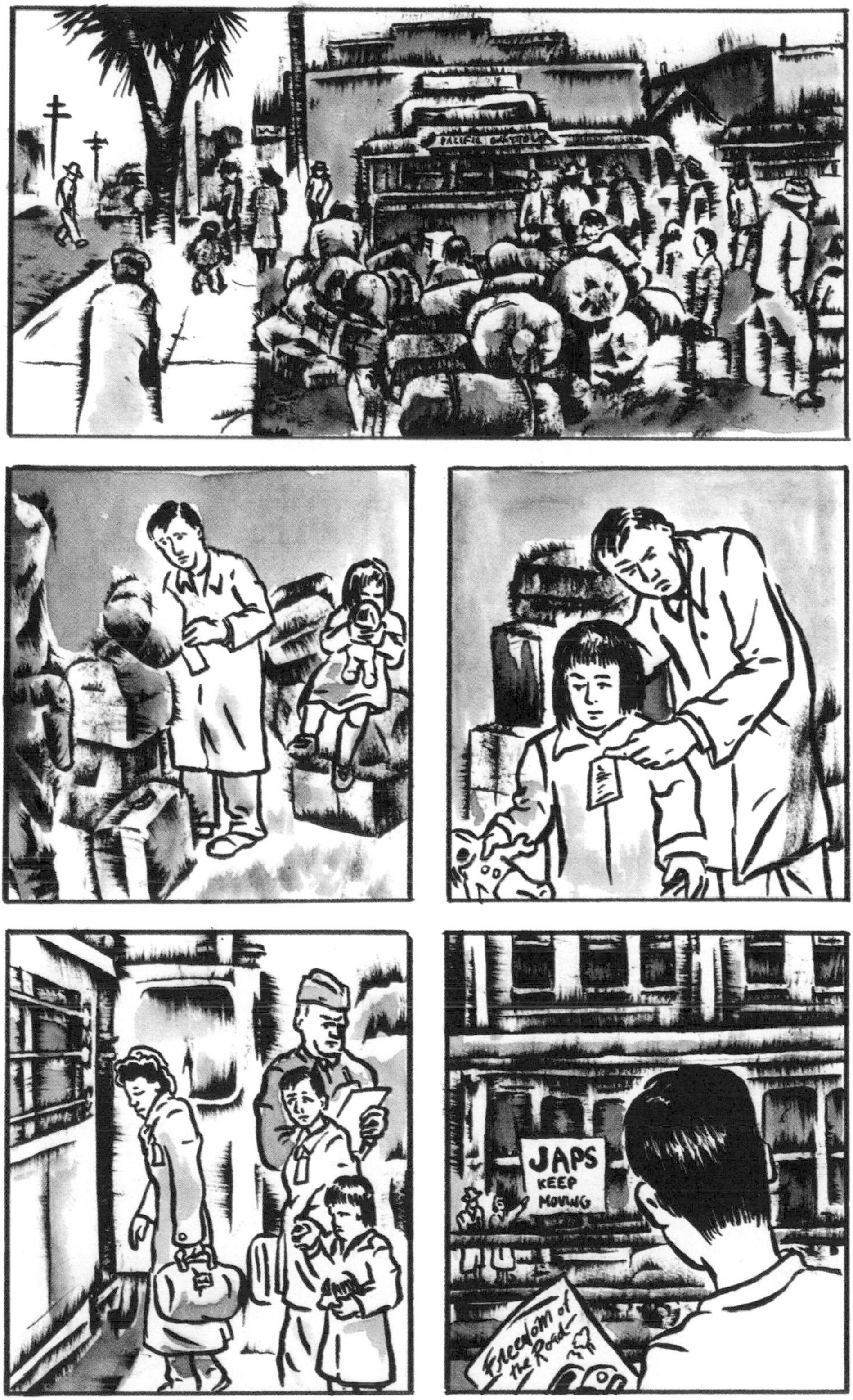
JAPS
KEEP
MOVING
Freedom of the Road

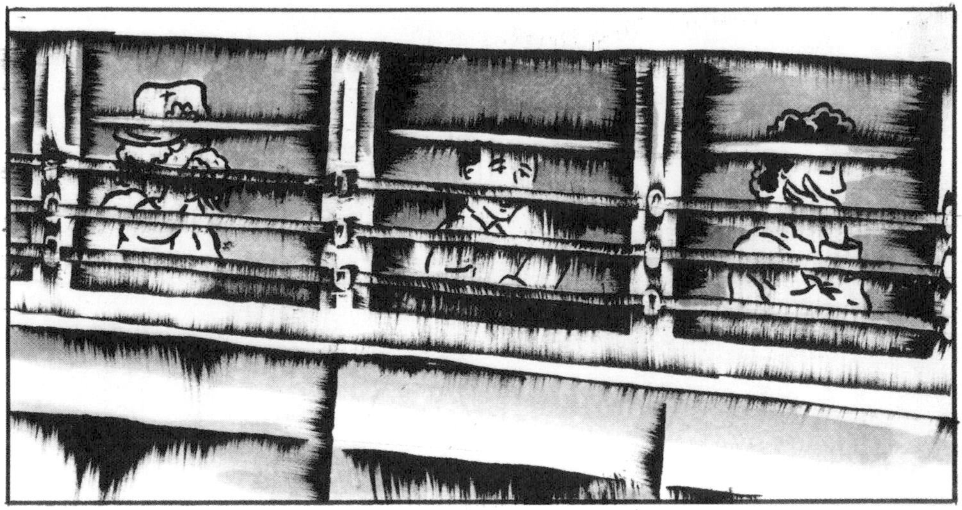

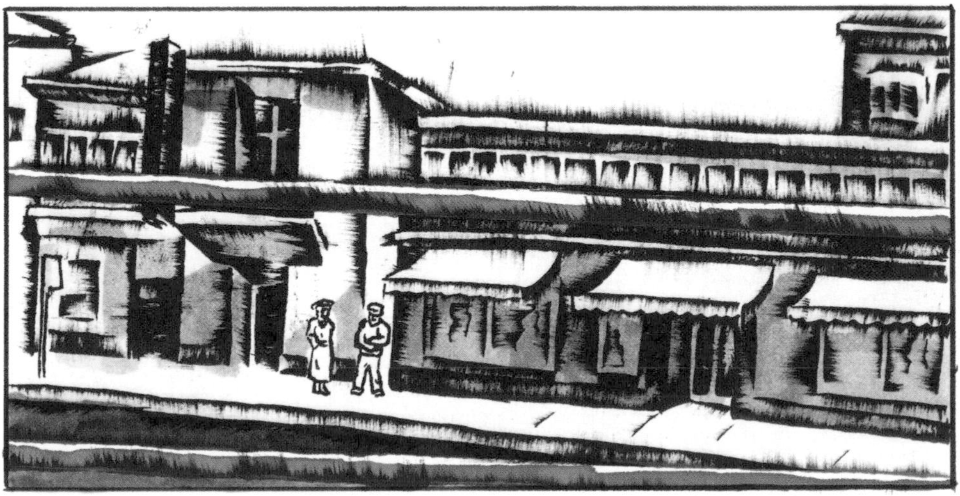

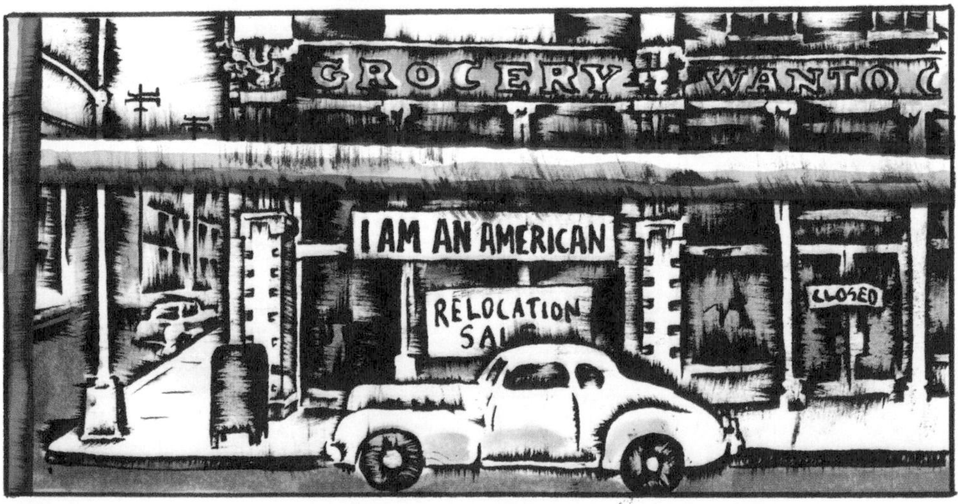
GROCERY
WANTO
I AM AN AMERICAN
RELOCATION SAL
CLOSED

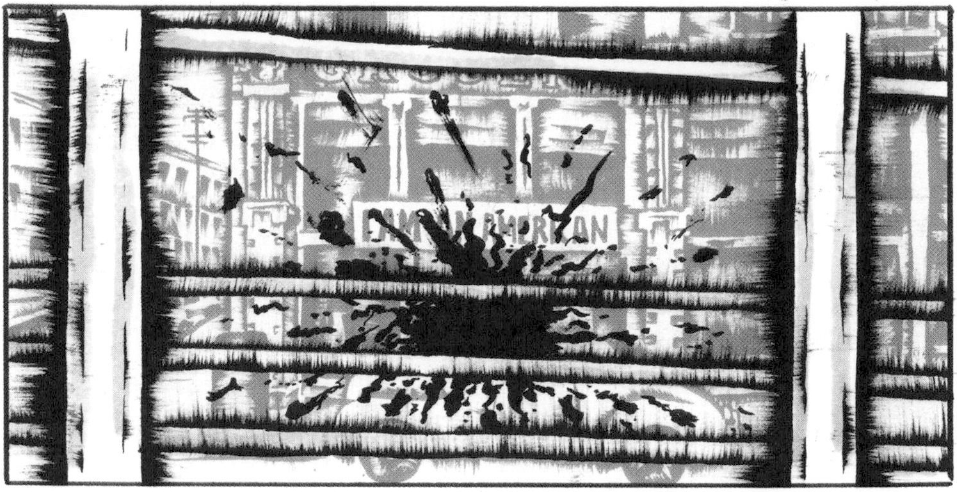

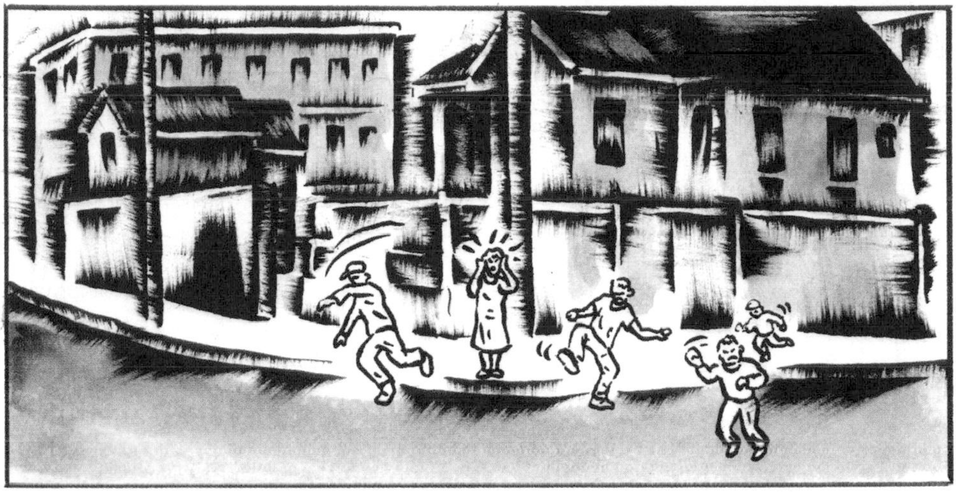

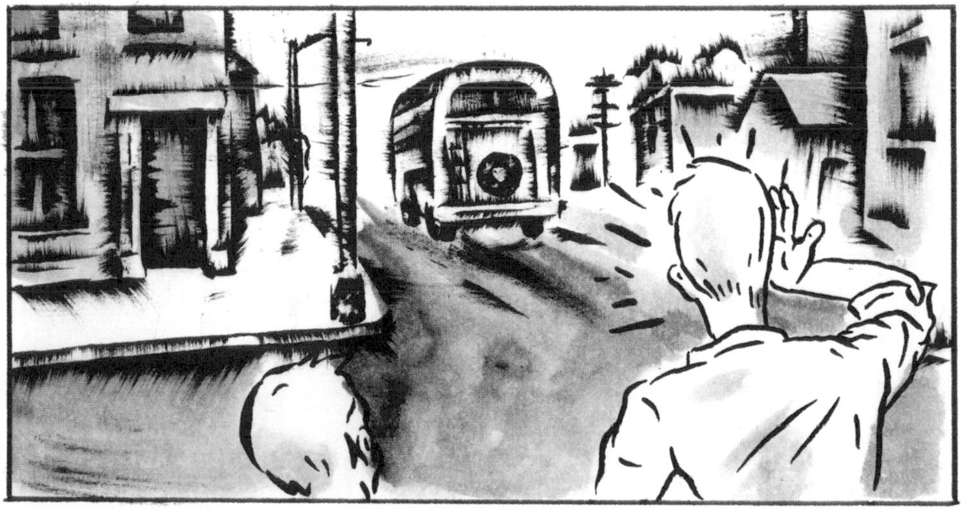

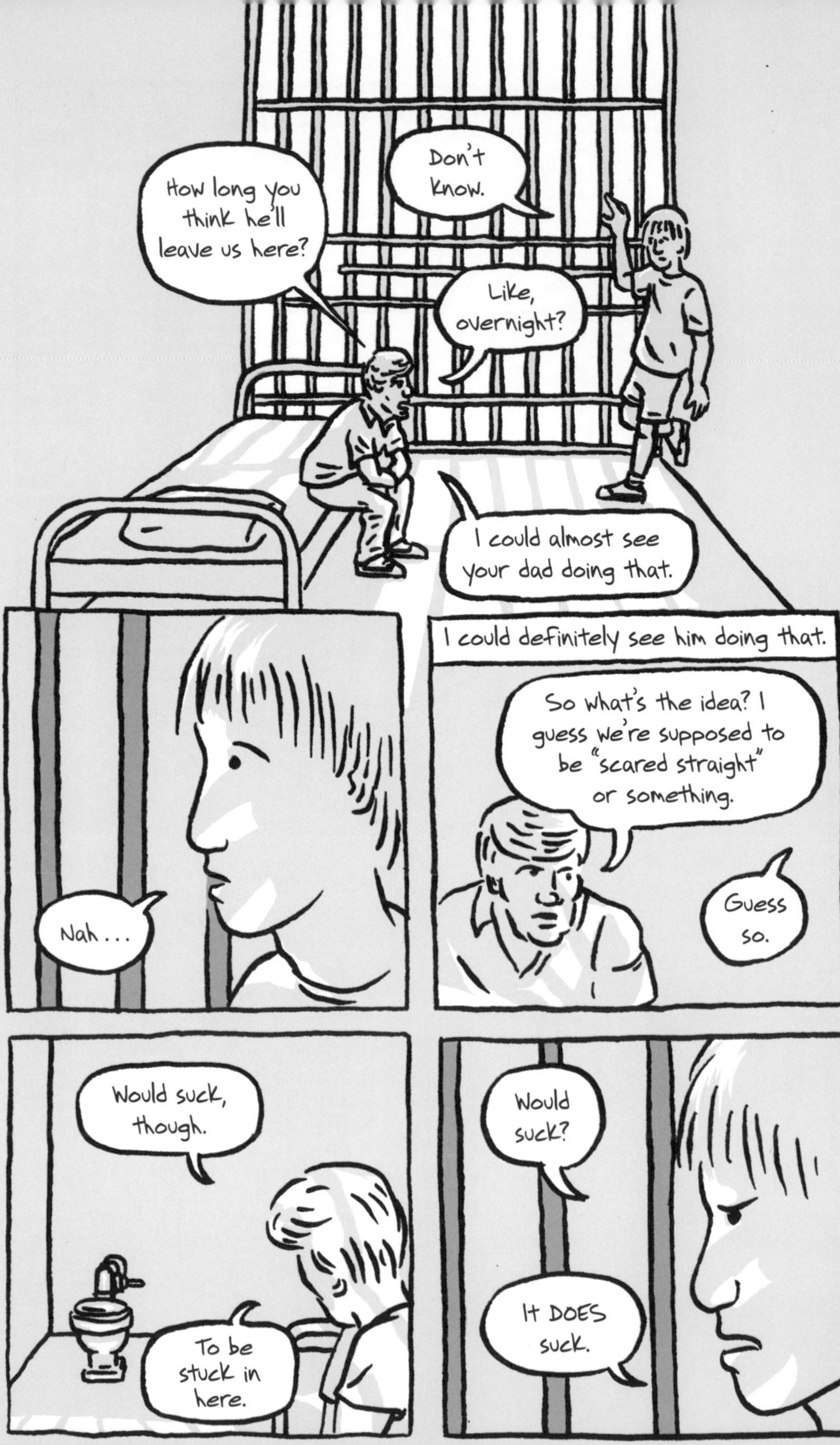
How long you think he'll leave us here?
Don't know.
Like, overnight?
I could almost see your dad doing that.
Nah...
I could definitely see him doing that.
So what's the idea? I guess we're supposed to be "scared straight" or something.
Guess so.
Would suck, though.
To be stuck in here.
Would suck?
It DOES suck.

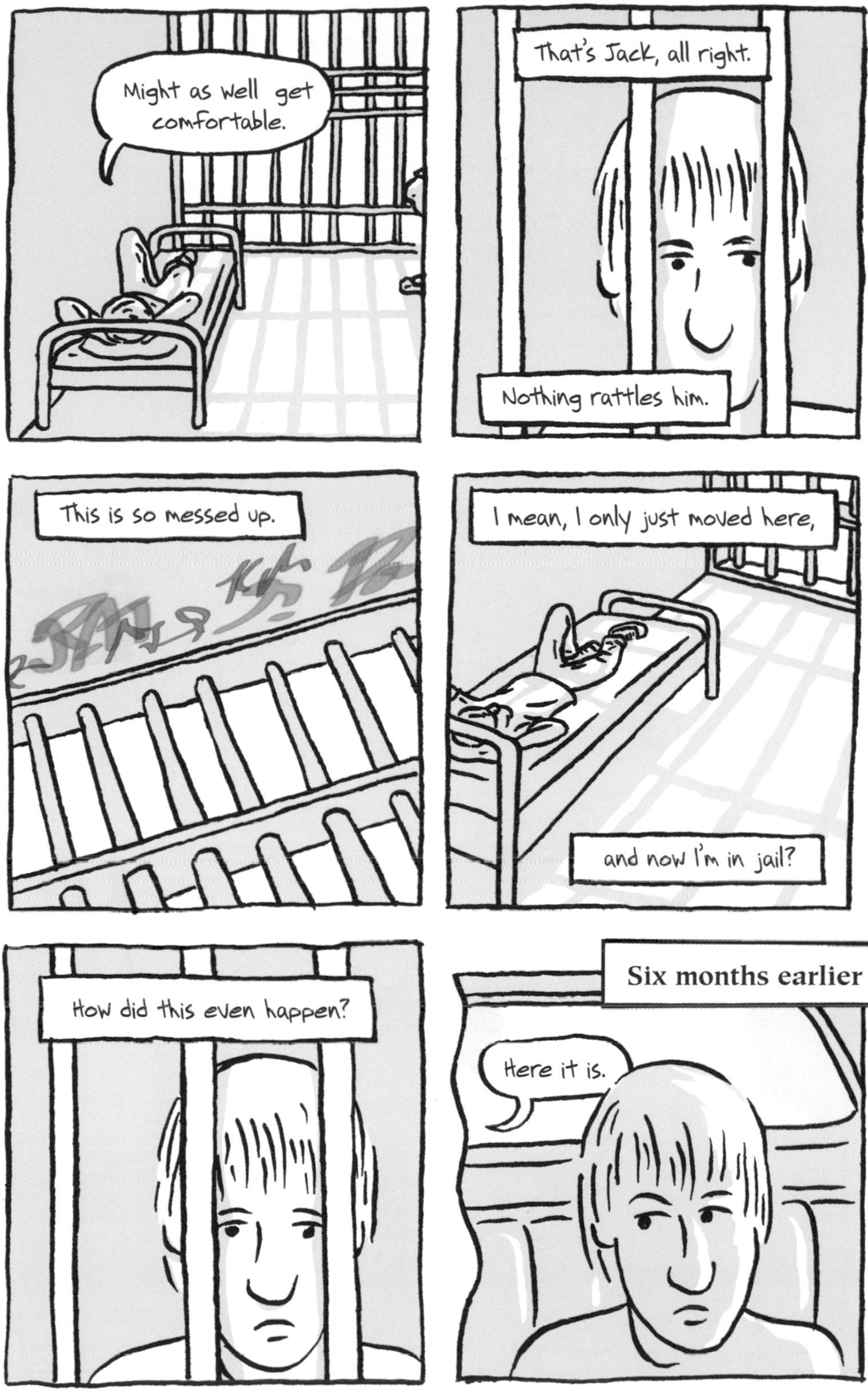
Might as well get comfortable.
That's Jack, all right.
Nothing rattles him.
This is so messed up.
I mean, I only just moved here,
and now I'm in jail?
How did this even happen?
Six months earlier
Here it is.

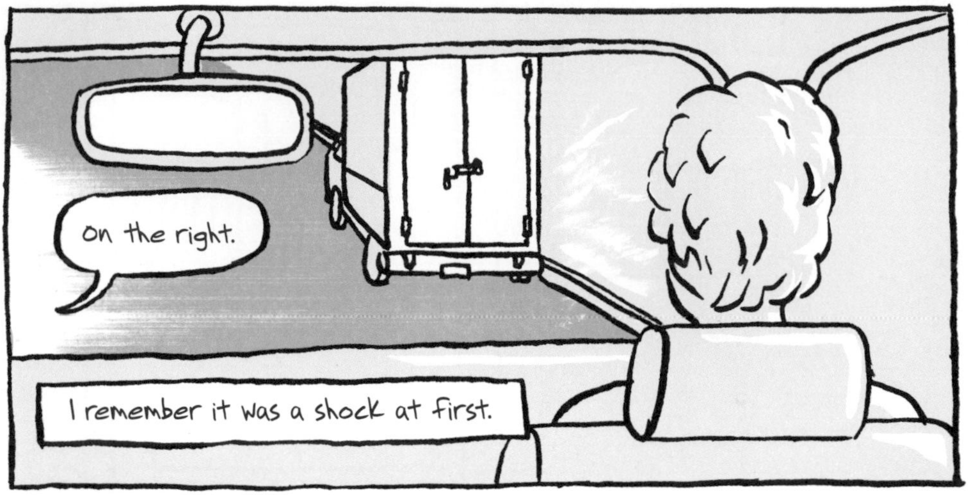
On the right.
I remember it was a shock at first.

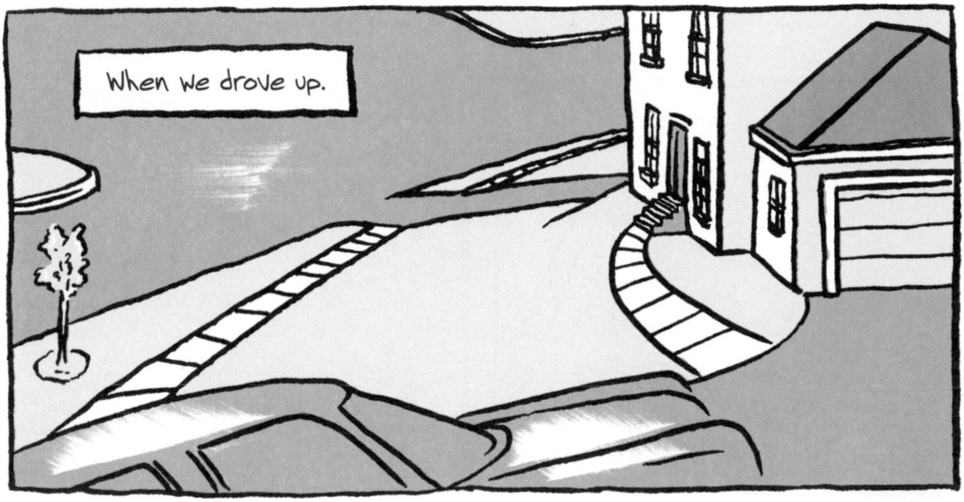
When we drove up.

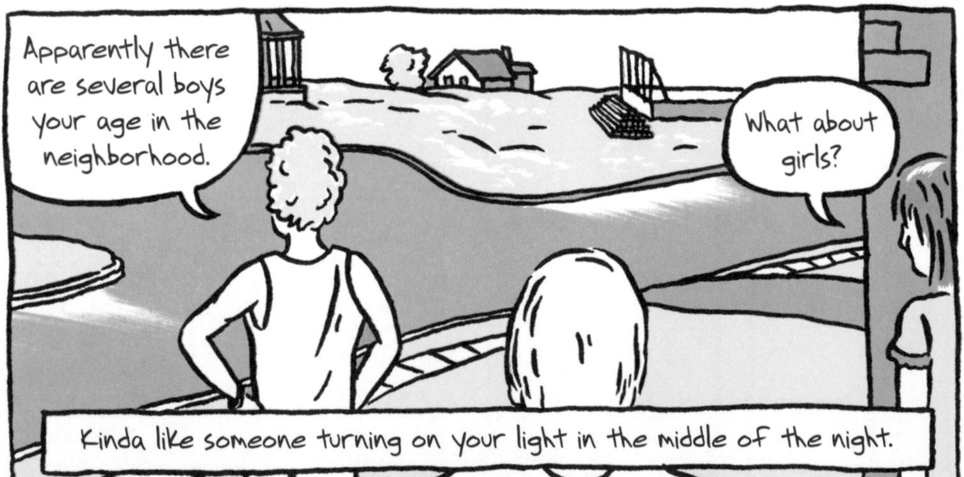
Apparently there are several boys your age in the neighborhood.
What about girls?
Kinda like someone turning on your light in the middle of the night.

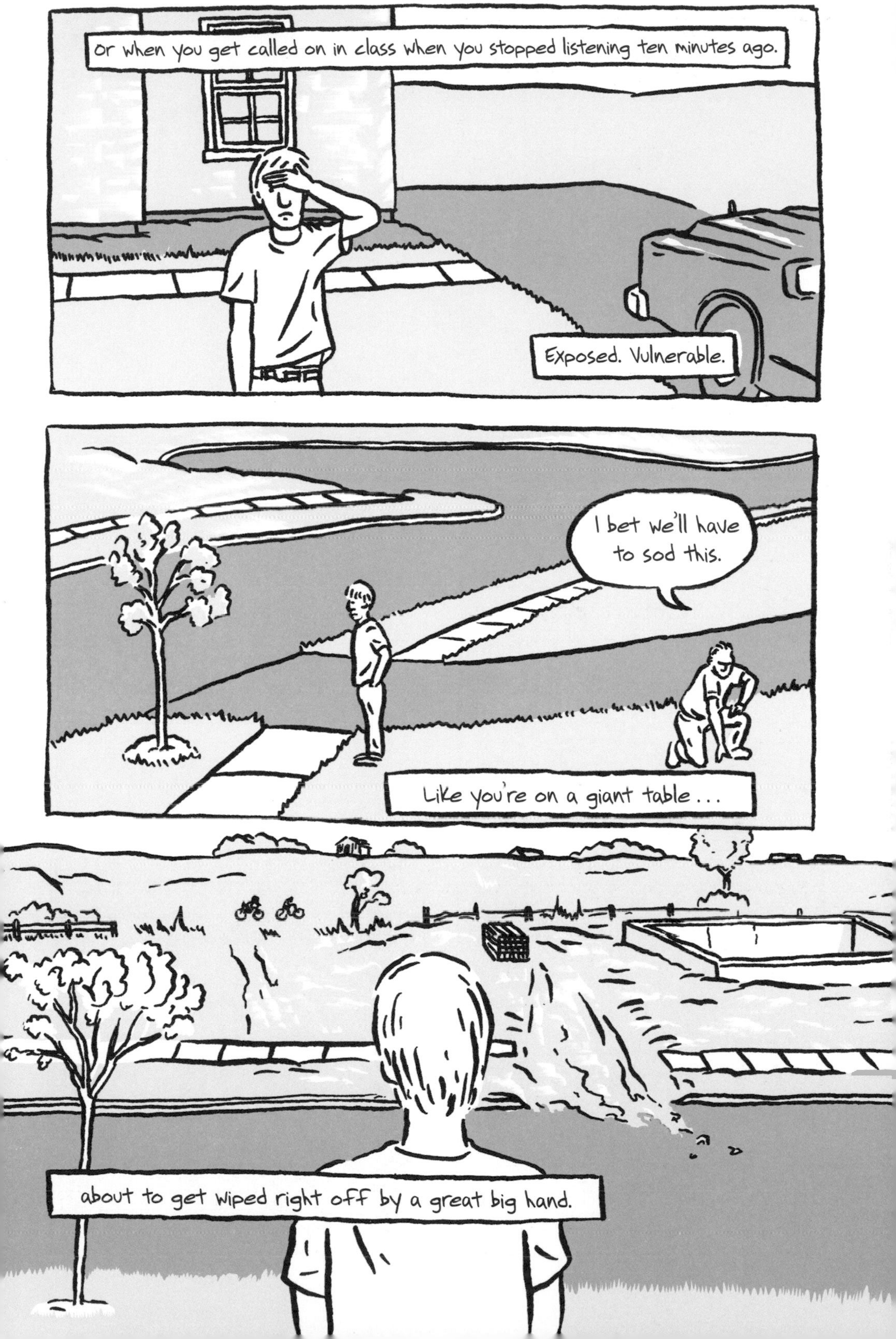
Or when you get called on in class when you stopped listening ten minutes ago.
Exposed. Vulnerable.
I bet we'll have to sod this.
Like you're on a giant table . . .
about to get wiped right off by a great big hand.

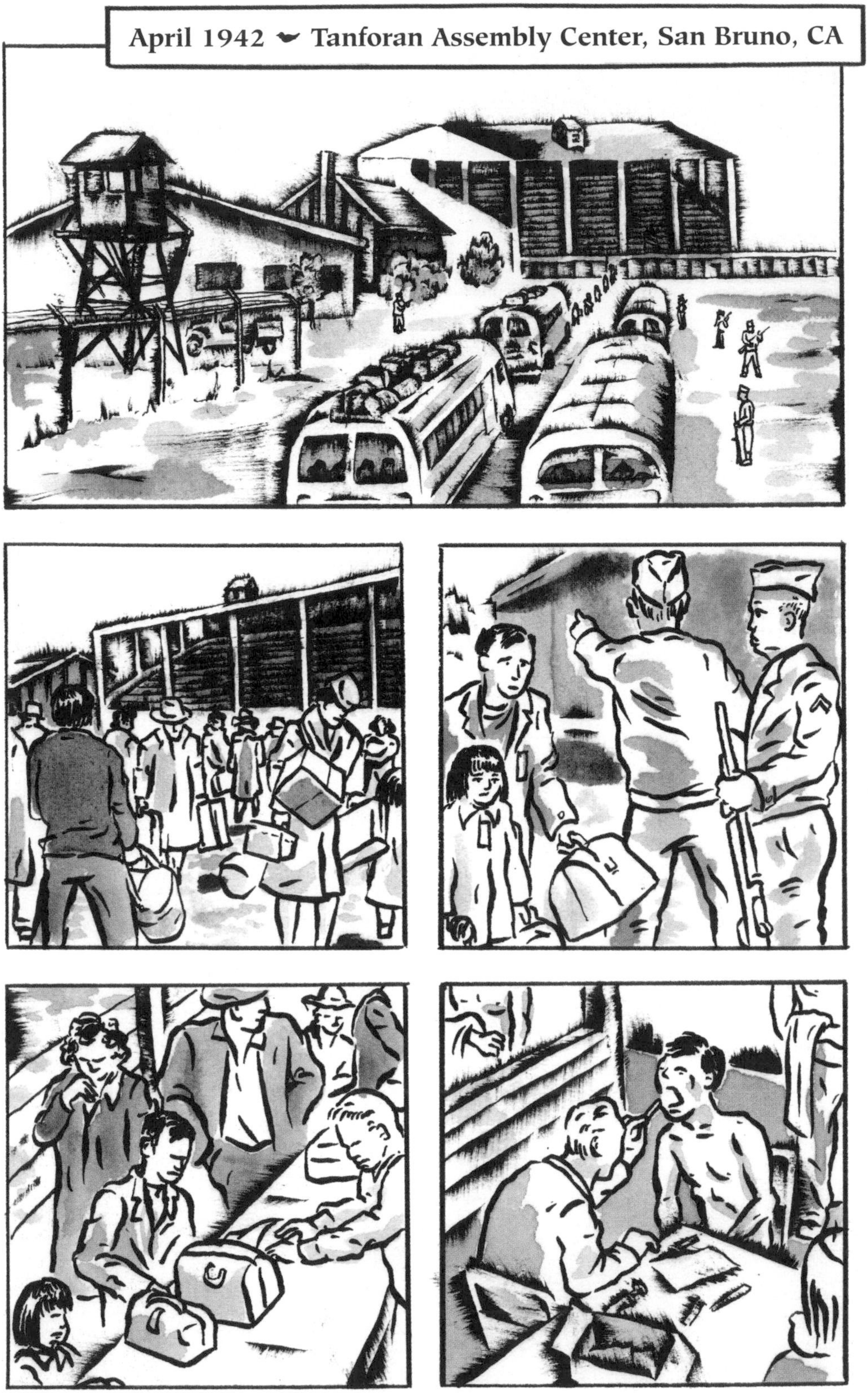
April 1942 ❧ Tanforan Assembly Center, San Bruno, CA

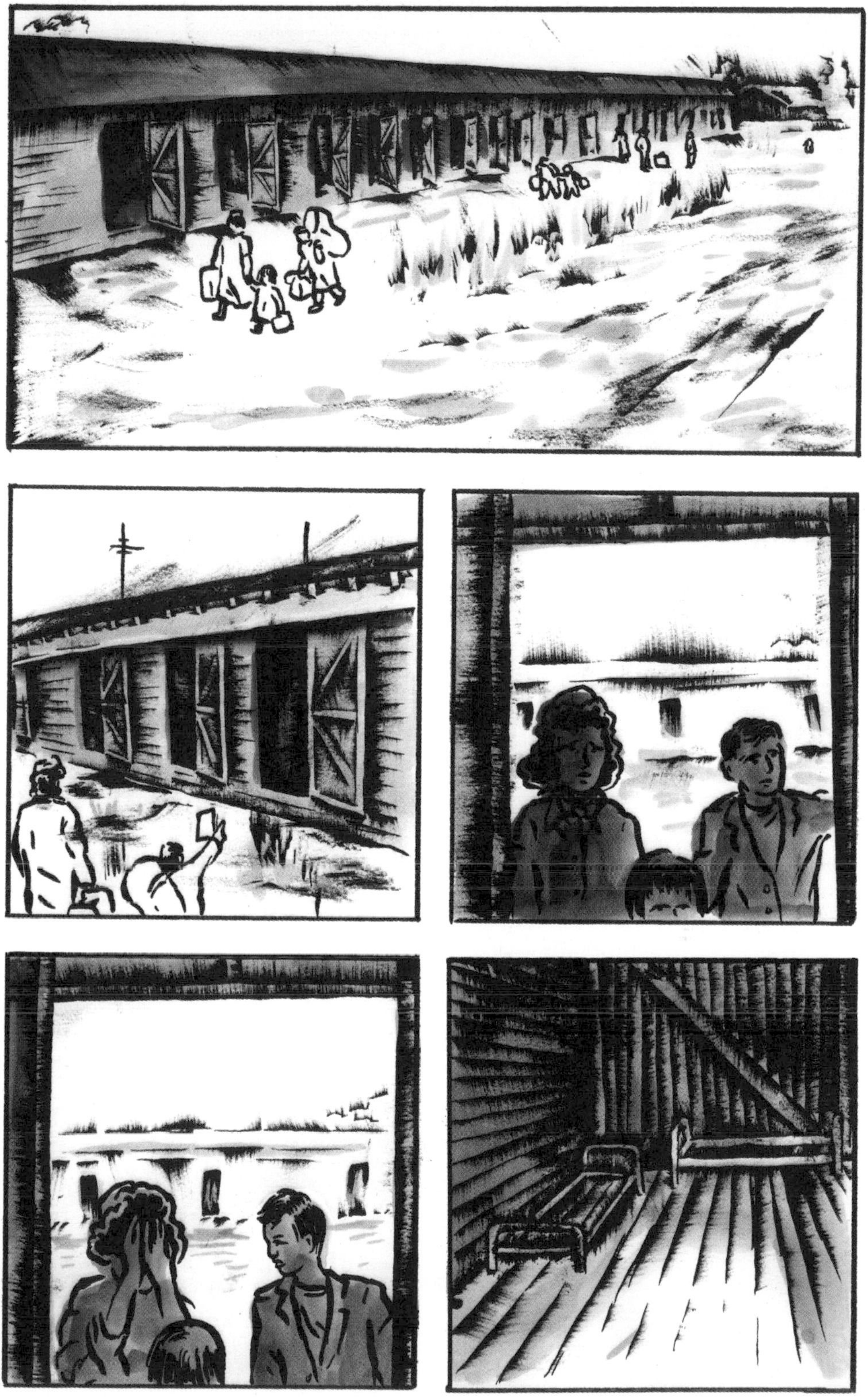

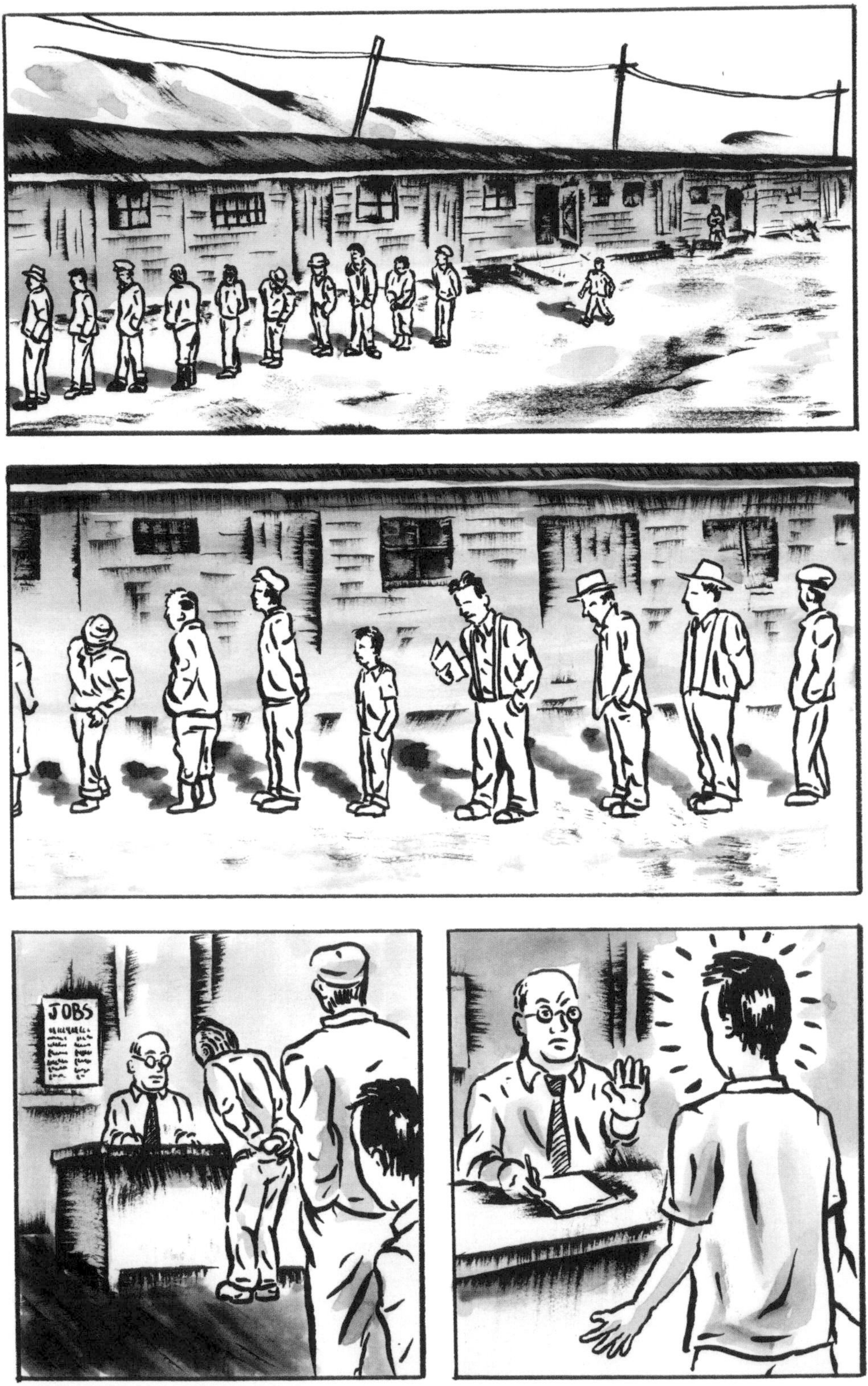
JOBS

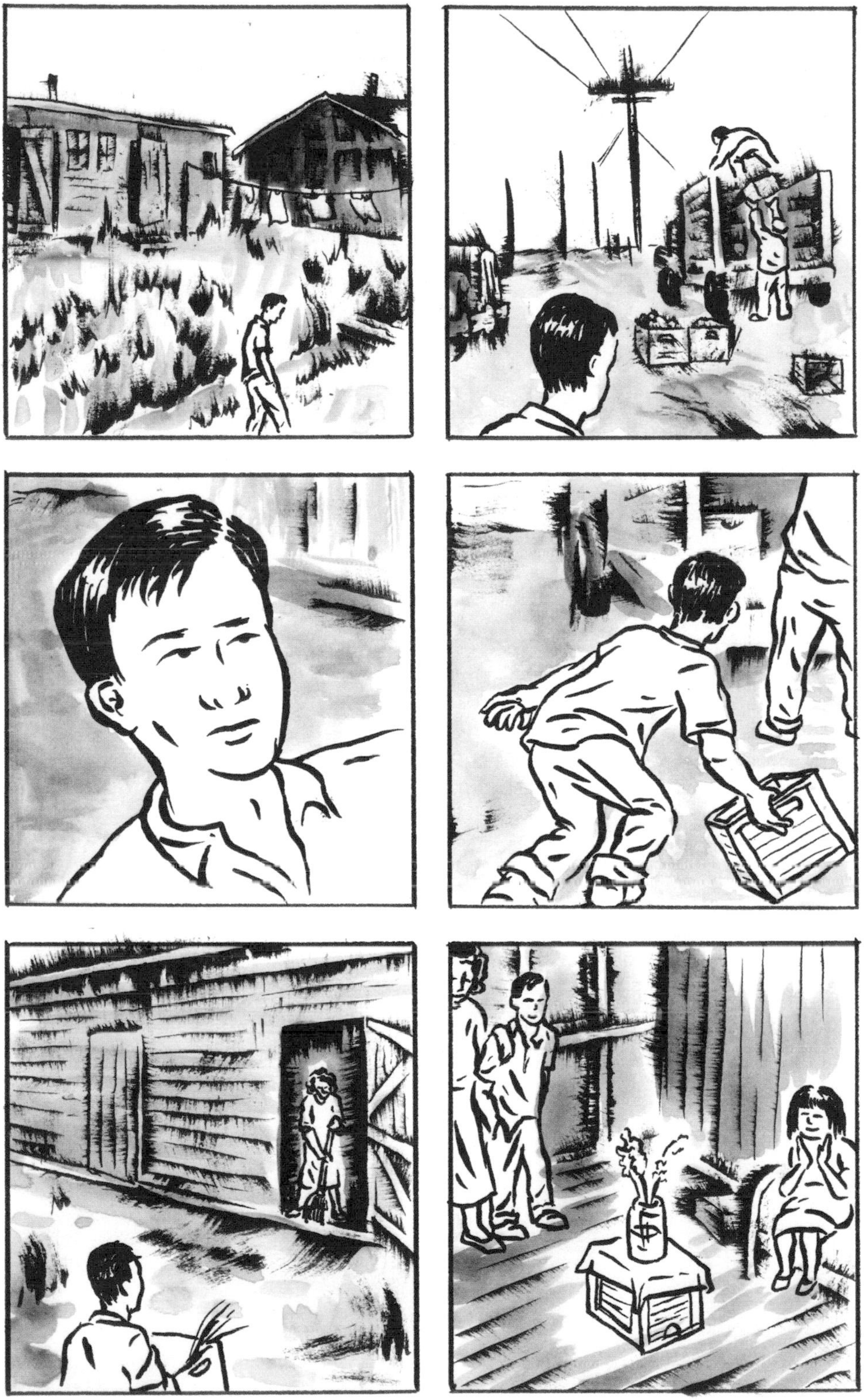

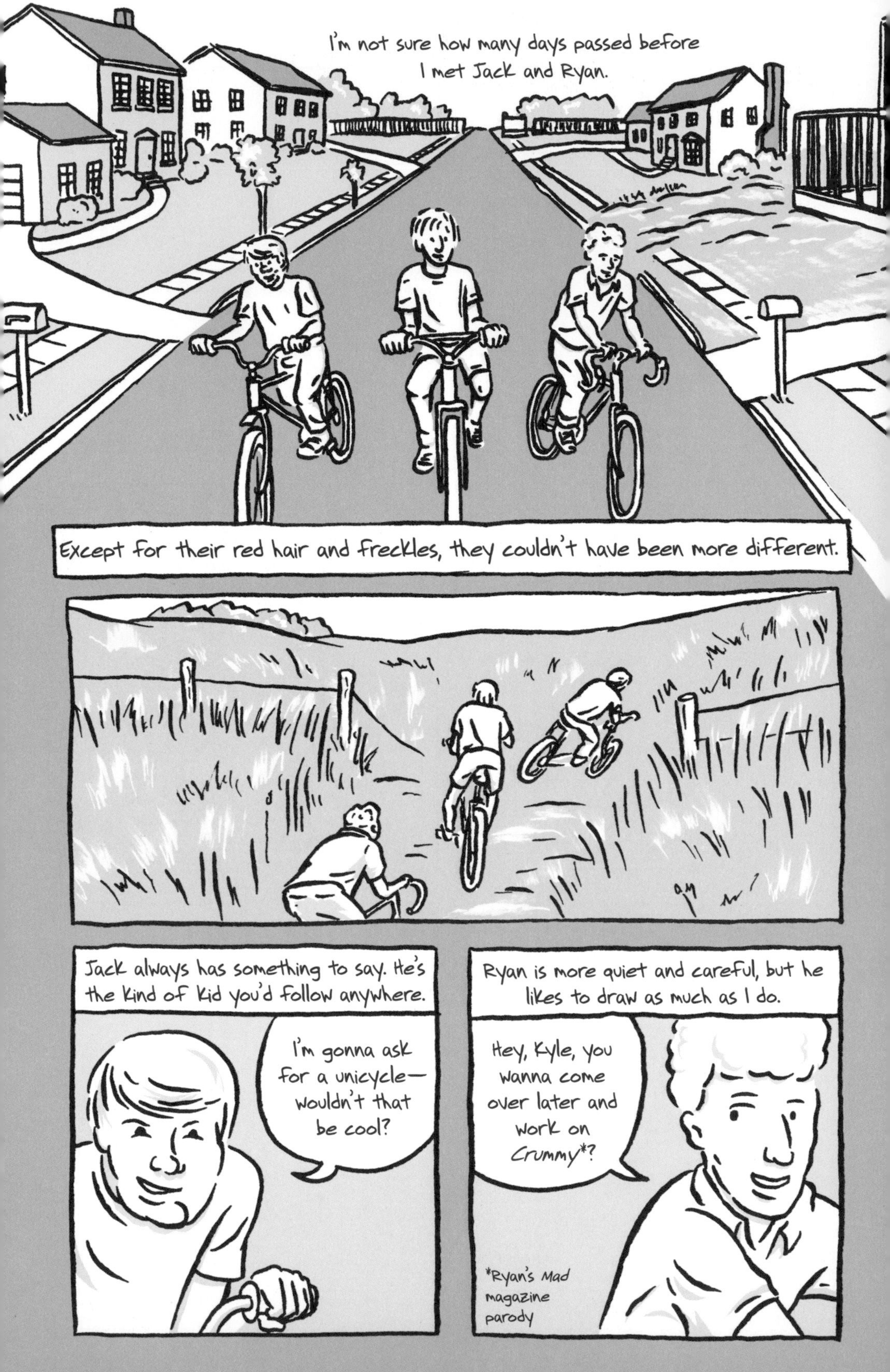

I'm not sure how many days passed before I met Jack and Ryan.
Except for their red hair and freckles, they couldn't have been more different.
Jack always has something to say. He's the kind of kid you'd follow anywhere.
I'm gonna ask for a unicycle— wouldn't that be cool?
Ryan is more quiet and careful, but he likes to draw as much as I do.
Hey, Kyle, you wanna come over later and work on Crummy*?
*Ryan's Mad magazine parody

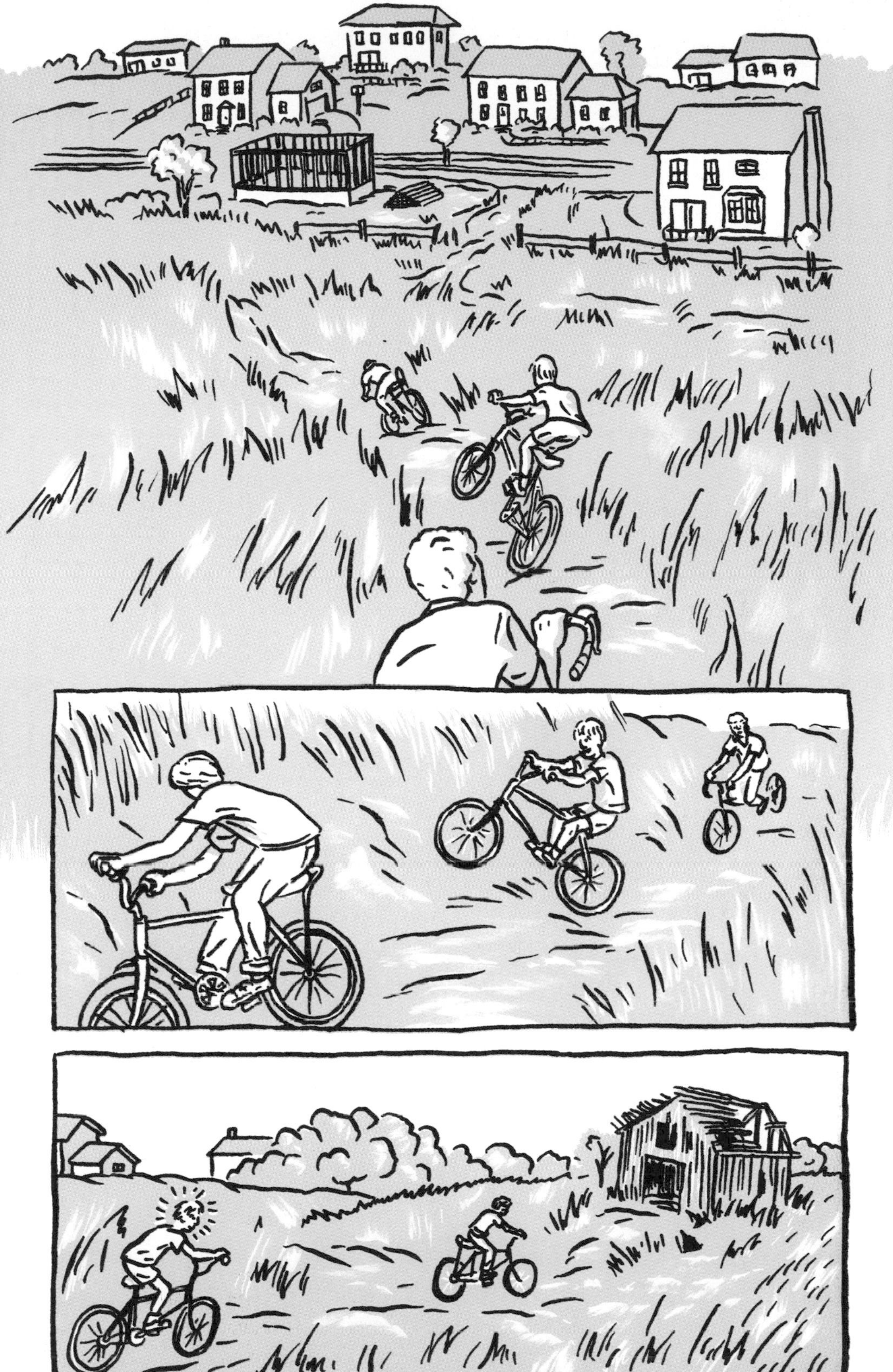

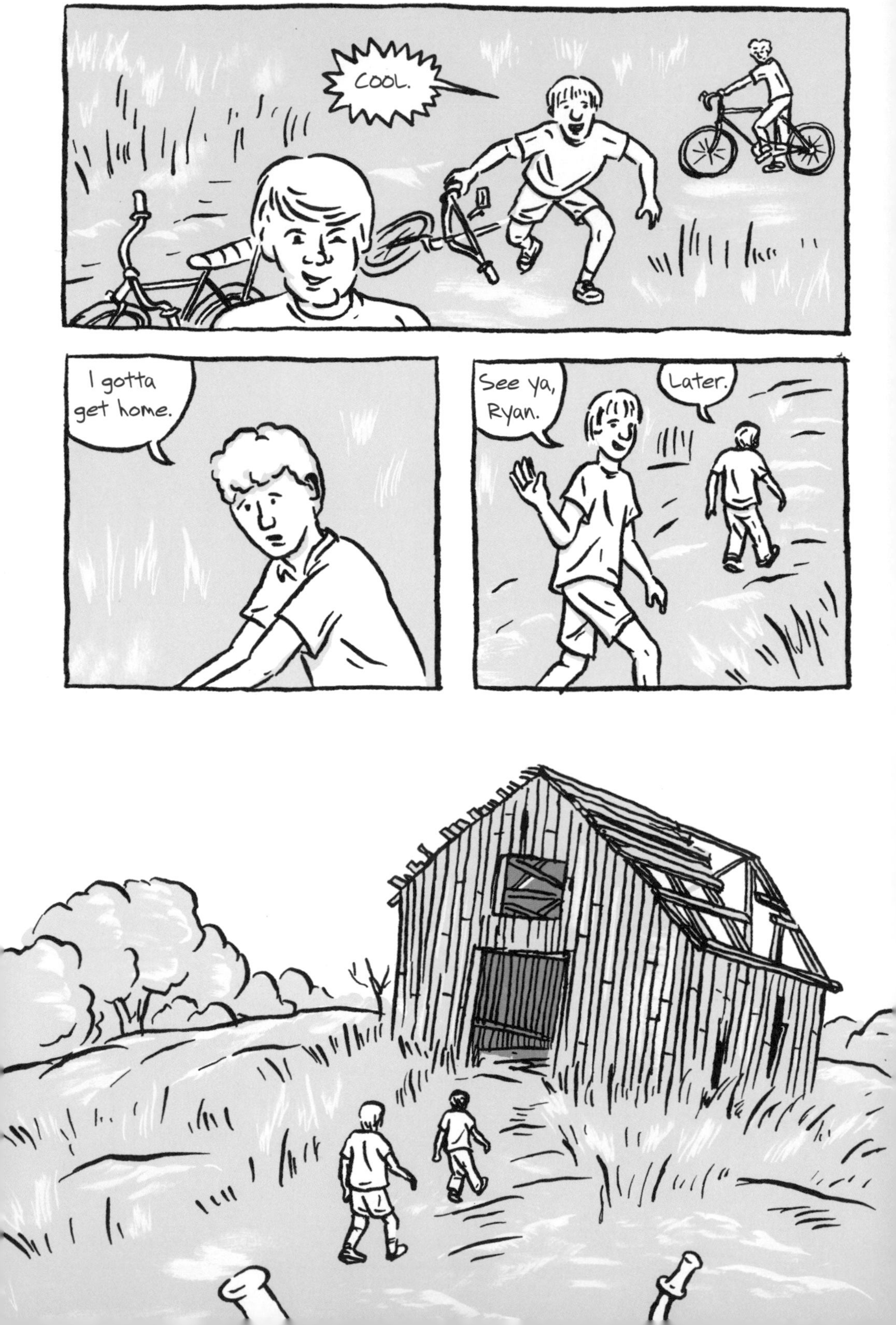
COOL.
I gotta get home.
See ya, Ryan.
Later.

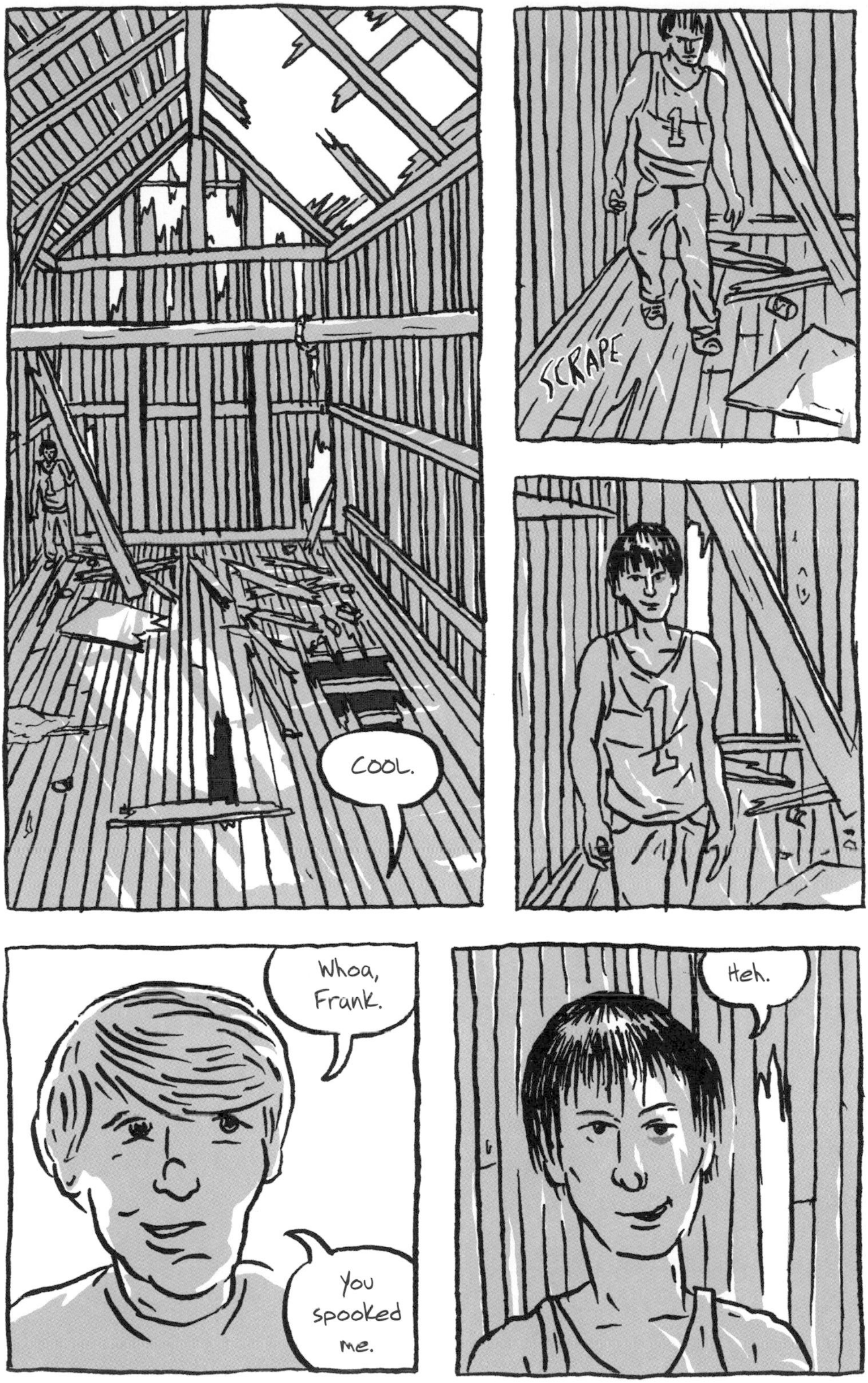
COOL.
SCRAPE
Whoa, Frank.
You spooked me.
Heh.

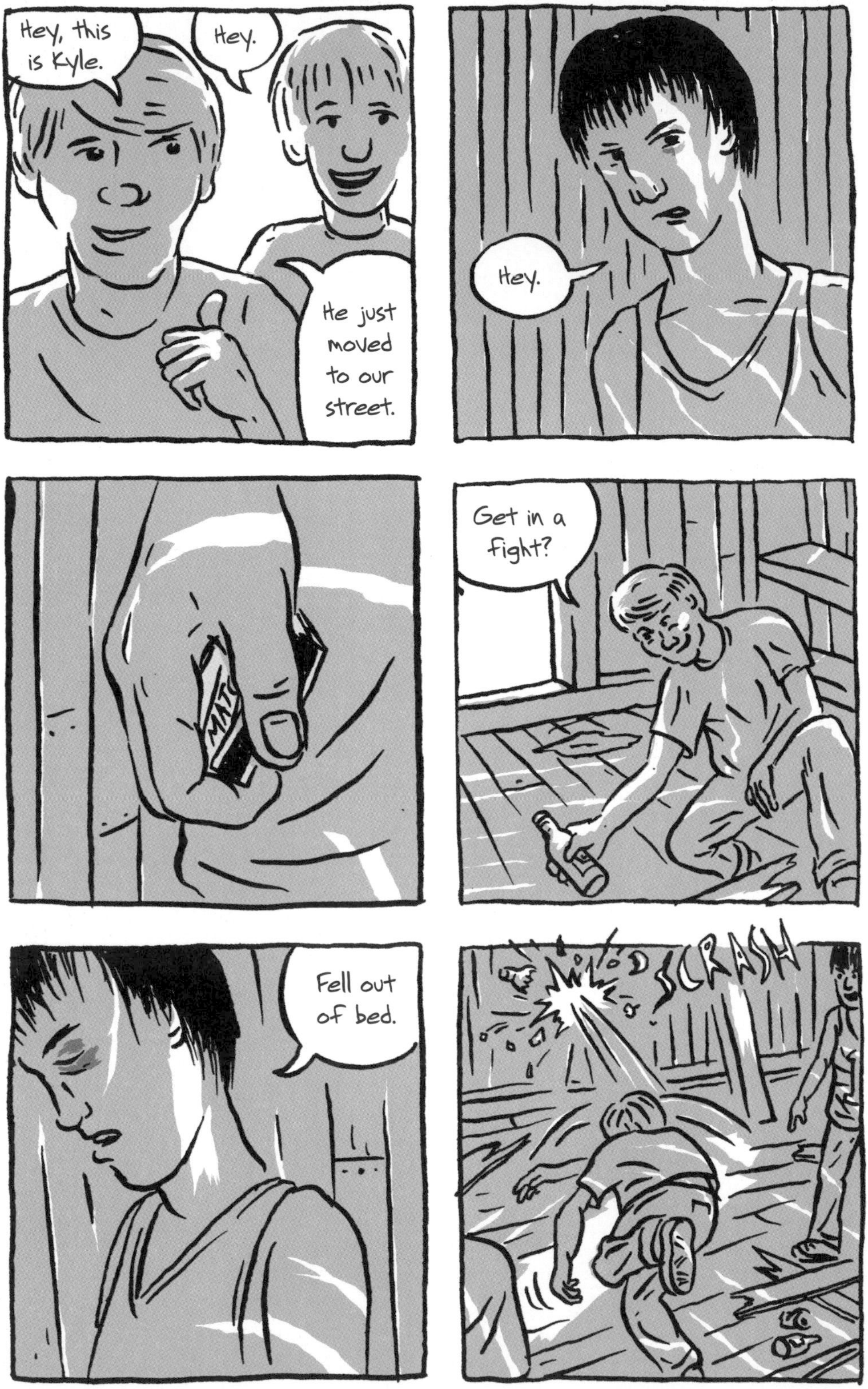
Hey, this is Kyle.
Hey.
He just moved to our street.
Hey.
MATC
Get in a fight?
Fell out of bed.
CRASH

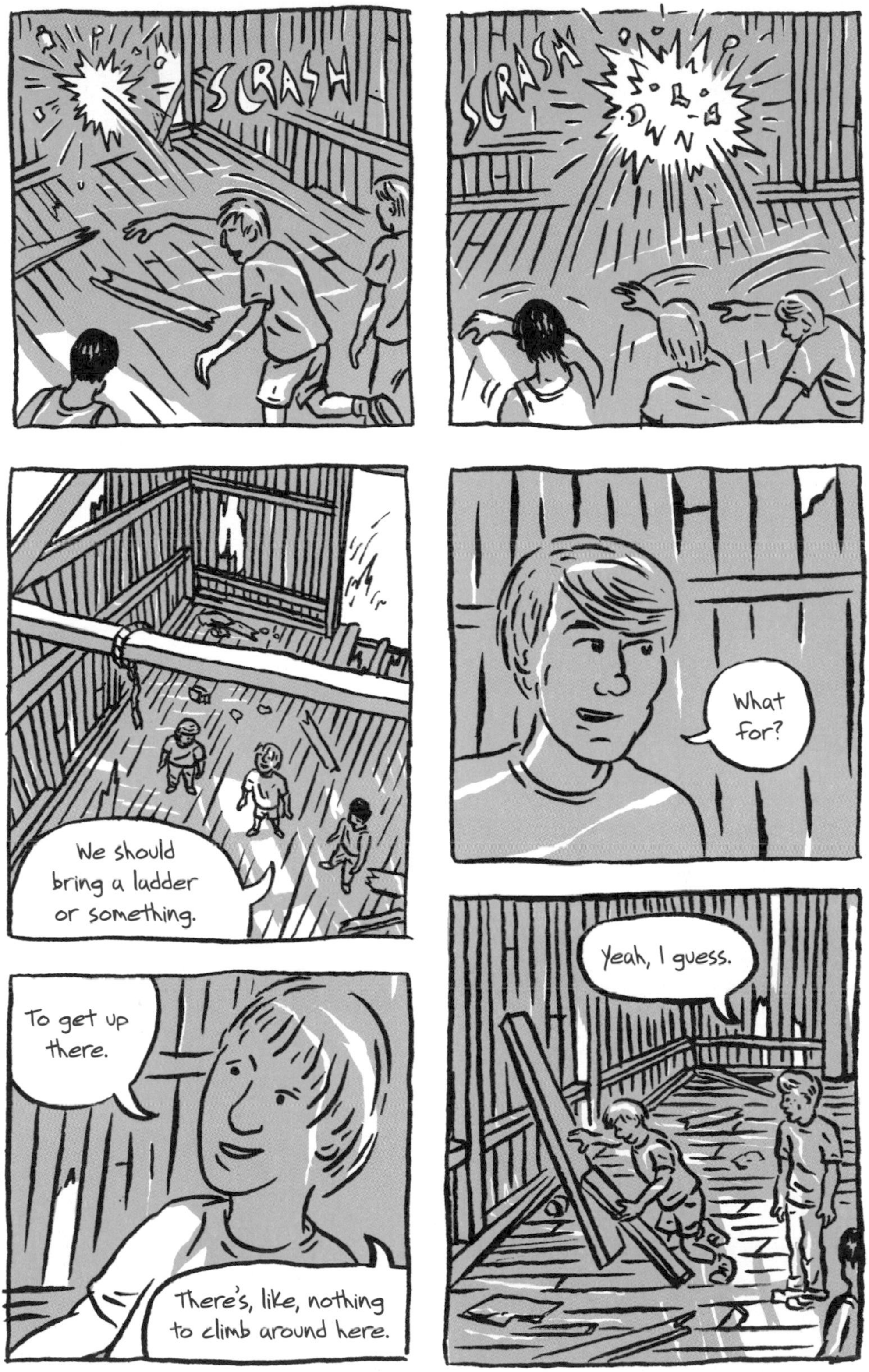
SCRASH
SCRASH
We should bring a ladder or something.
What for?
To get up there.
There's, like, nothing to climb around here.
Yeah, I guess.

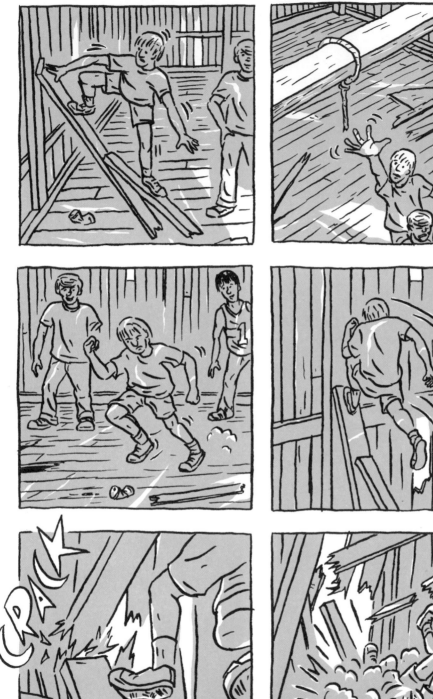

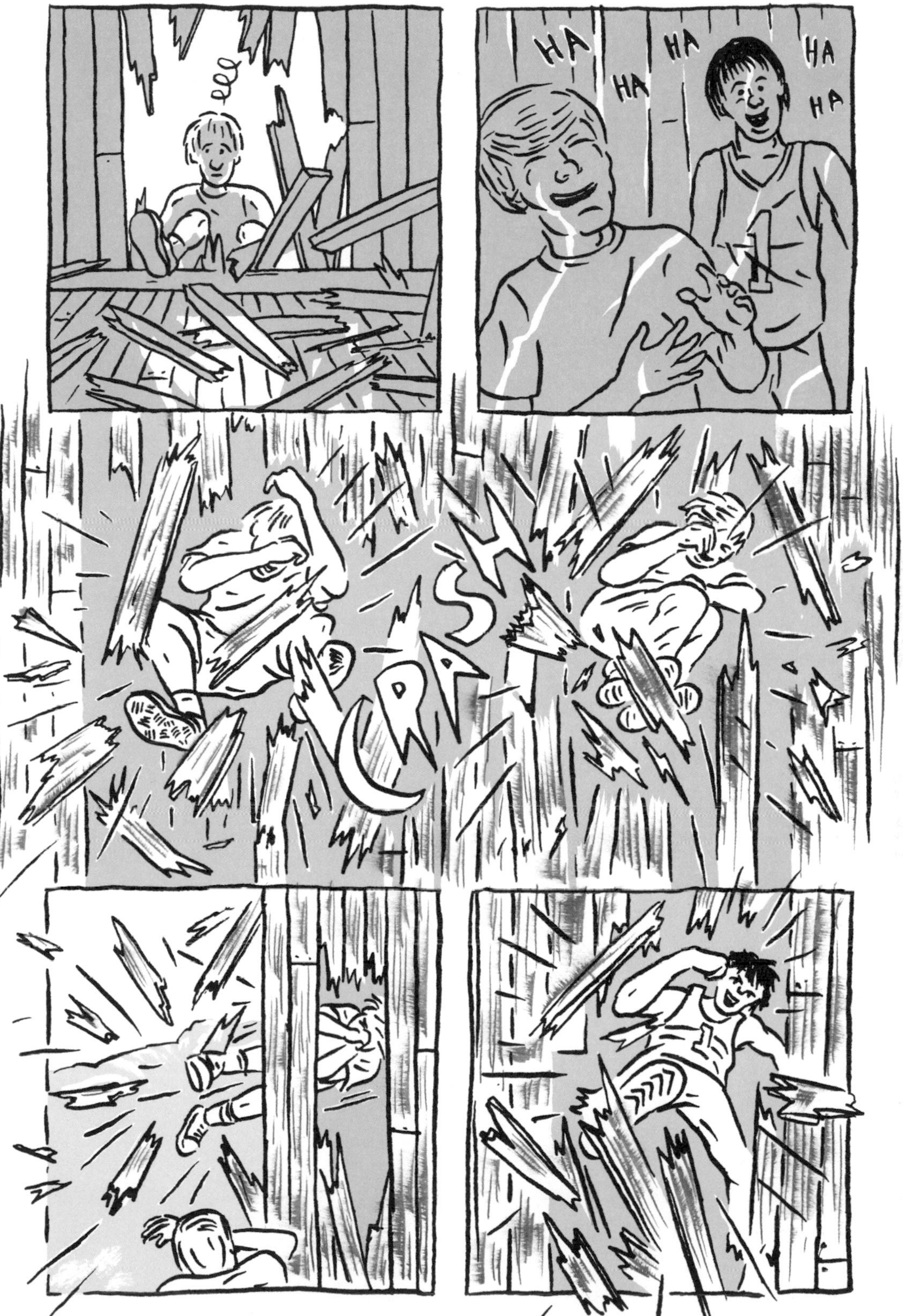

HA
HA
HA
HA
HA
CRASH

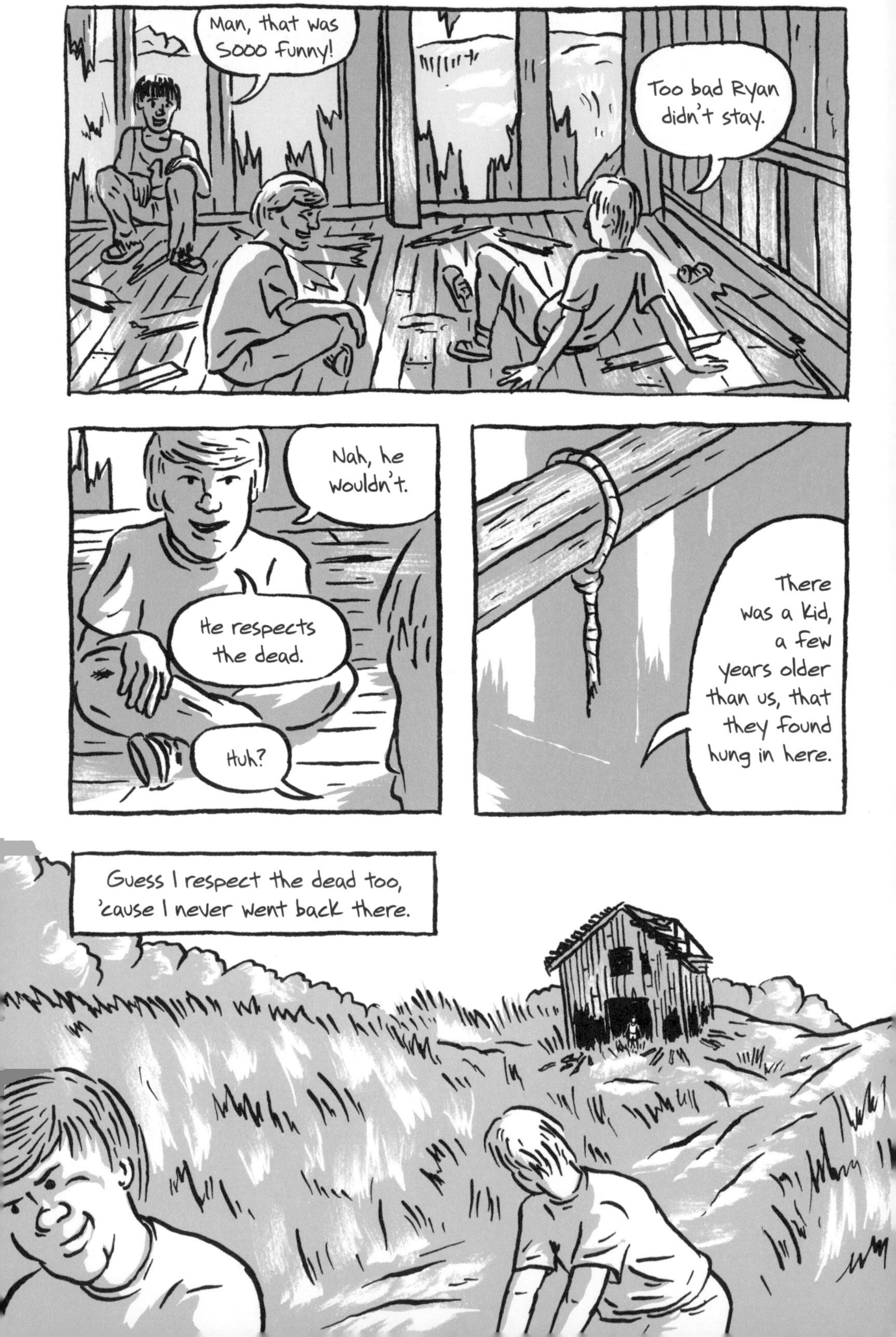
Man, that was Sooo funny!
Too bad Ryan didn't stay.
Nah, he wouldn't.
He respects the dead.
Huh?
There was a kid, a few years older than us, that they found hung in here.
Guess I respect the dead too, 'cause I never went back there.

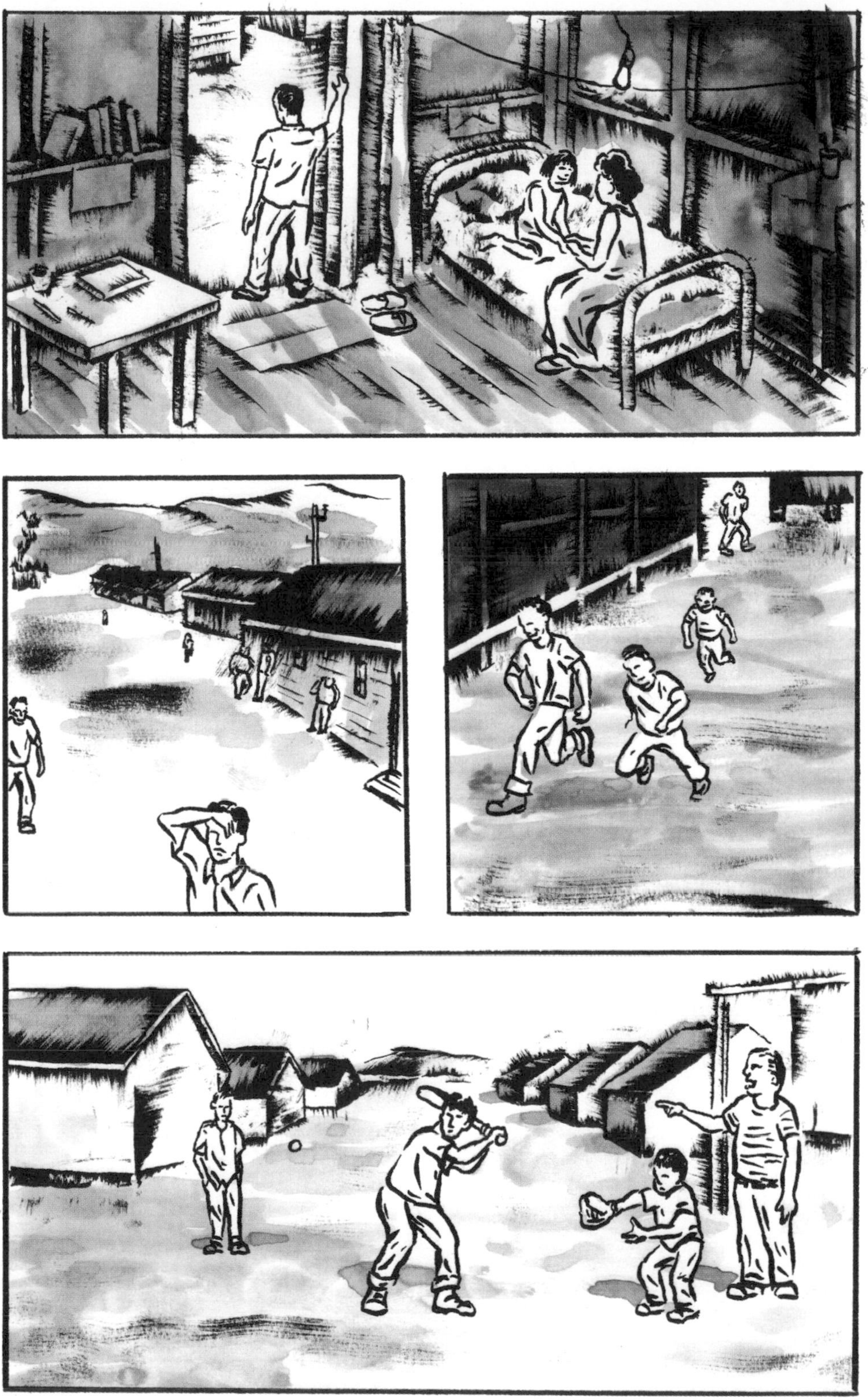

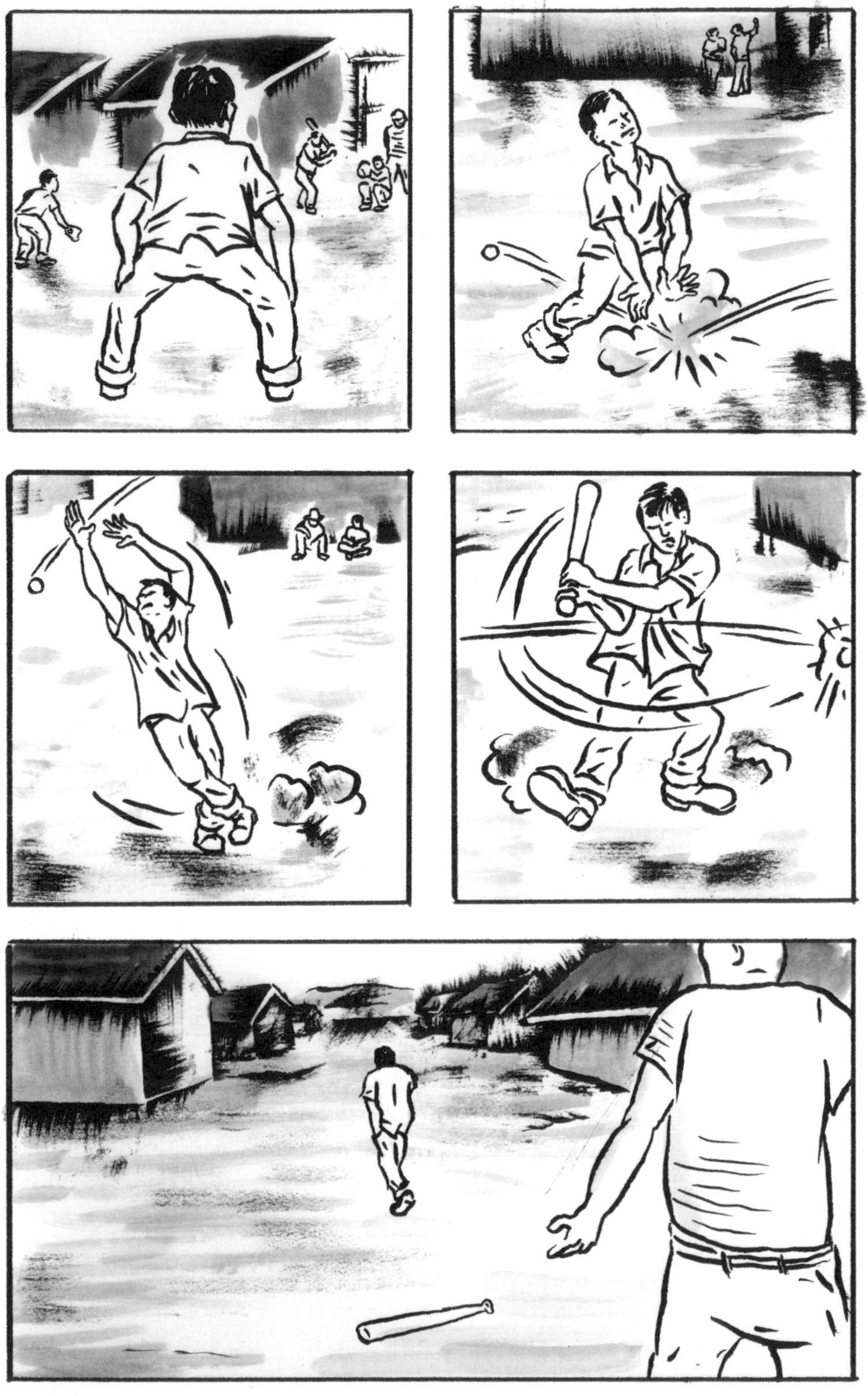

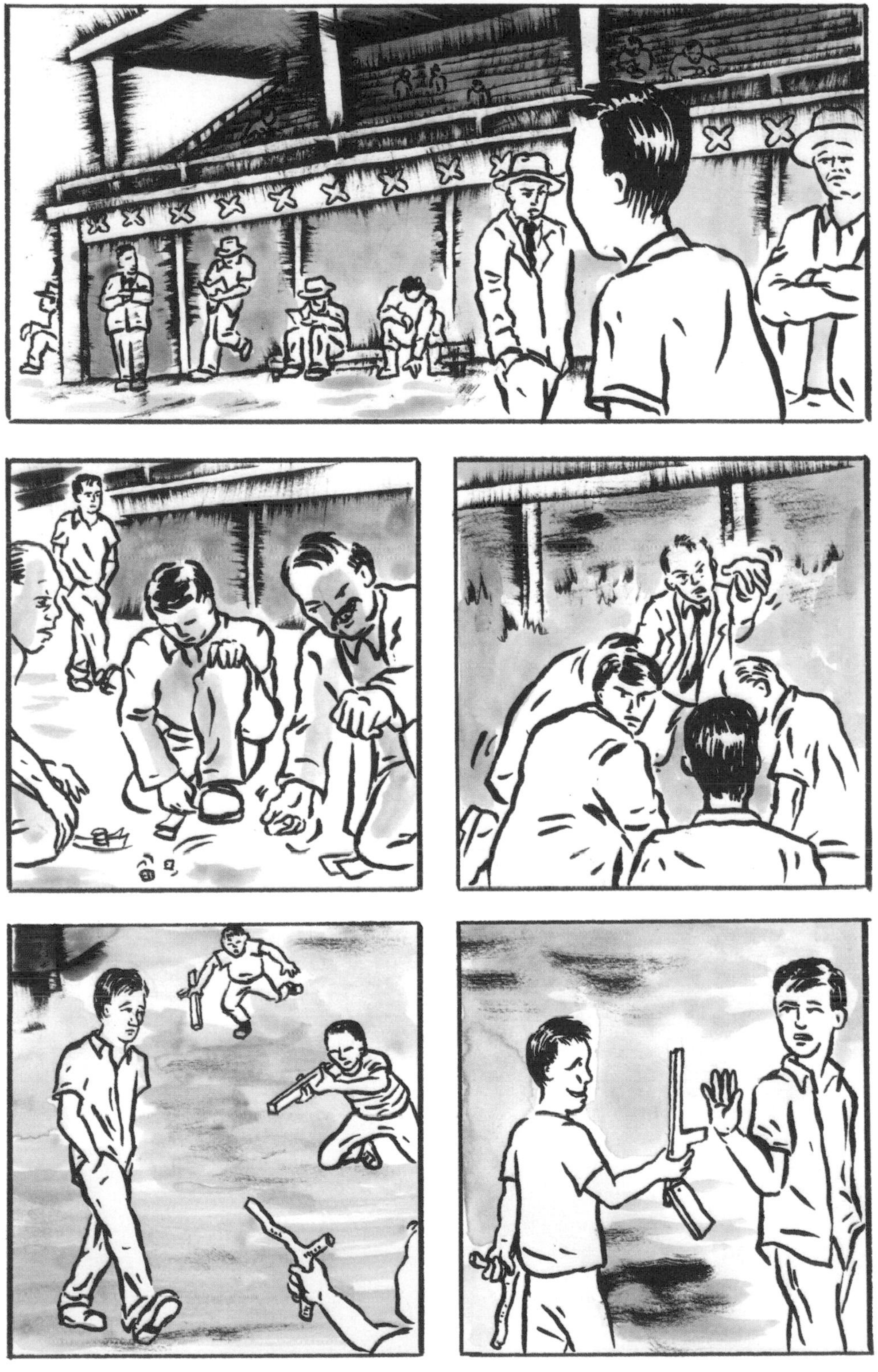

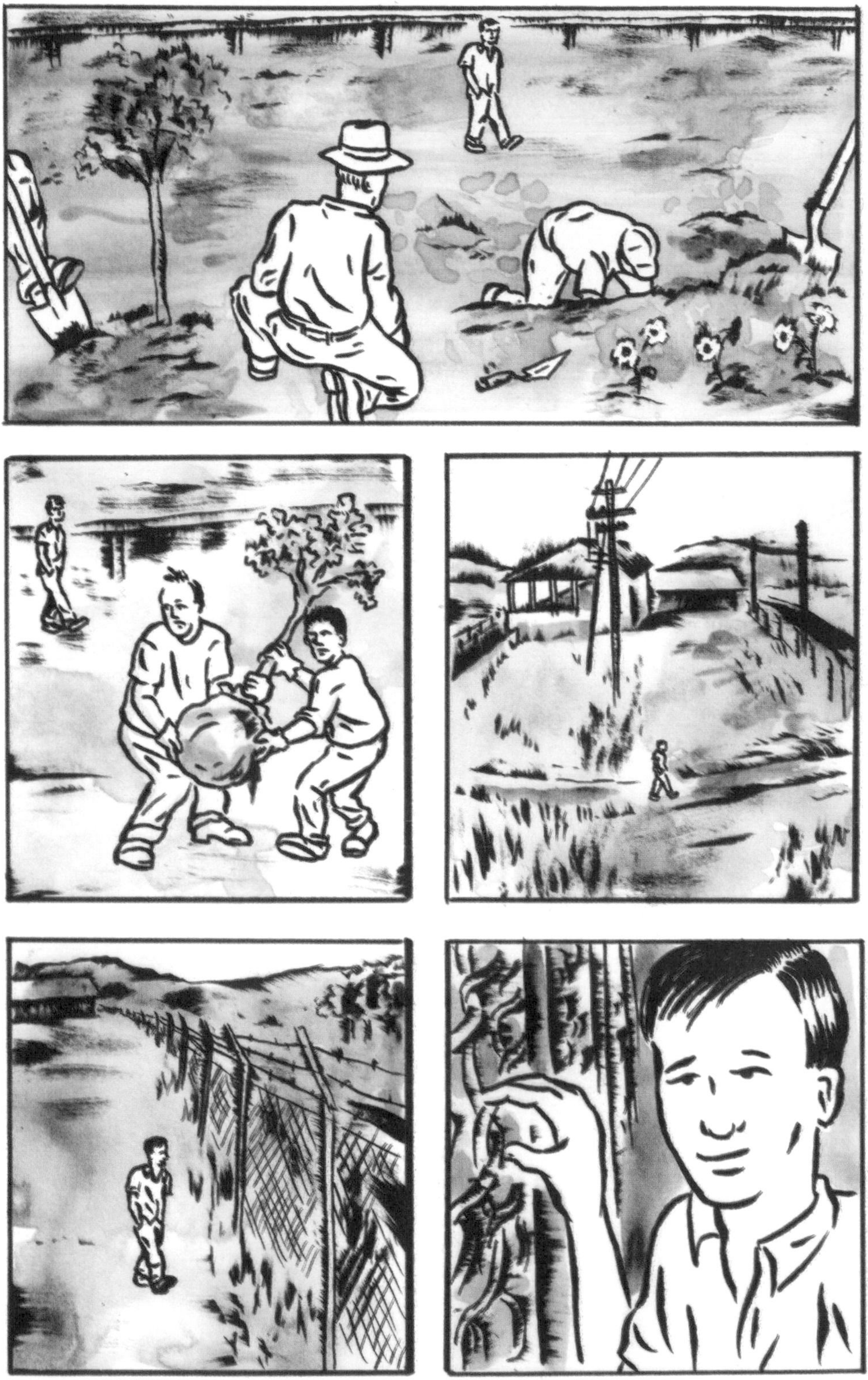

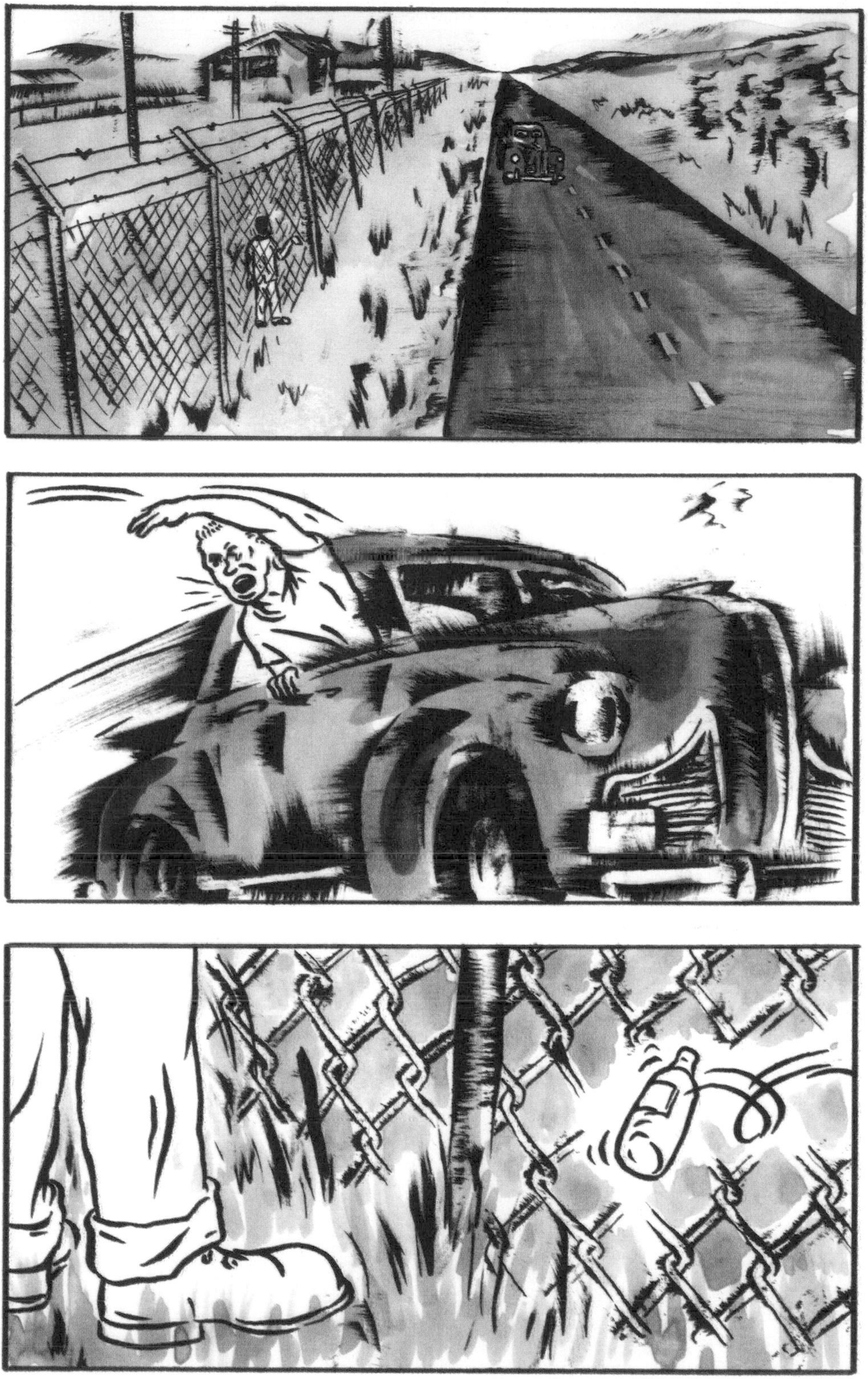

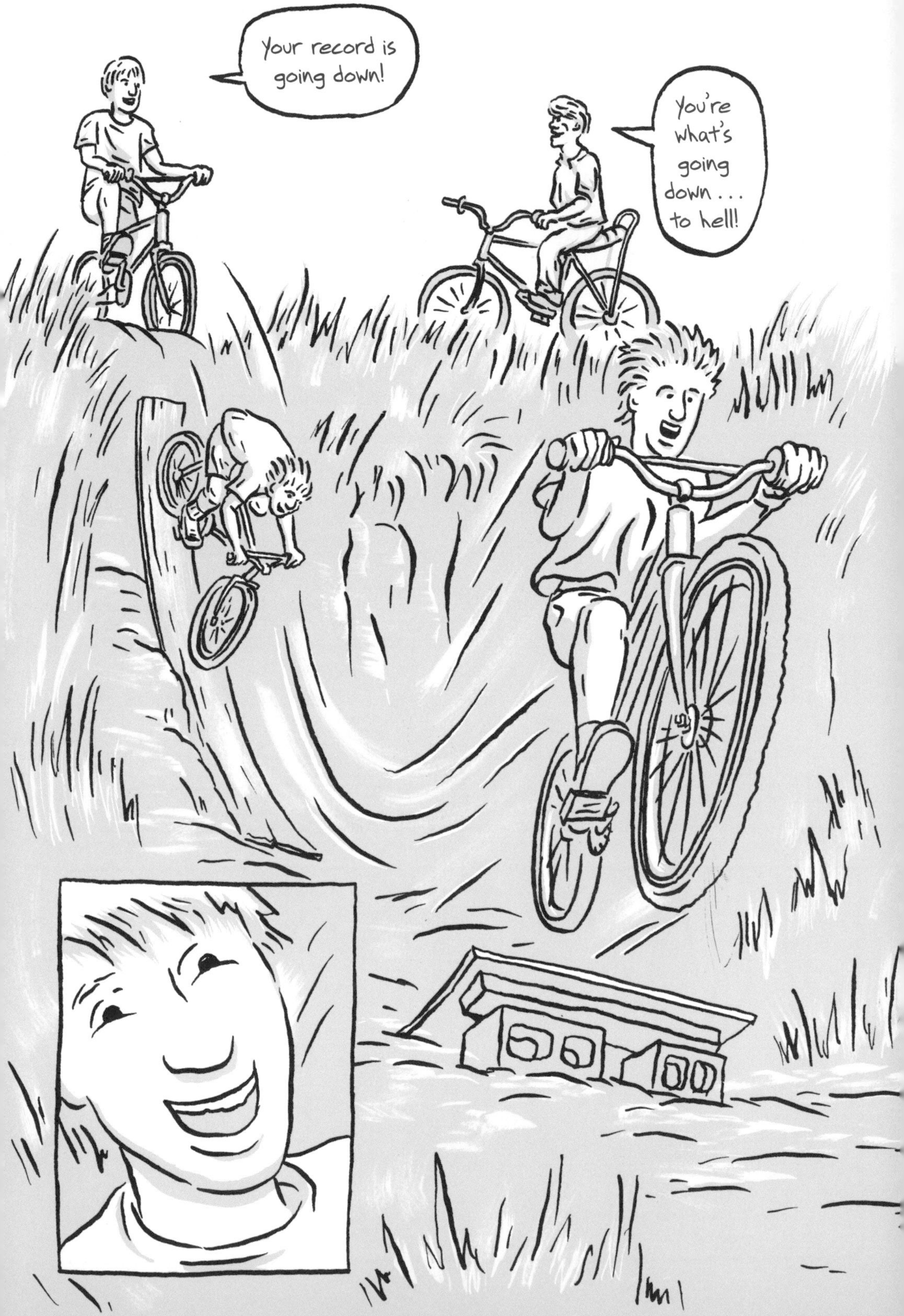
Your record is going down!
You're what's going down . . . to hell!

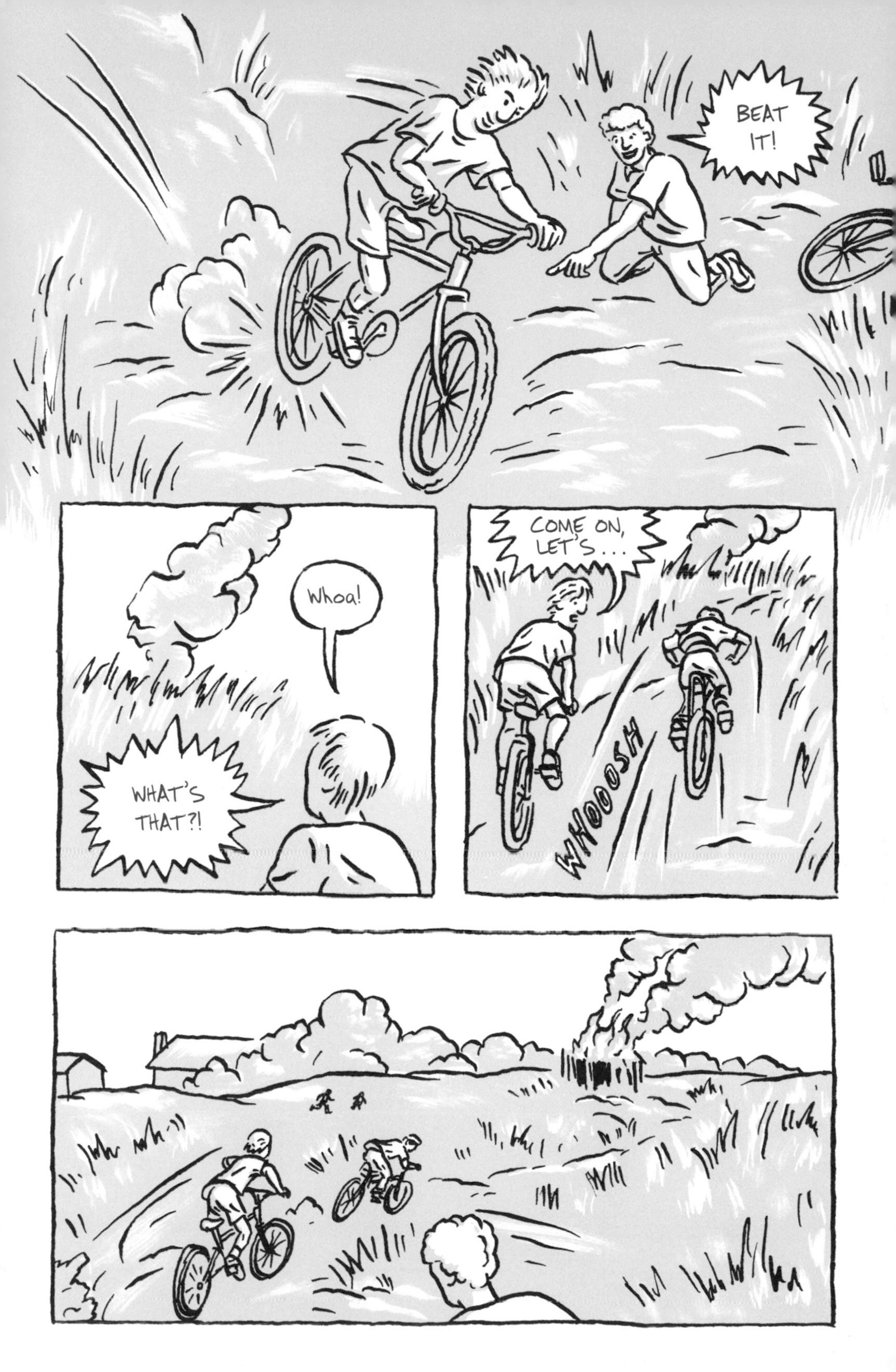
BEAT IT!
Whoa!
WHAT'S THAT?!
COME ON, LET'S . . .
WHOOOSH

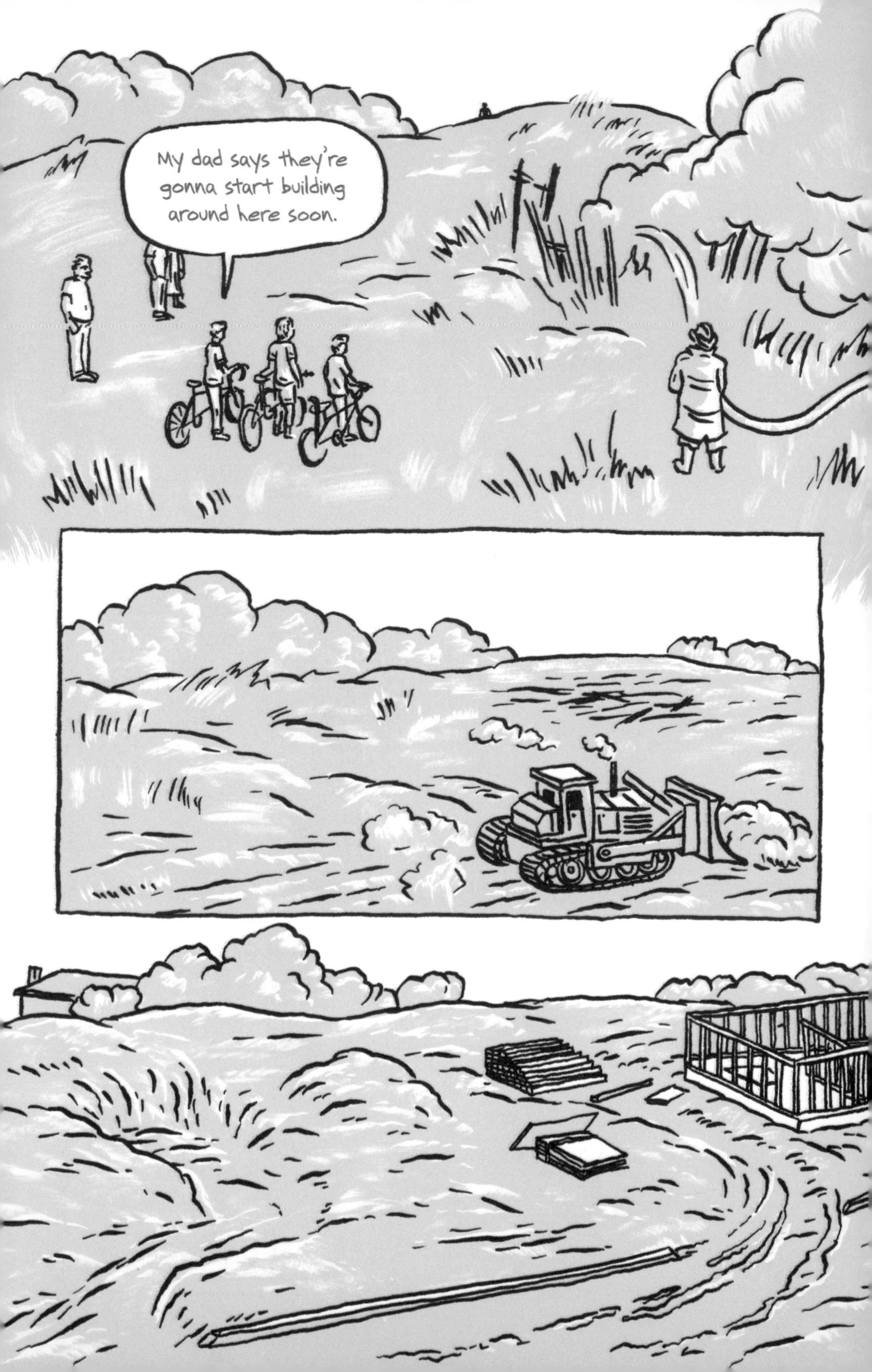
My dad says they're gonna start building around here soon.

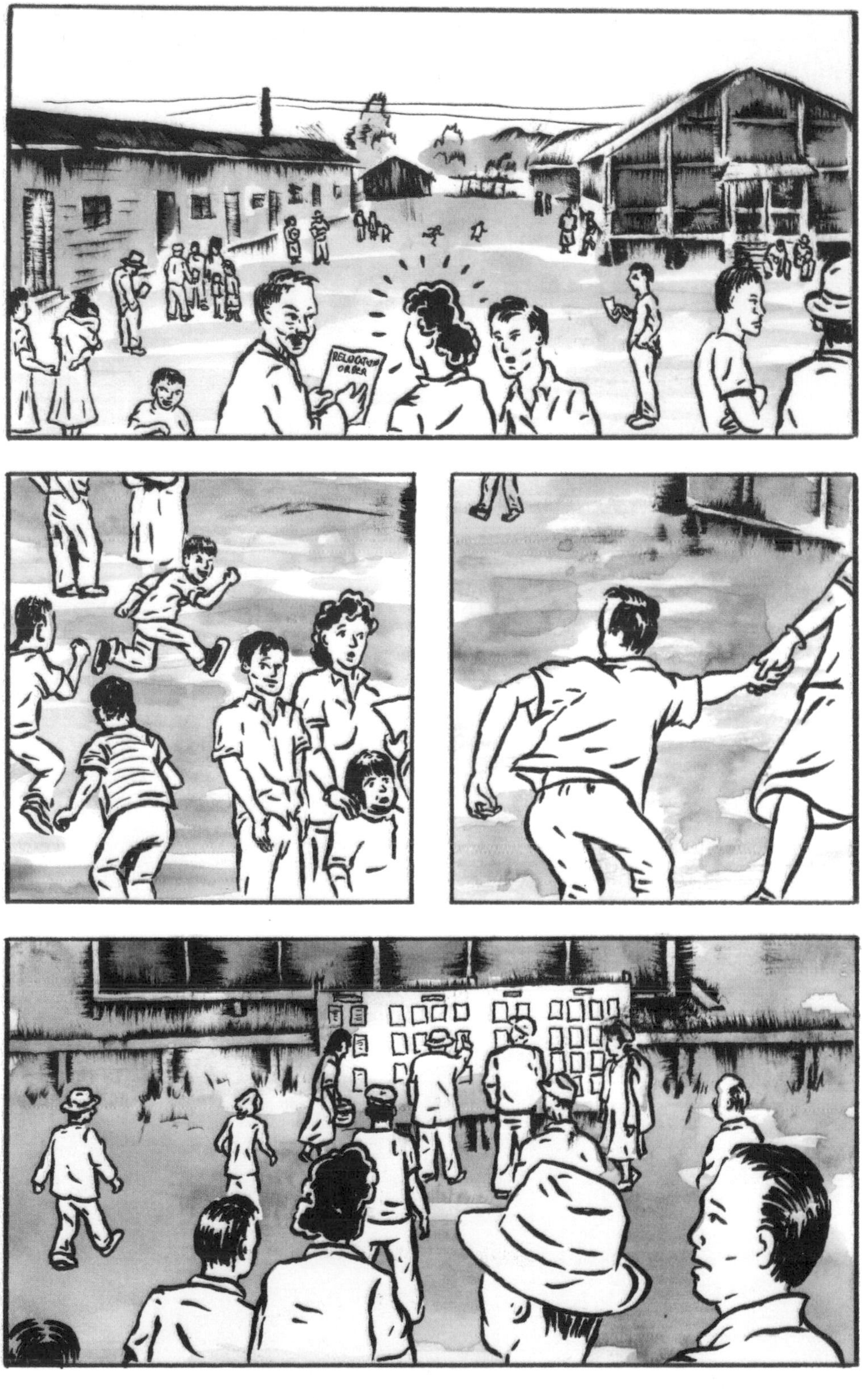
RELOCATION ORDER

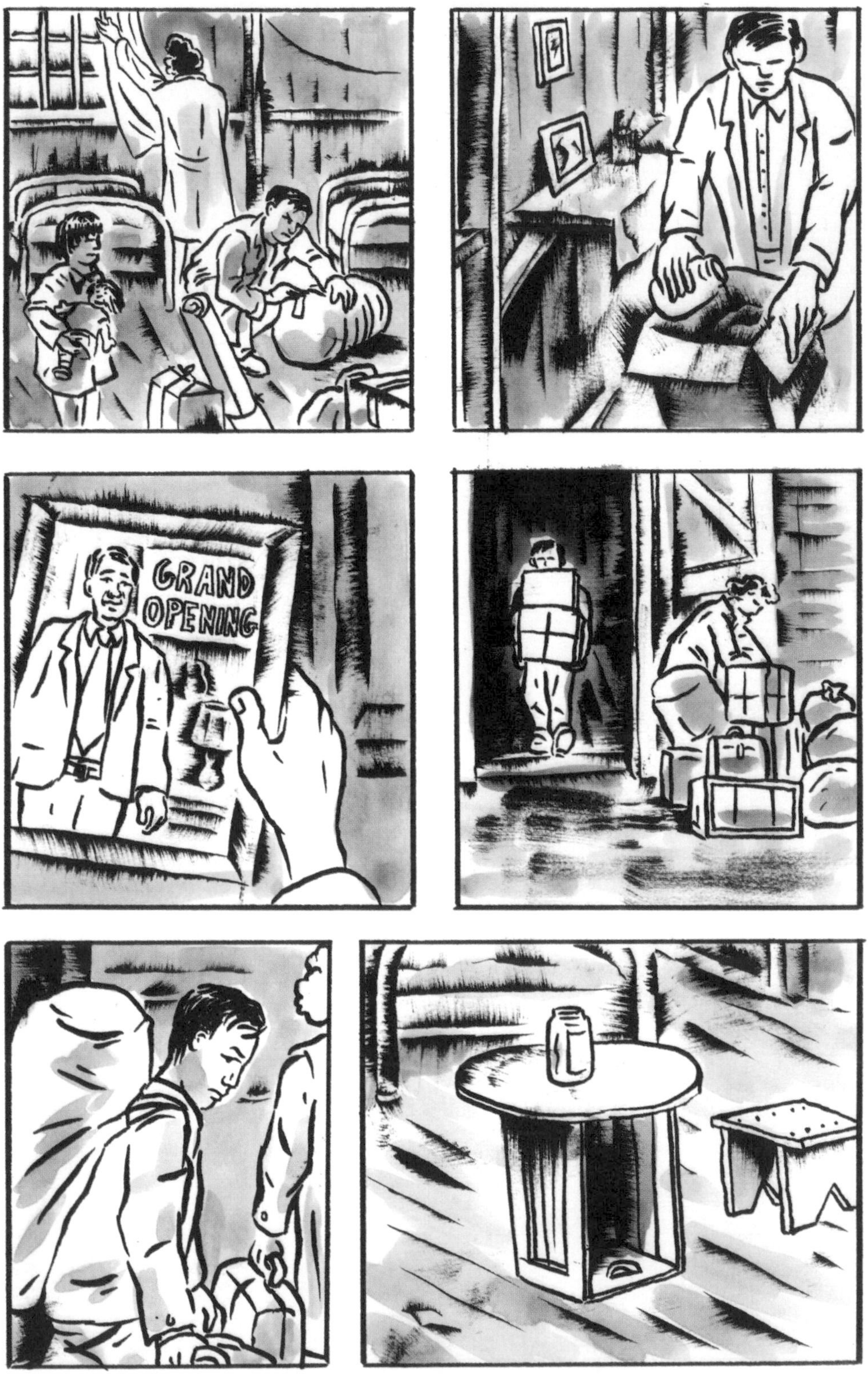
GRAND
OPENING

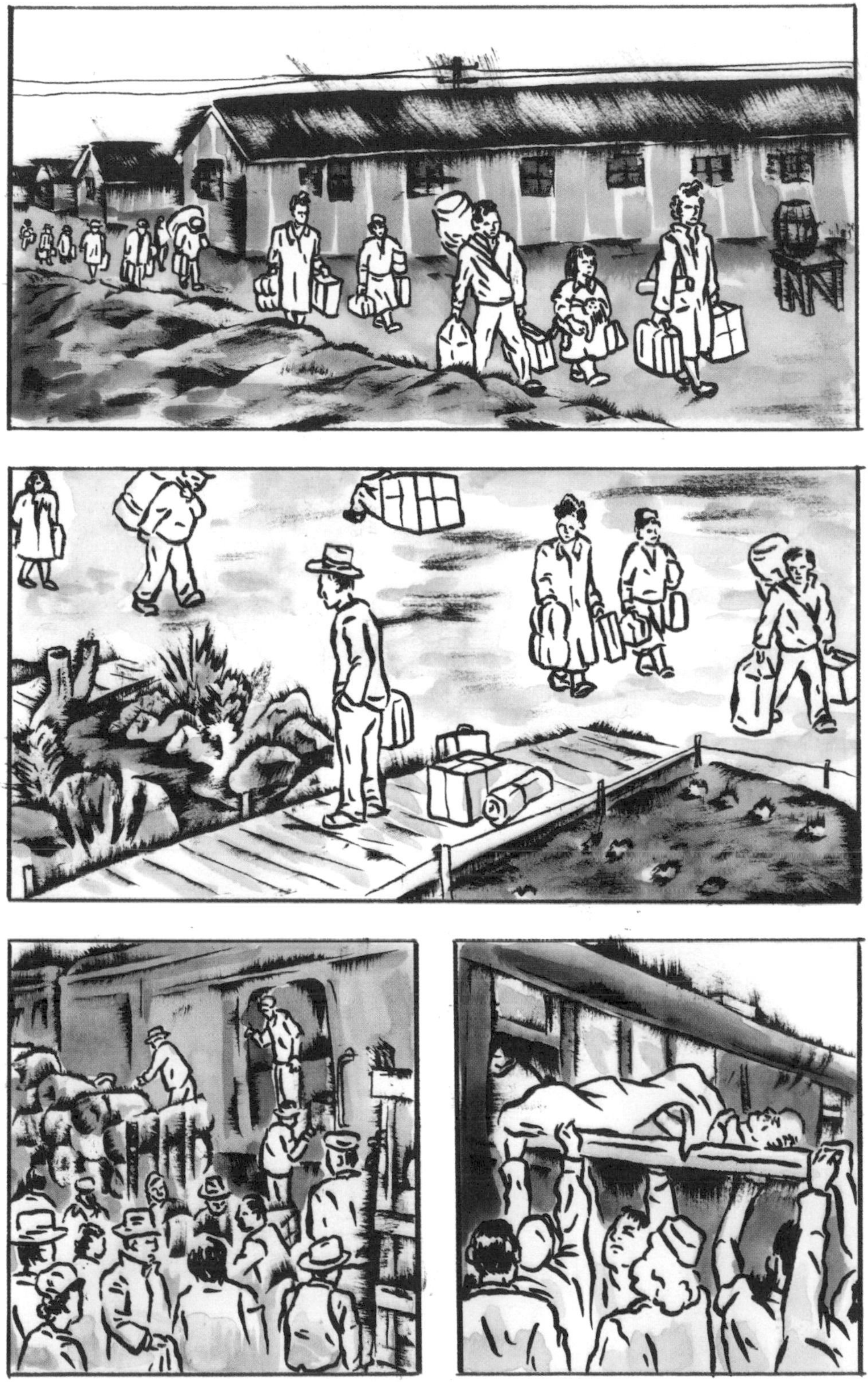

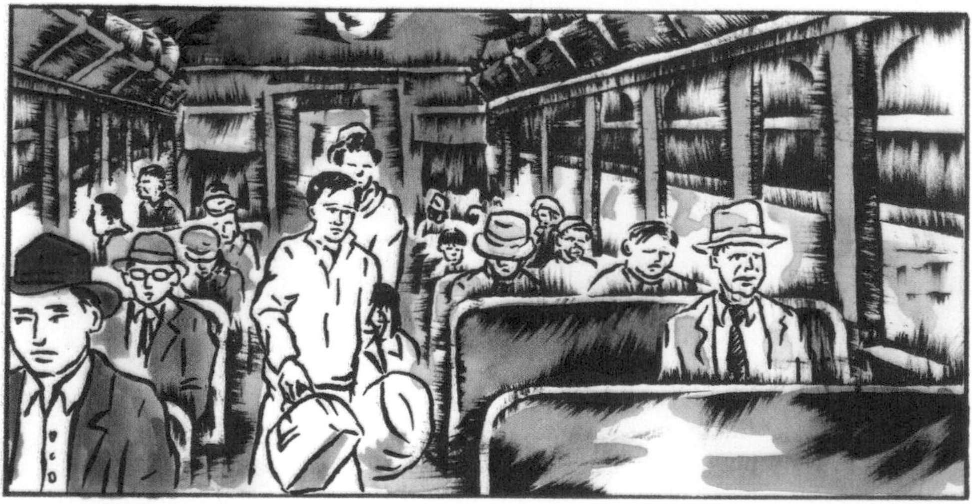
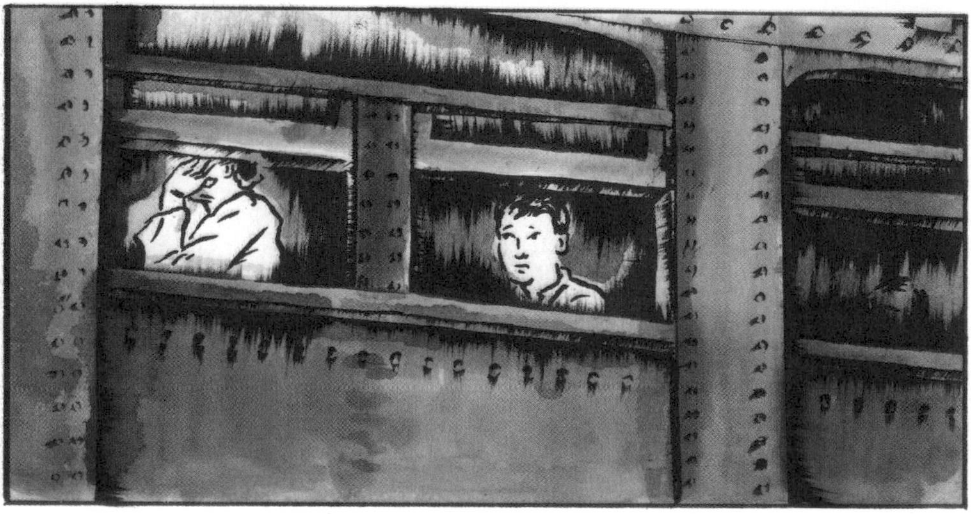
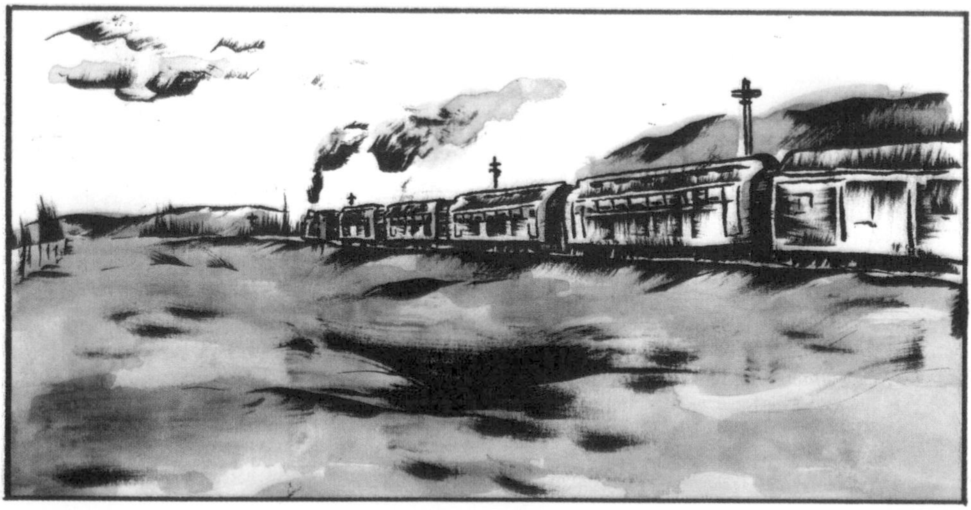

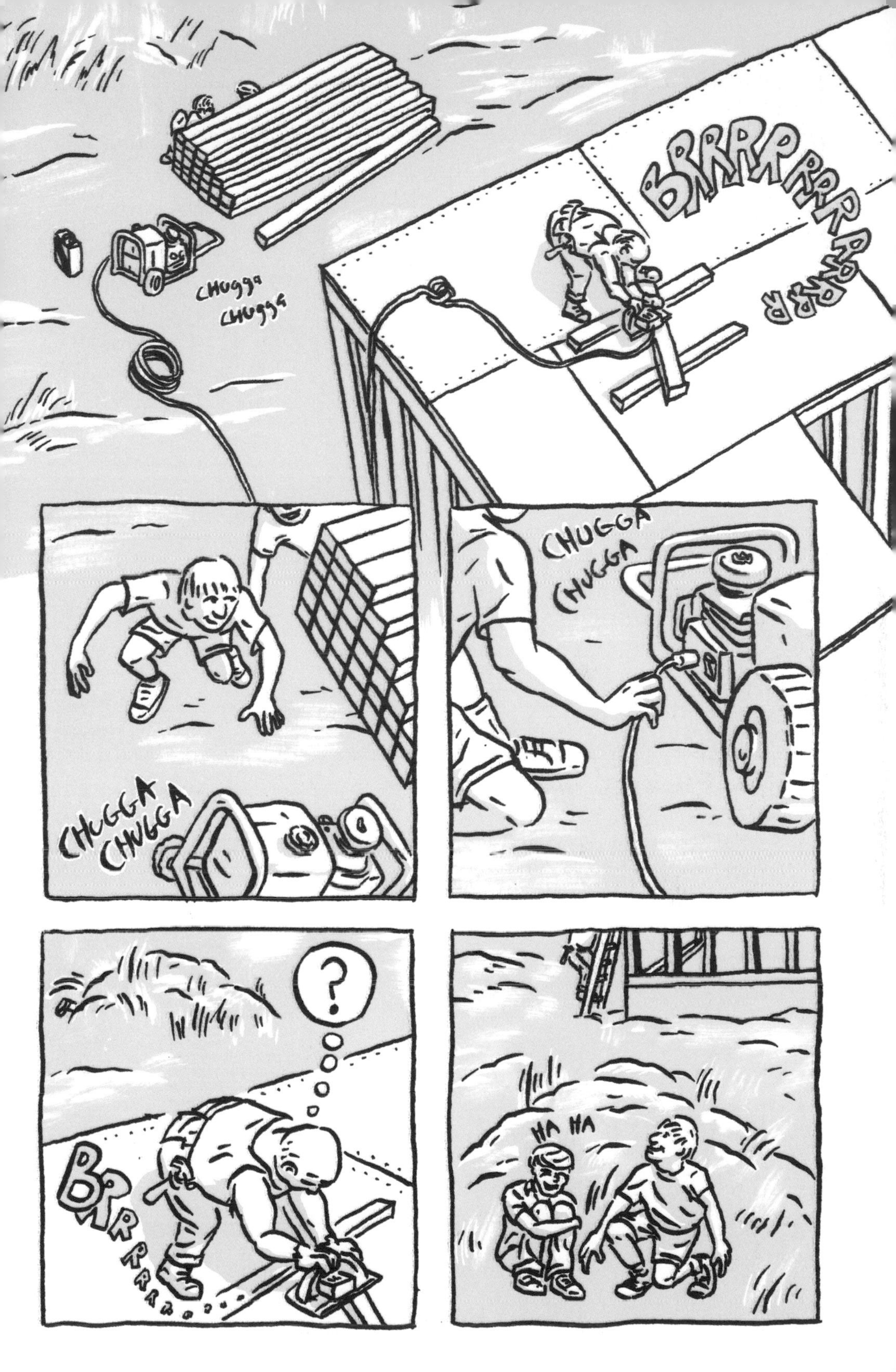

BRRRRRRRRRRRRRR
CHUGGA CHUGGA
CHUGGA CHUGGA
CHUGGA CHUGGA
?
BRRRR
HA HA

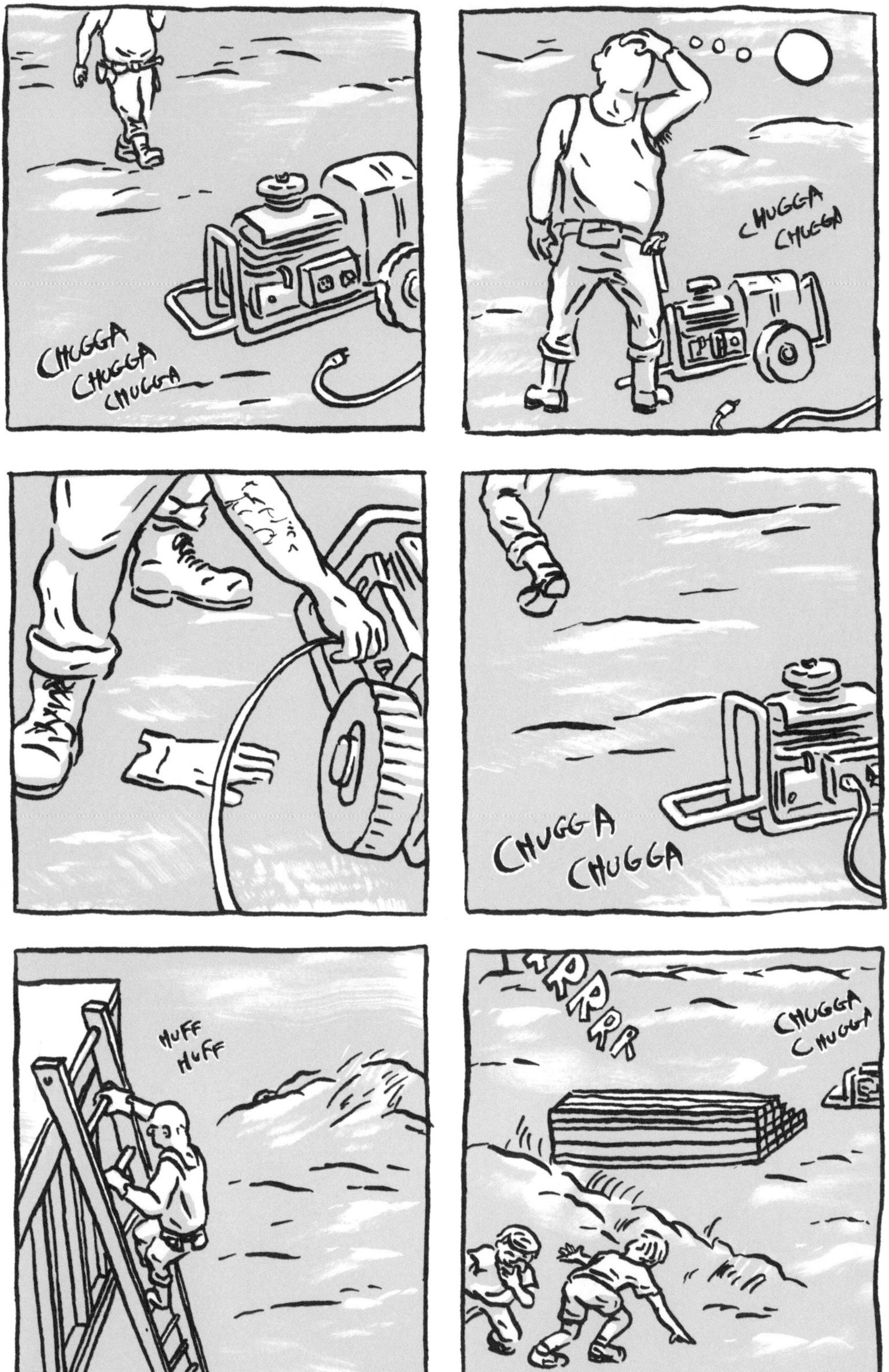
CHUGGA
CHUGGA
CHUGGA
CHUGGA
CHUGGA
CHUGGA
CHUGGA
HUFF
HUFF
RRRR
CHUGGA
CHUGGA

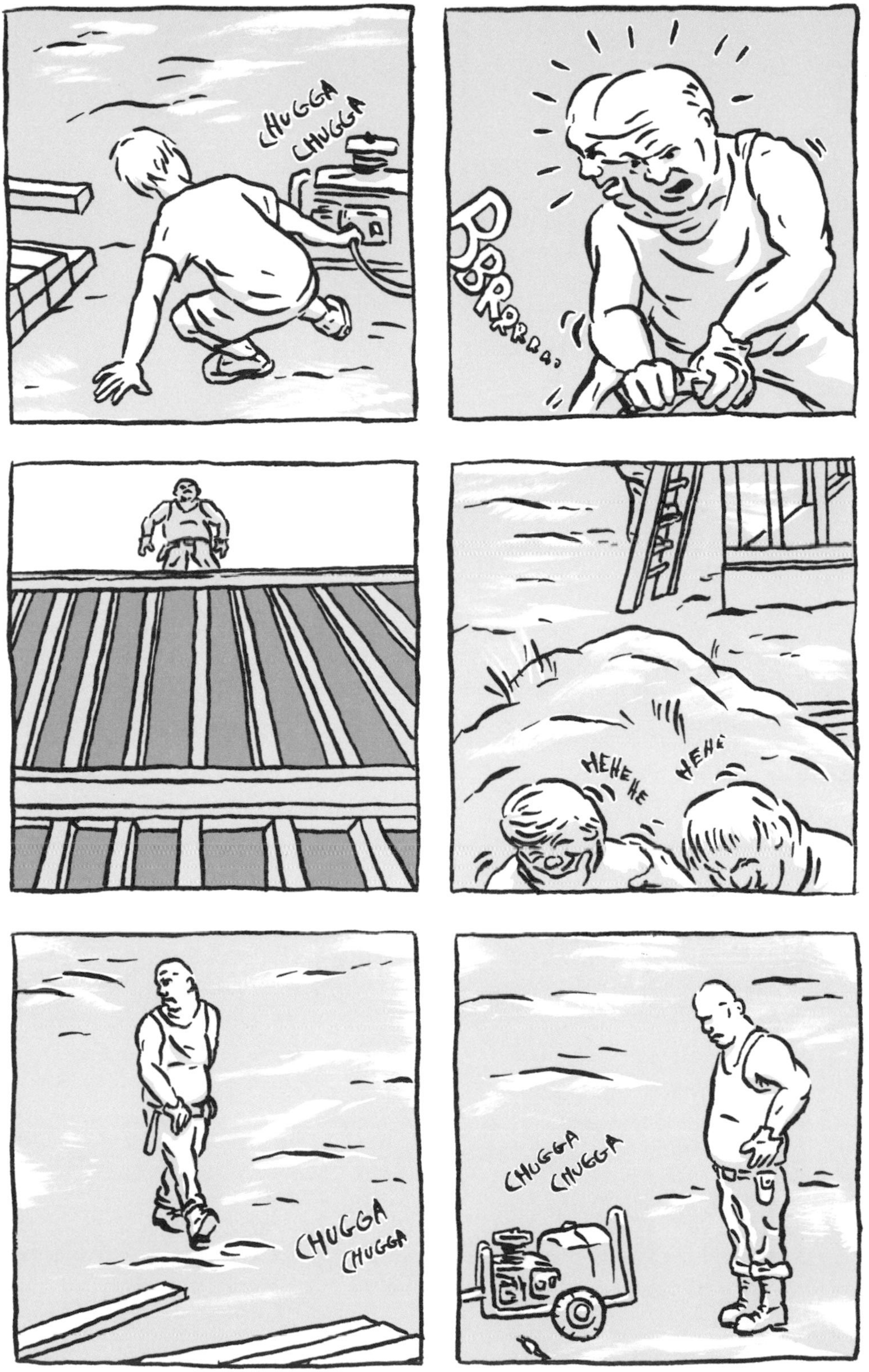
CHUGGA CHUGGA
BBRRRRRR...
HEHEHEHE
HEHE
CHUGGA CHUGGA
CHUGGA CHUGGA

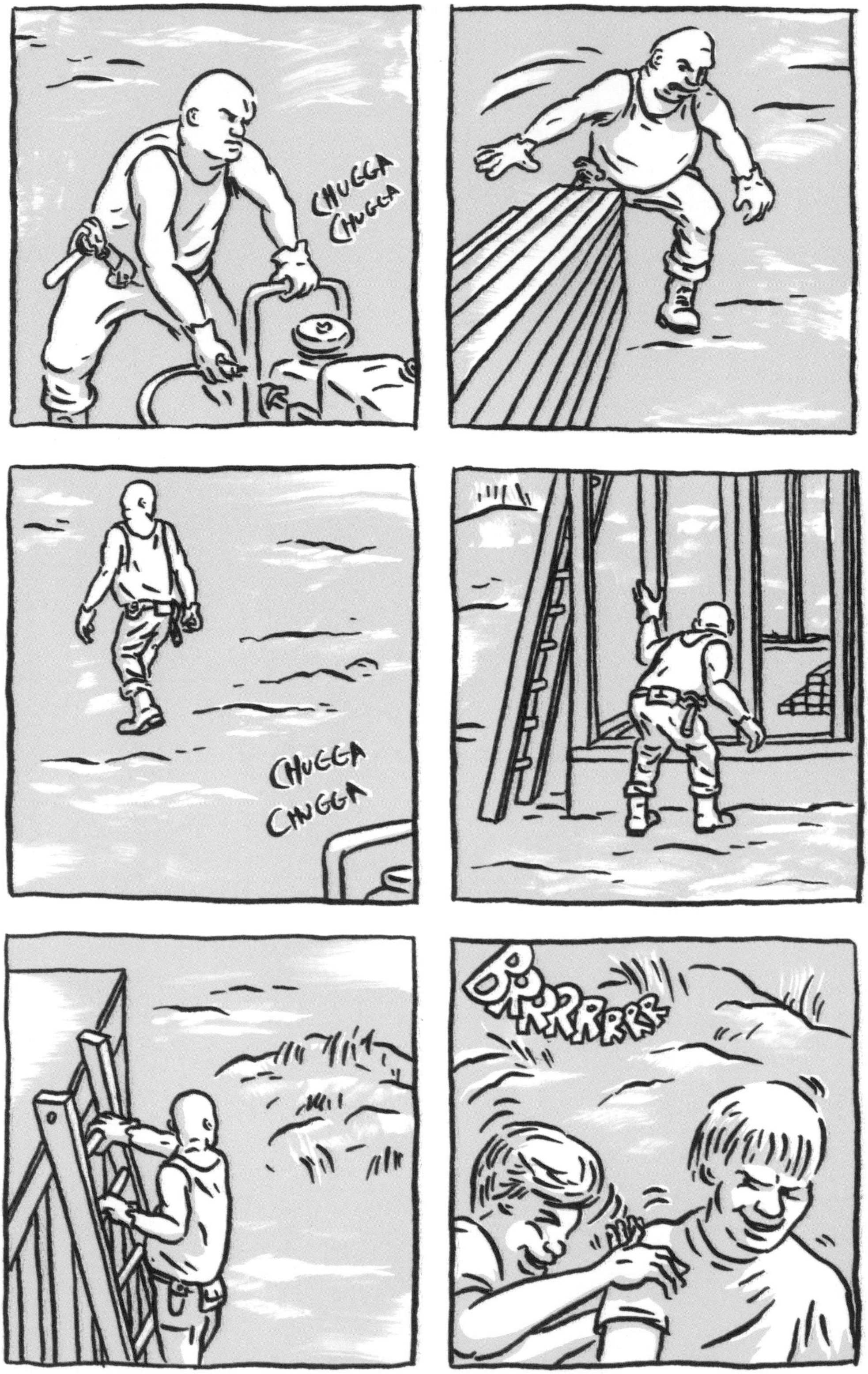
CHUGGA CHUGGA
CHUGGA CHUGGA
BRRRRRR

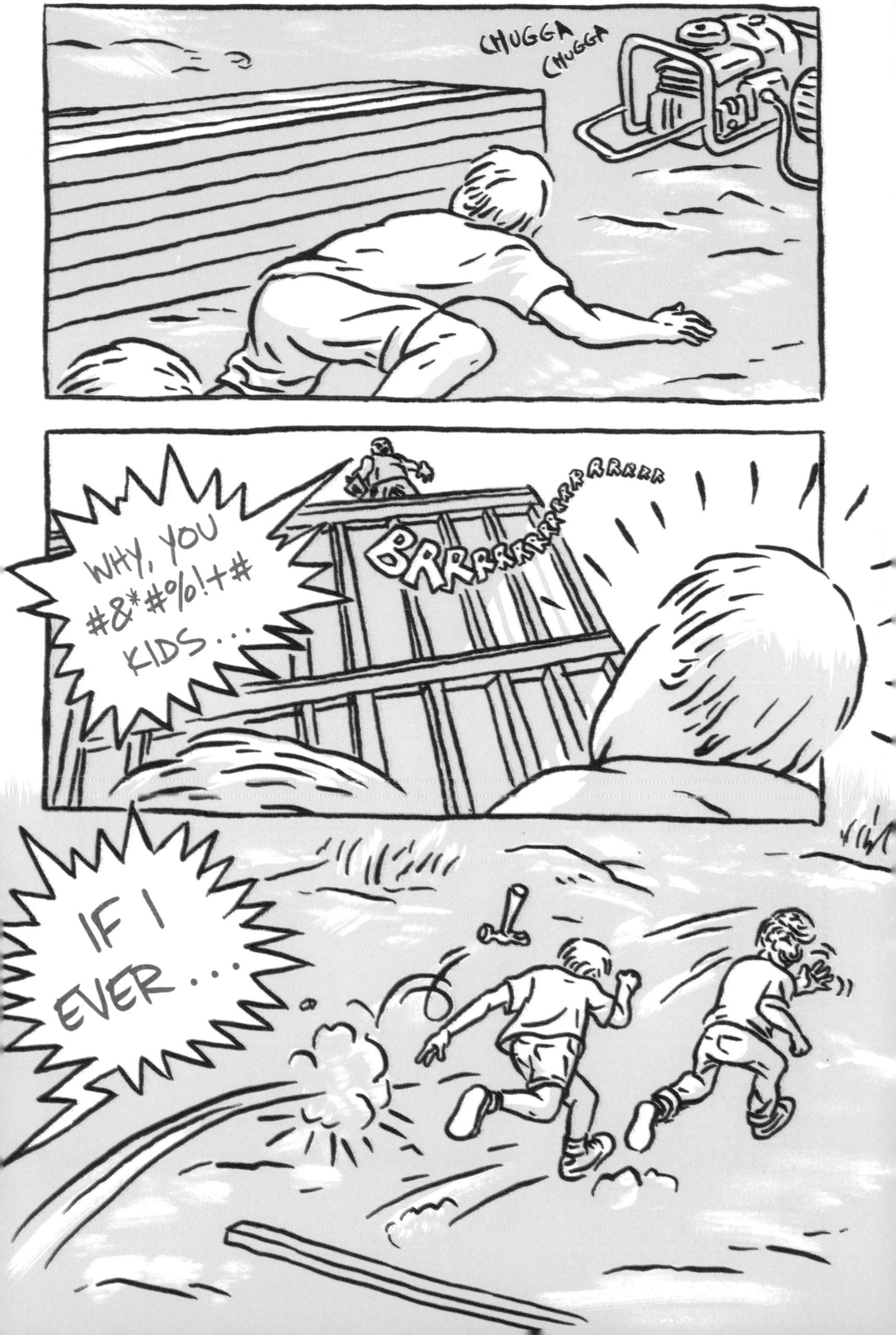
CHUGGA CHUGGA
BRRRRRRRRRRRRRRRRRR
WHY, YOU #&*#%!+# KIDS...
IF I EVER...

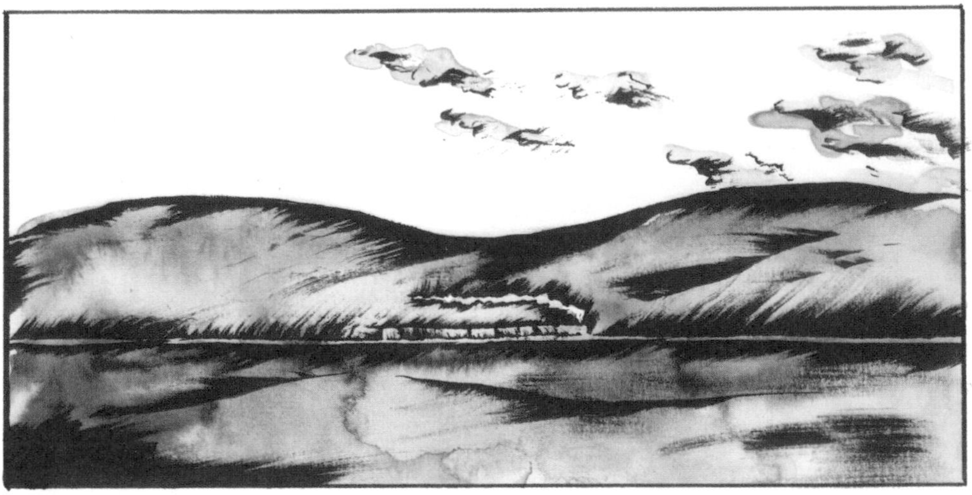
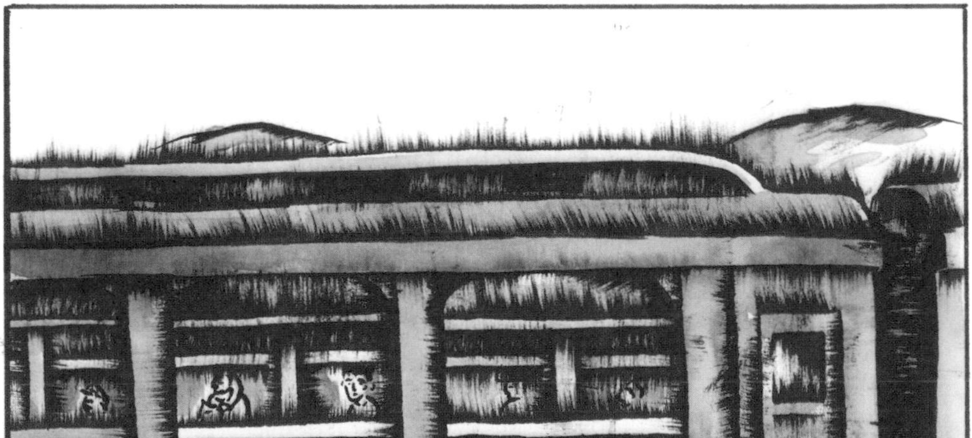
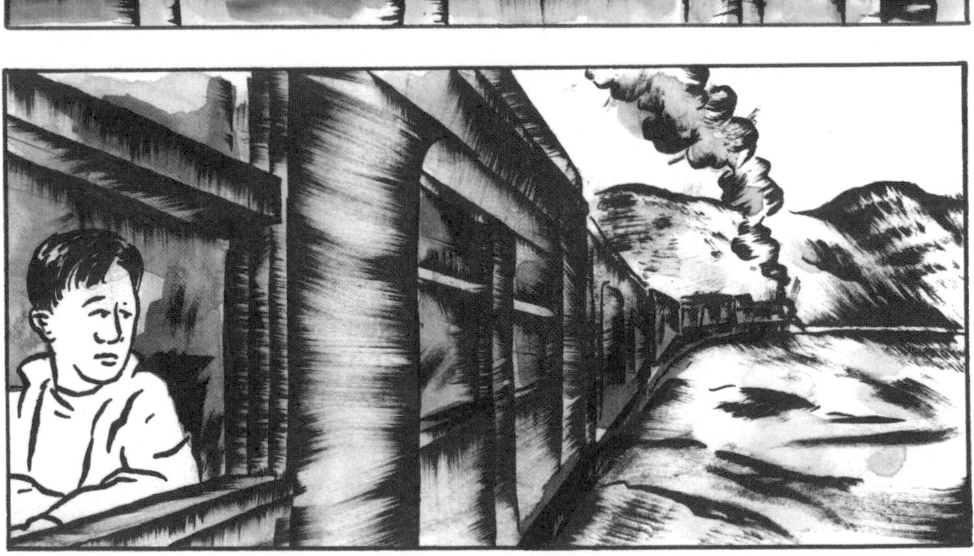

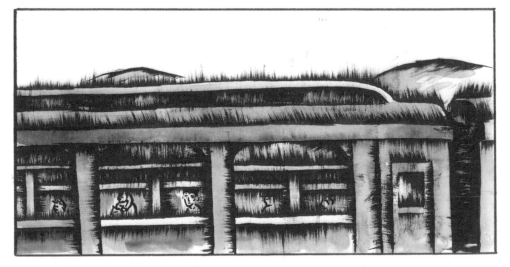

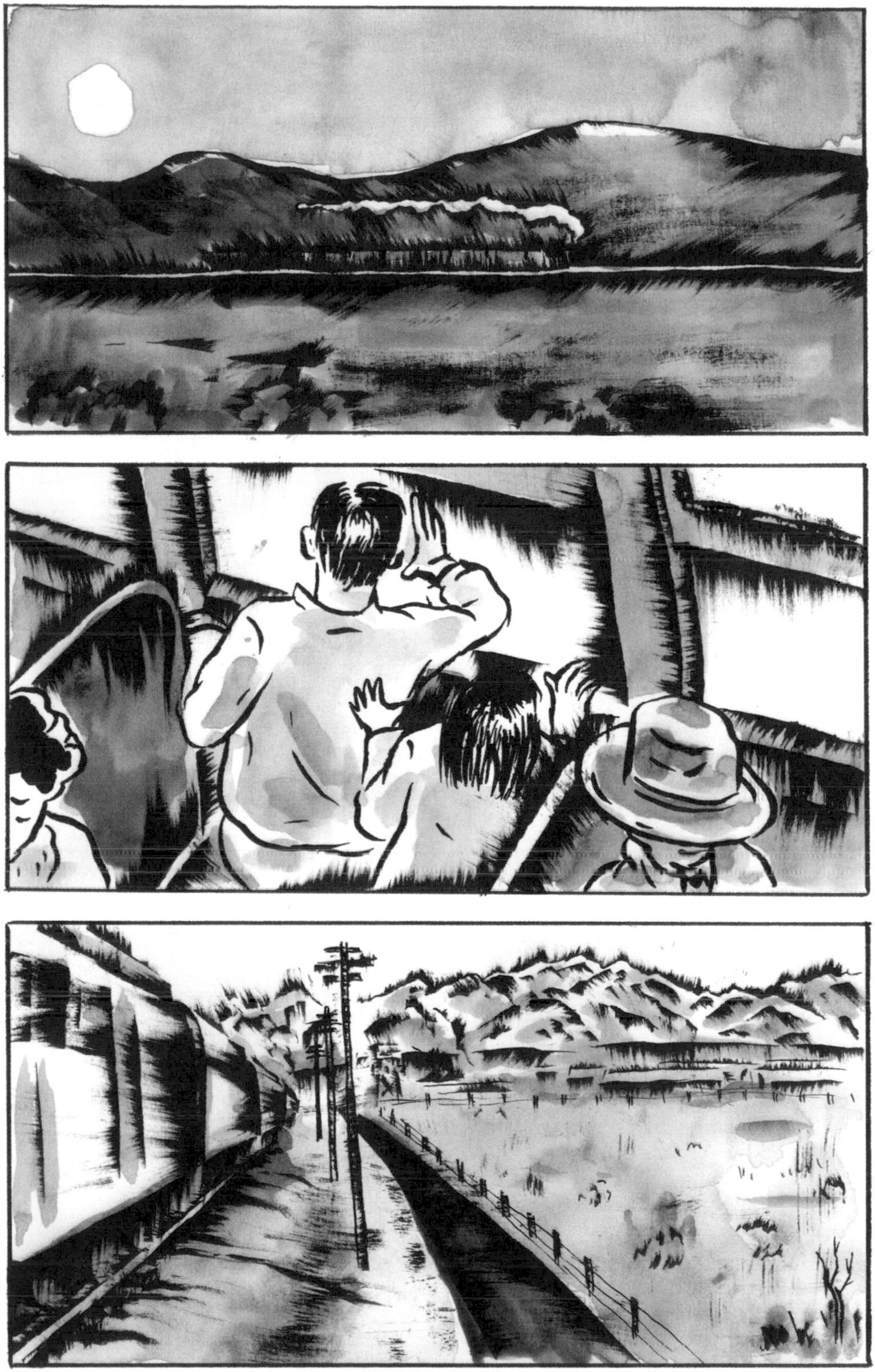

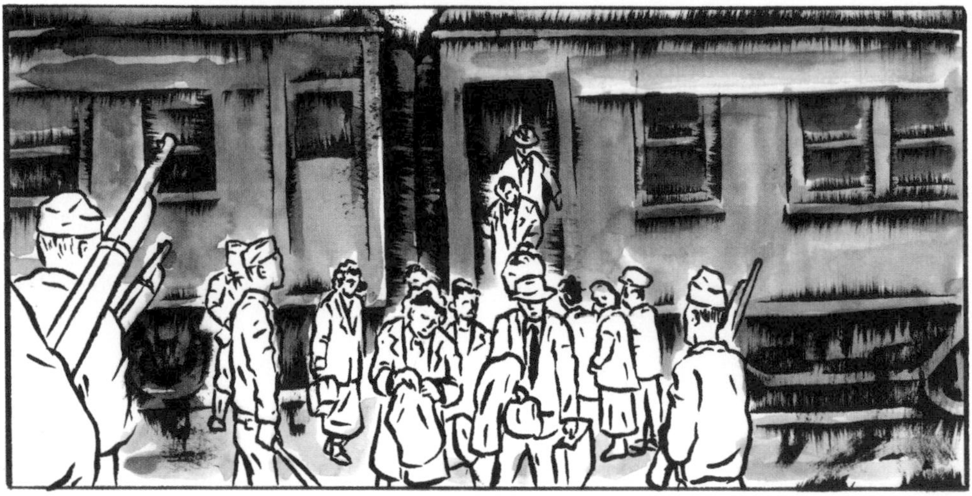

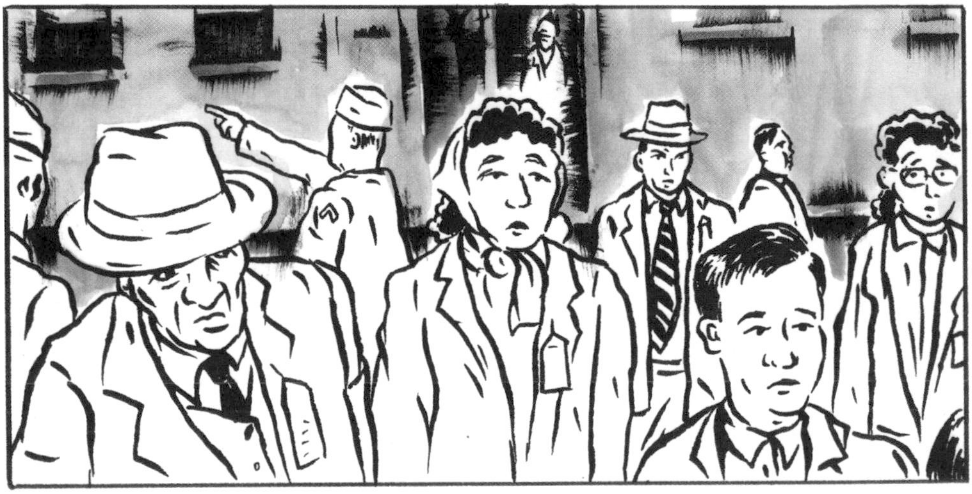

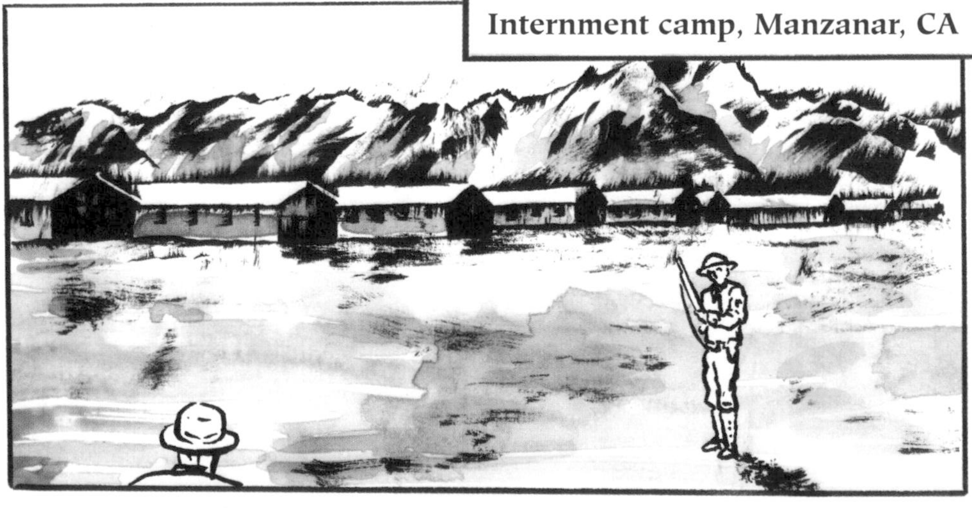
Internment camp, Manzanar, CA

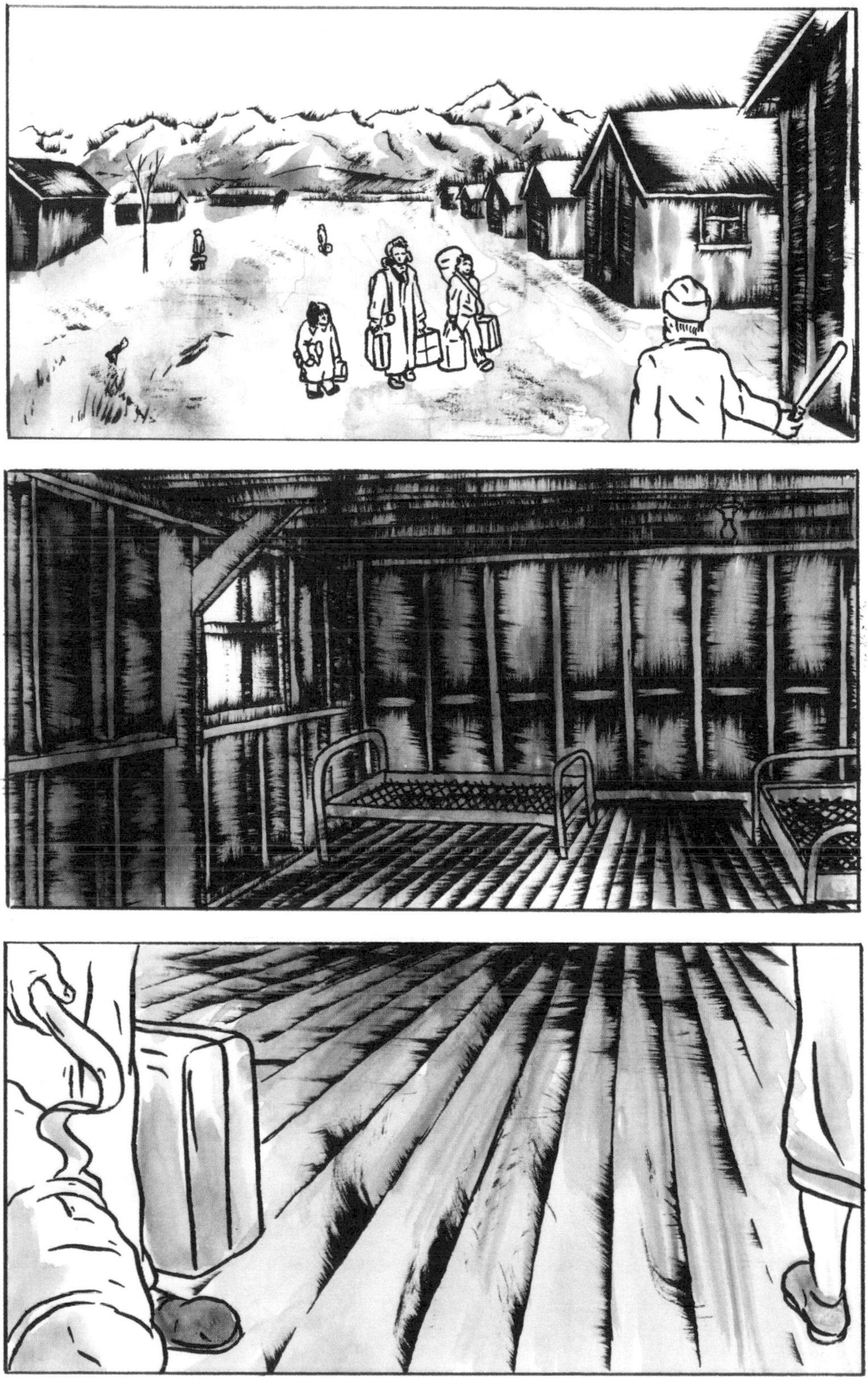

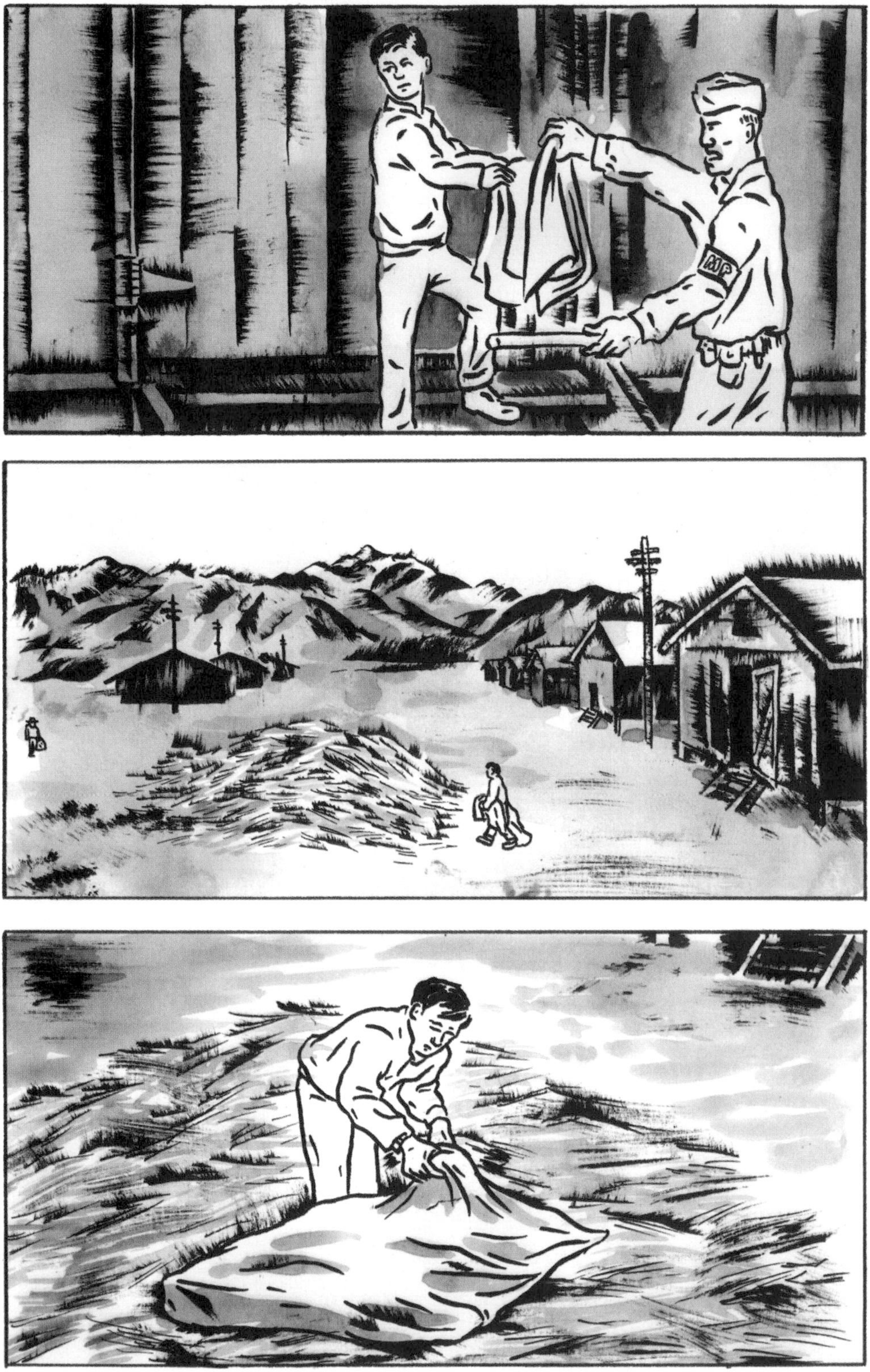
MP

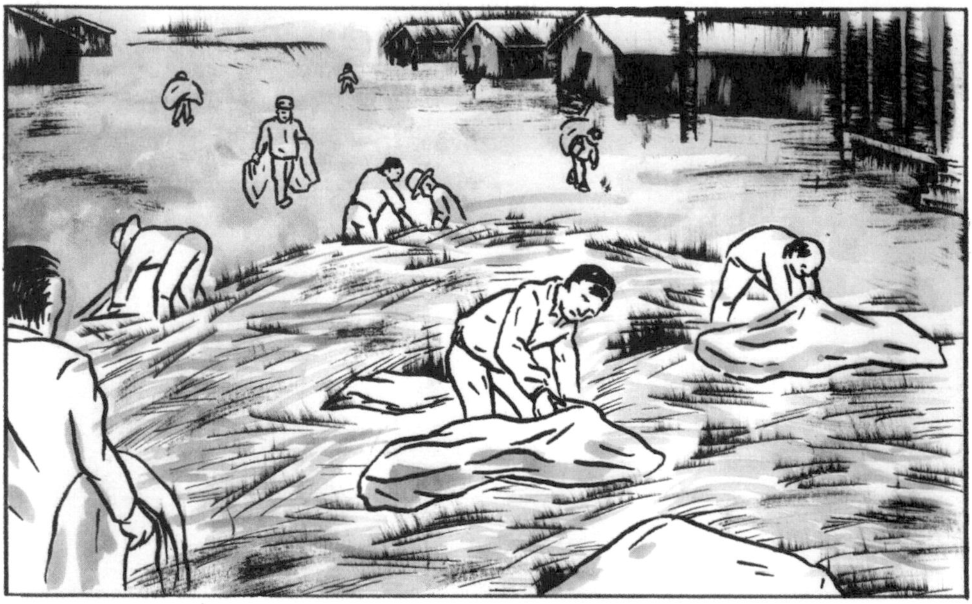

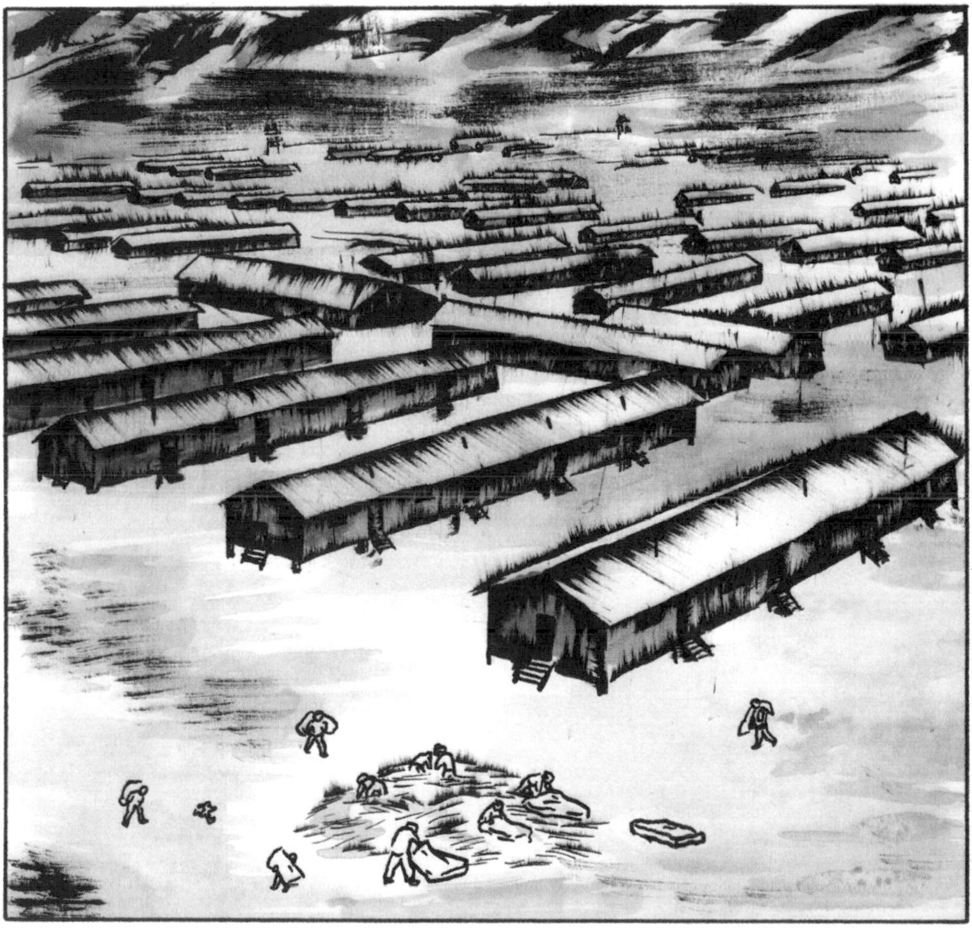

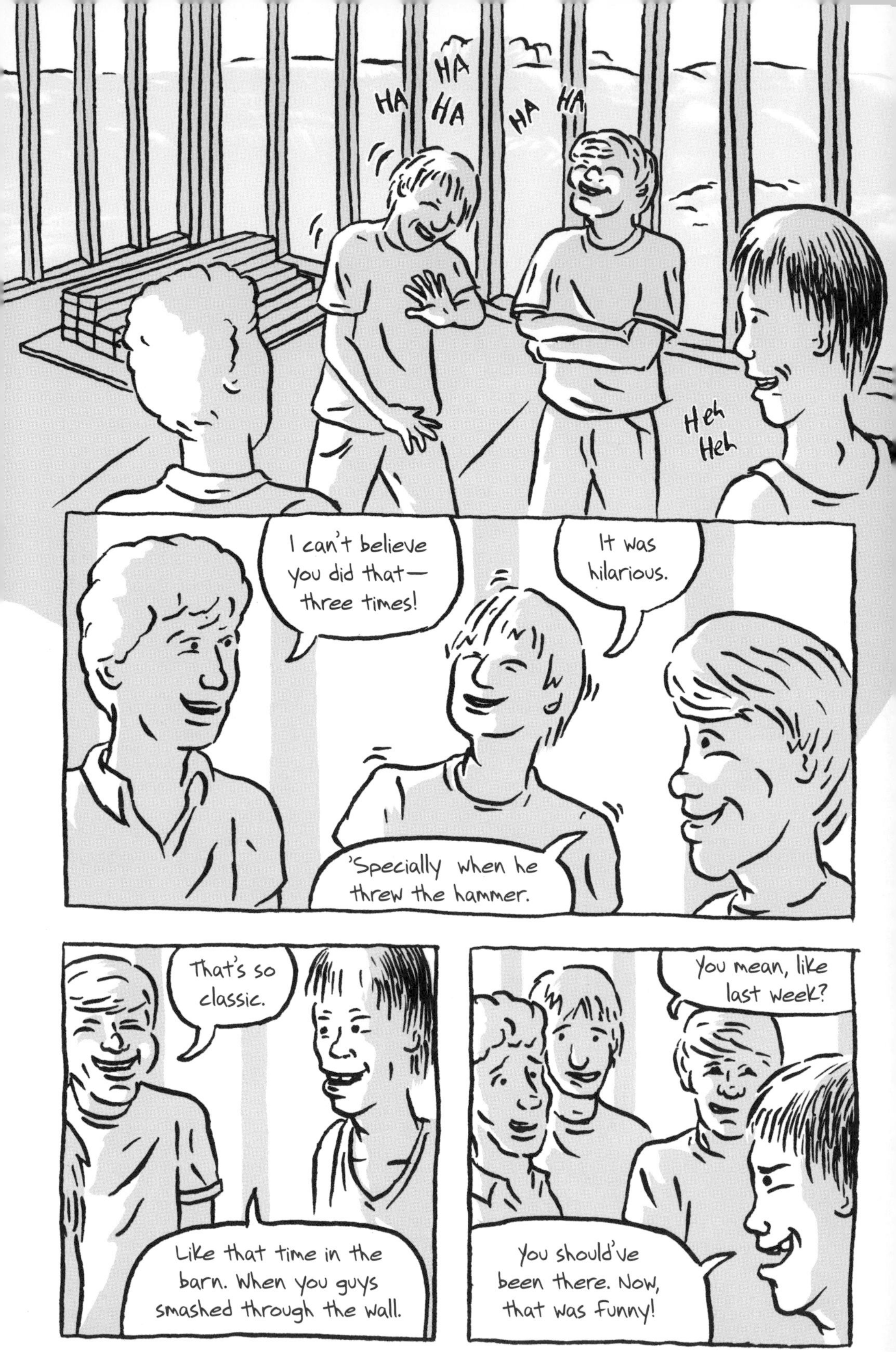
HA
HA
HA
HA
HA
Heh
Heh
I can't believe you did that— three times!
It was hilarious.
'Specially when he threw the hammer.
That's so classic.
Like that time in the barn. When you guys smashed through the wall.
You mean, like last week?
You should've been there. Now, that was funny!

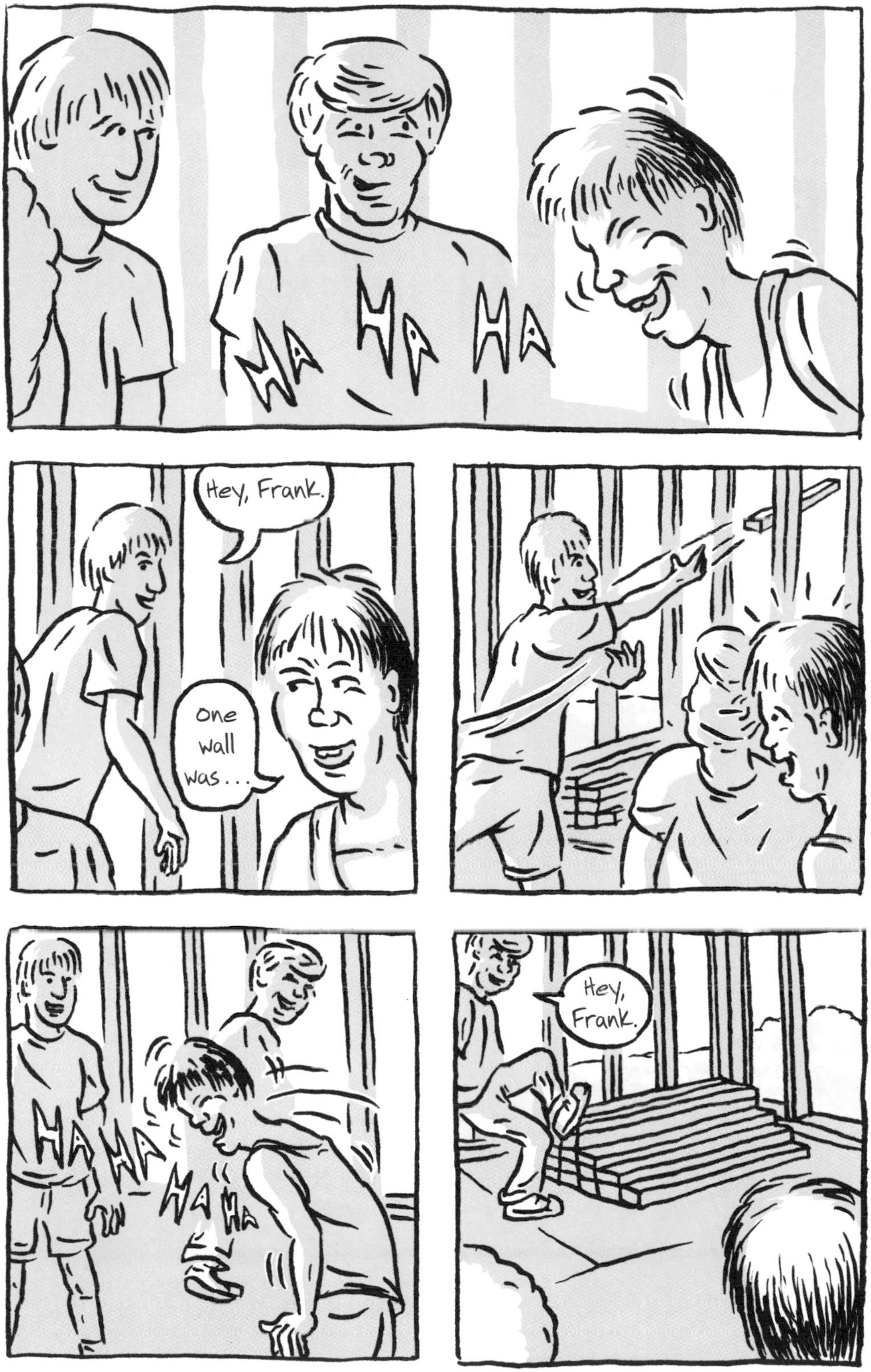
HA HA HA
Hey, Frank.
One wall was...
HA HA HA HA
Hey, Frank.

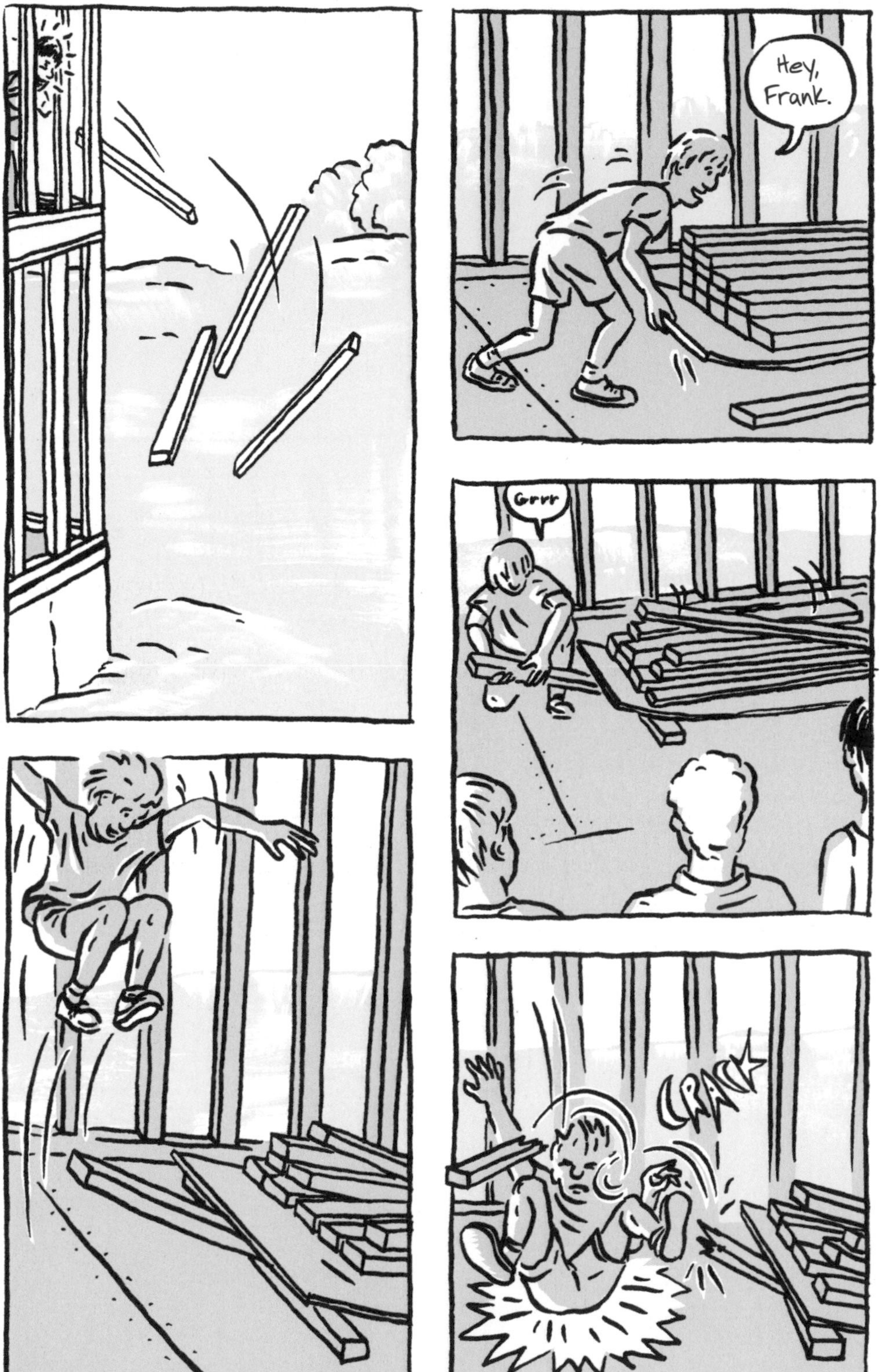
Hey, Frank.
Grrr
CRACK

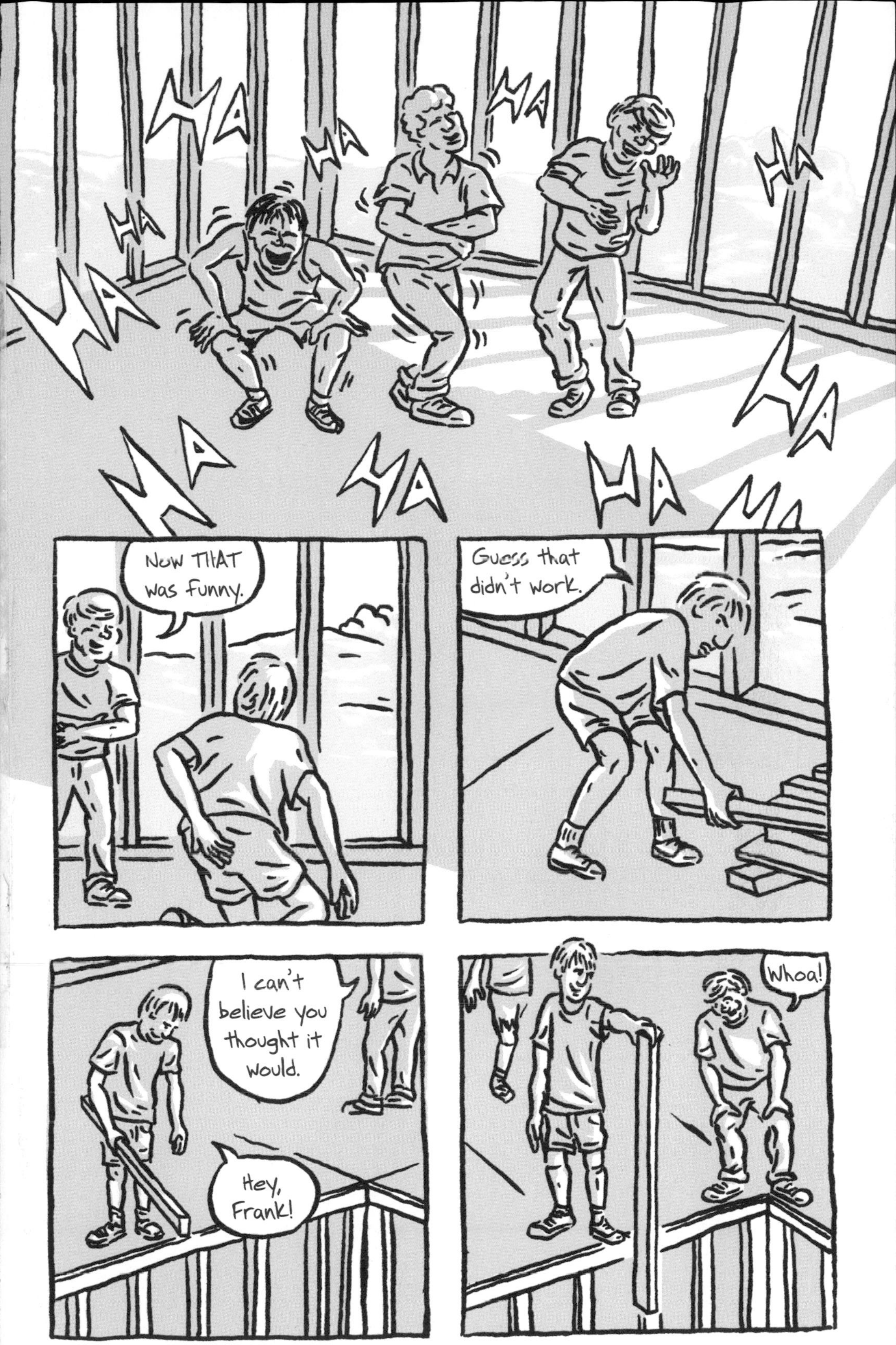
HA
HA
HA
HA
HA
HA
HA
HA
HA
HA
Now THAT was funny.
Guess that didn't work.
I can't believe you thought it would.
Hey, Frank!
Whoa!

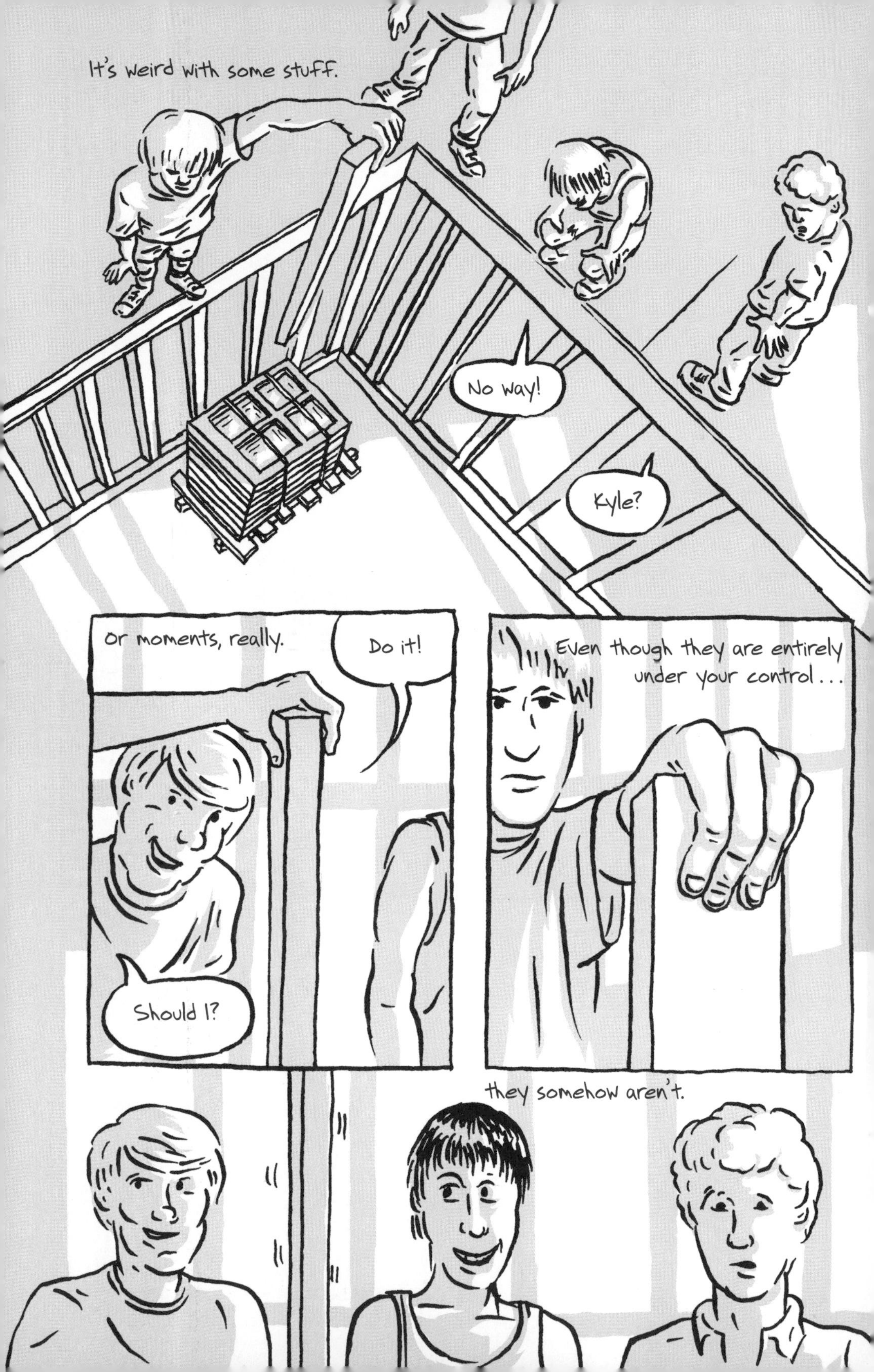
It's weird with some stuff.
No way!
Kyle?
Or moments, really.
Do it!
Should I?
Even though they are entirely under your control . . .
they somehow aren't.

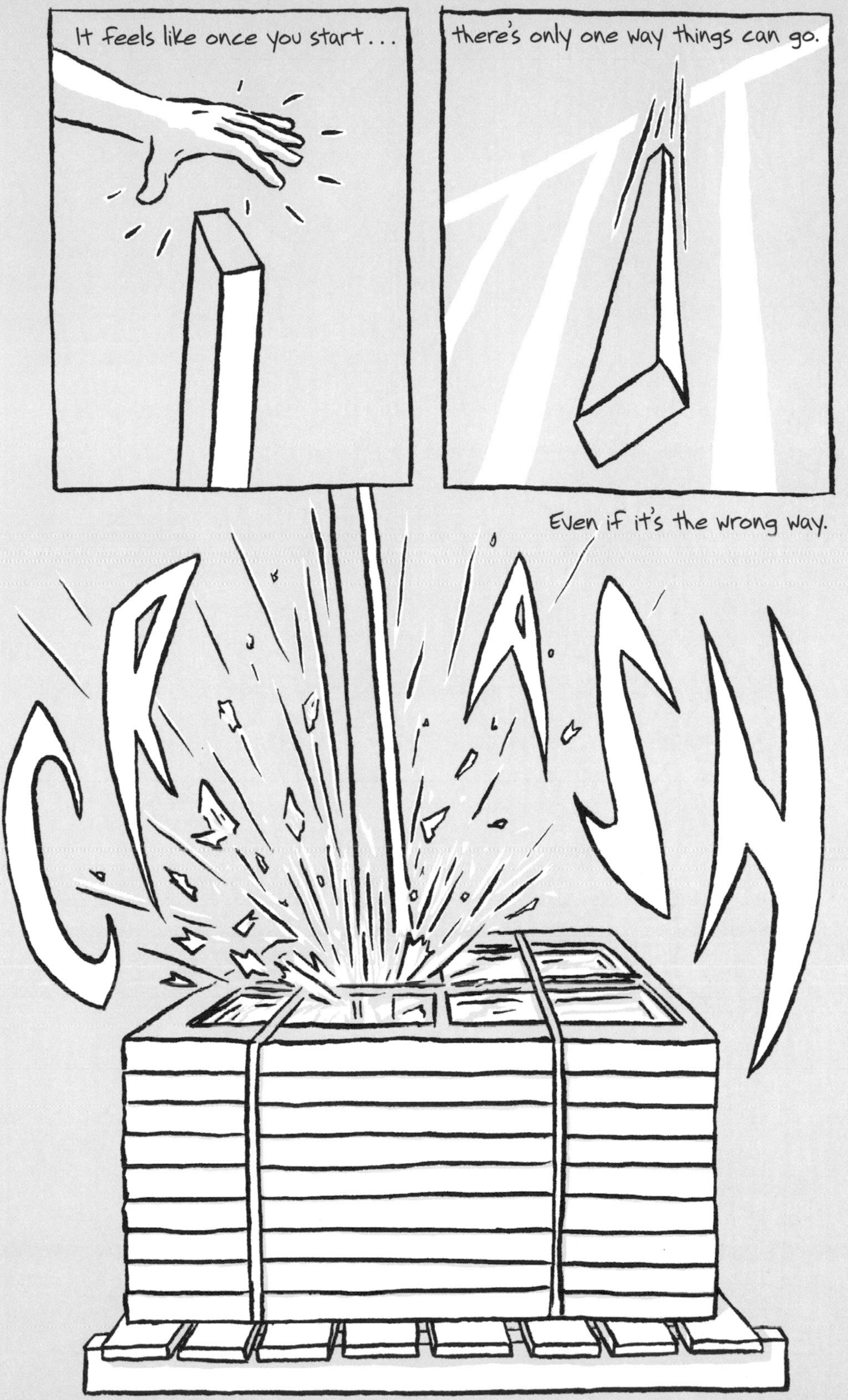

It feels like once you start...
there's only one way things can go.
Even if it's the wrong way.
CRASH

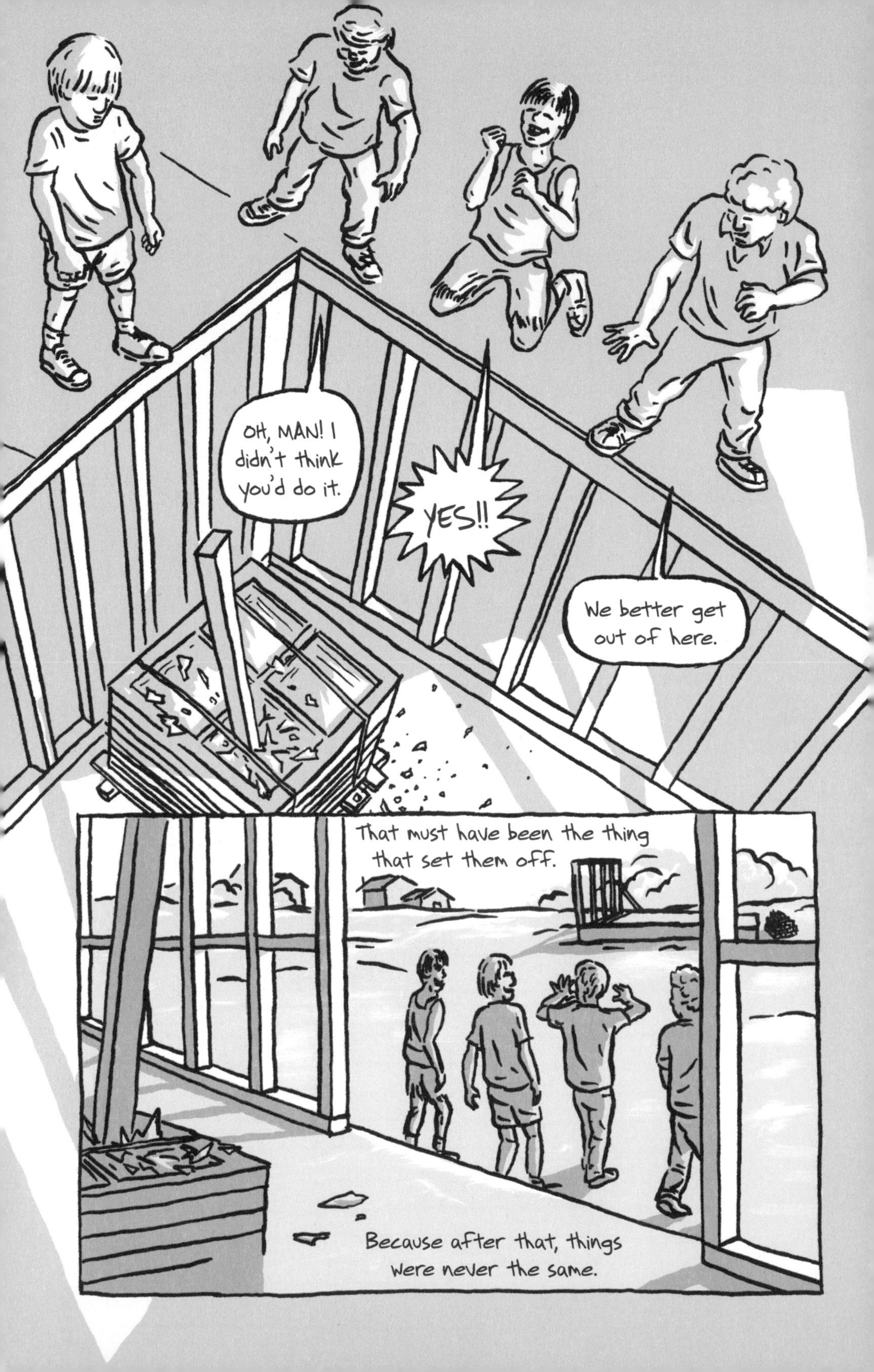
OH, MAN! I didn't think you'd do it.
YES!!
We better get out of here.
That must have been the thing that set them off.
Because after that, things were never the same.

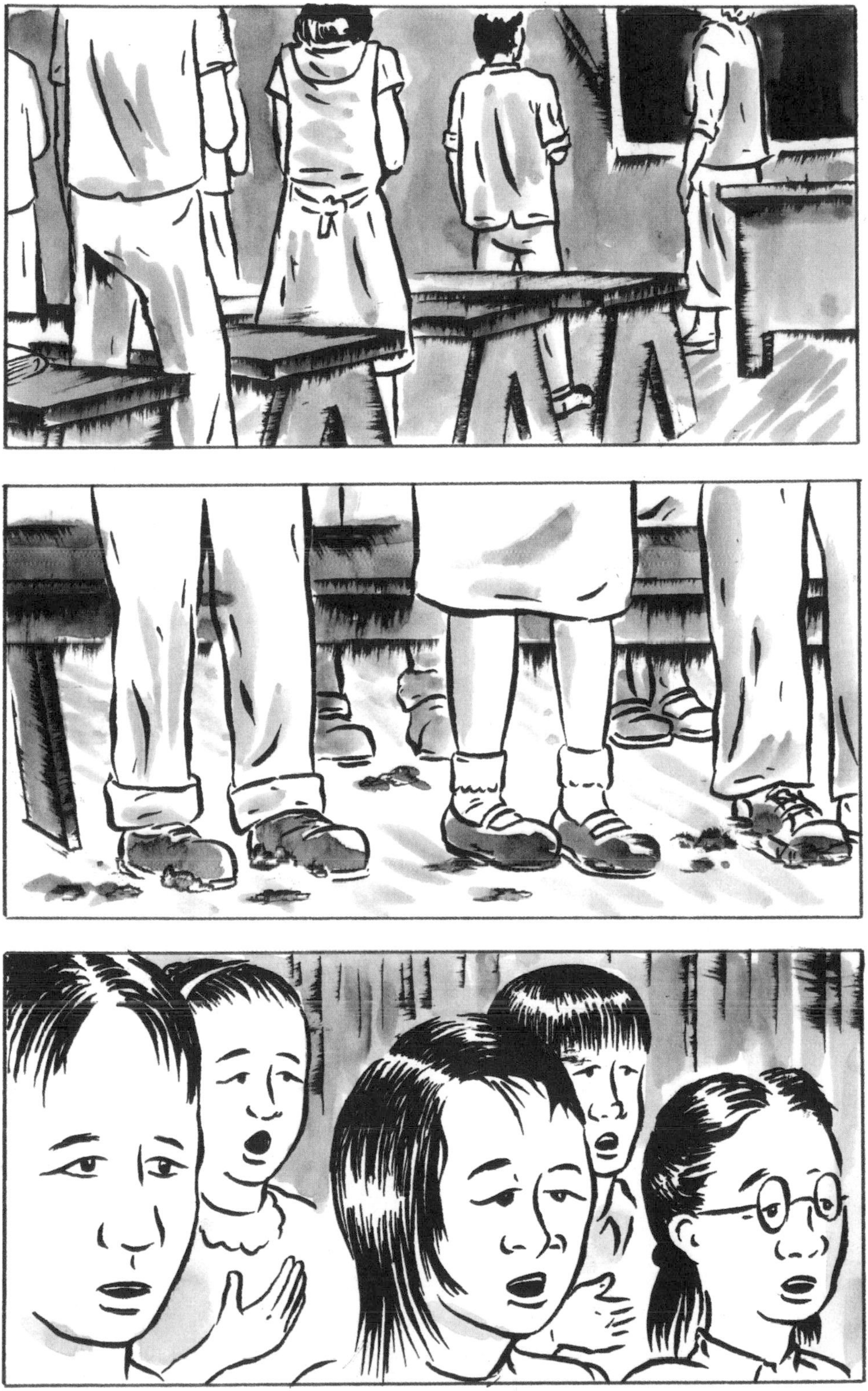

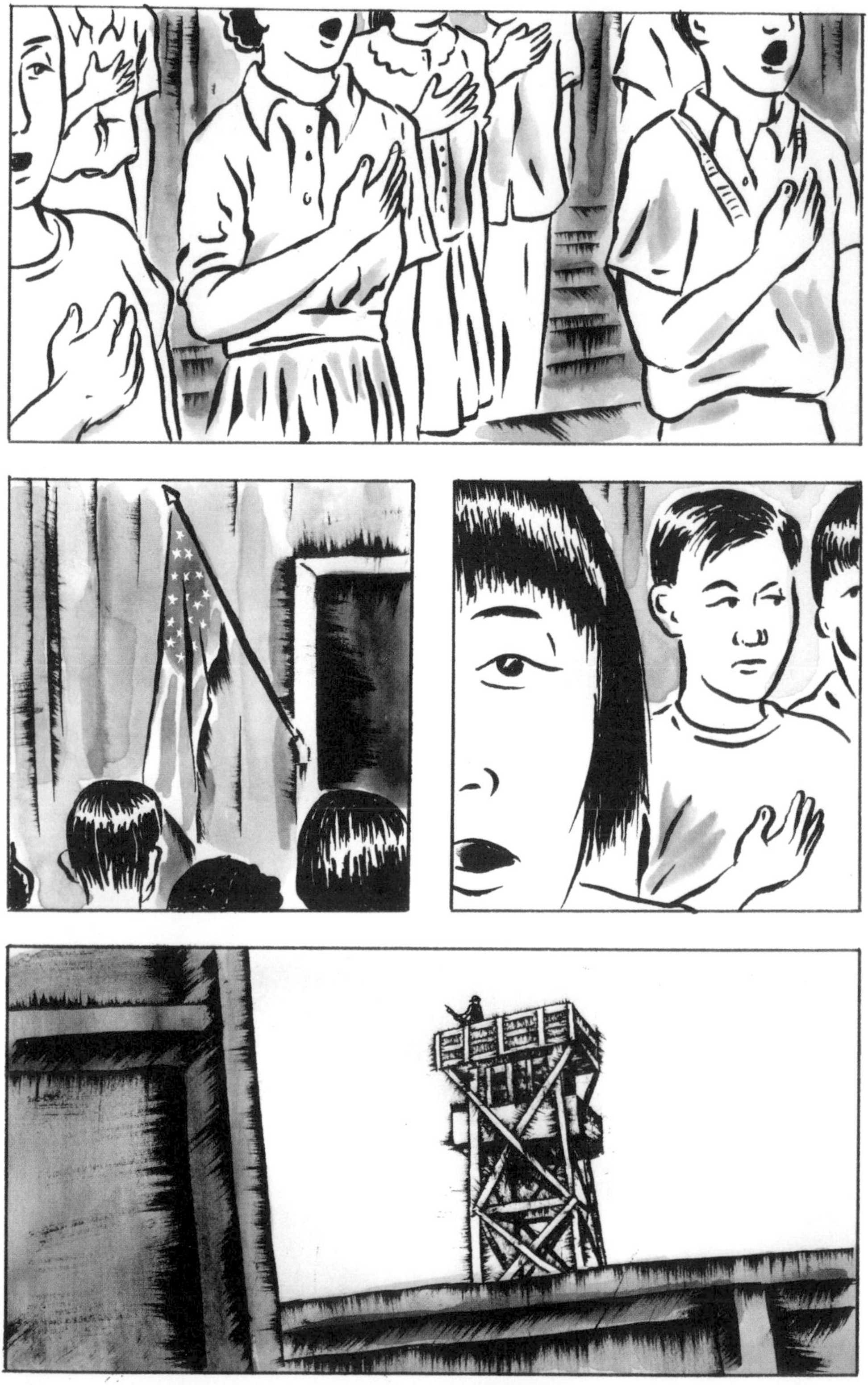

From then on, a guy we called "the jeep creep" would patrol on weekends.

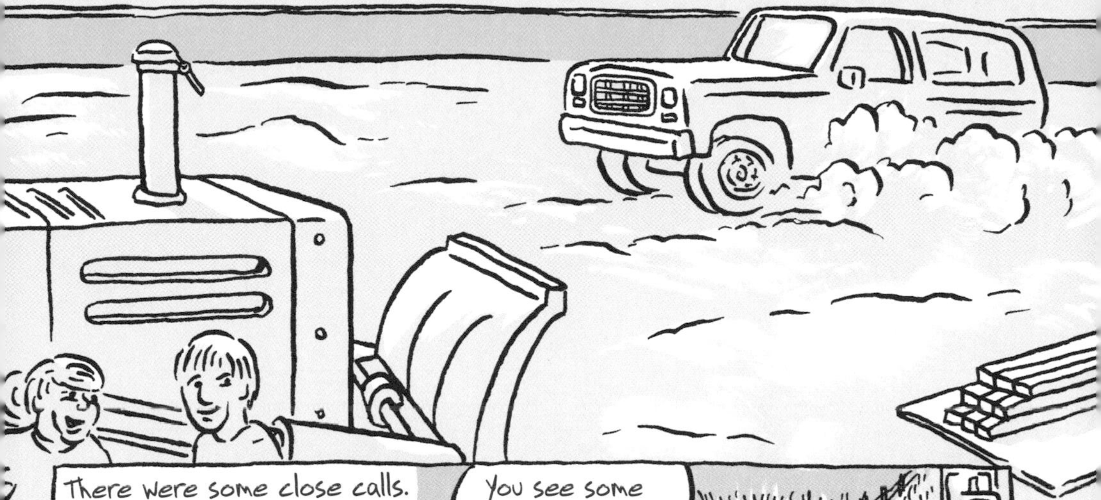

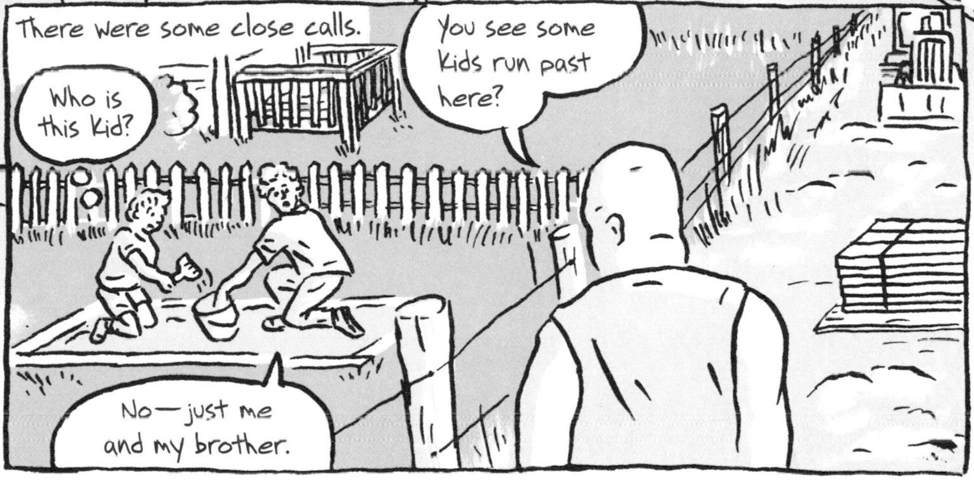
There were some close calls.
Who is this kid?
You see some kids run past here?
No—just me and my brother.

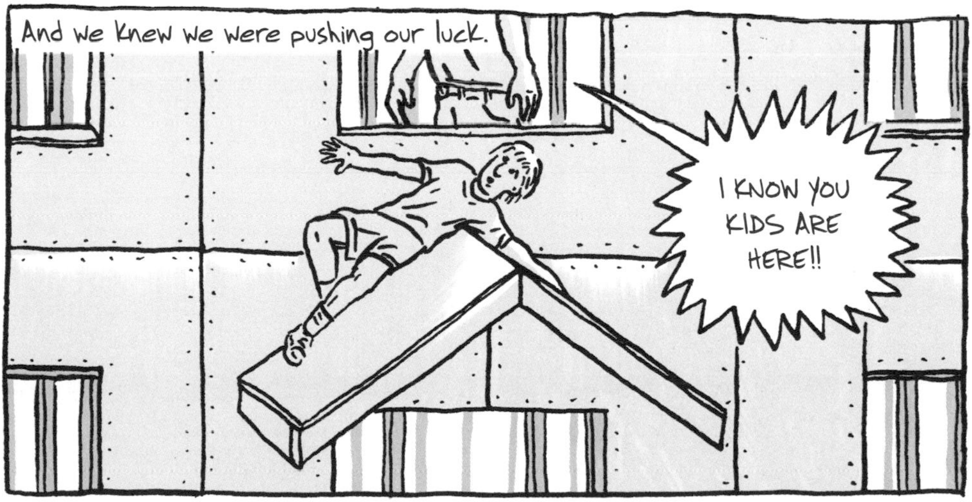
And we knew we were pushing our luck.
I KNOW YOU KIDS ARE HERE!!

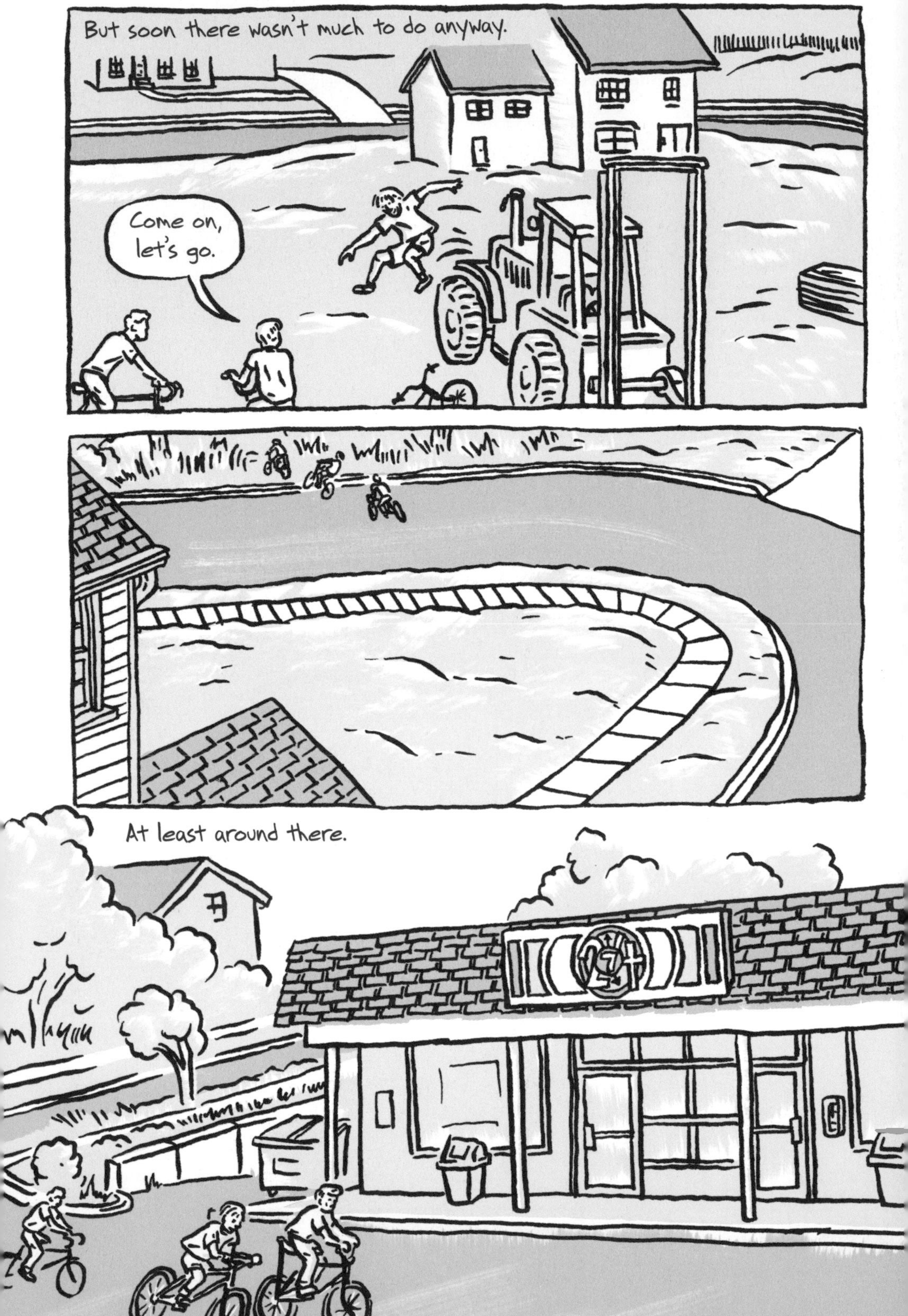
But soon there wasn't much to do anyway.
Come on, let's go.
At least around there.

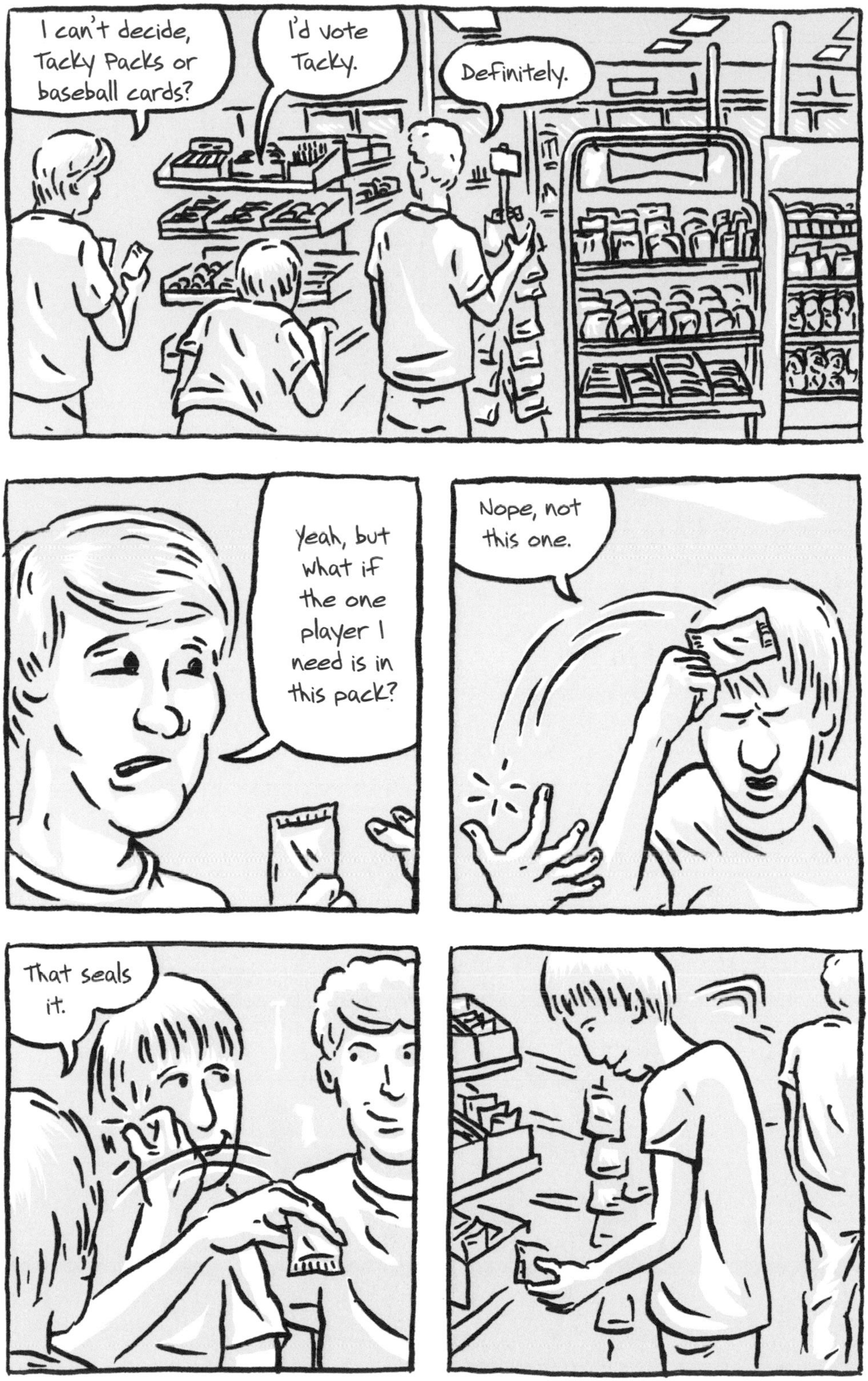
I can't decide, Tacky Packs or baseball cards?
I'd vote Tacky.
Definitely.
Yeah, but what if the one player I need is in this pack?
Nope, not this one.
That seals it.

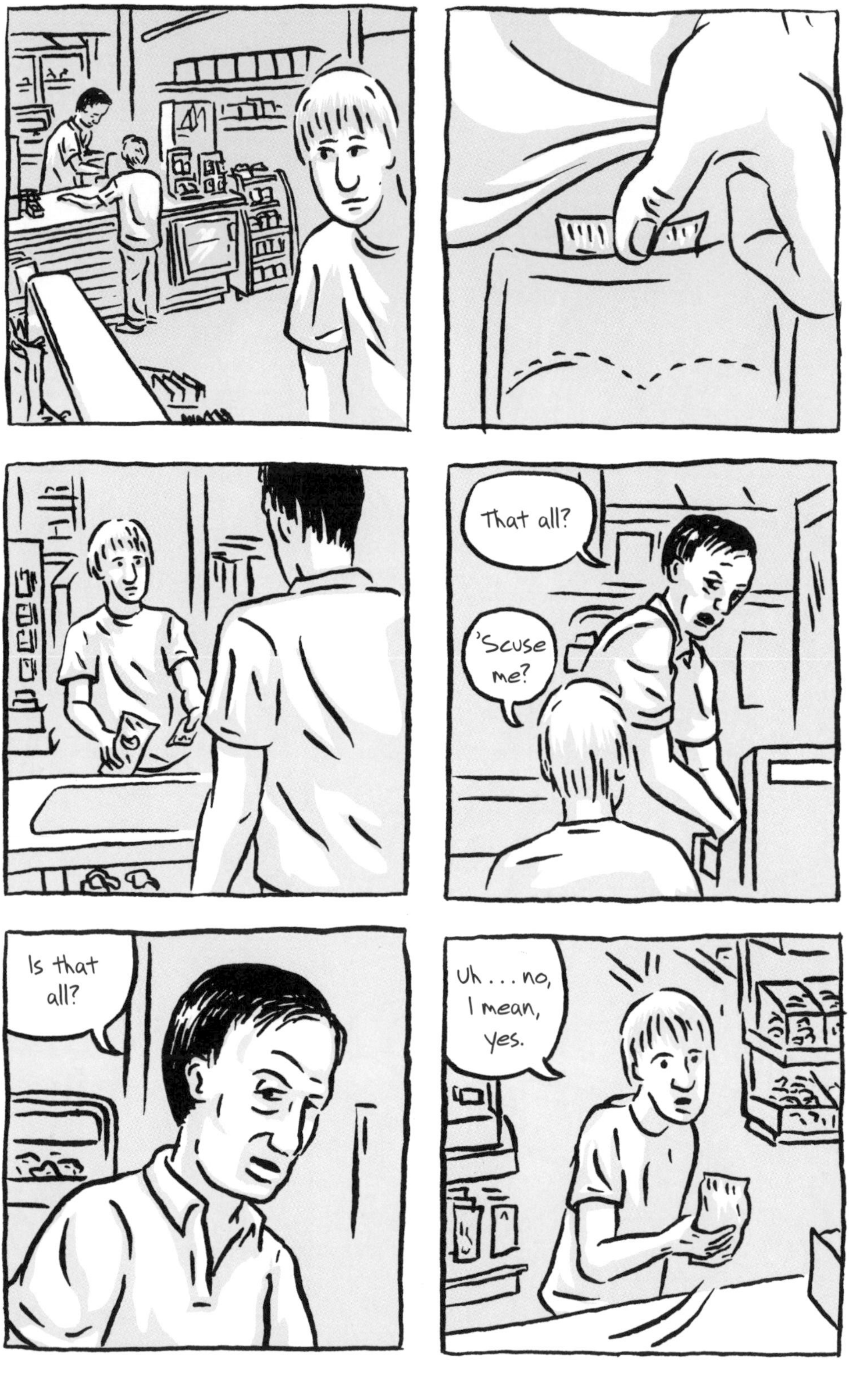
That all?
'Scuse me?
Is that all?
Uh . . . no, I mean, yes.

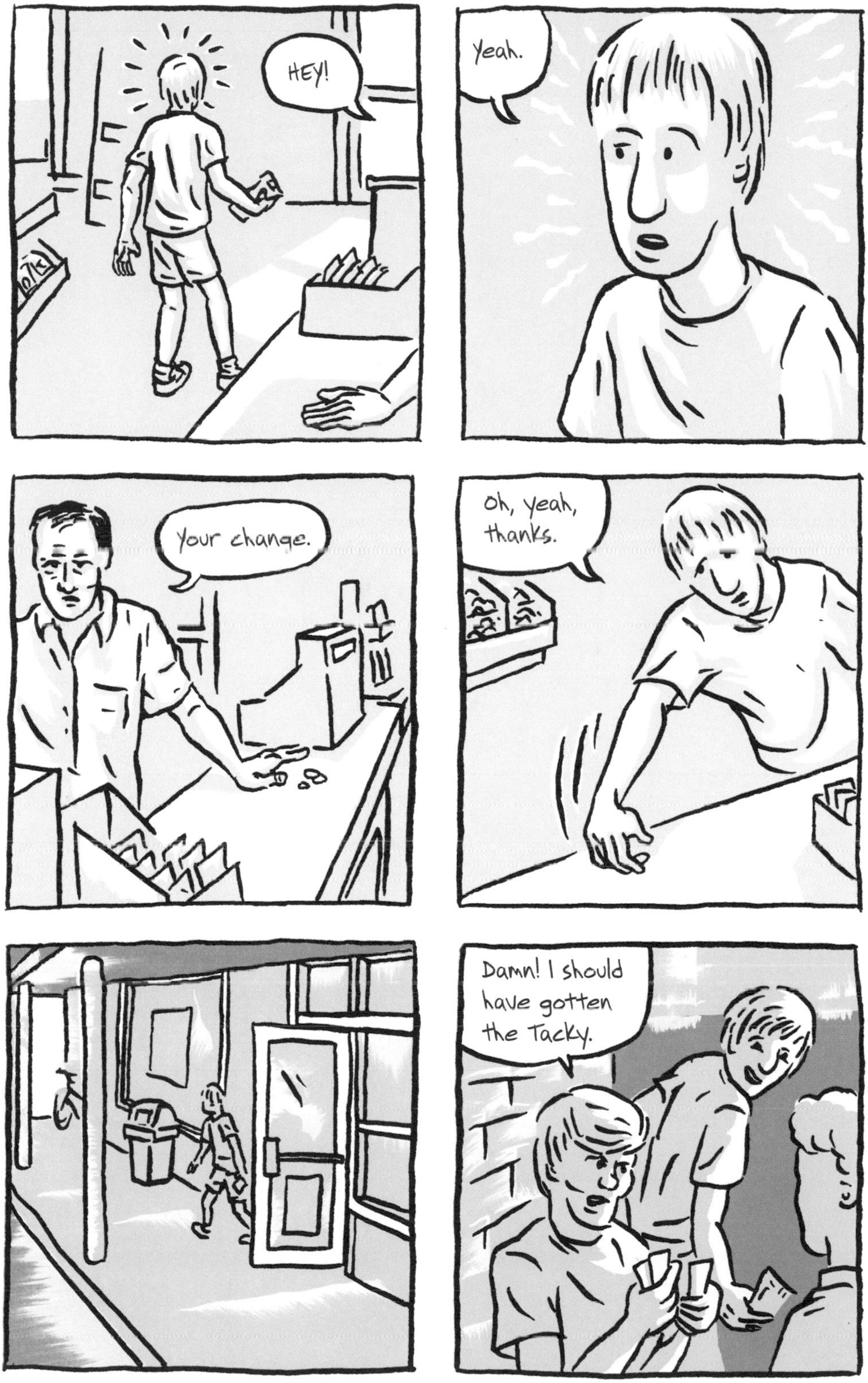
HEY!
Yeah.
Your change.
Oh, yeah, thanks.
Damn! I should have gotten the Tacky.

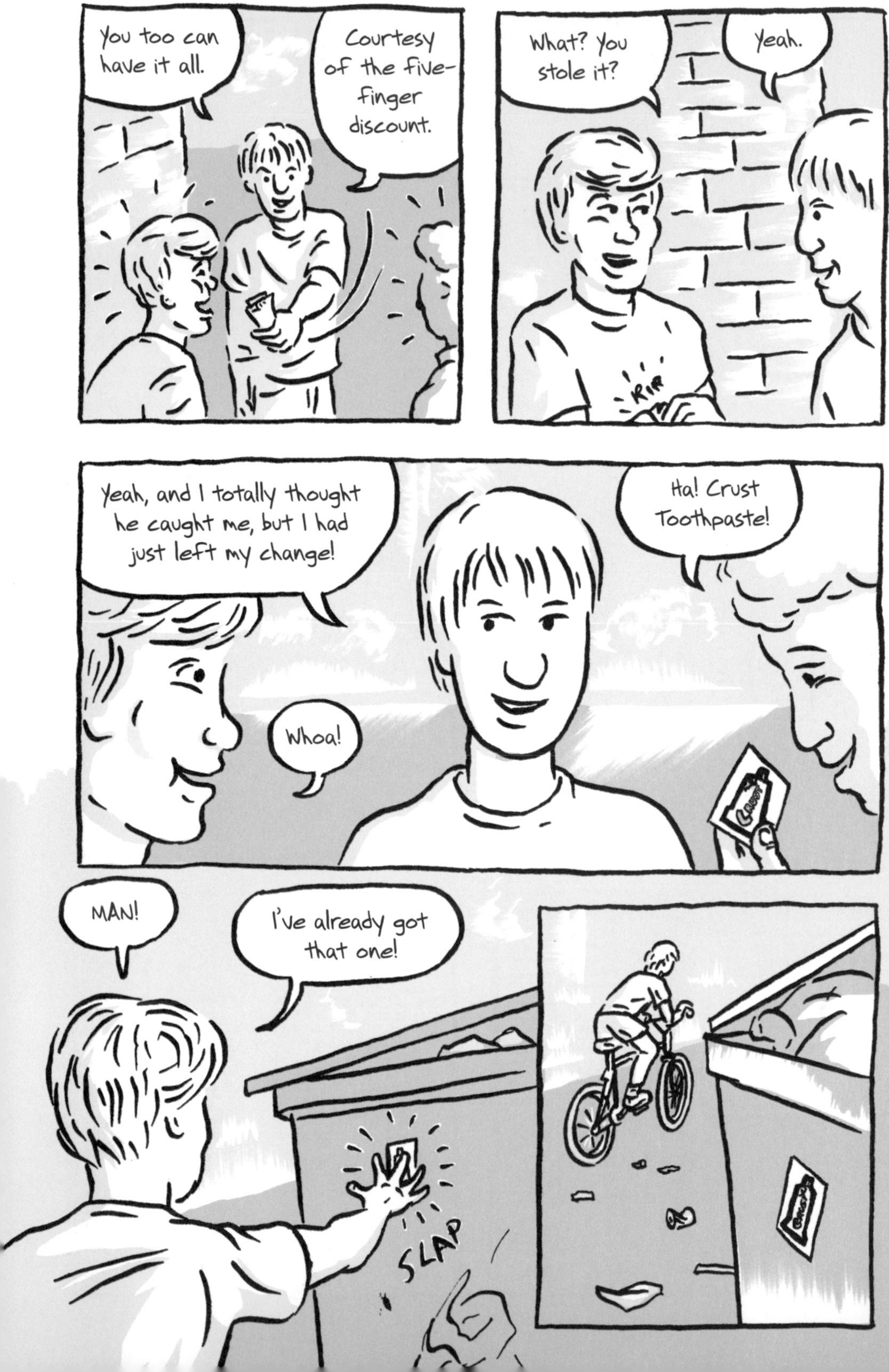
You too can have it all.
Courtesy of the five-finger discount.
What? You stole it?
Yeah.
RIP
Yeah, and I totally thought he caught me, but I had just left my change!
Ha! Crust Toothpaste!
Whoa!
MAN!
I've already got that one!
SLAP

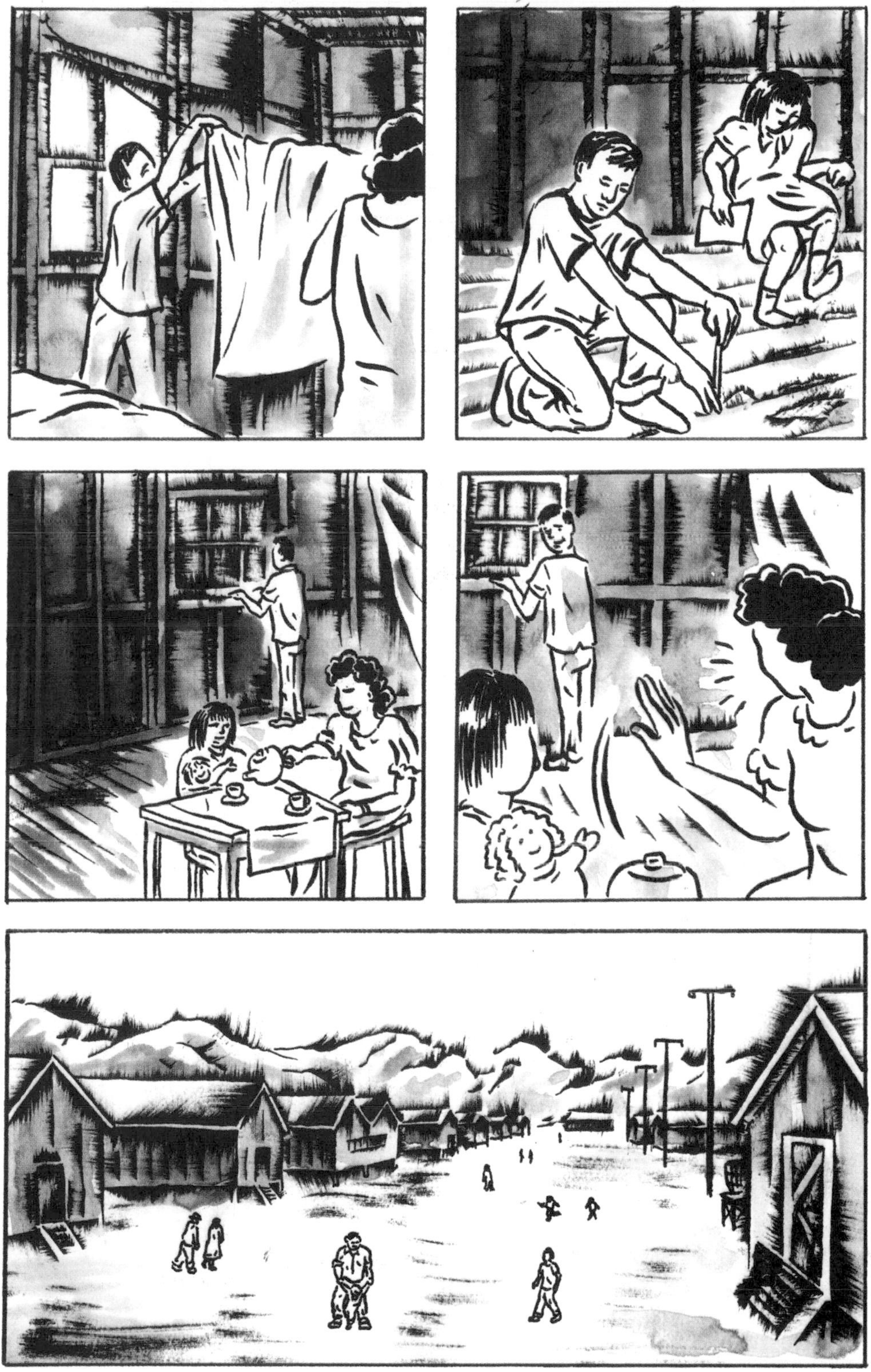

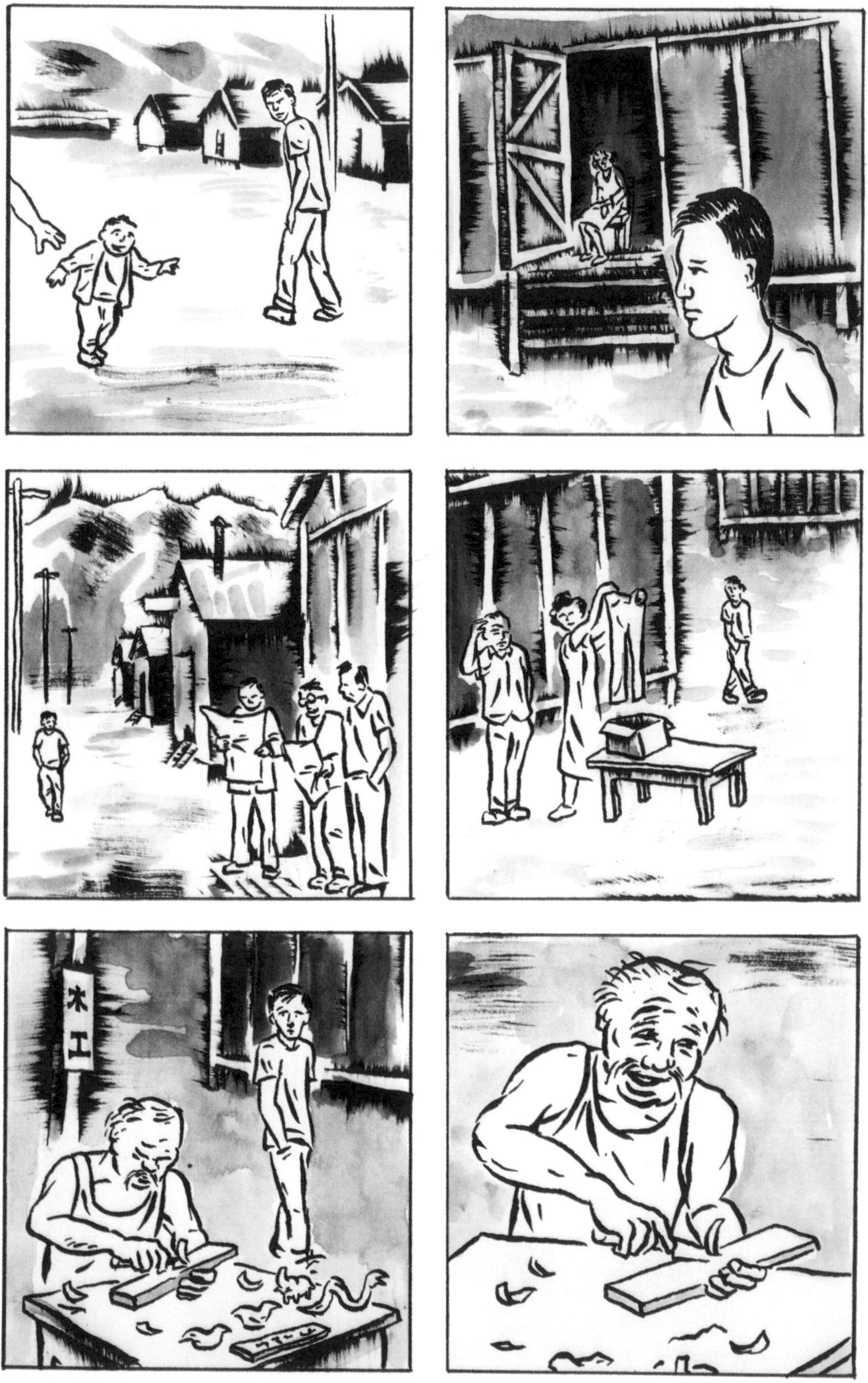
木工

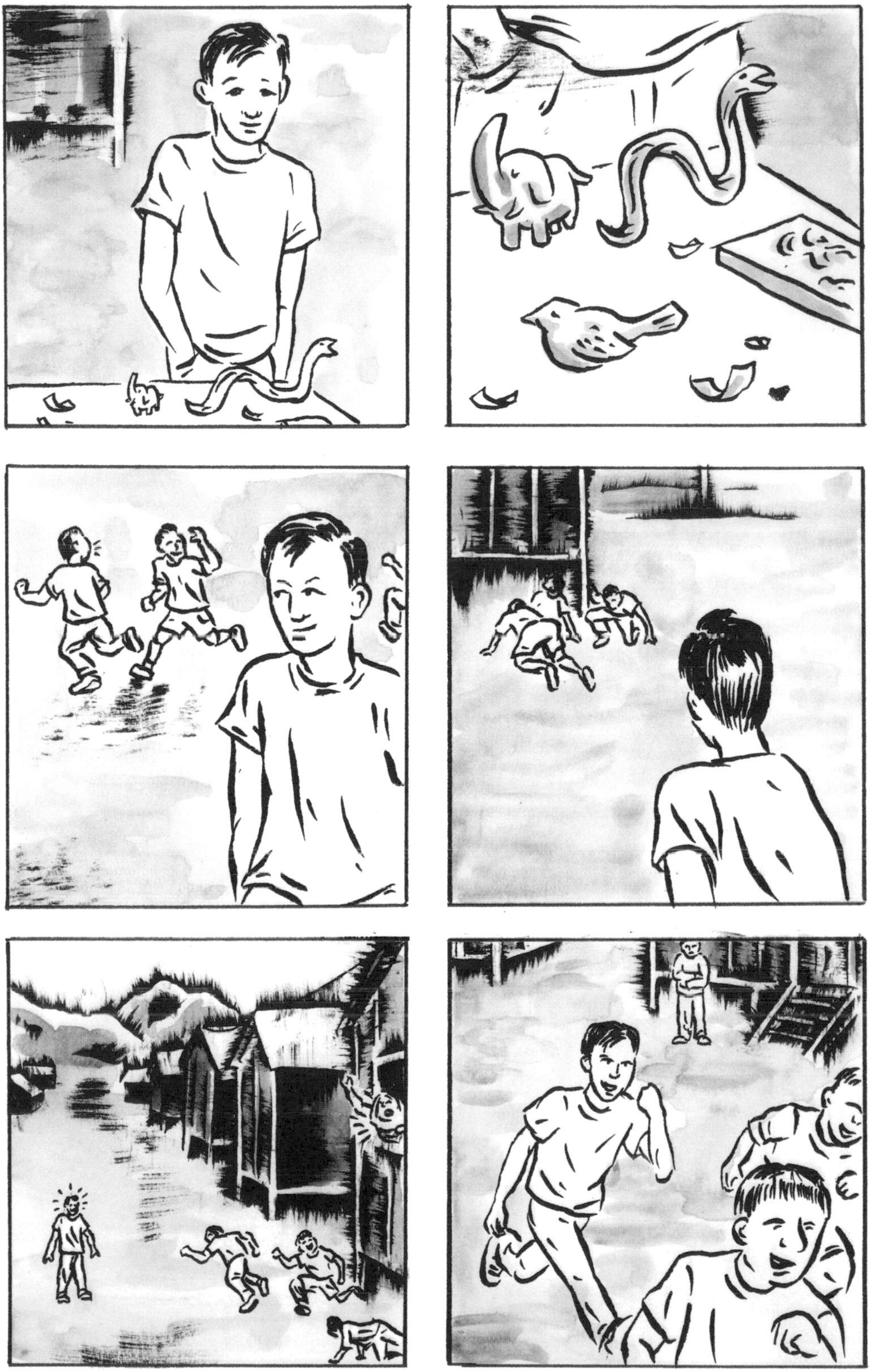

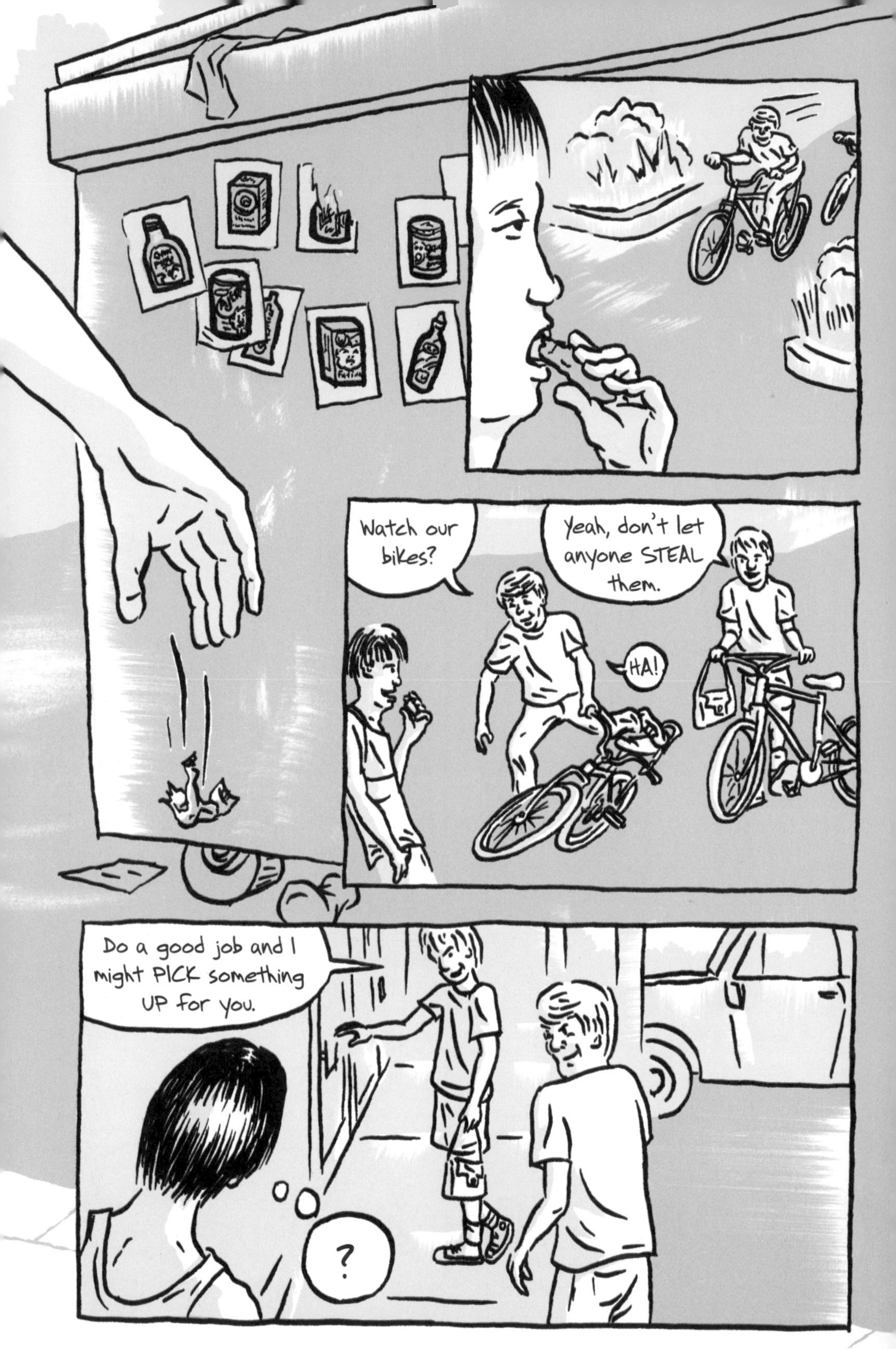
Watch our bikes?
Yeah, don't let anyone STEAL them.
HA!
Do a good job and I might PICK something UP for you.
?

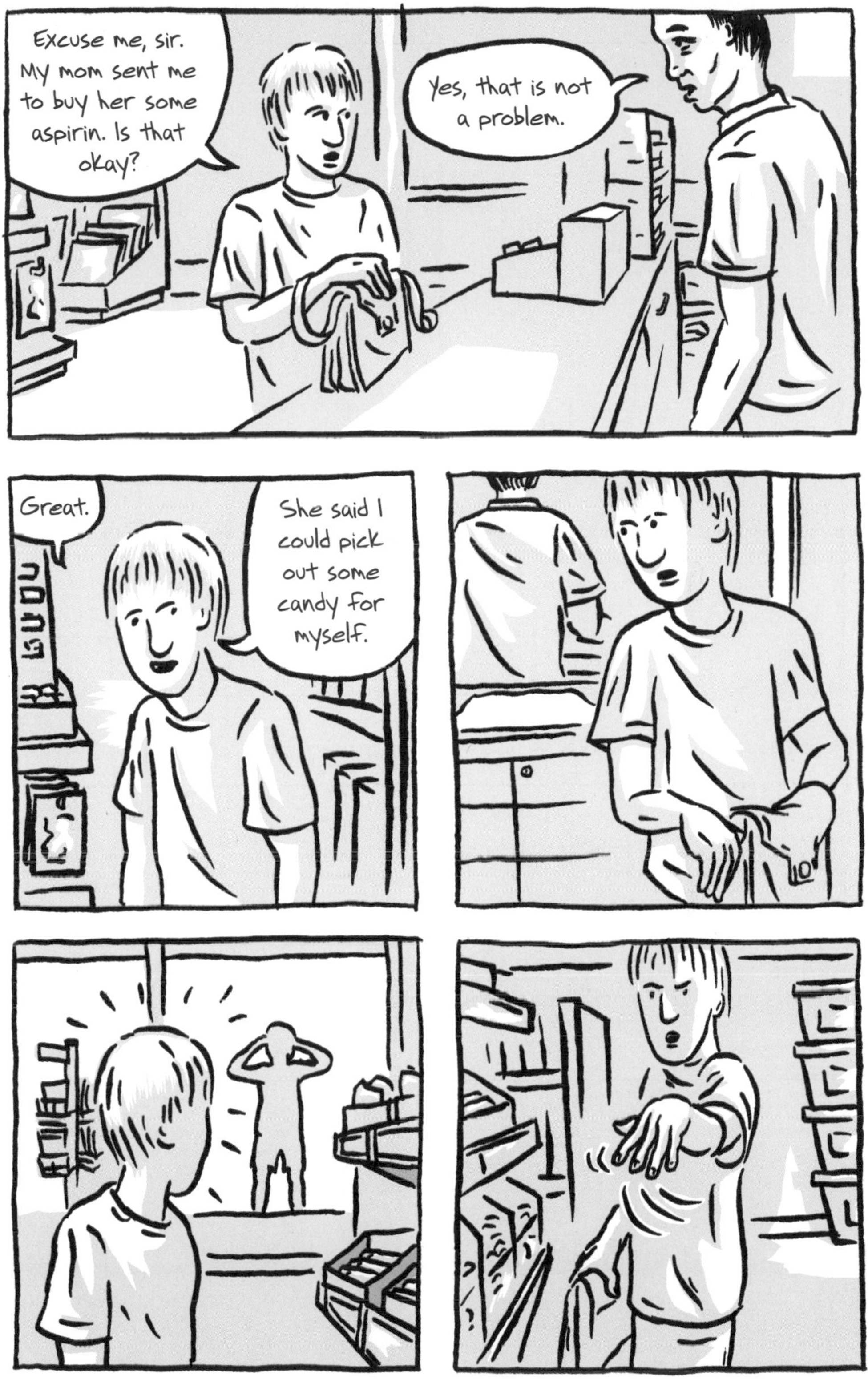
Excuse me, sir. My mom sent me to buy her some aspirin. Is that okay?
Yes, that is not a problem.
Great.
She said I could pick out some candy for myself.

Thanks.
You idiot!
You almost blew my cover!
What?

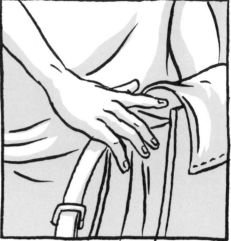

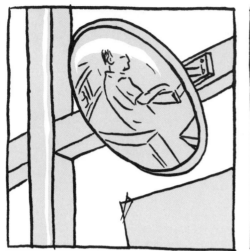

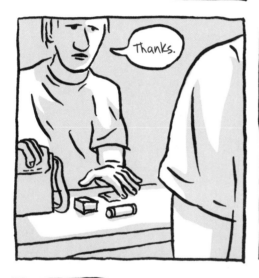

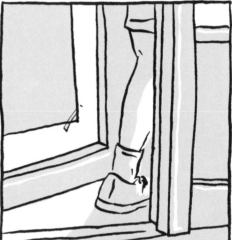

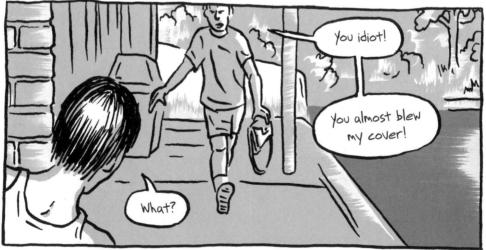

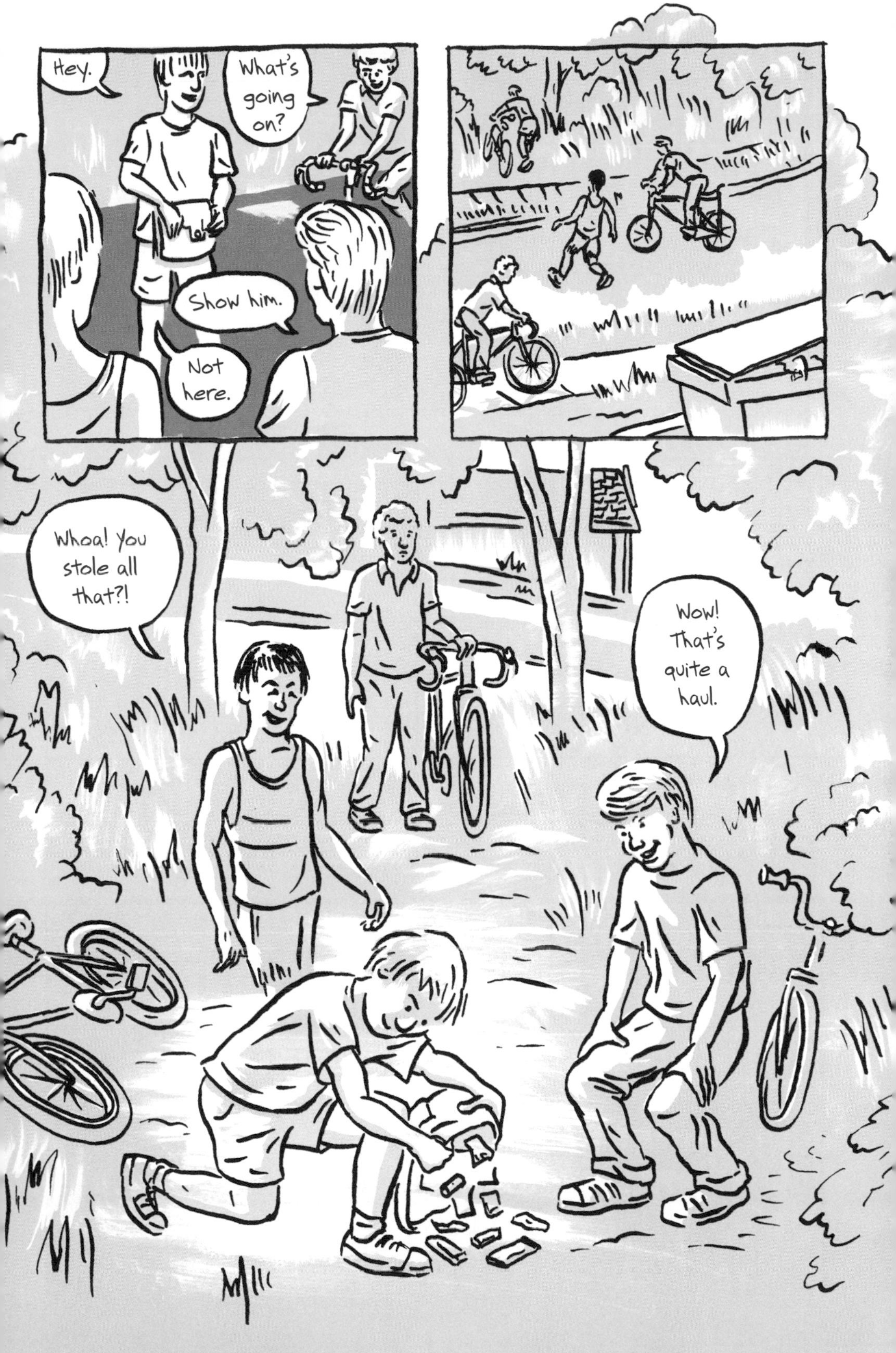
Hey.
What's going on?
Show him.
Not here.
Whoa! You stole all that?!
Wow! That's quite a haul.

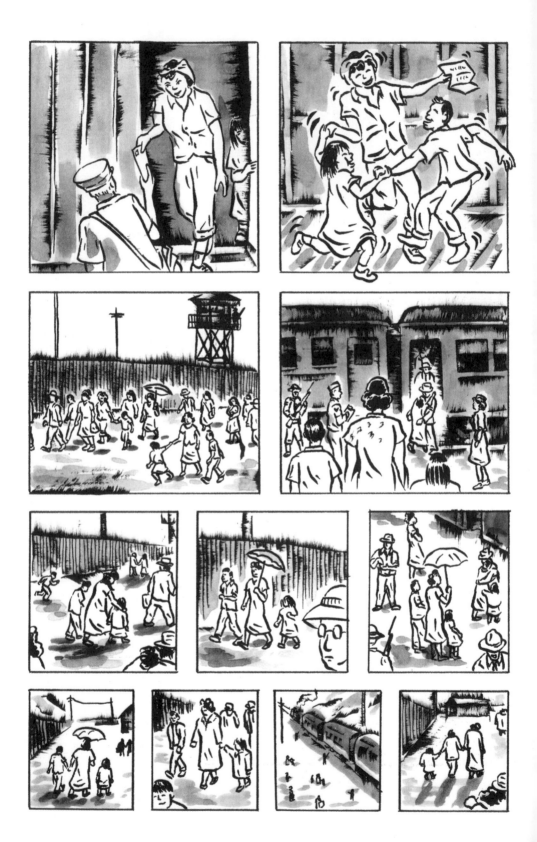

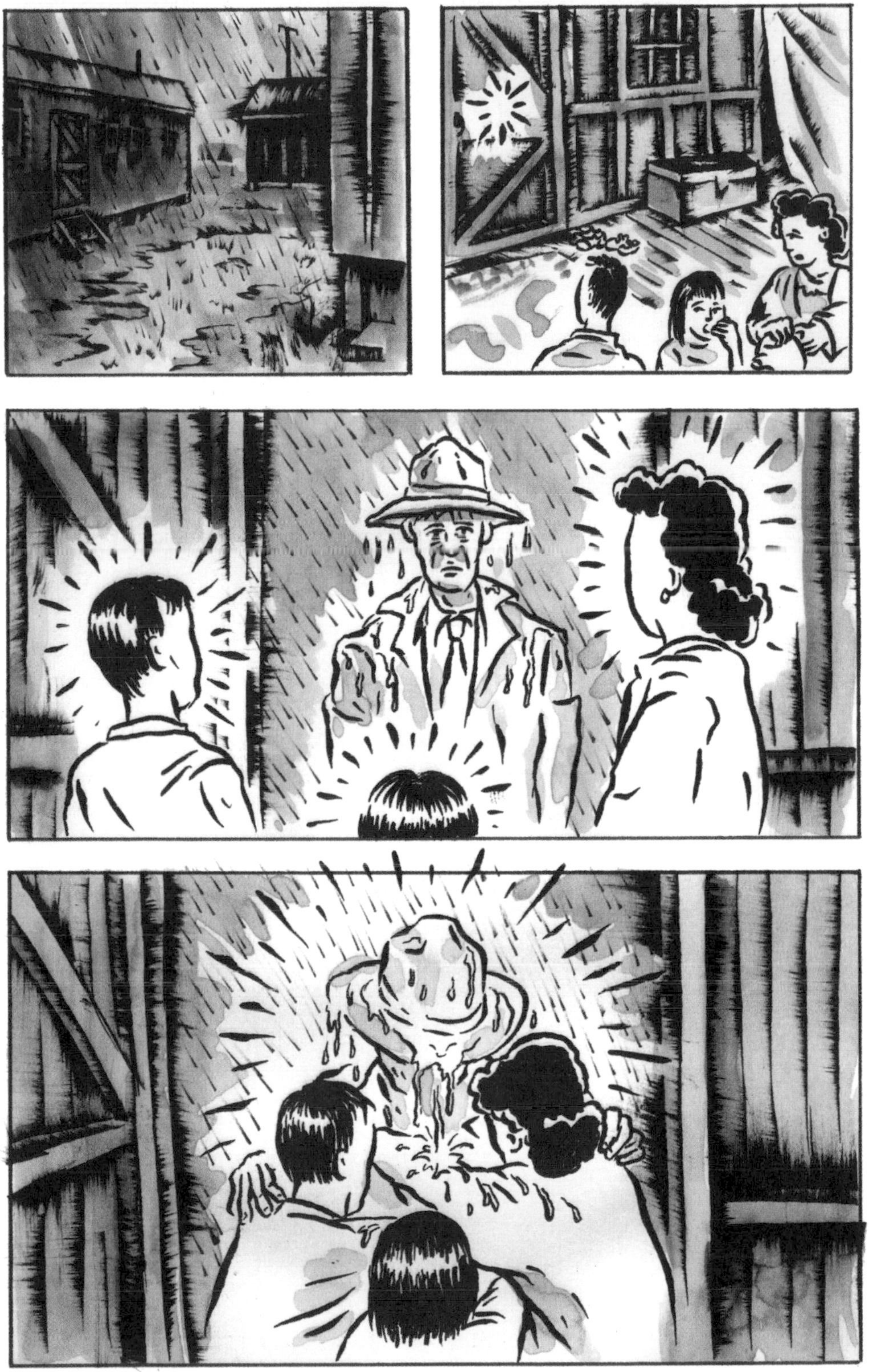

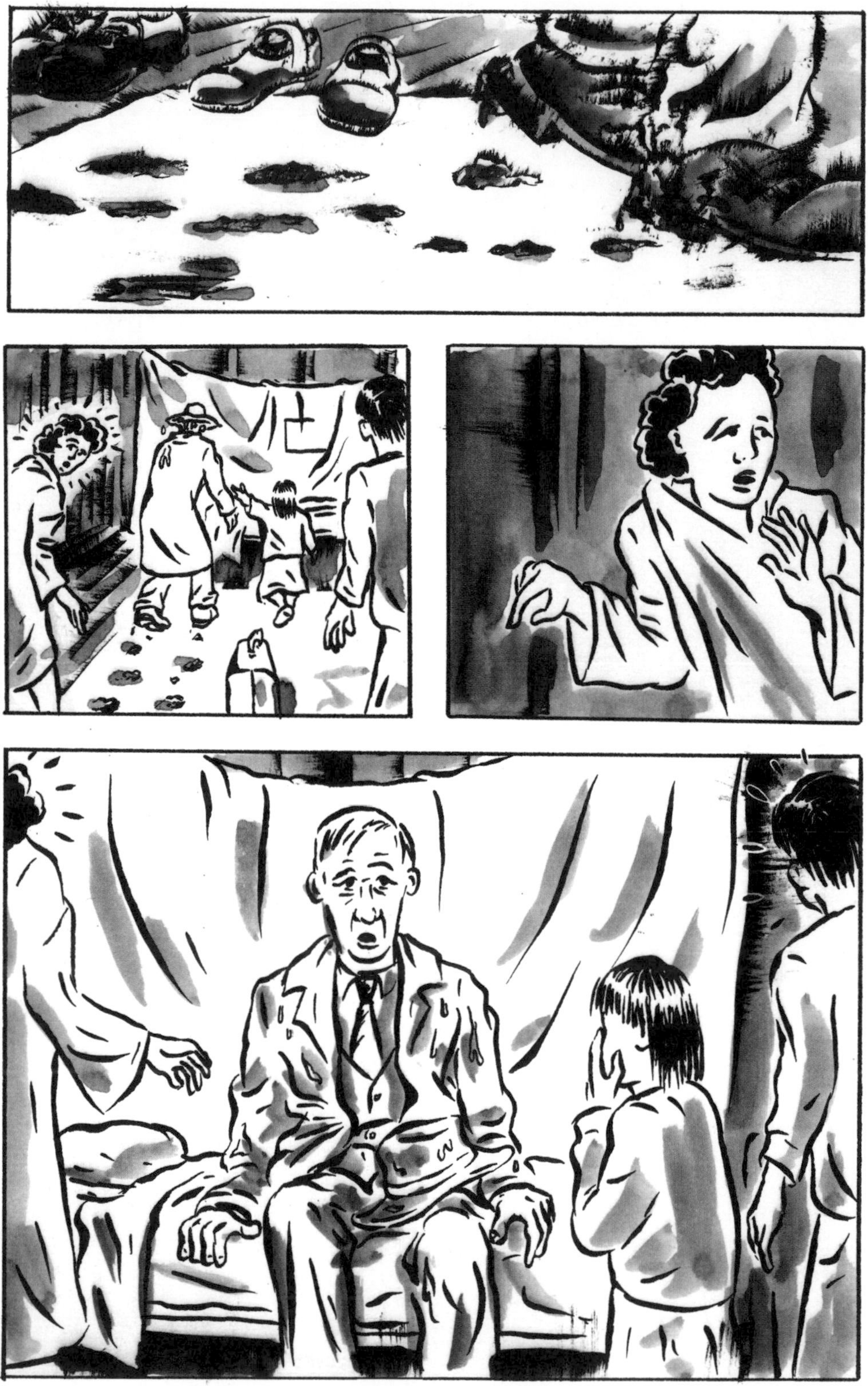

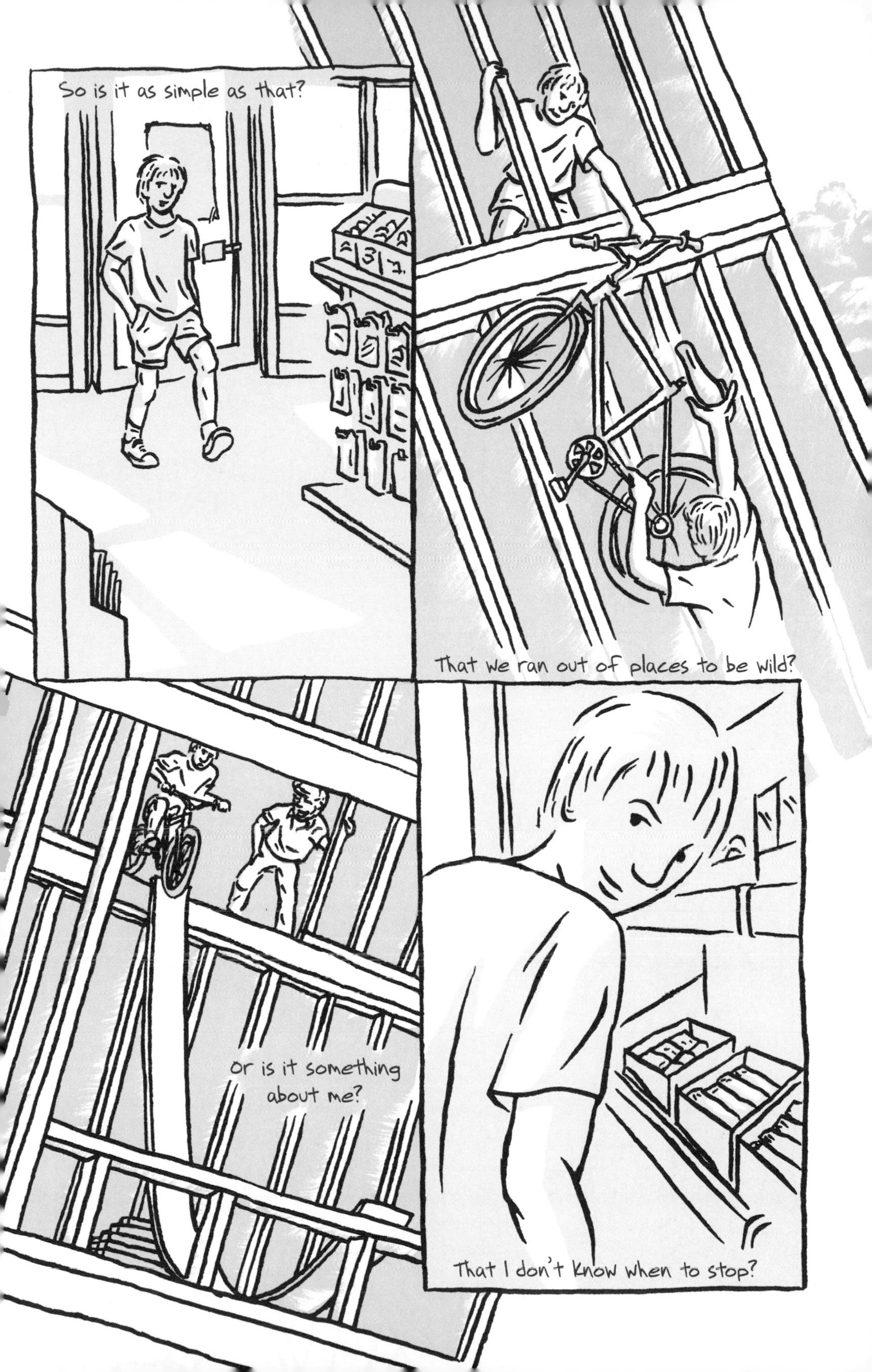
So is it as simple as that?
That we ran out of places to be wild?
Or is it something about me?
That I don't know when to stop?

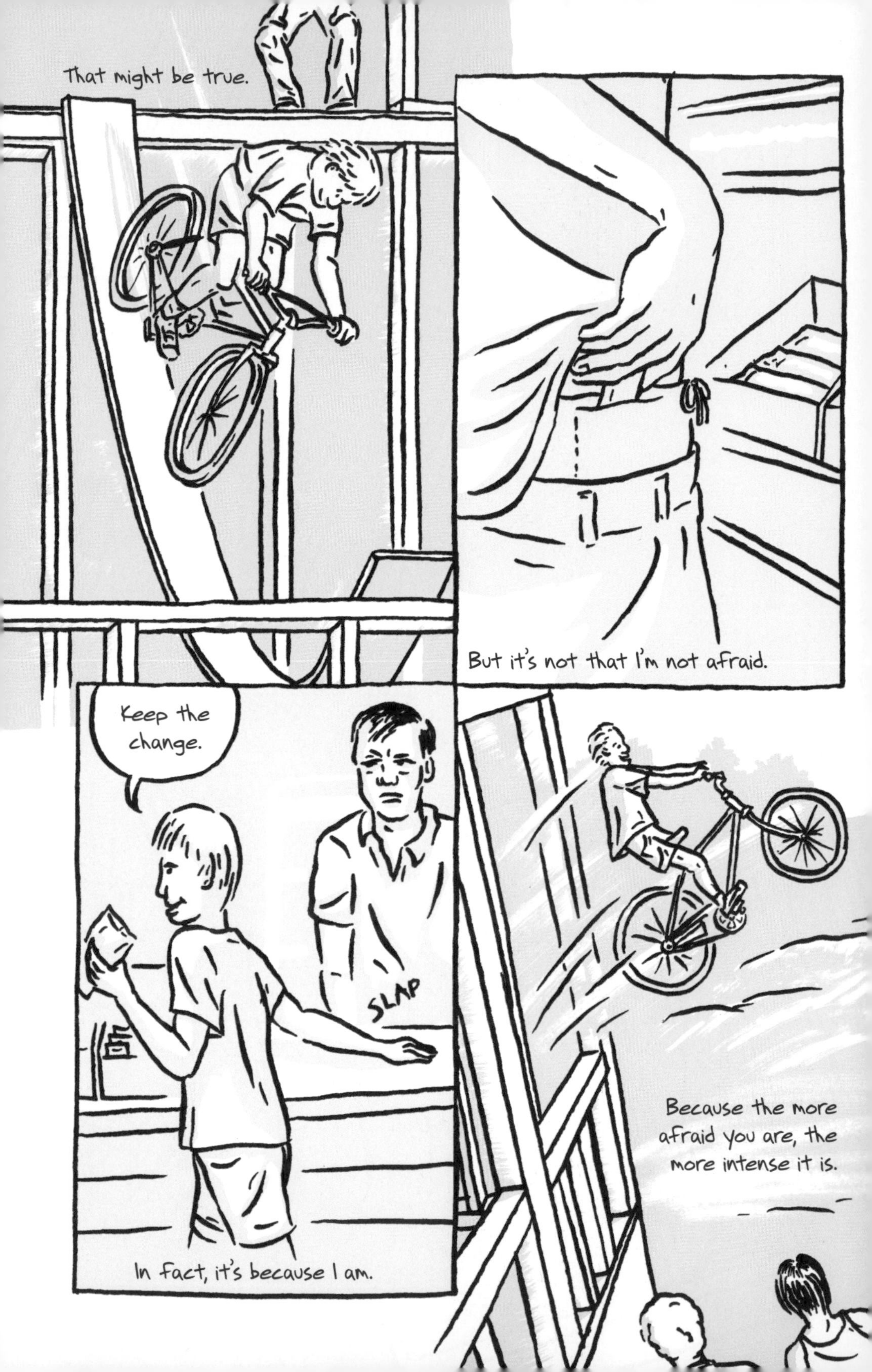
That might be true.
But it's not that I'm not afraid.
Keep the change.
SLAP
In fact, it's because I am.
Because the more afraid you are, the more intense it is.

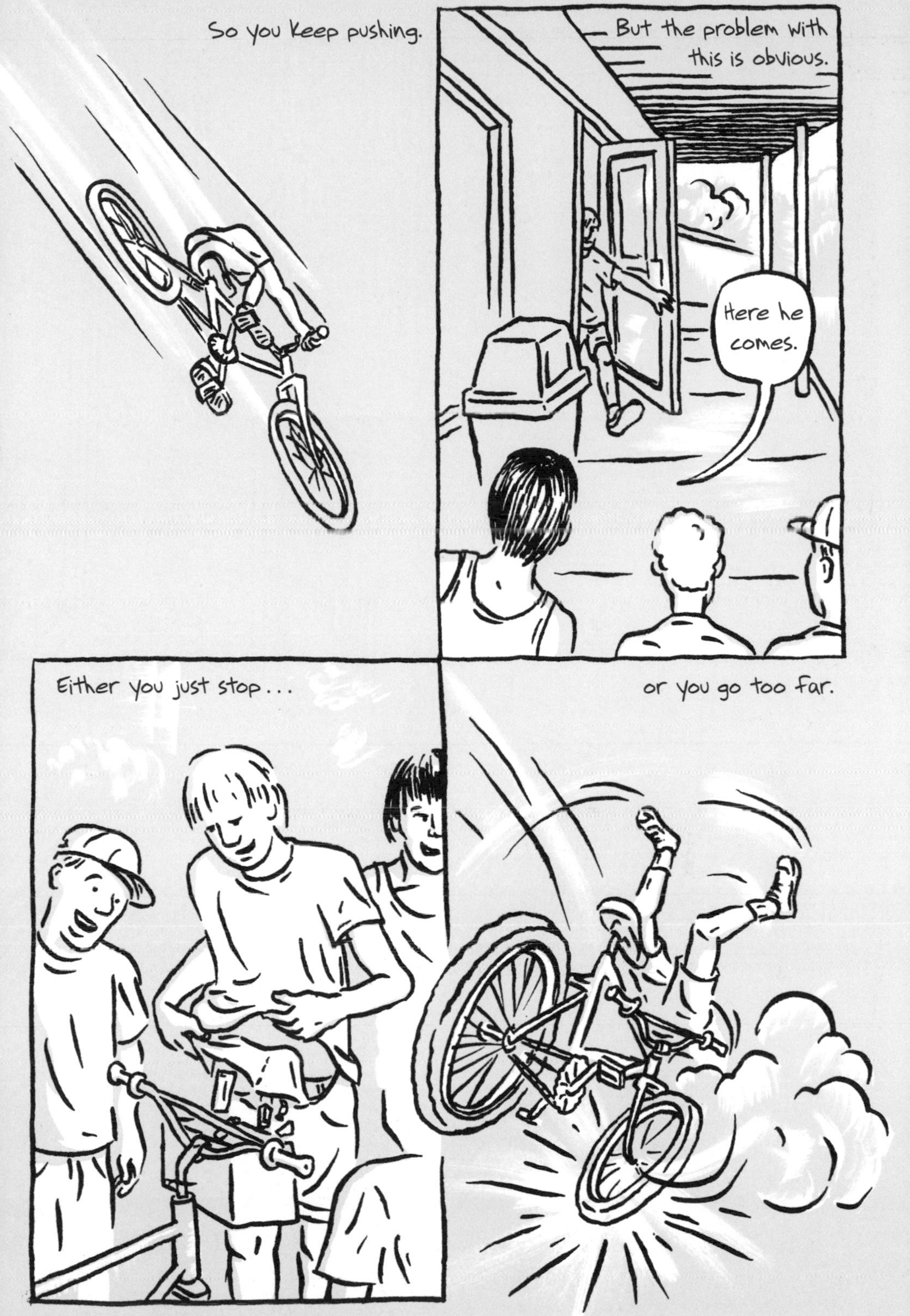
So you keep pushing.
But the problem with this is obvious.
Here he comes.
Either you just stop . . .
or you go too far.

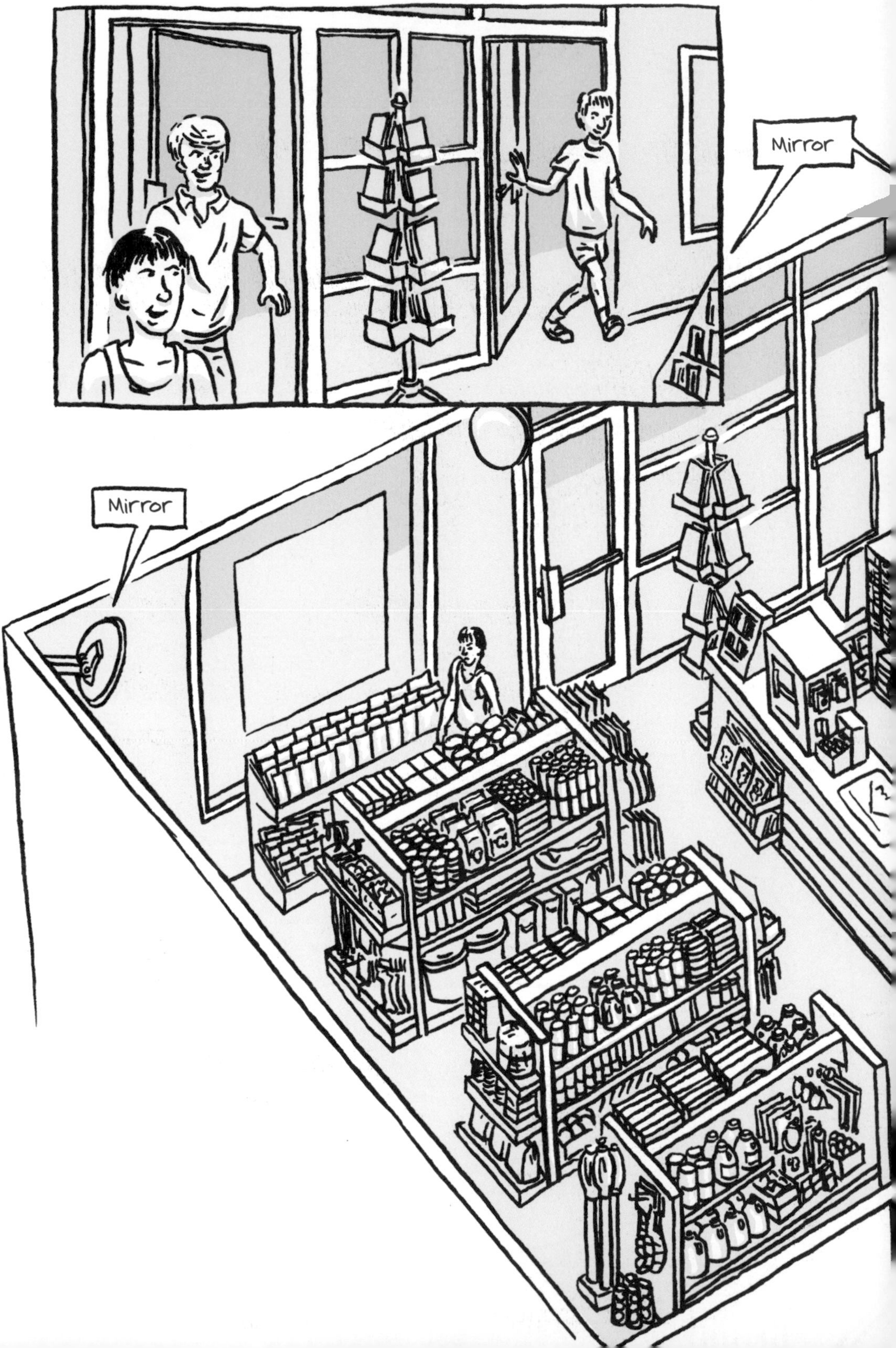
Mirror
Mirror

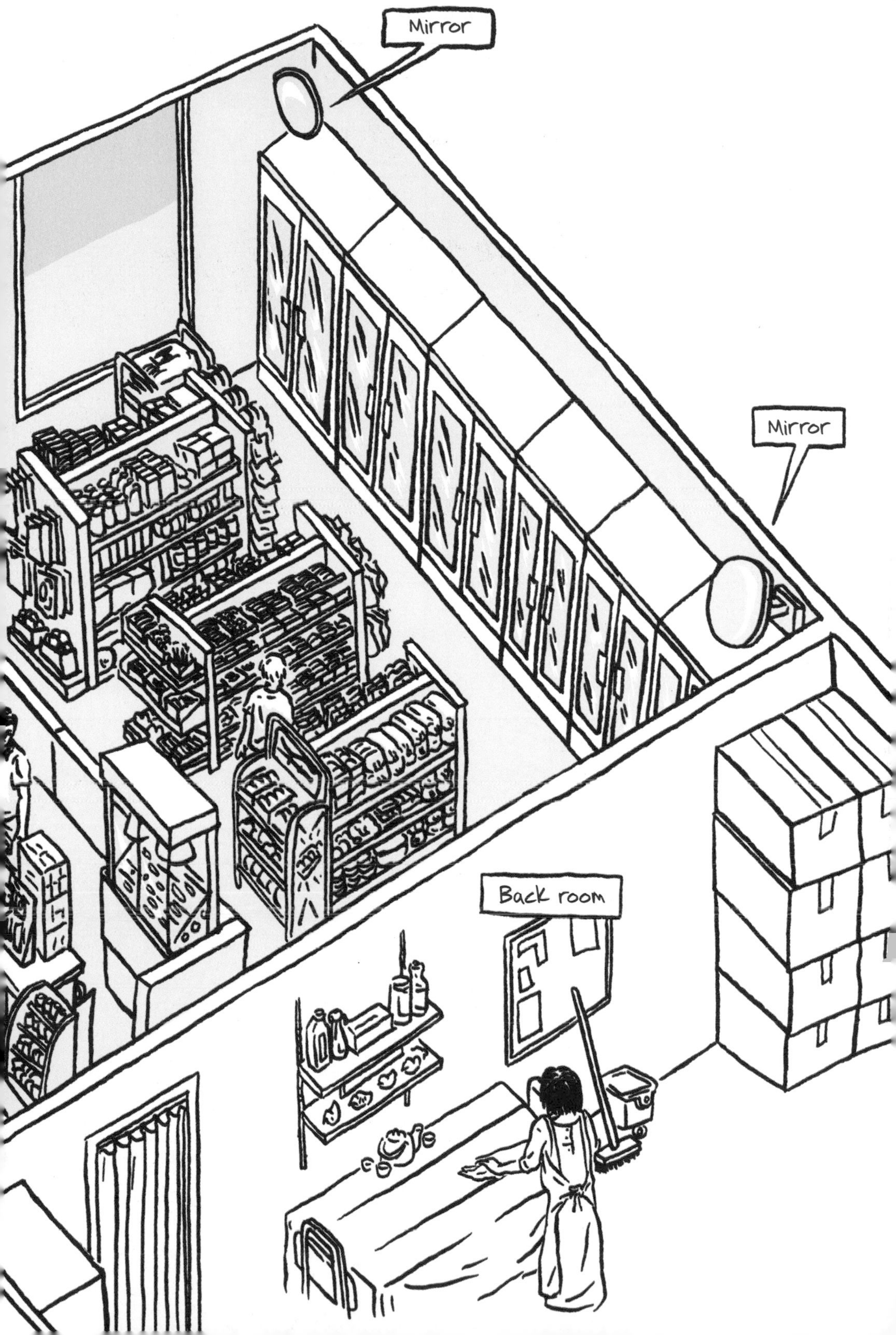
Mirror
Mirror
Back room

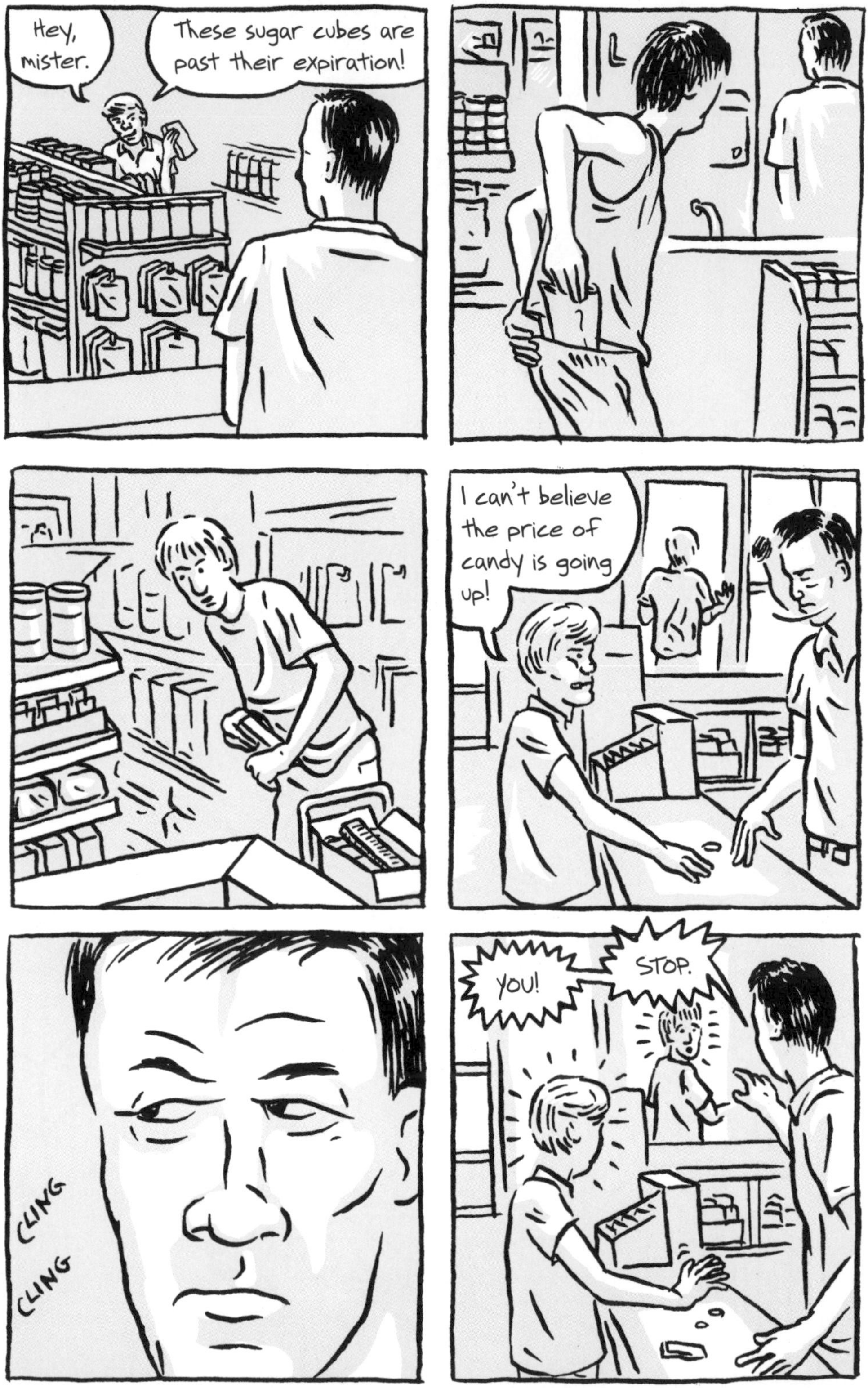
Hey, mister.
These sugar cubes are past their expiration!
I can't believe the price of candy is going up!
CLING
CLING
YOU!
STOP.

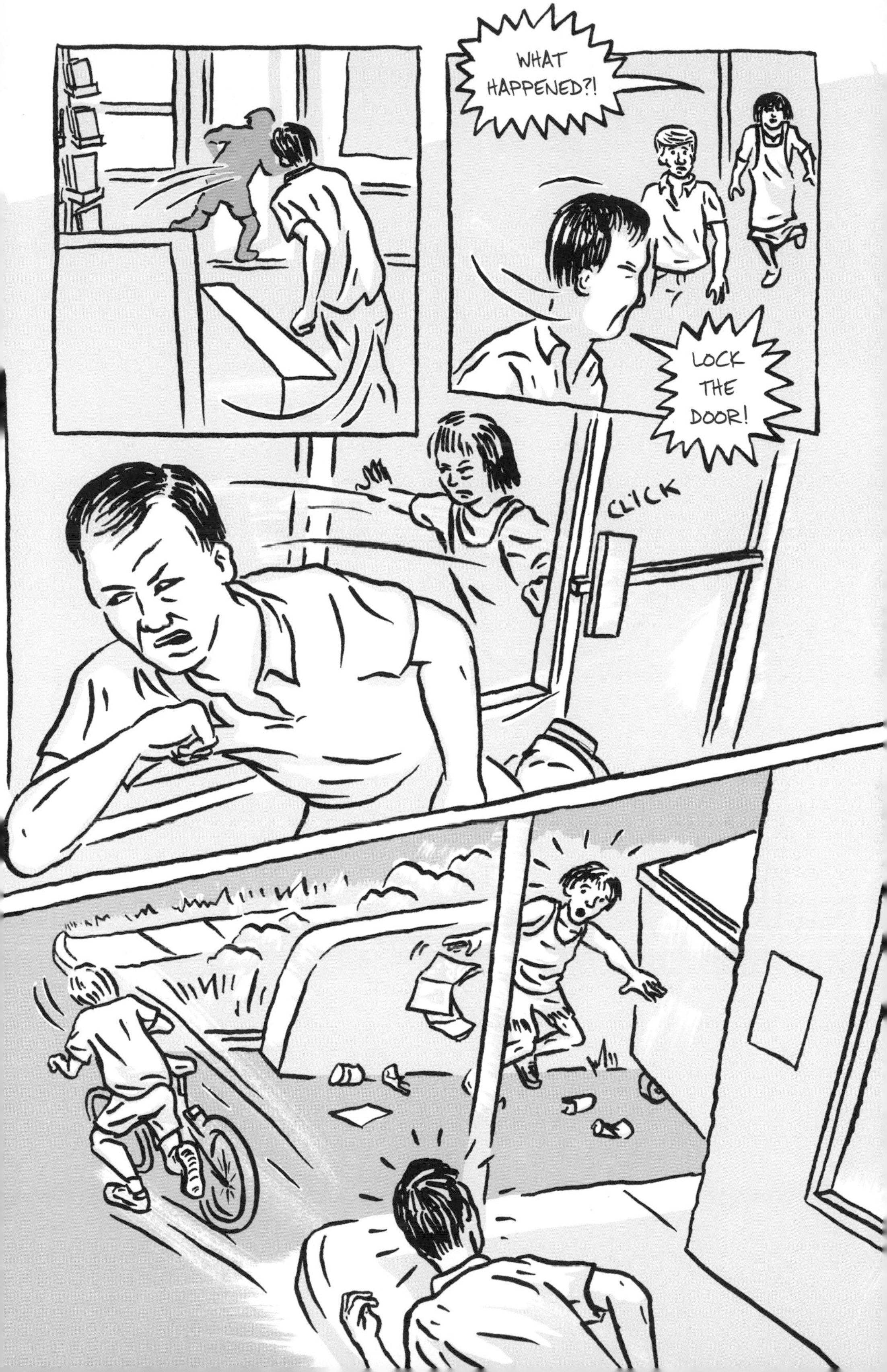
WHAT HAPPENED?!
LOCK THE DOOR!
CLICK

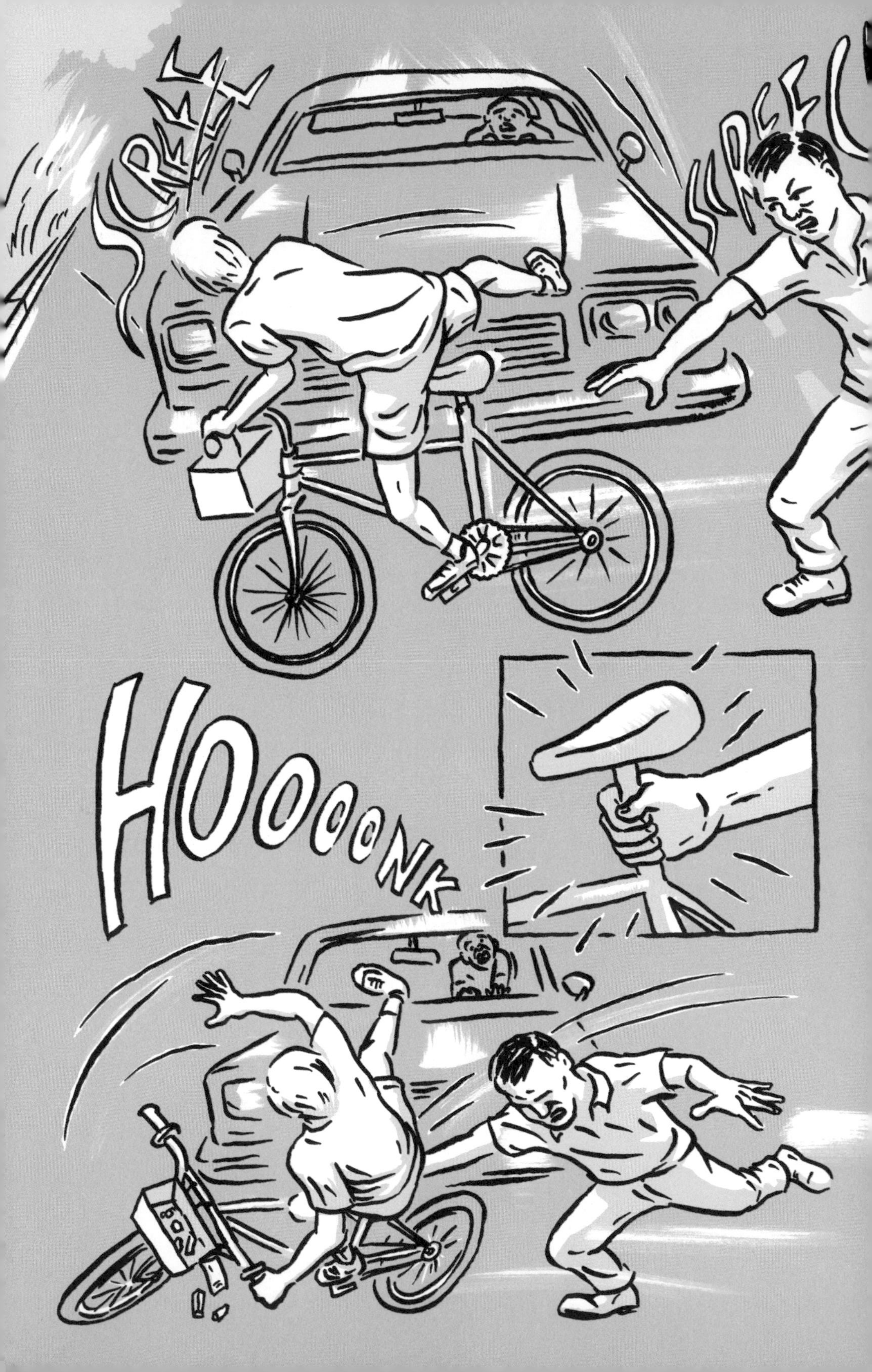
SCREEEE
HOOOONK

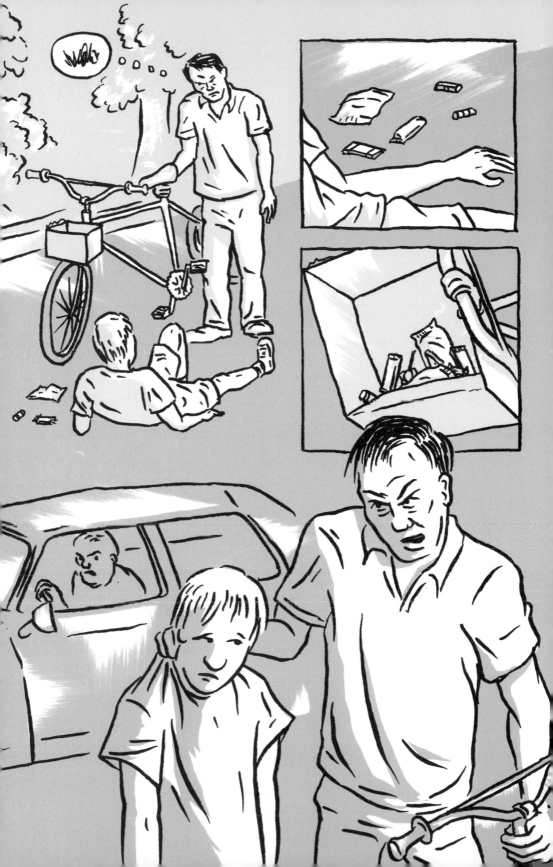

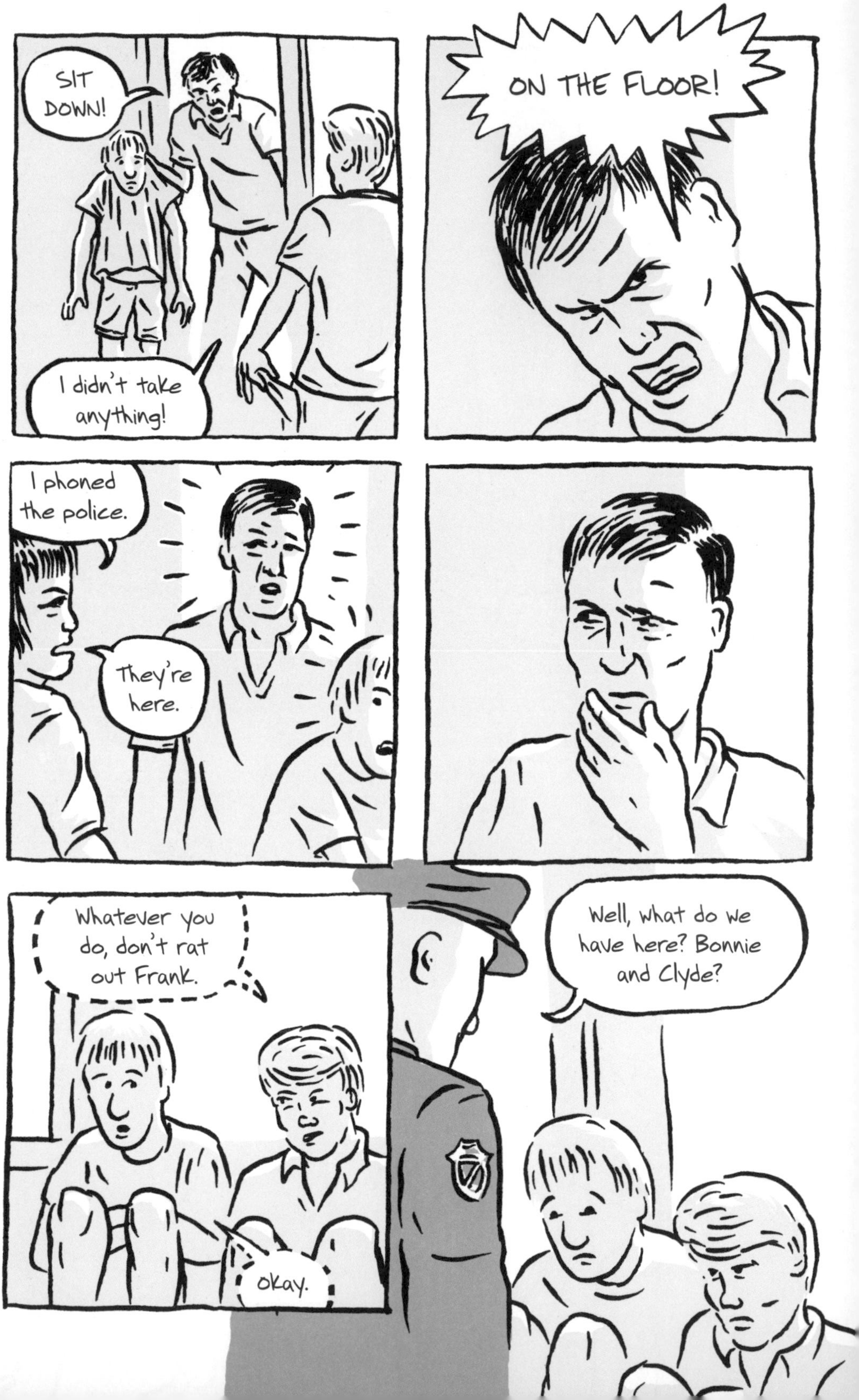
SIT DOWN!
I didn't take anything!
ON THE FLOOR!
I phoned the police.
They're here.
Whatever you do, don't rat out Frank.
okay.
Well, what do we have here? Bonnie and Clyde?

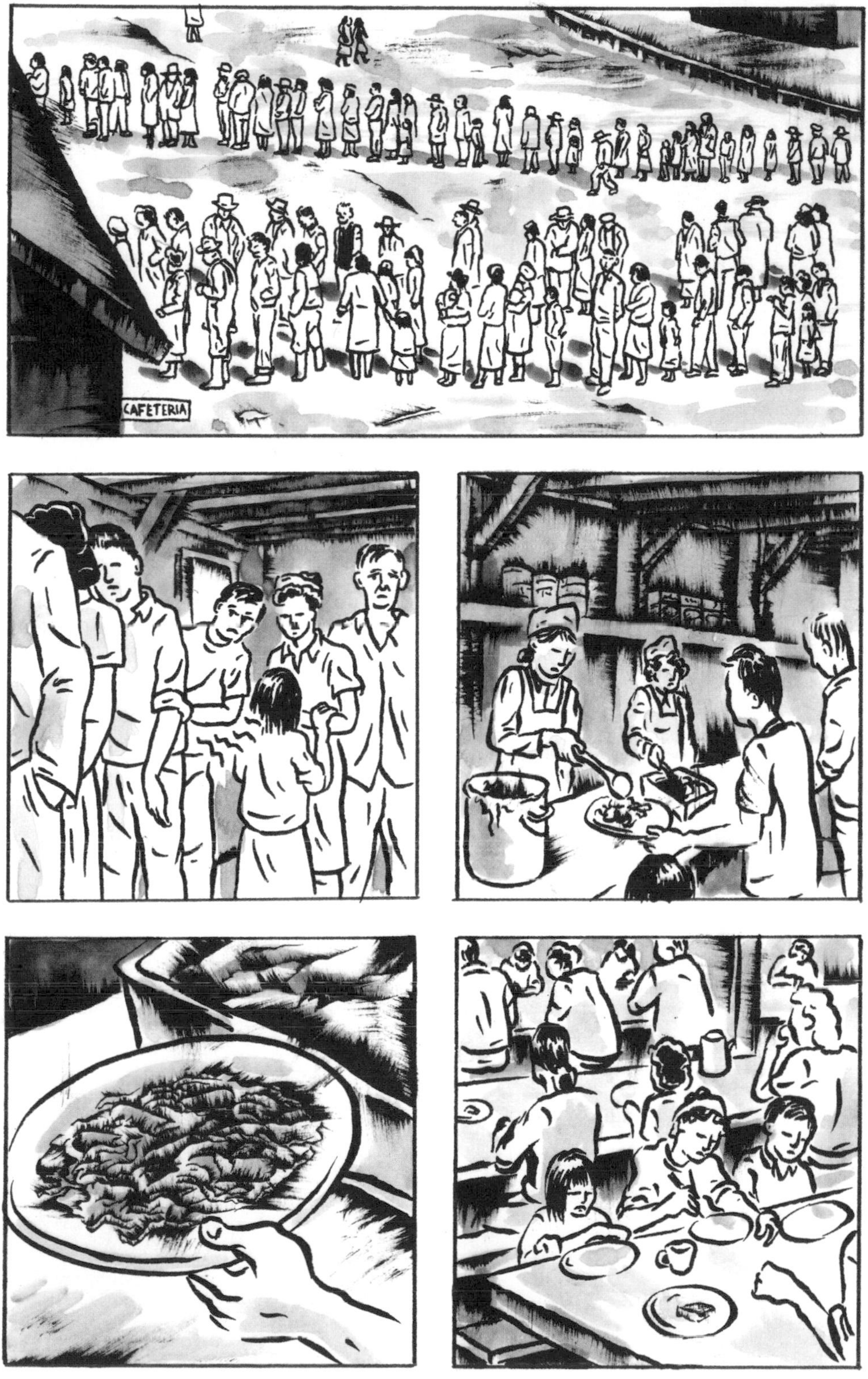
CAFETERIA

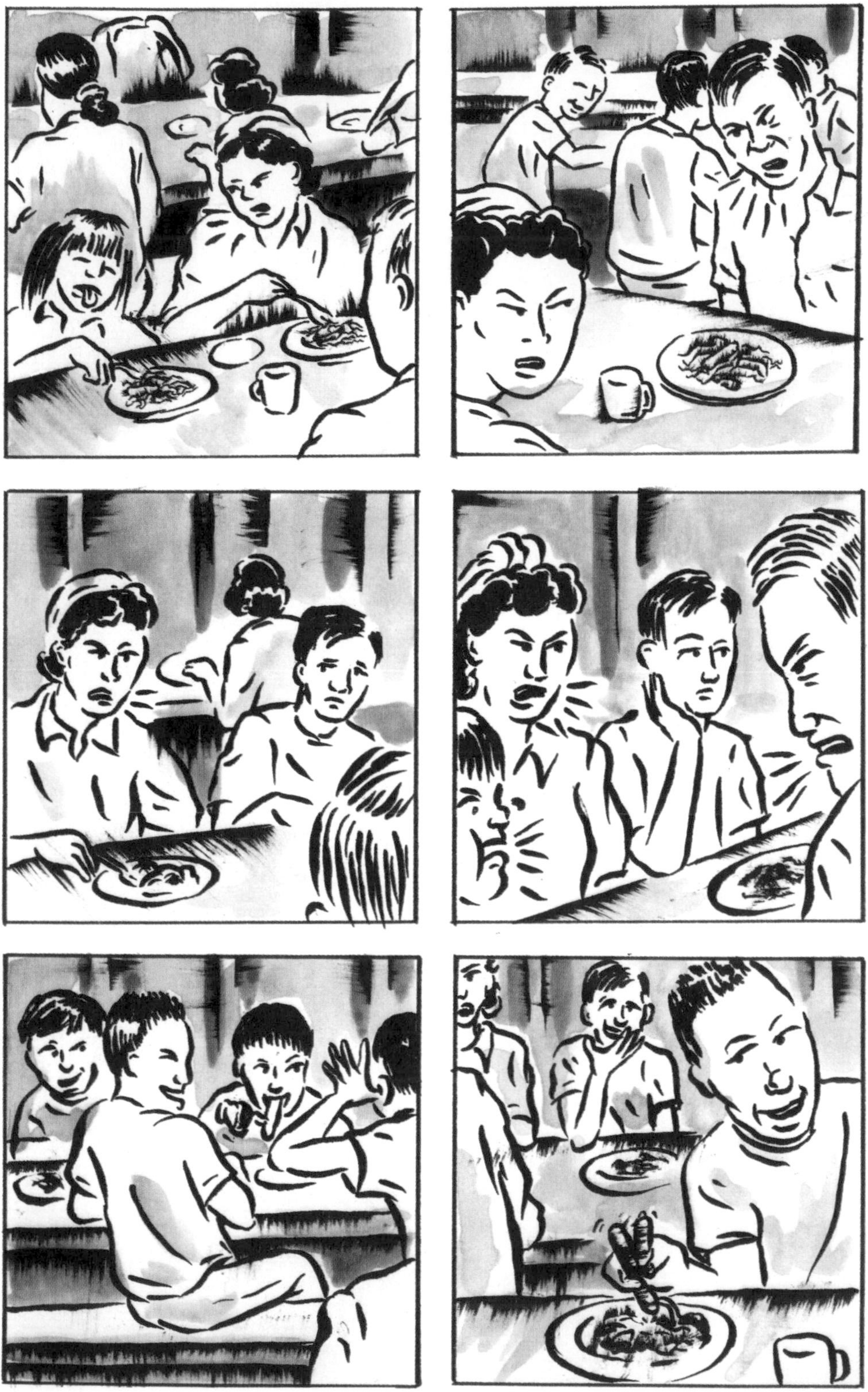

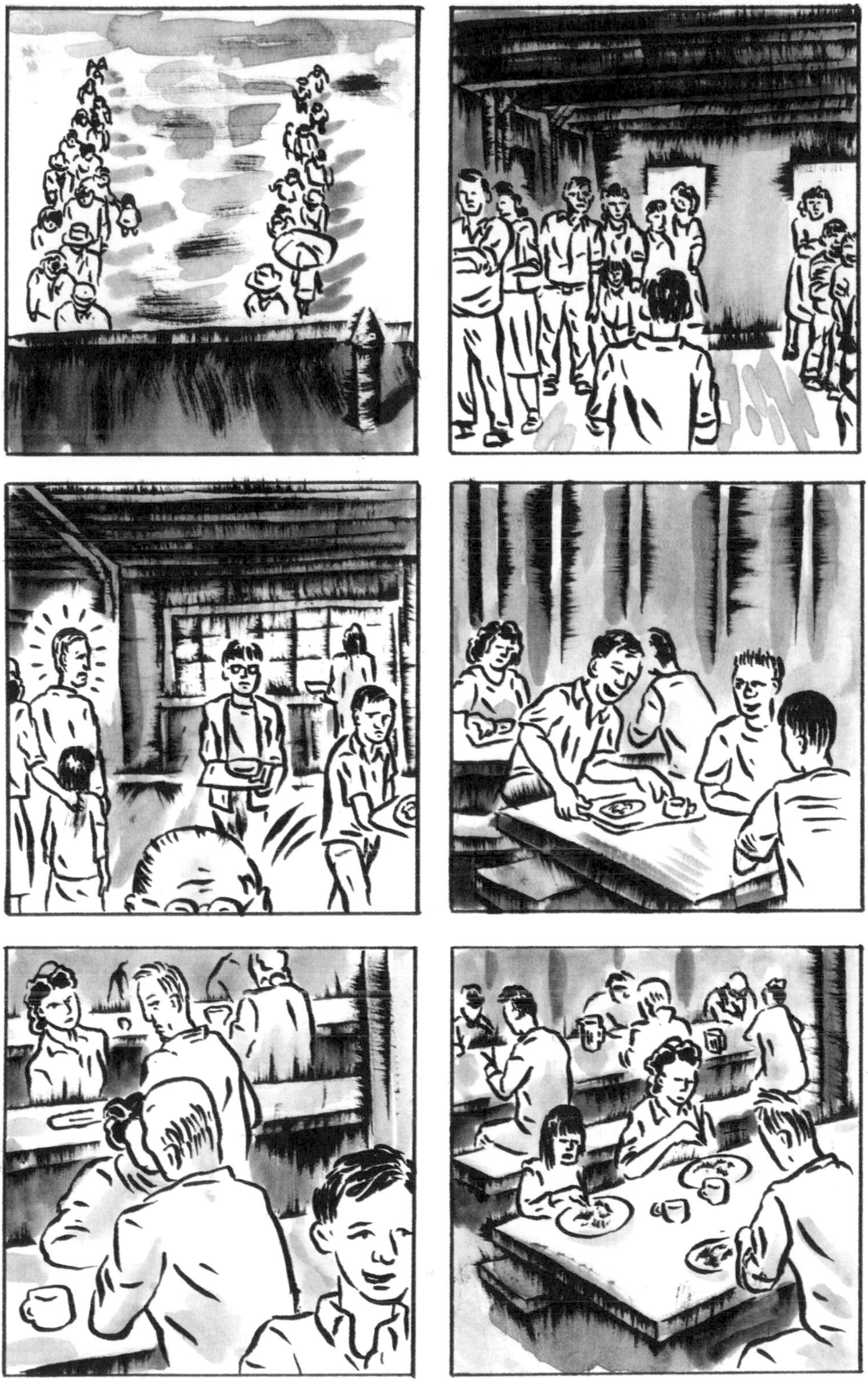

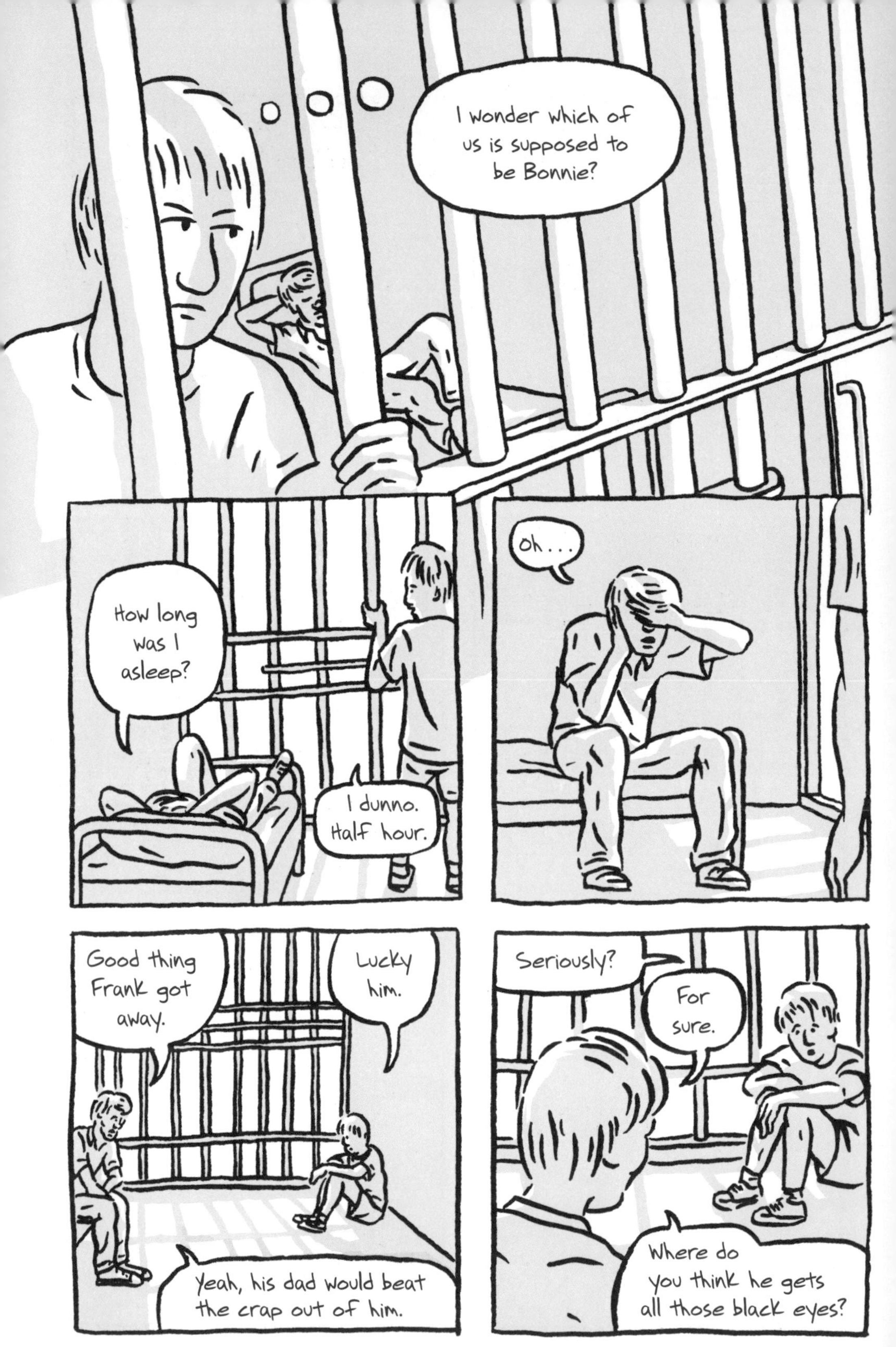
I wonder which of us is supposed to be Bonnie?
How long was I asleep?
I dunno. Half hour.
Oh....
Good thing Frank got away.
Lucky him.
Yeah, his dad would beat the crap out of him.
Seriously?
For sure.
Where do you think he gets all those black eyes?

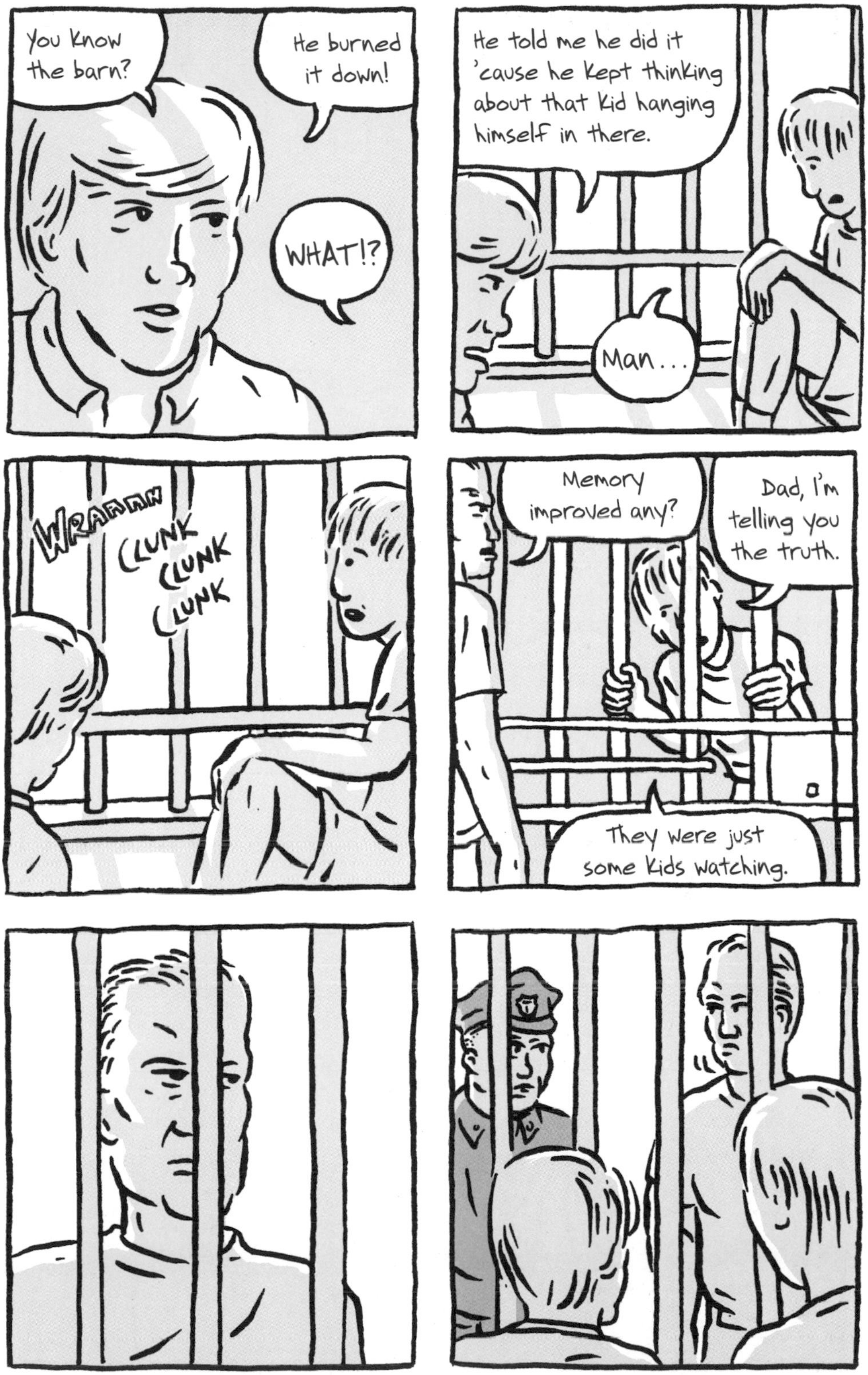
You know the barn?
He burned it down!
WHAT!?
He told me he did it 'cause he kept thinking about that kid hanging himself in there.
Man...
WRAAAAH
CLUNK
CLUNK
CLUNK
Memory improved any?
Dad, I'm telling you the truth.
They were just some kids watching.

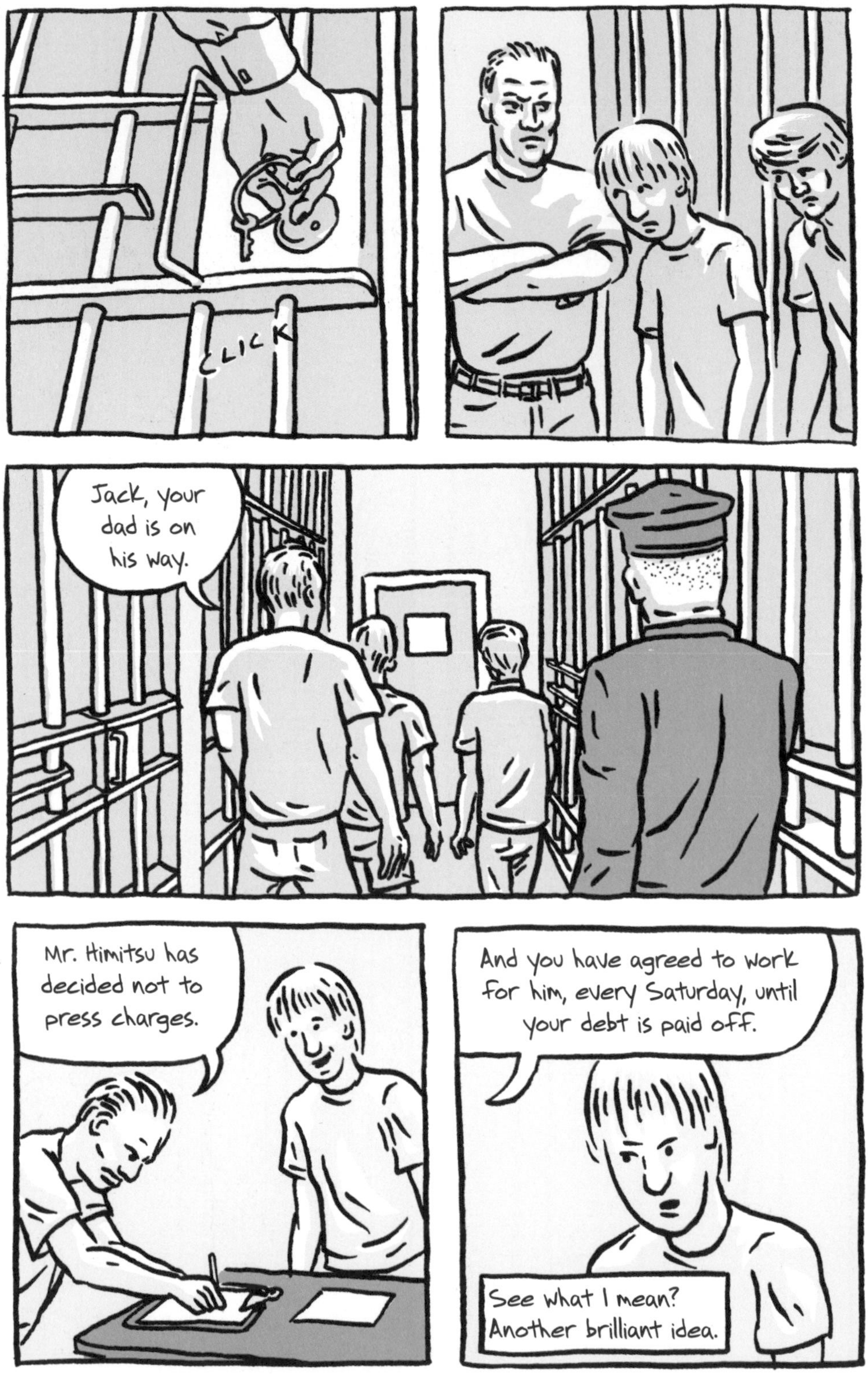
CLICK
Jack, your dad is on his way.
Mr. Himitsu has decided not to press charges.
And you have agreed to work for him, every Saturday, until your debt is paid off.
See what I mean? Another brilliant idea.

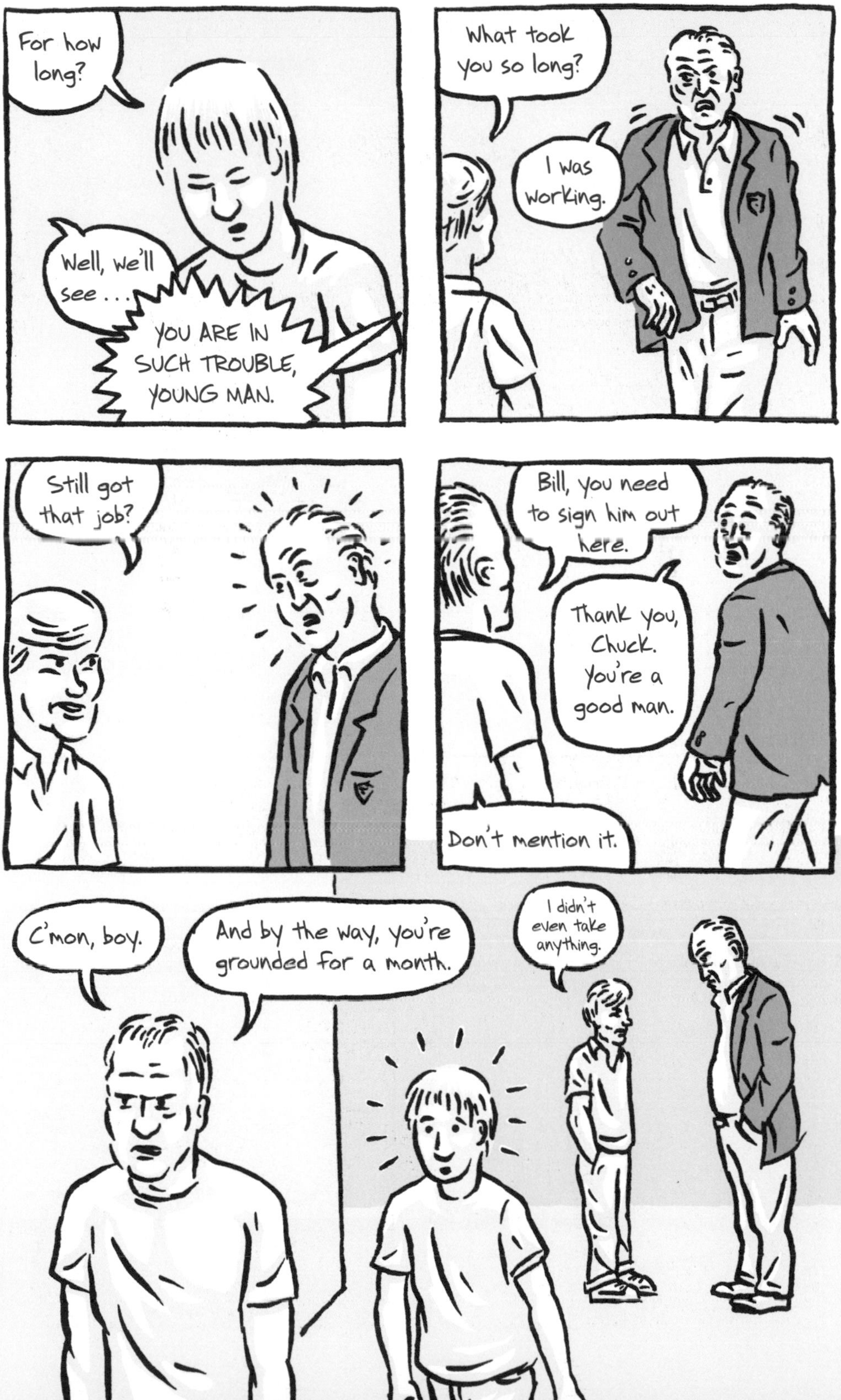
For how long?
Well, we'll see . . .
YOU ARE IN SUCH TROUBLE, YOUNG MAN.
What took you so long?
I was working.
Still got that job?
Bill, you need to sign him out here.
Thank you, Chuck. You're a good man.
Don't mention it.
C'mon, boy.
And by the way, you're grounded for a month.
I didn't even take anything.

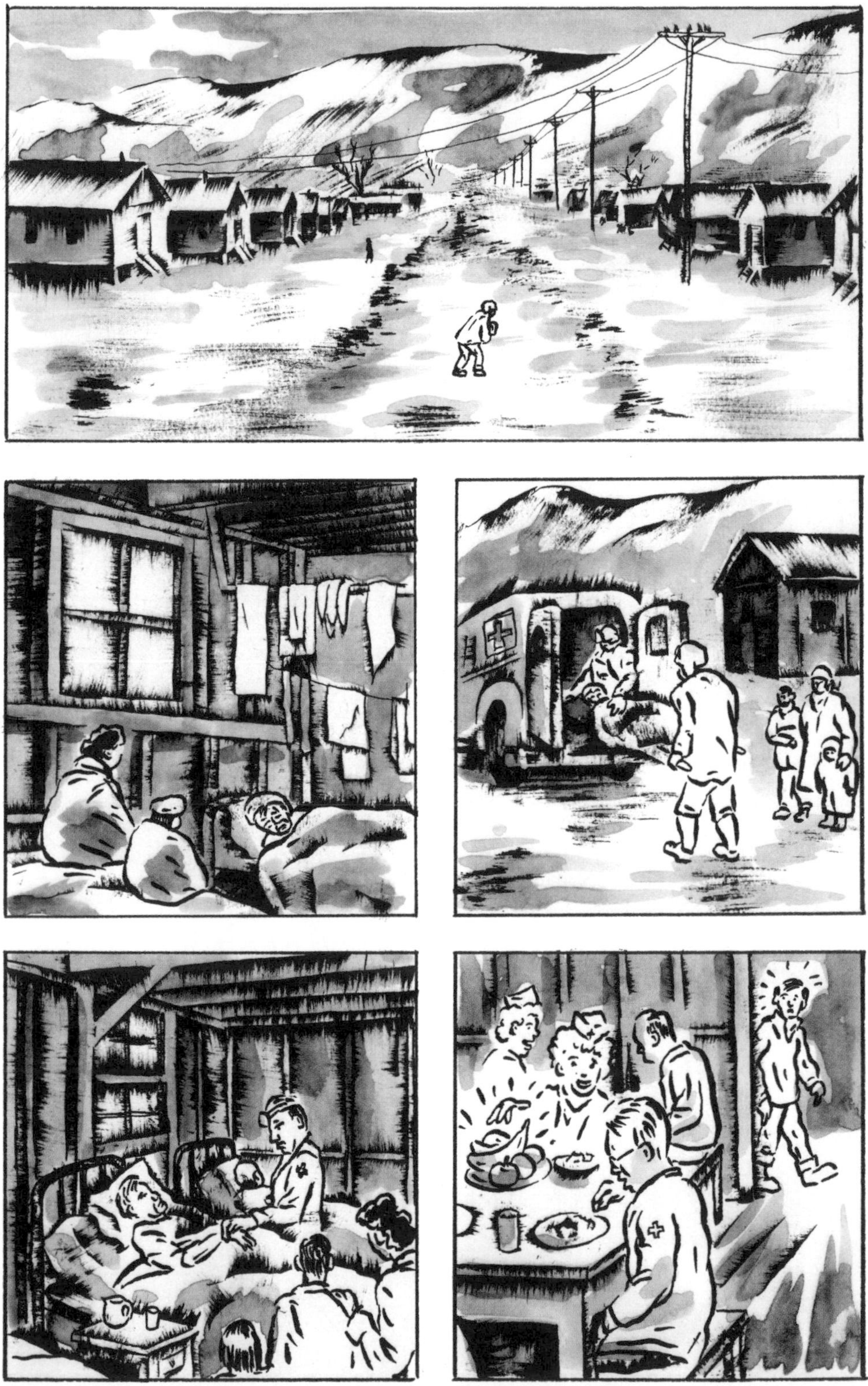

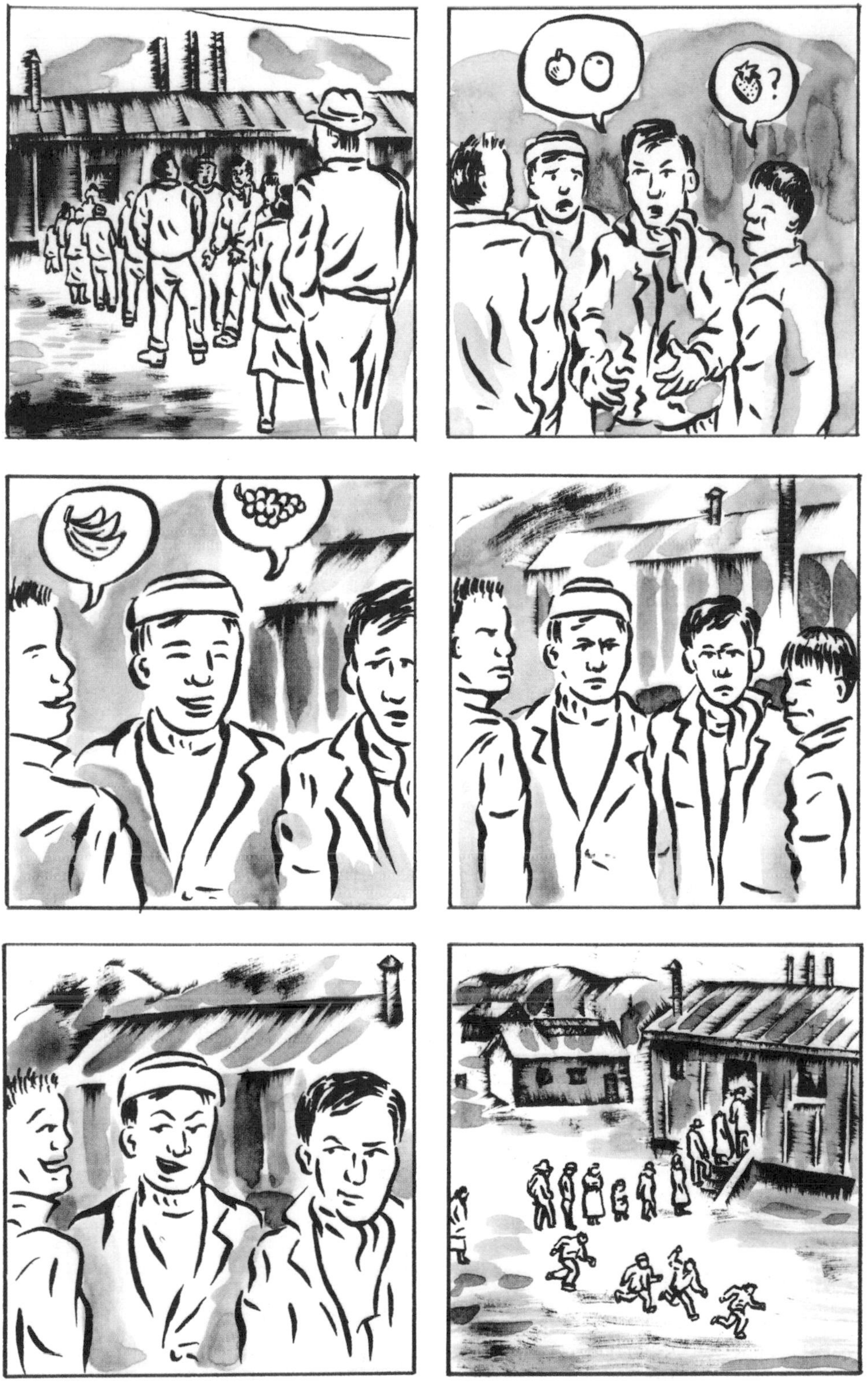
?

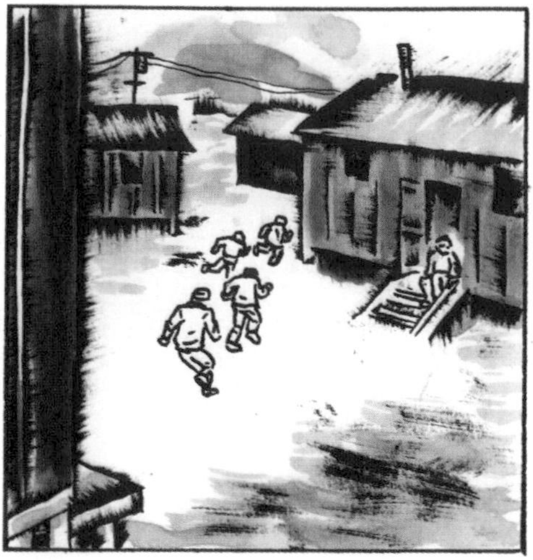
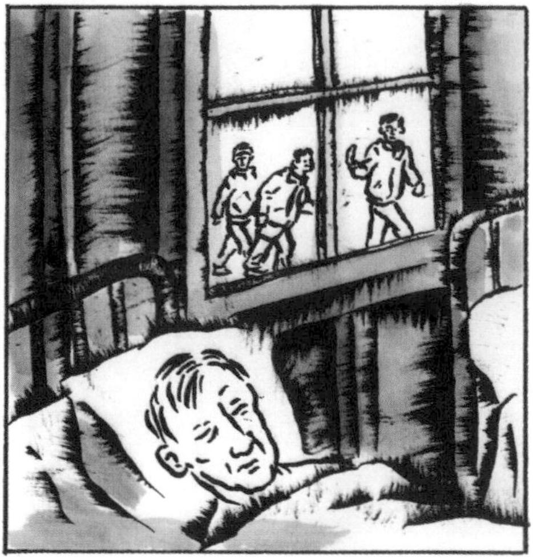
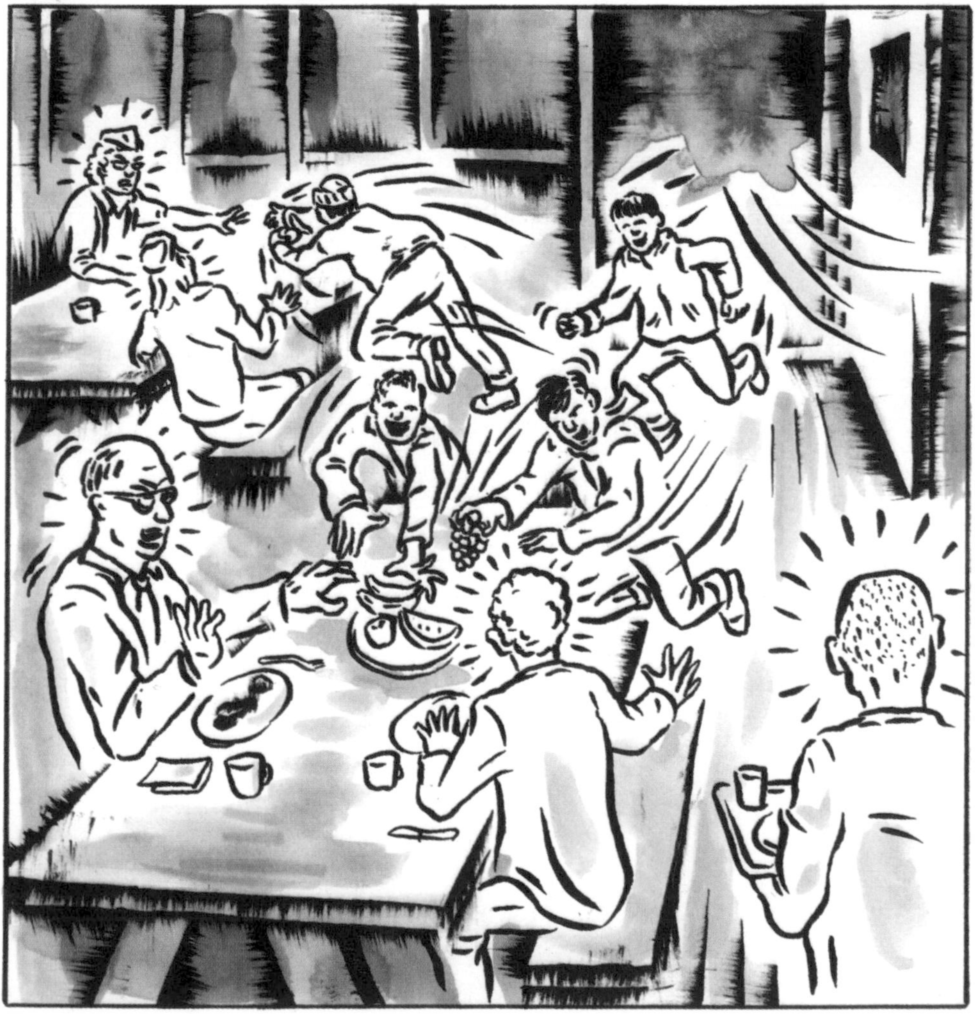

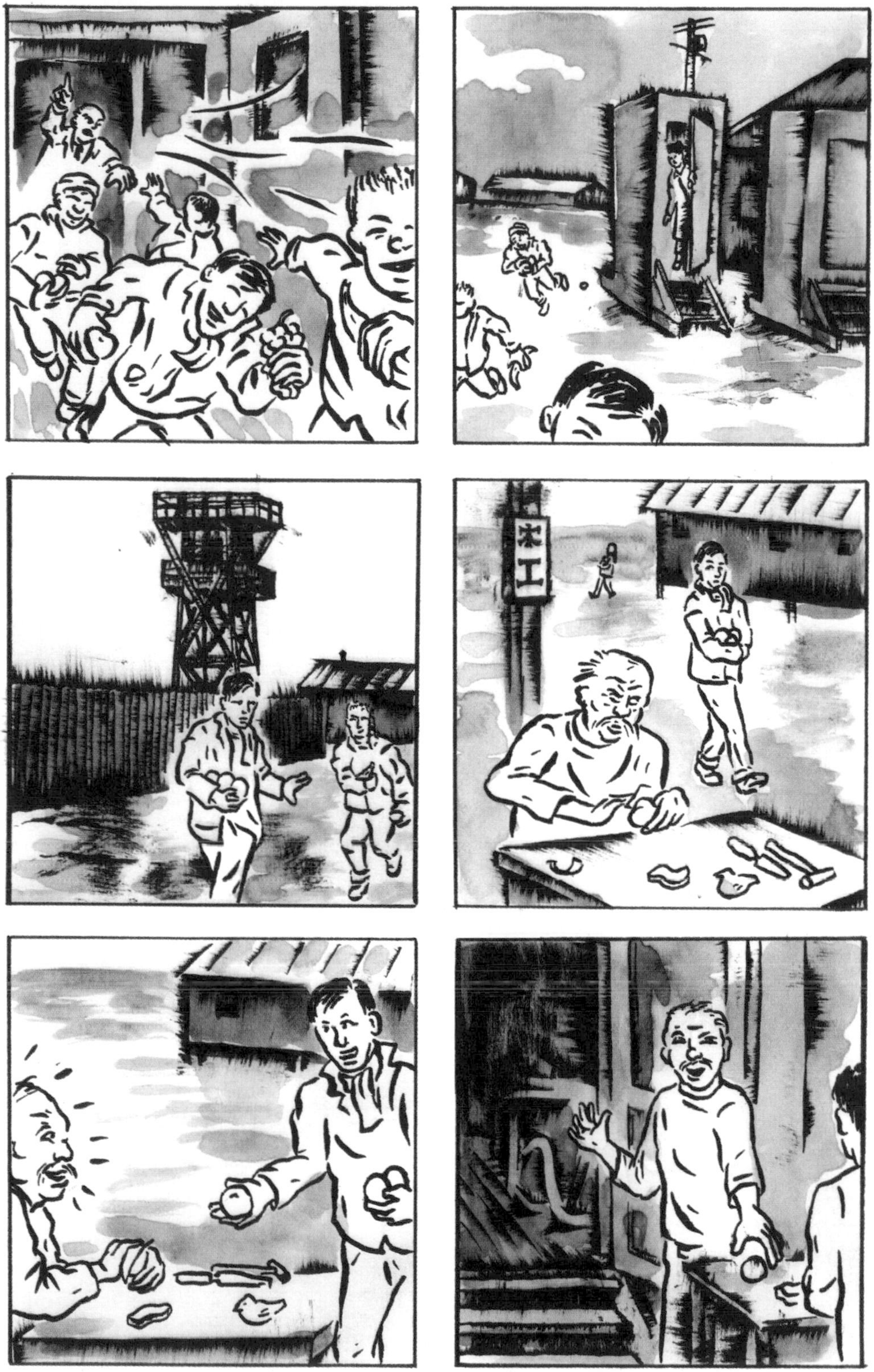
木工

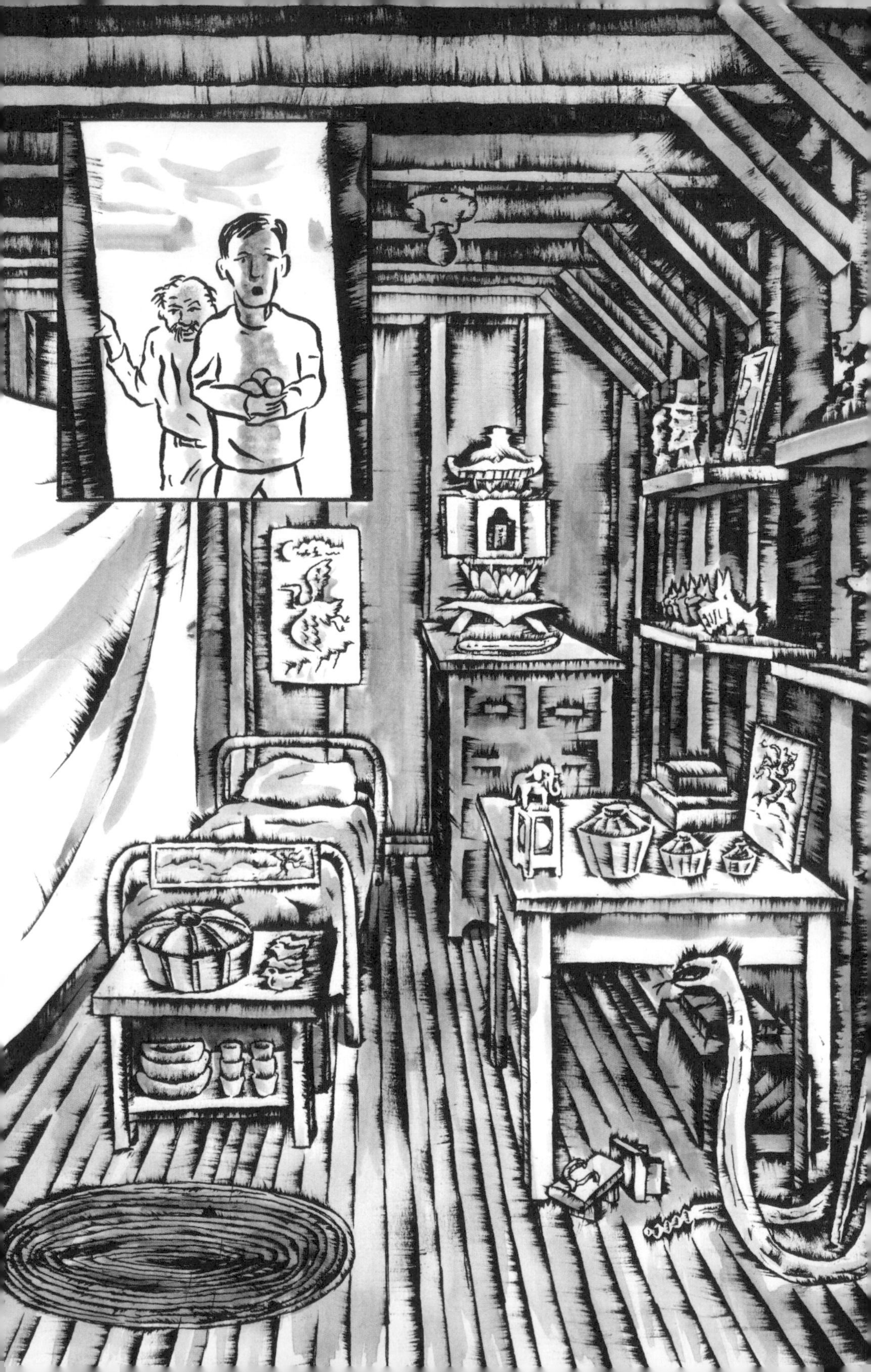

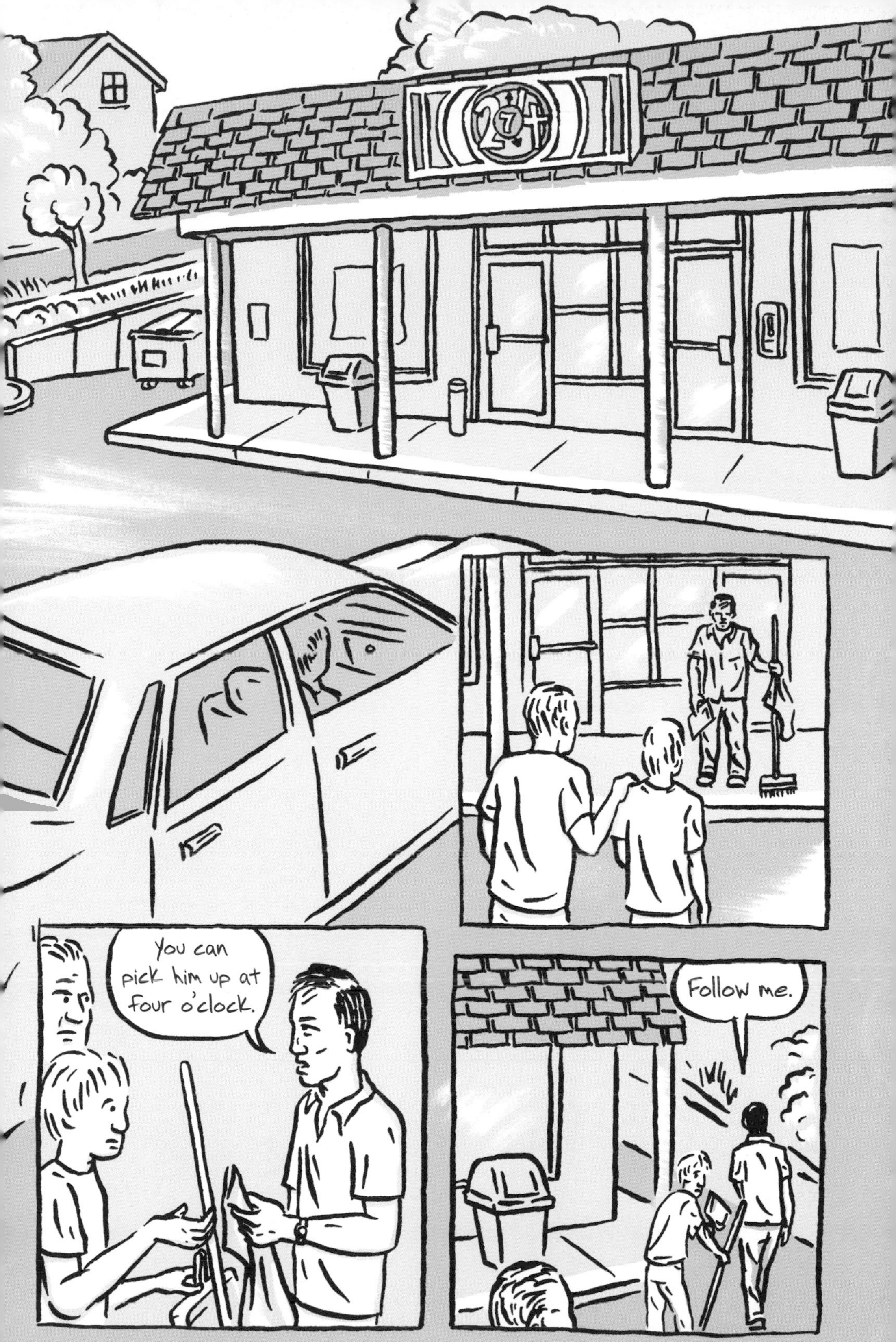
You can pick him up at four o'clock.
Follow me.

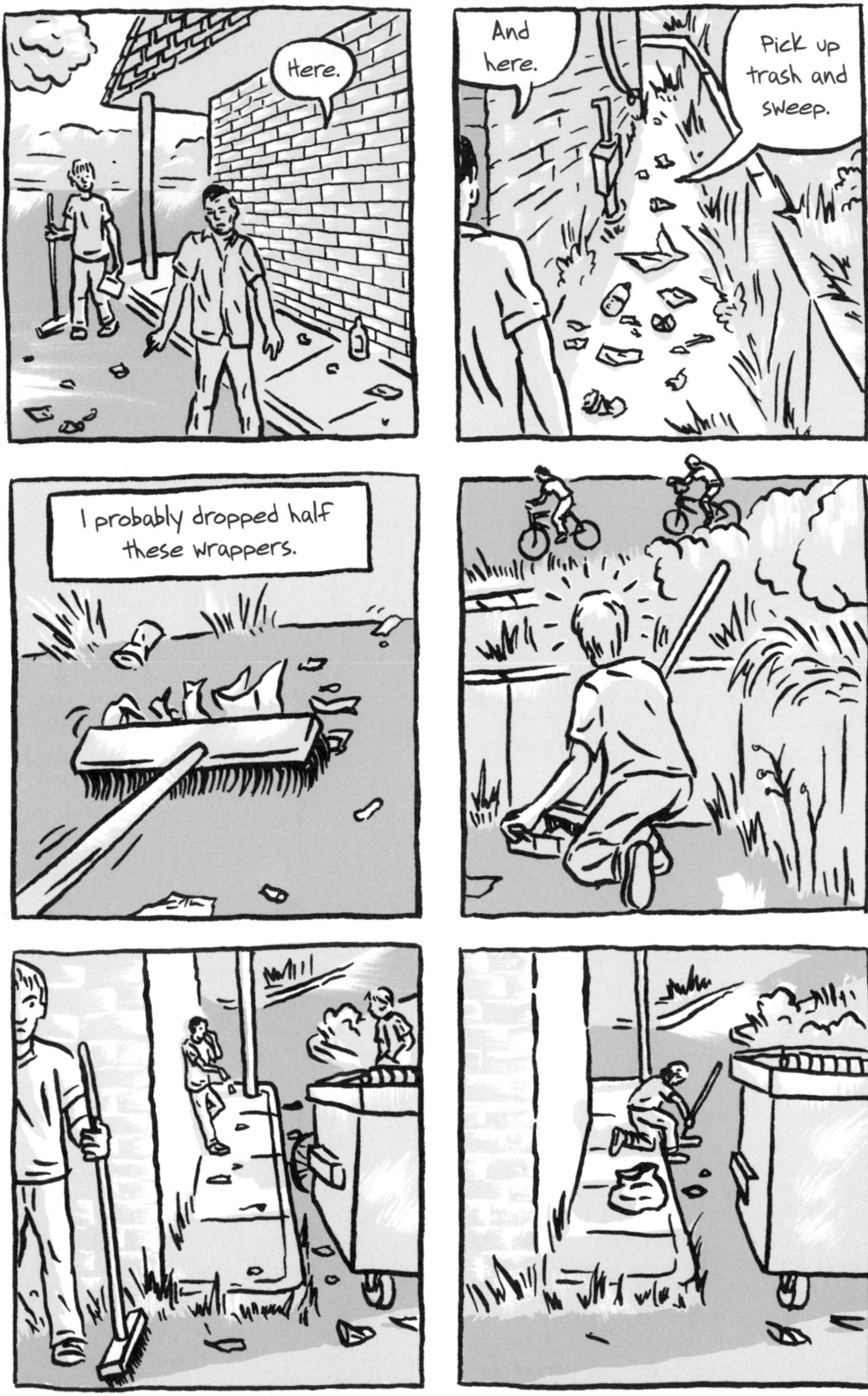
Here.
And here.
Pick up trash and sweep.
I probably dropped half these wrappers.

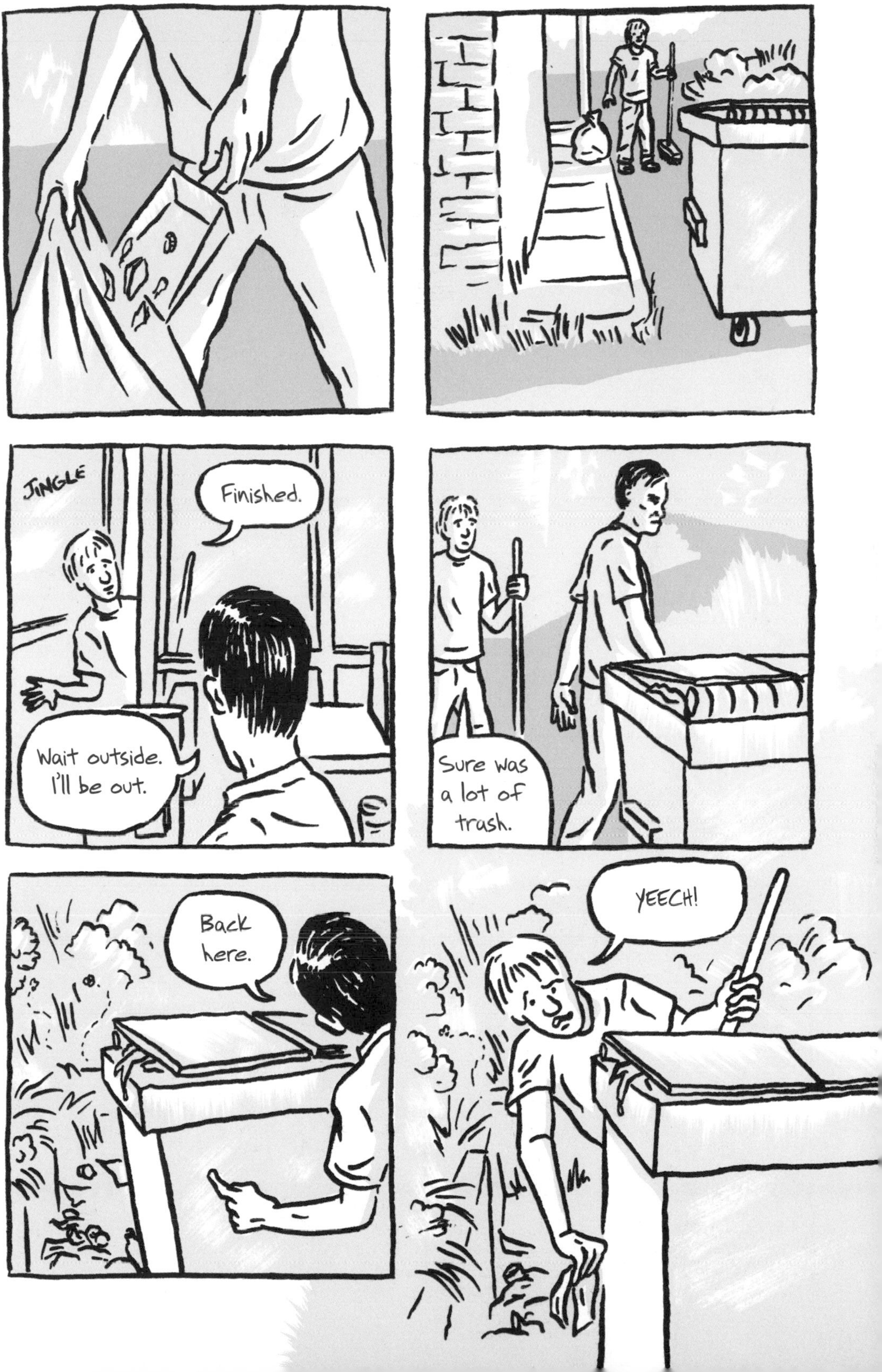
JINGLE
Finished.
Wait outside. I'll be out.
Sure was a lot of trash.
Back here.
YEECH!

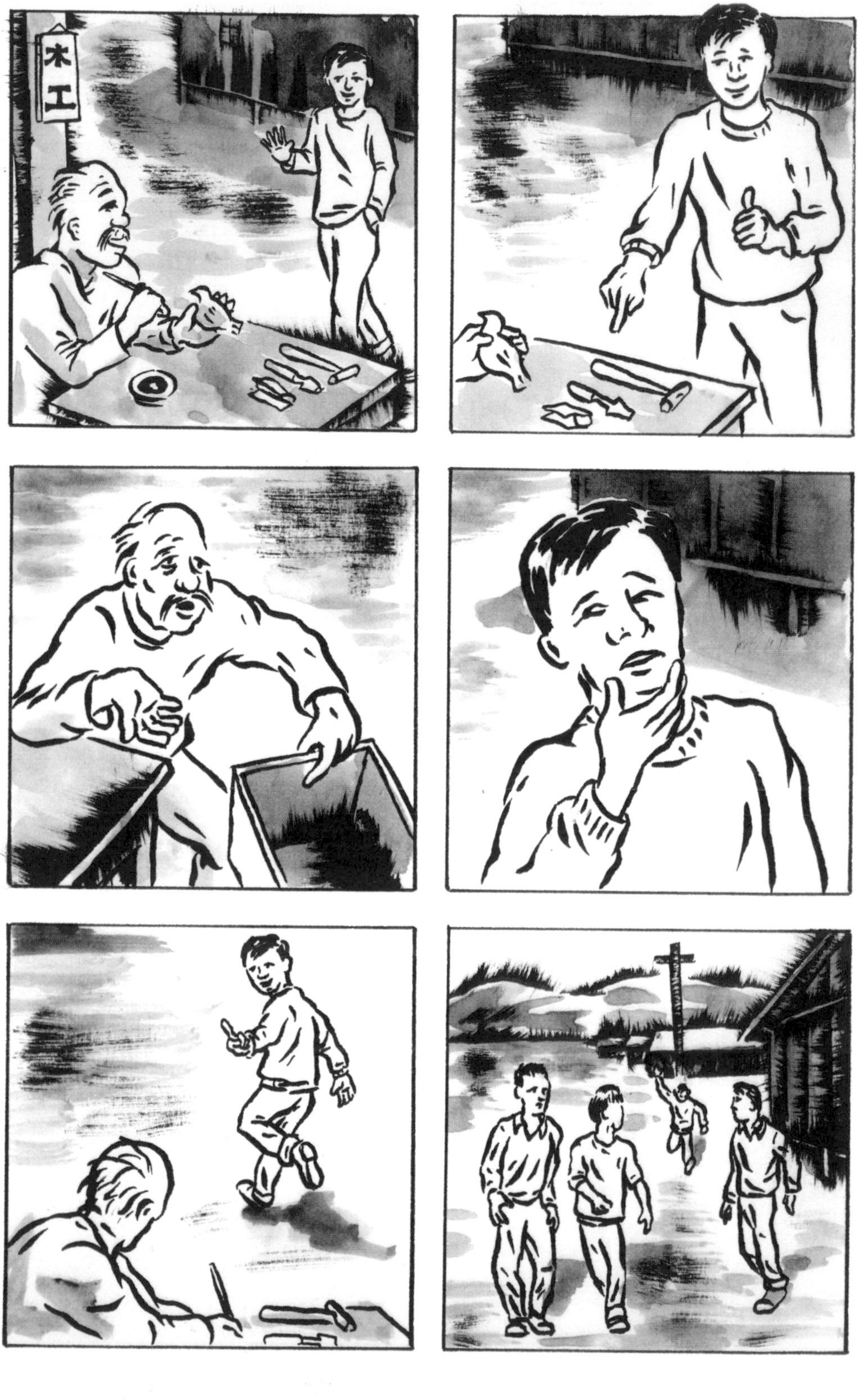
木工

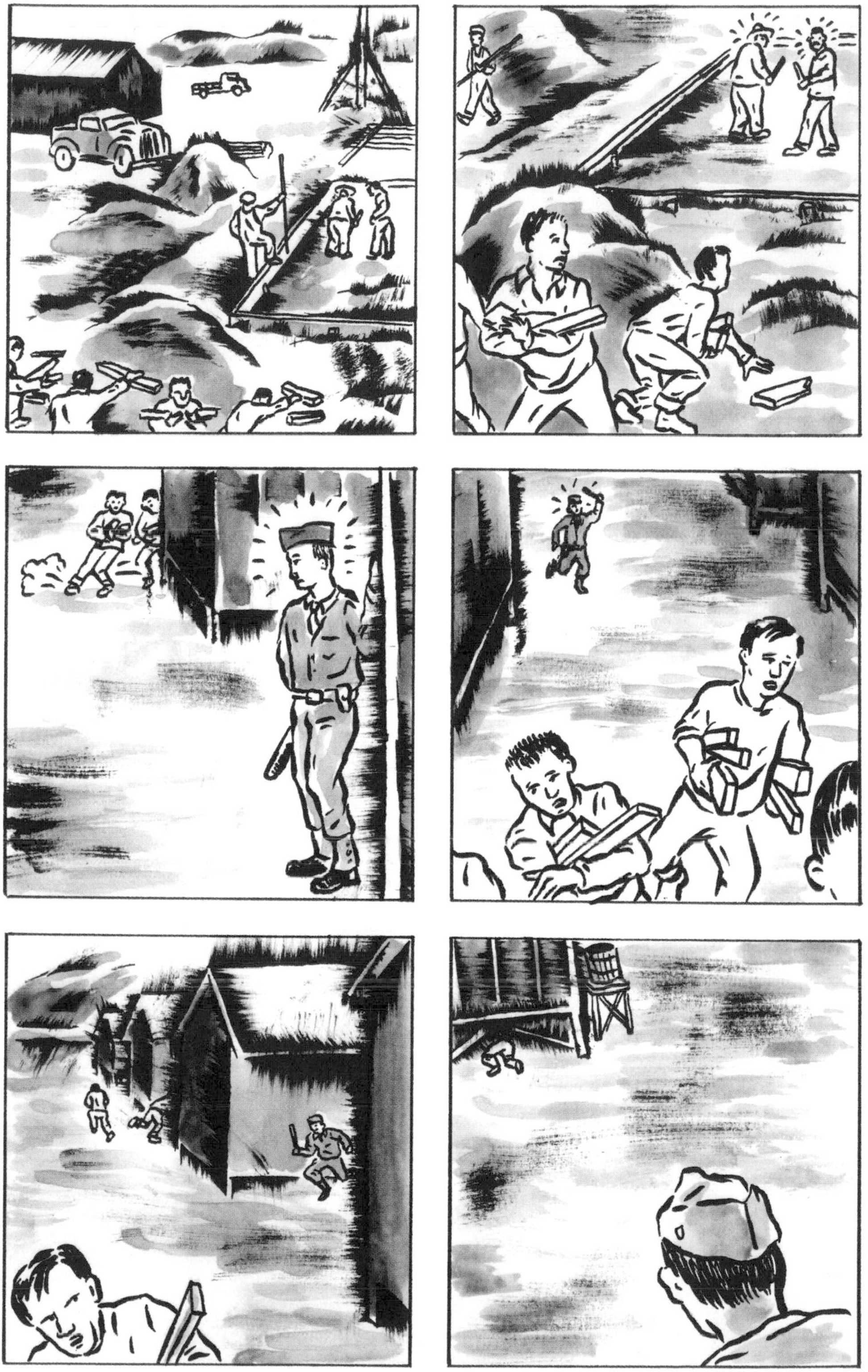

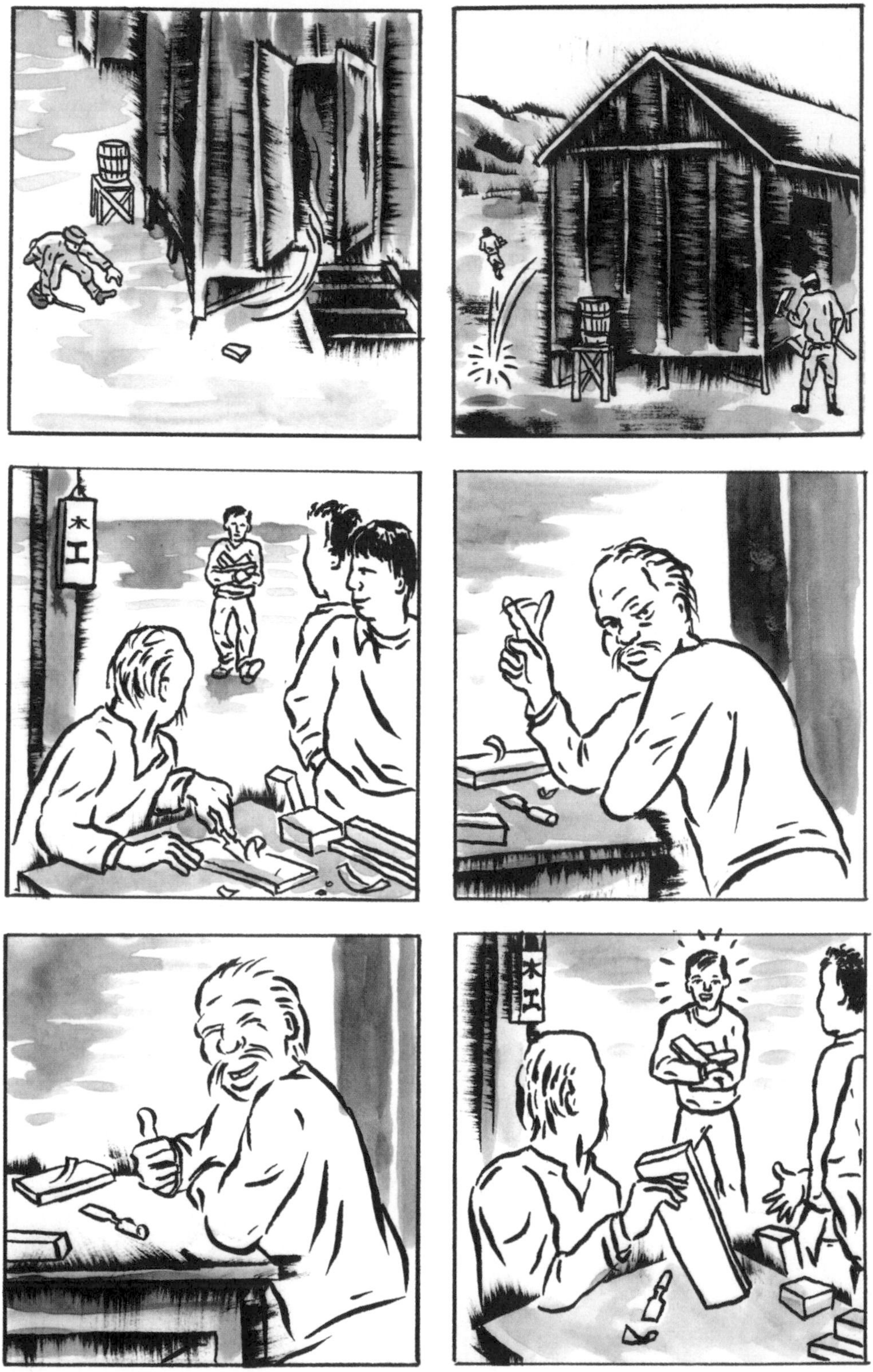
木工
木工

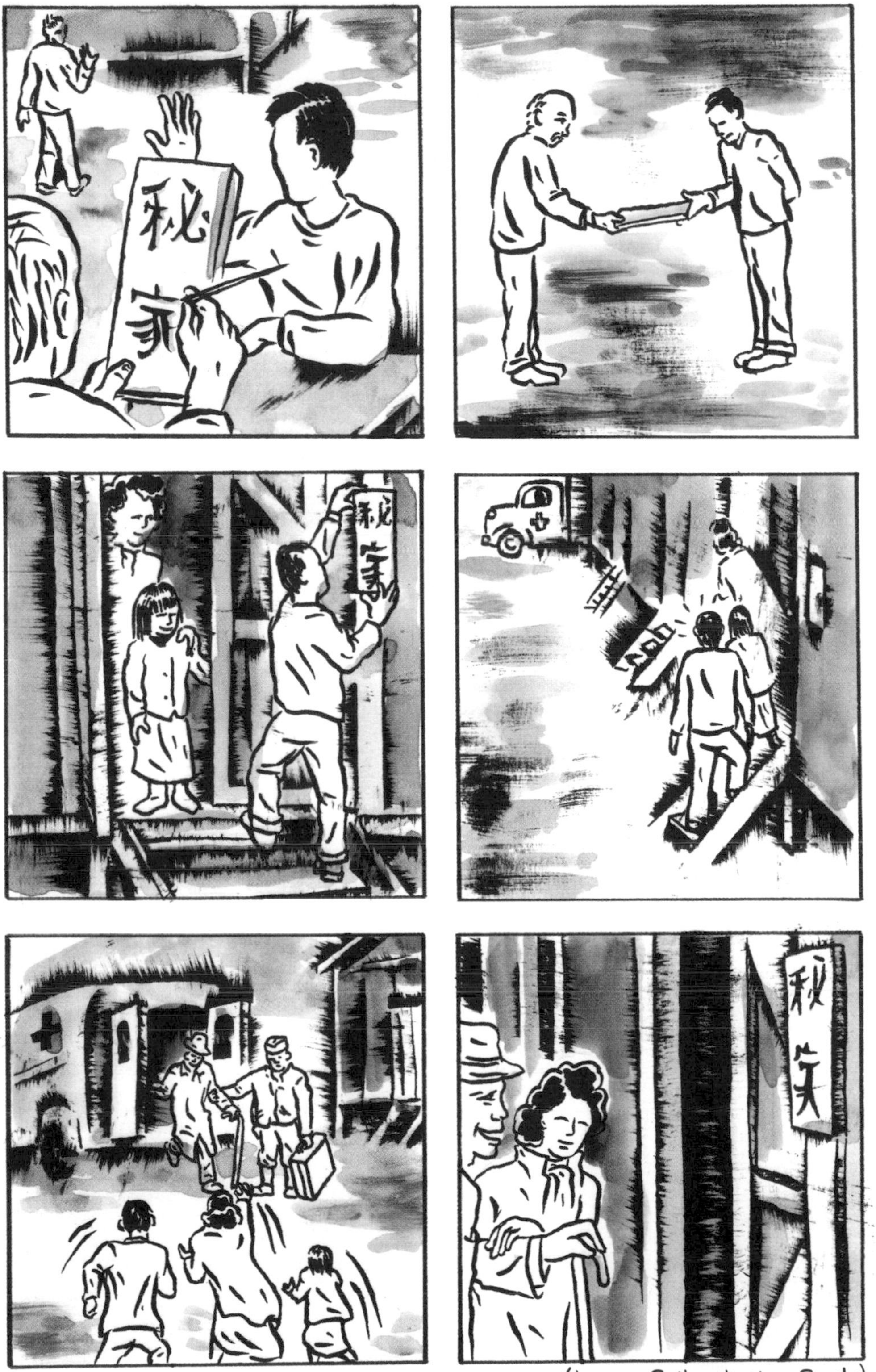
秘
家
(Home of the Himitsu family)

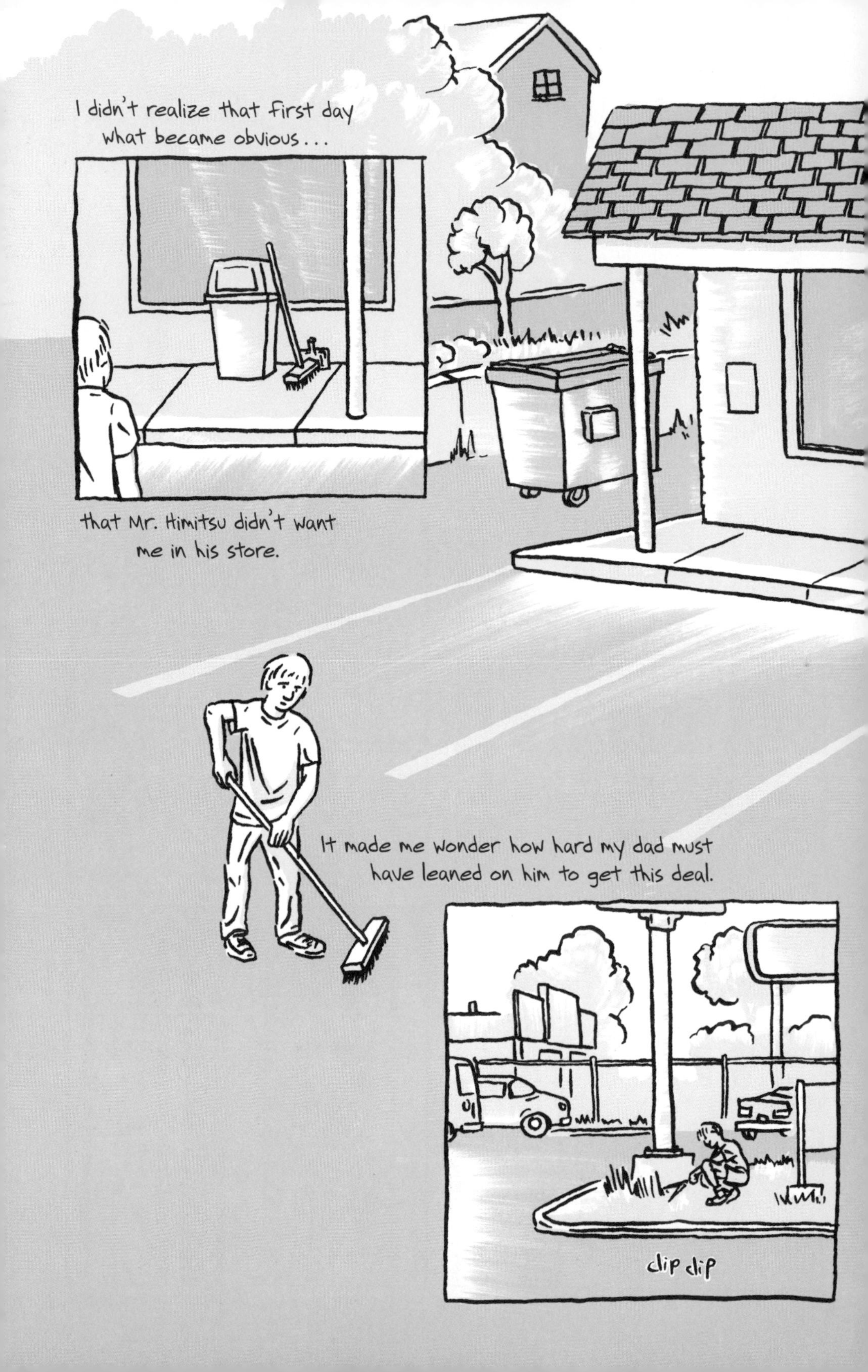
I didn't realize that first day what became obvious . . .
that Mr. Himitsu didn't want me in his store.
It made me wonder how hard my dad must have leaned on him to get this deal.
clip clip

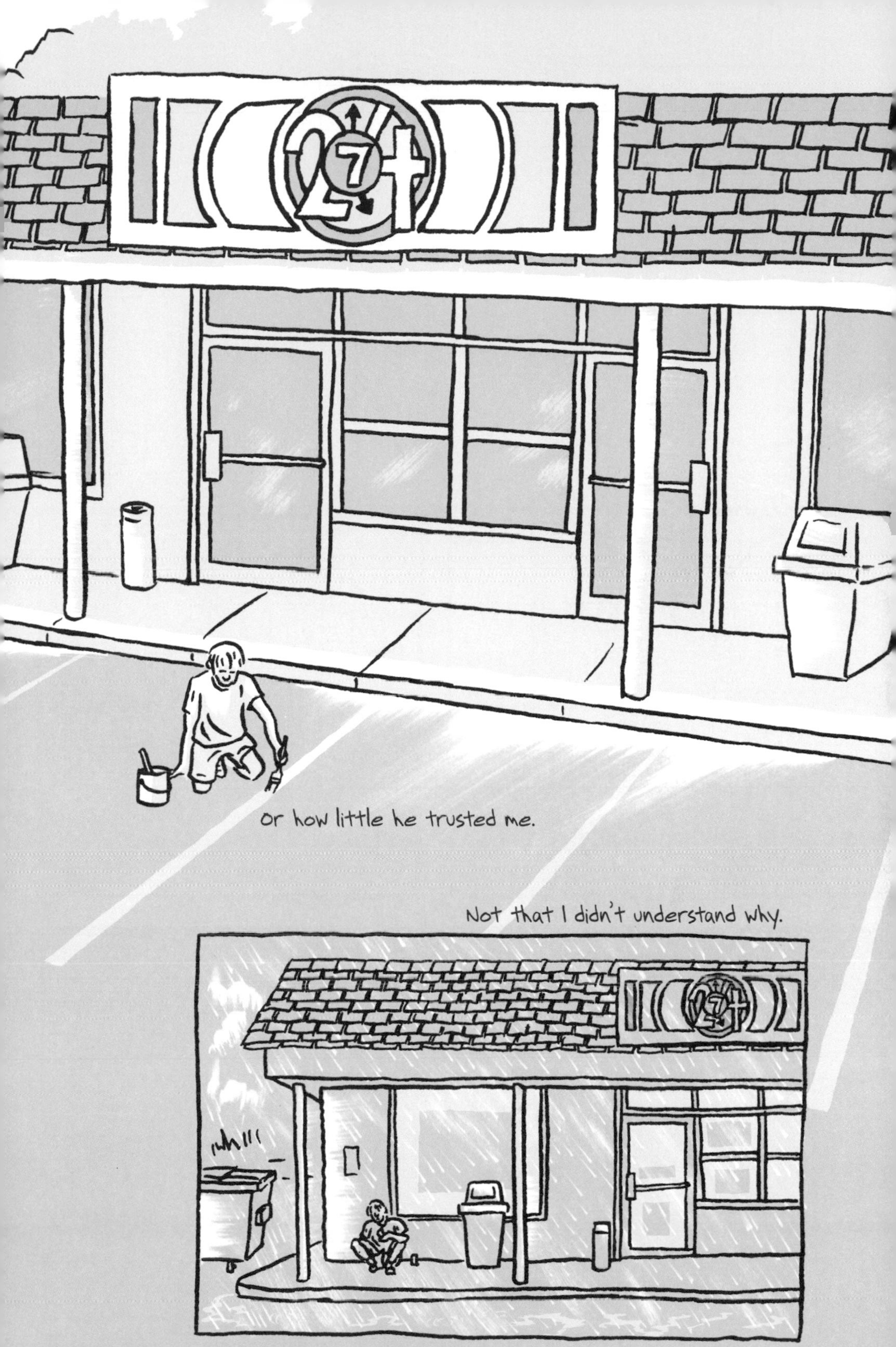
Or how little he trusted me.
Not that I didn't understand why.

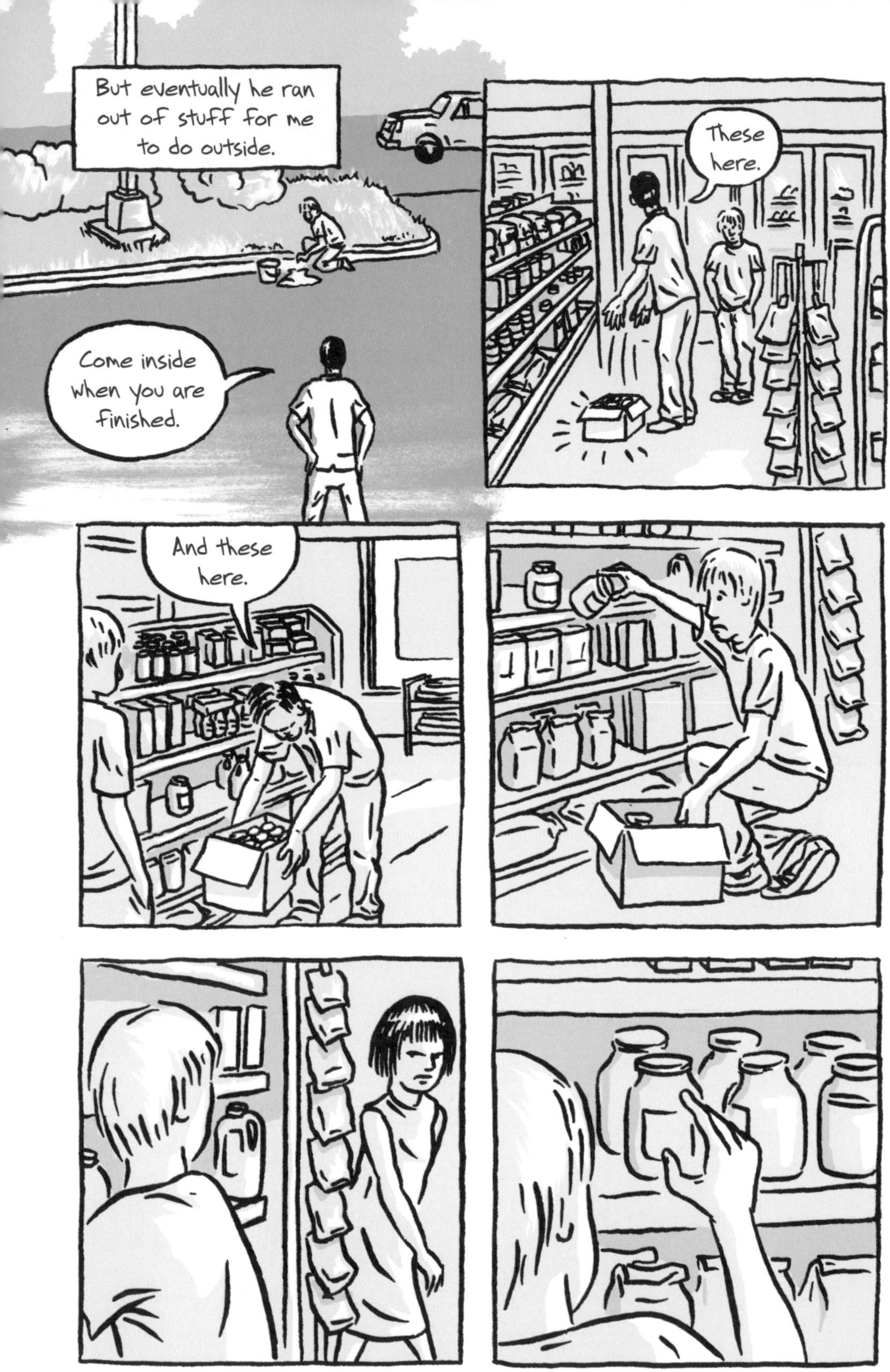

But eventually he ran out of stuff for me to do outside.
Come inside when you are finished.
These here.
And these here.

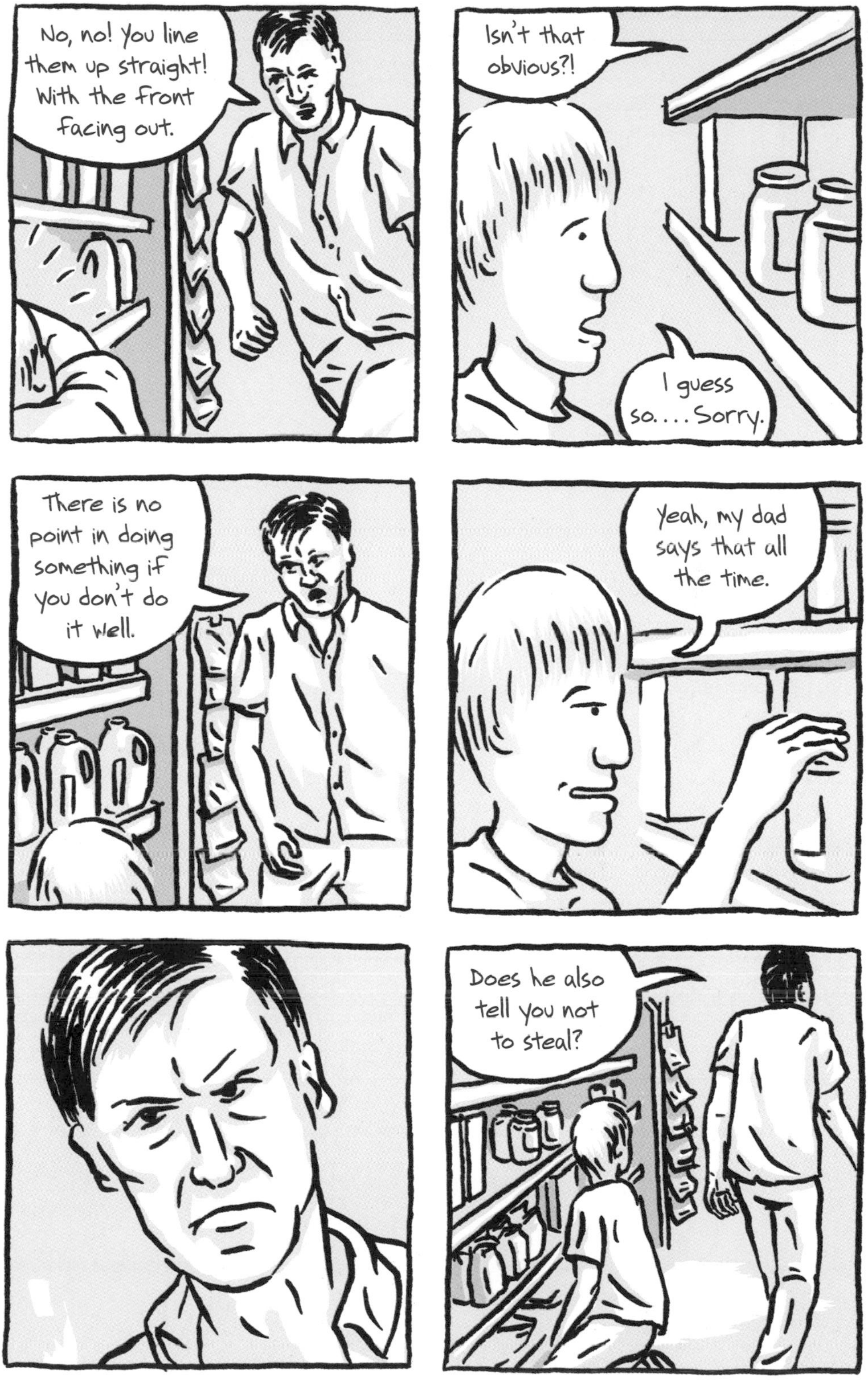
No, no! You line them up straight! With the front facing out.
Isn't that obvious?!
I guess so.... Sorry.
There is no point in doing something if you don't do it well.
Yeah, my dad says that all the time.
Does he also tell you not to steal?

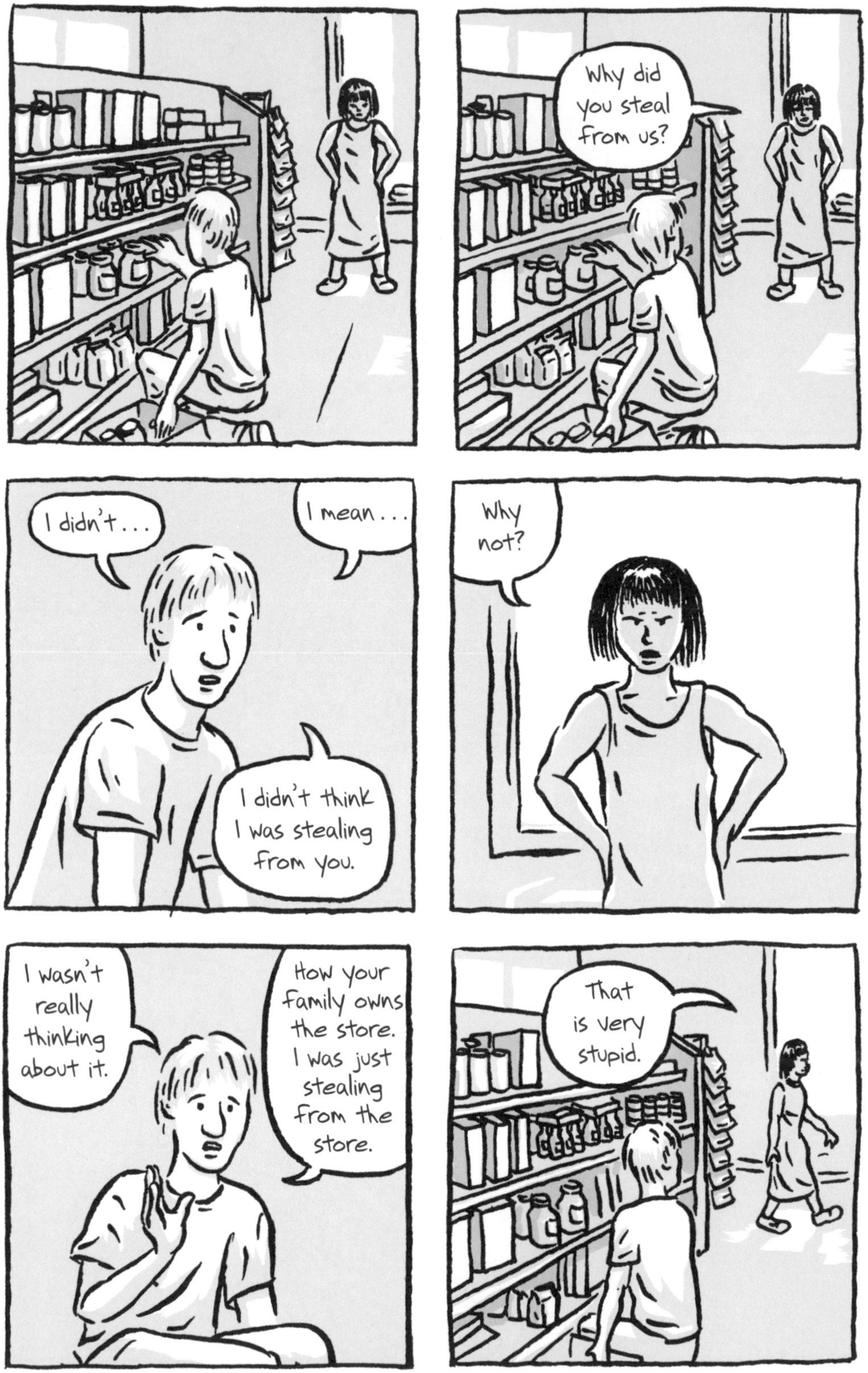
Why did you steal from us?
I didn't . . .
I mean . . .
I didn't think I was stealing from you.
Why not?
I wasn't really thinking about it.
How your family owns the store. I was just stealing from the store.
That is very stupid.

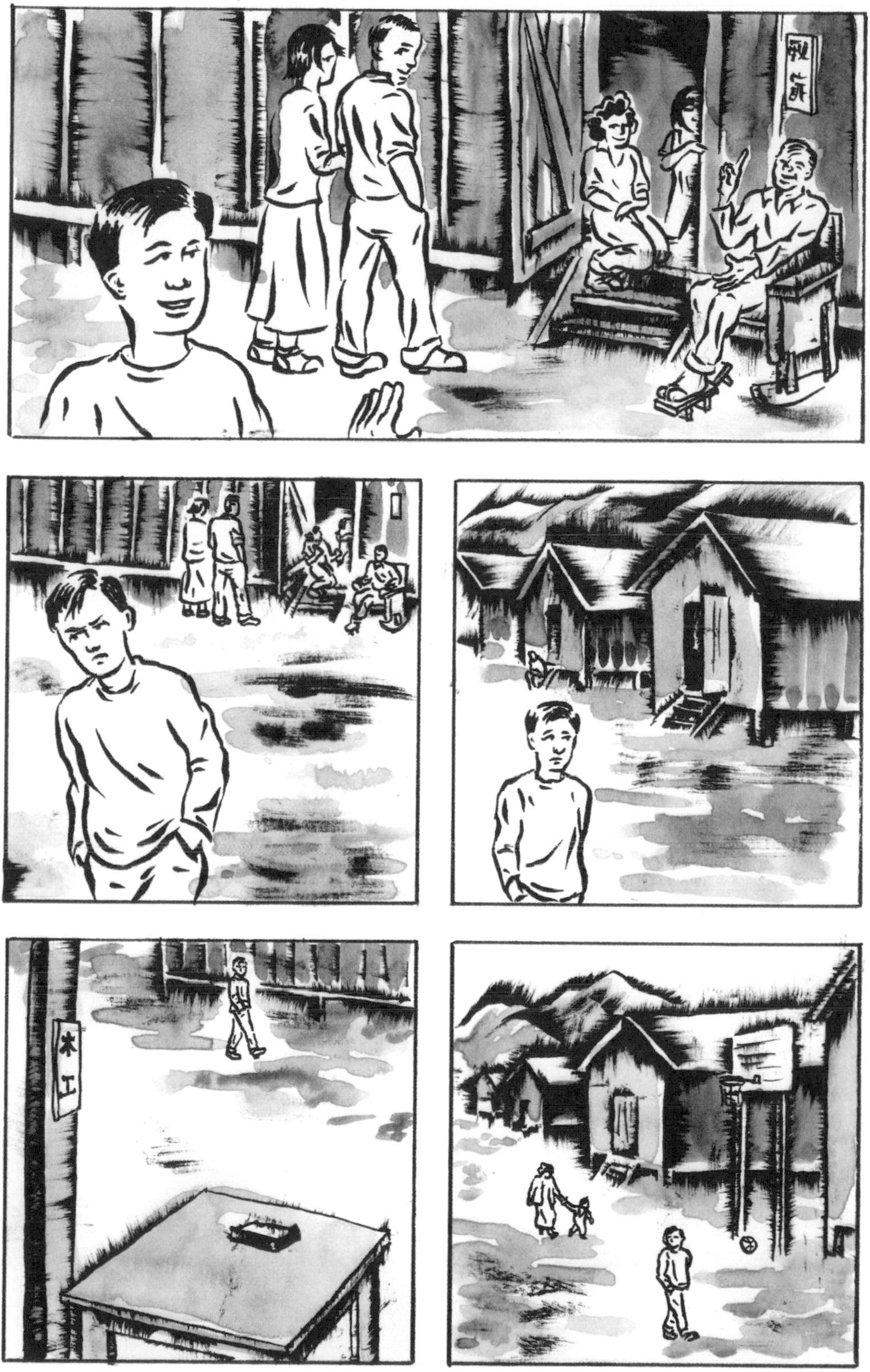
木工

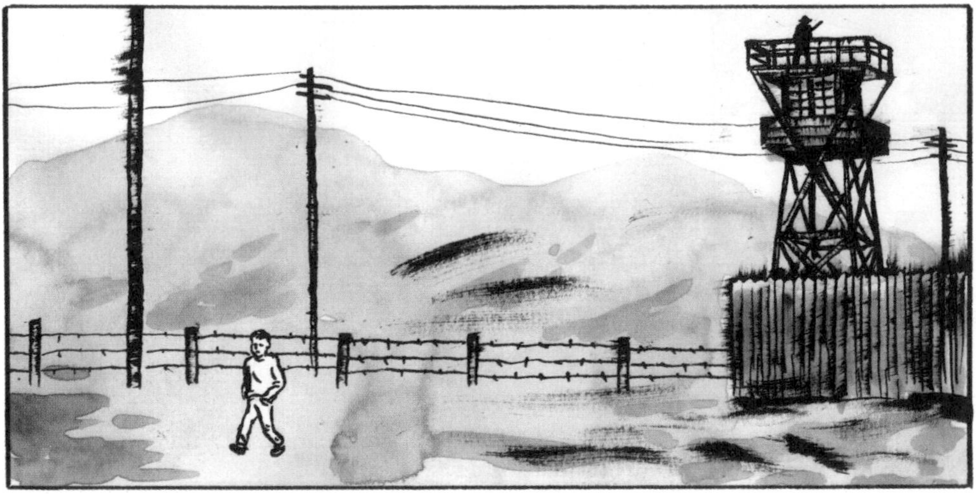

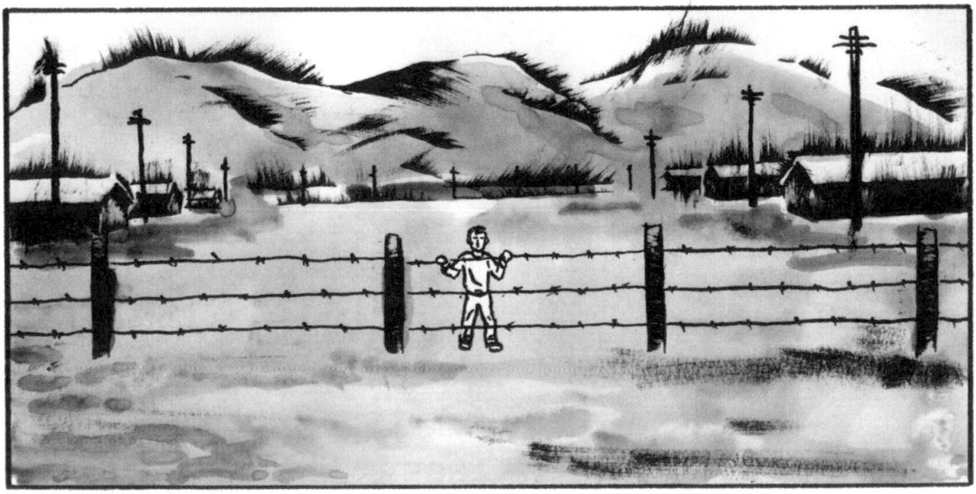

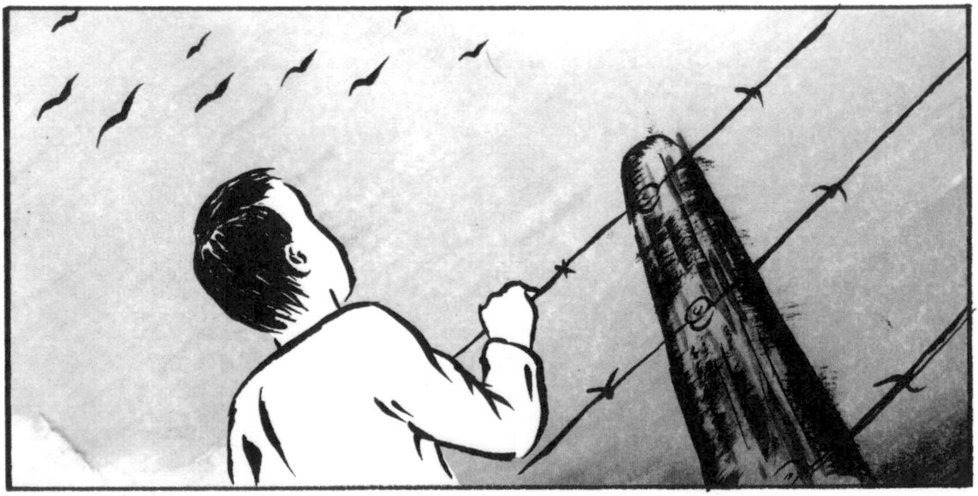

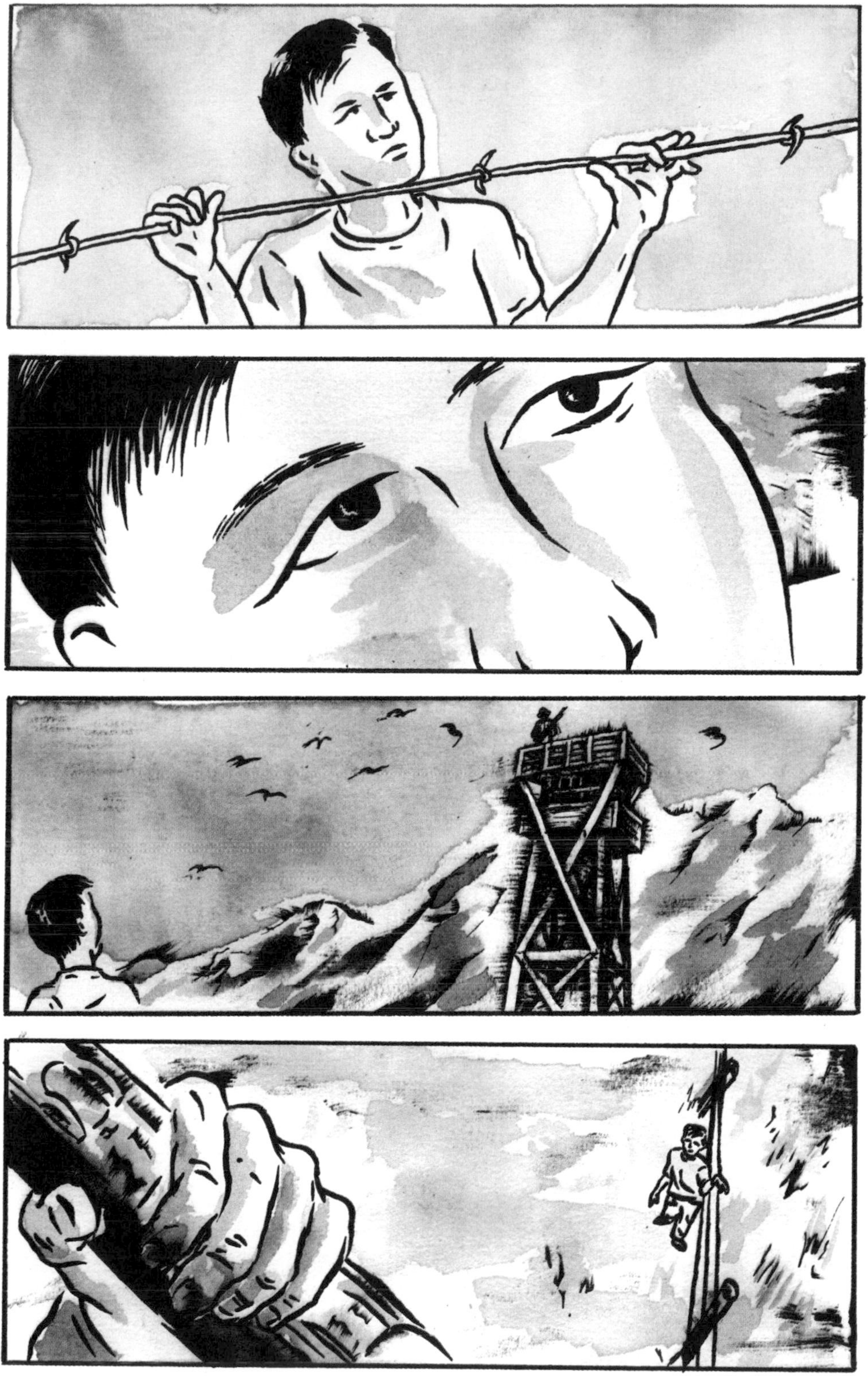

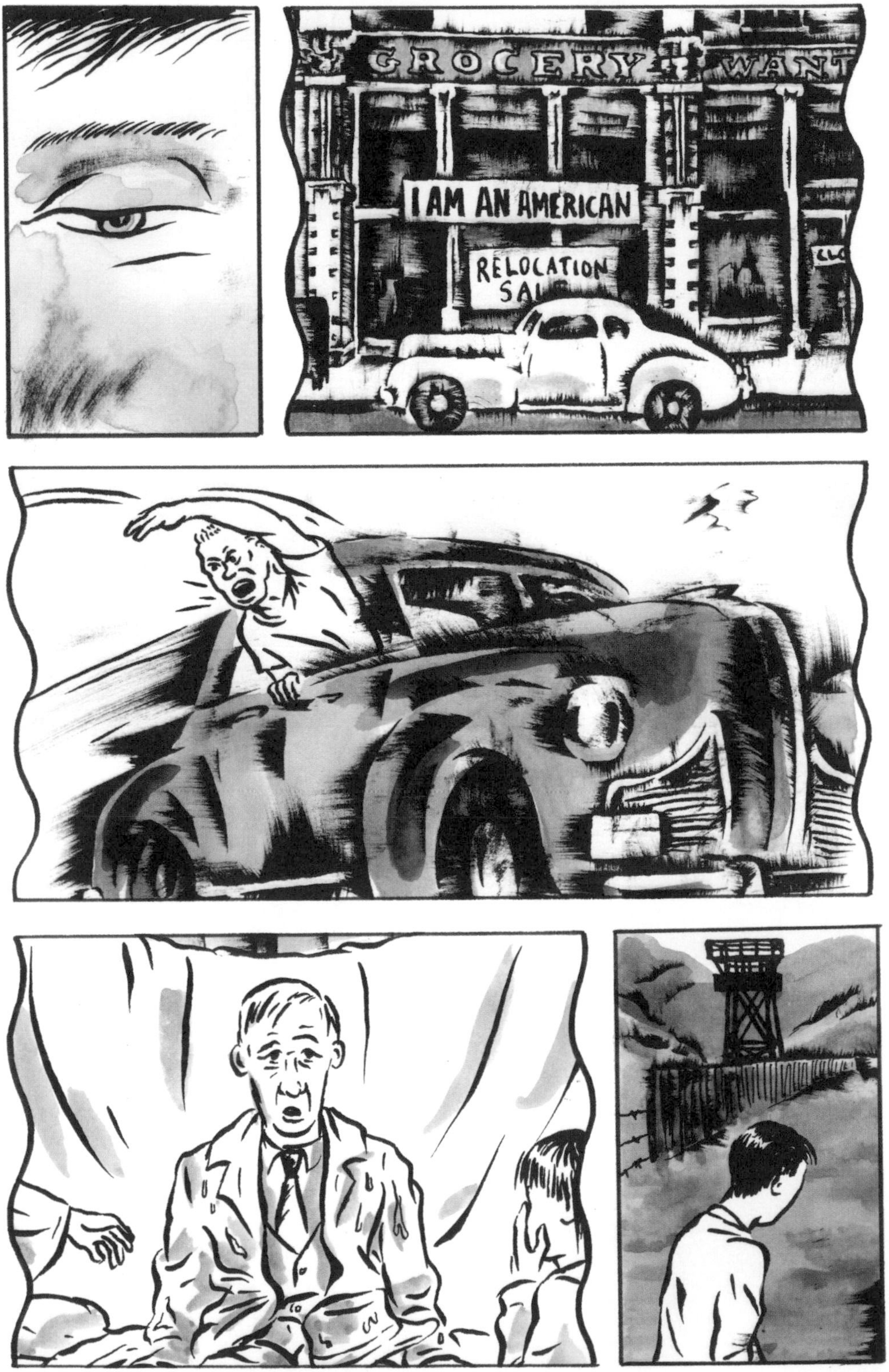
GROCERY
WANT
I AM AN AMERICAN
RELOCATION SAL

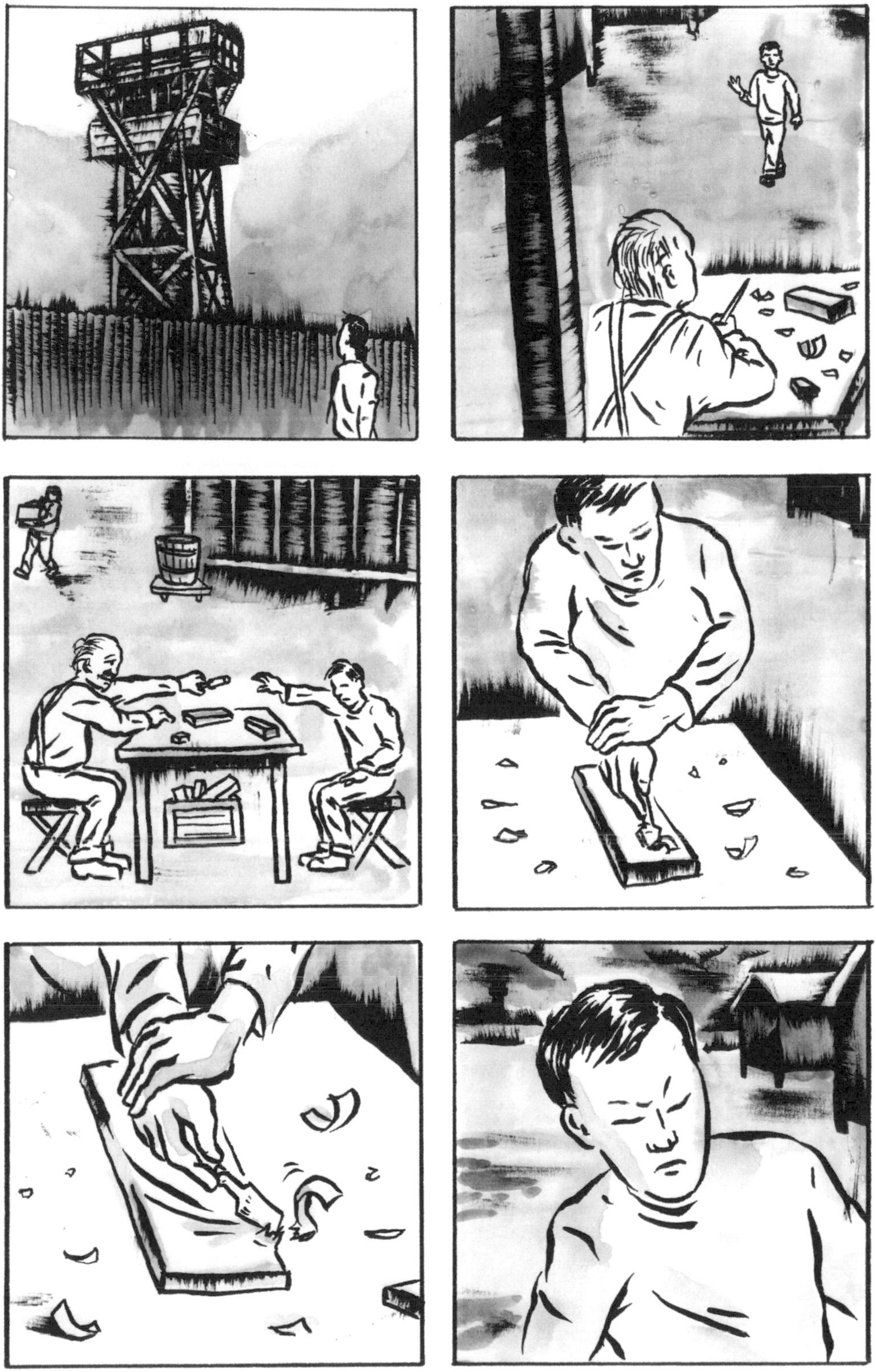

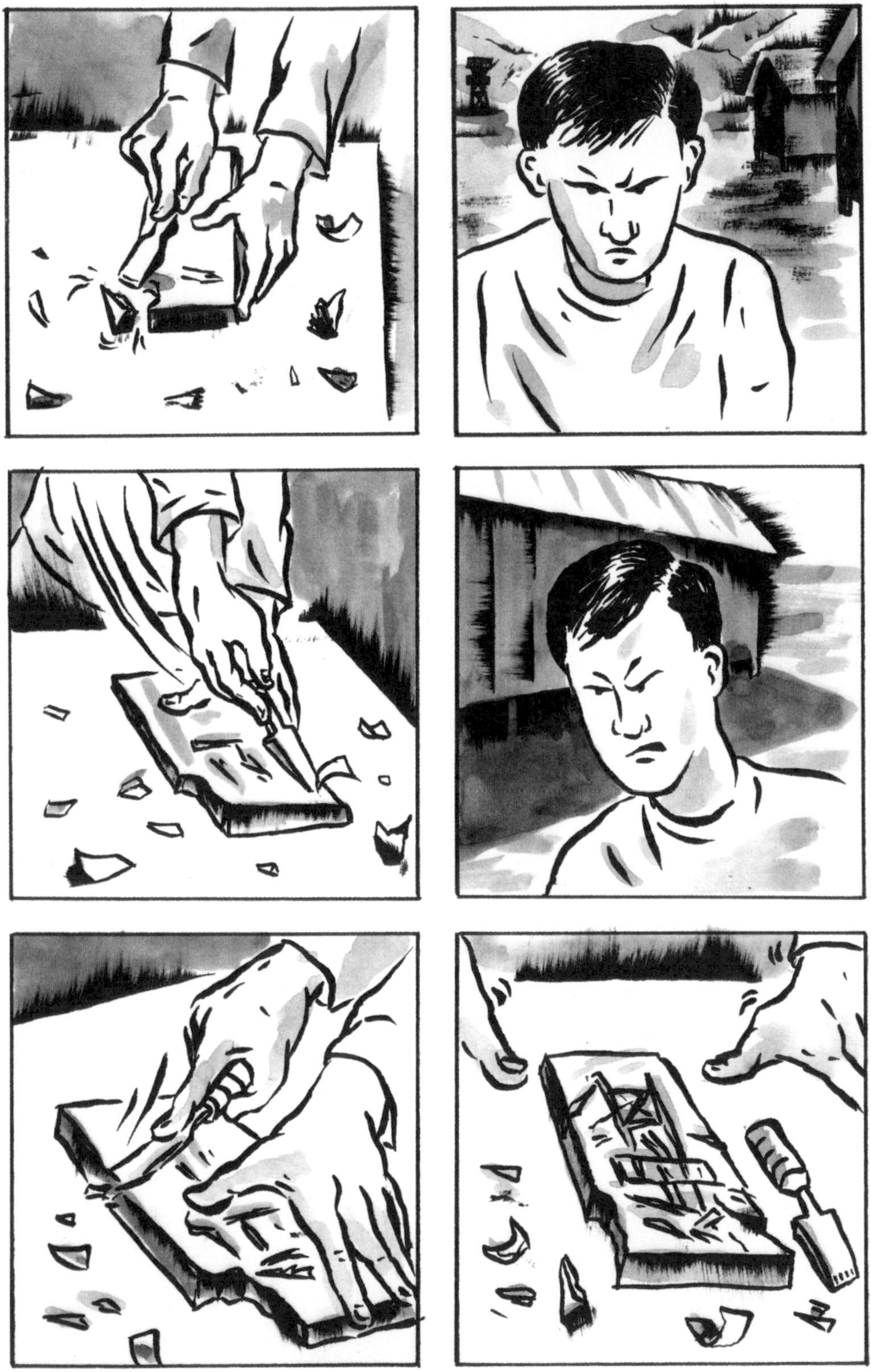

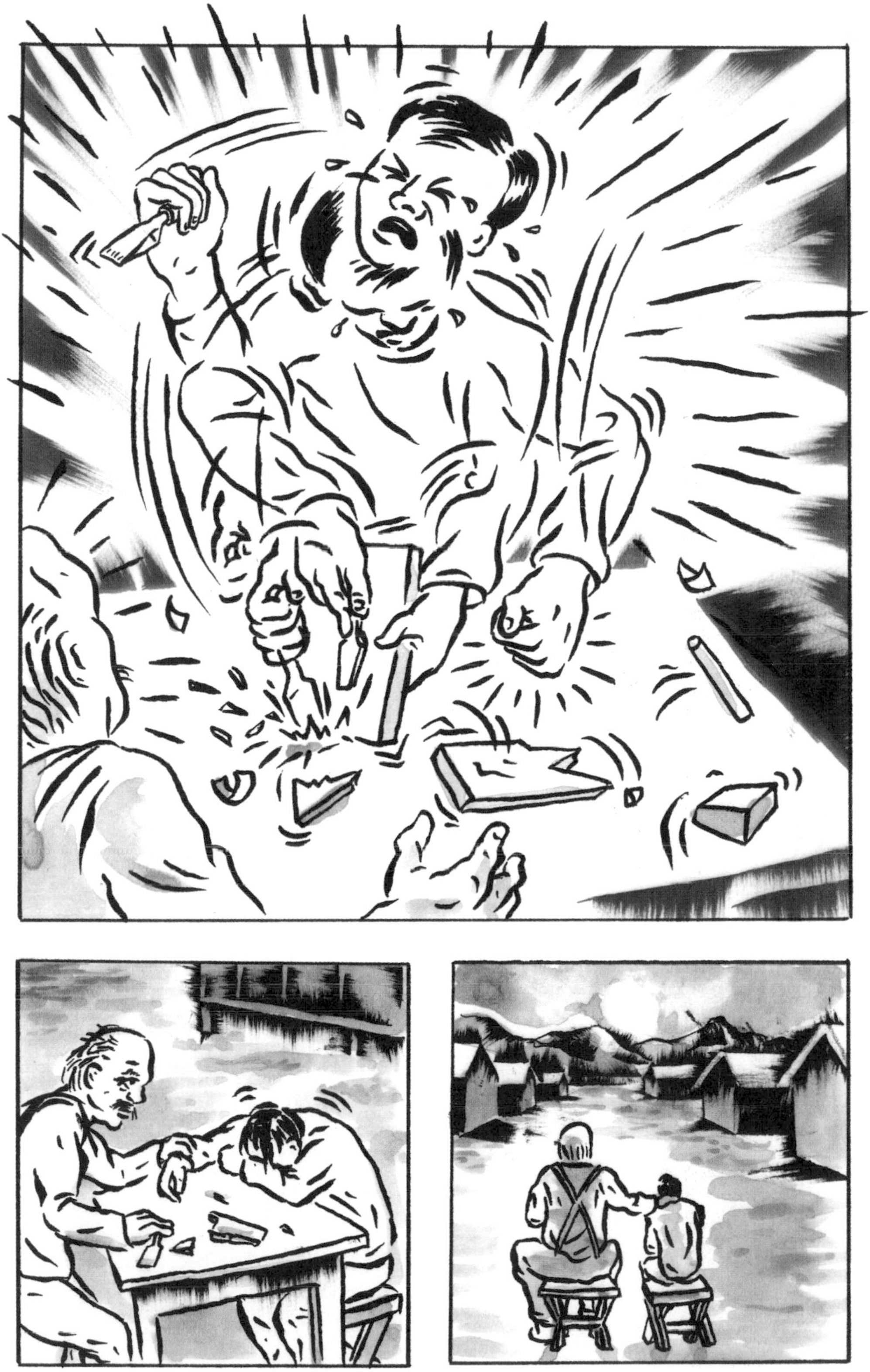

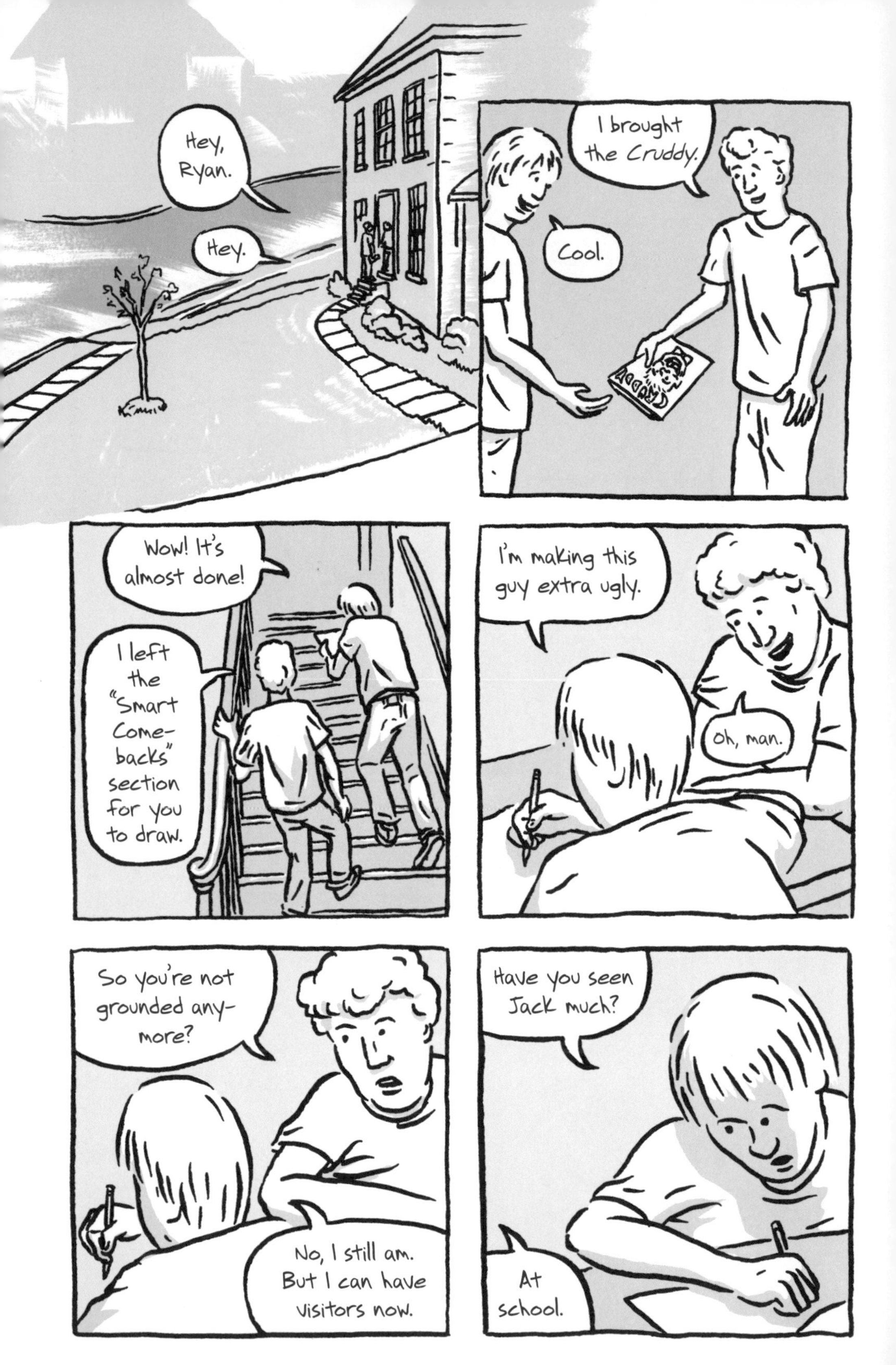
Hey, Ryan.
Hey.
I brought the Cruddy.
Cool.
Wow! It's almost done!
I left the "Smart Come-backs" section for you to draw.
I'm making this guy extra ugly.
Oh, man.
So you're not grounded any-more?
No, I still am. But I can have visitors now.
Have you seen Jack much?
At school.

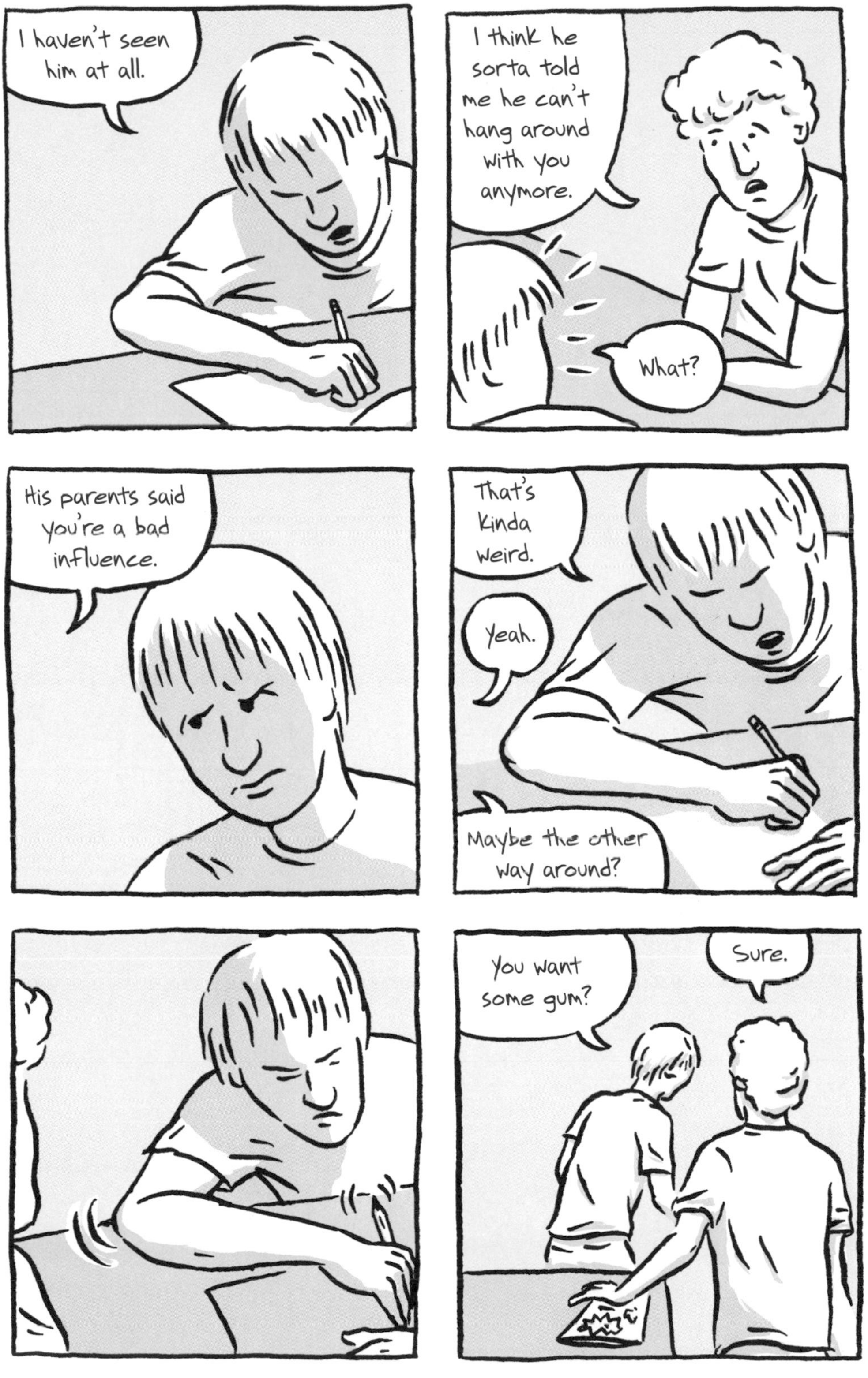
I haven't seen him at all.
I think he sorta told me he can't hang around with you anymore.
What?
His parents said you're a bad influence.
That's kinda weird.
Yeah.
Maybe the other way around?
You want some gum?
Sure.

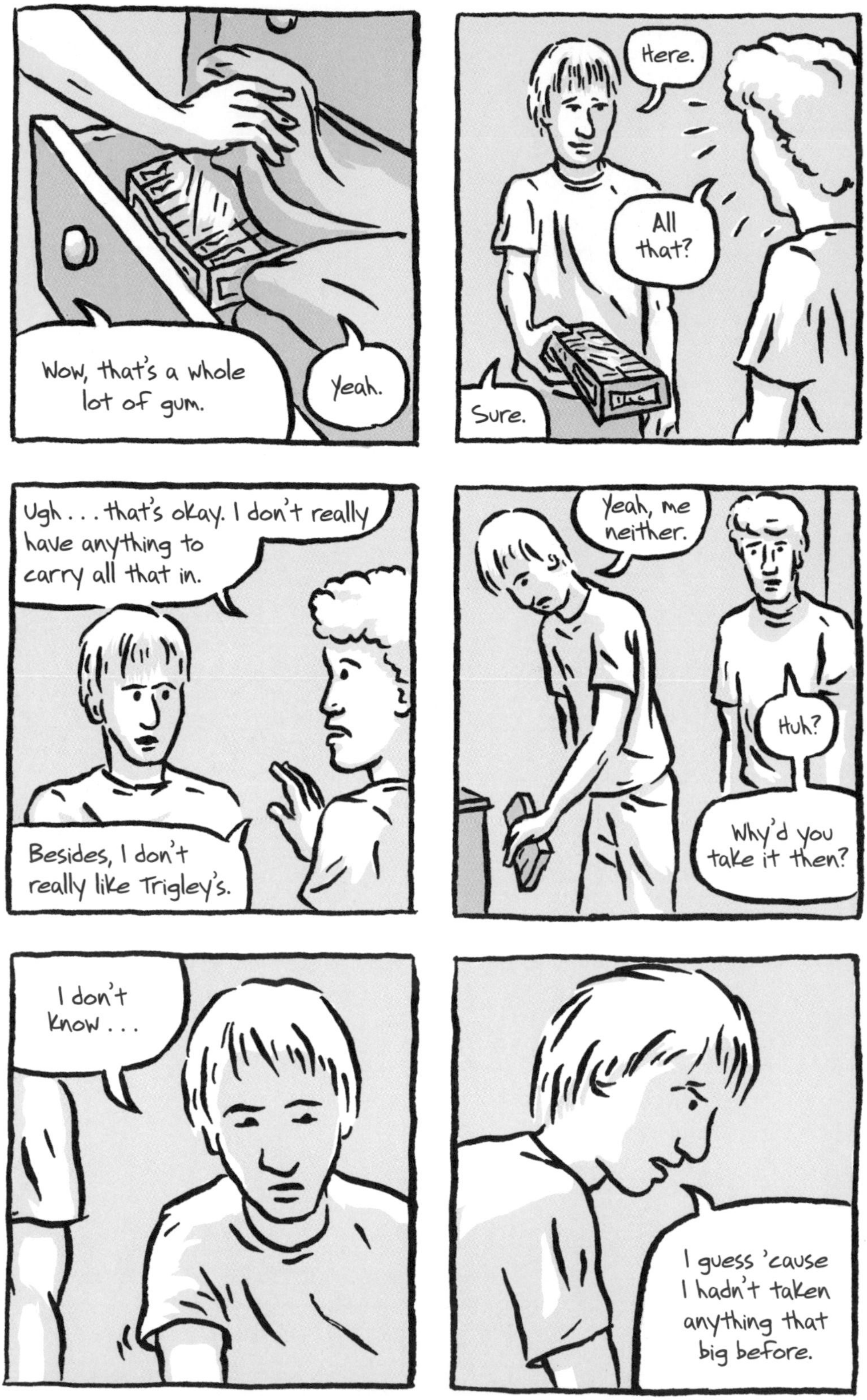
Wow, that's a whole lot of gum.
Yeah.
Here.
All that?
Sure.
Ugh . . . that's okay. I don't really have anything to carry all that in.
Besides, I don't really like Trigley's.
Yeah, me neither.
Huh?
Why'd you take it then?
I don't know . . .
I guess 'cause I hadn't taken anything that big before.

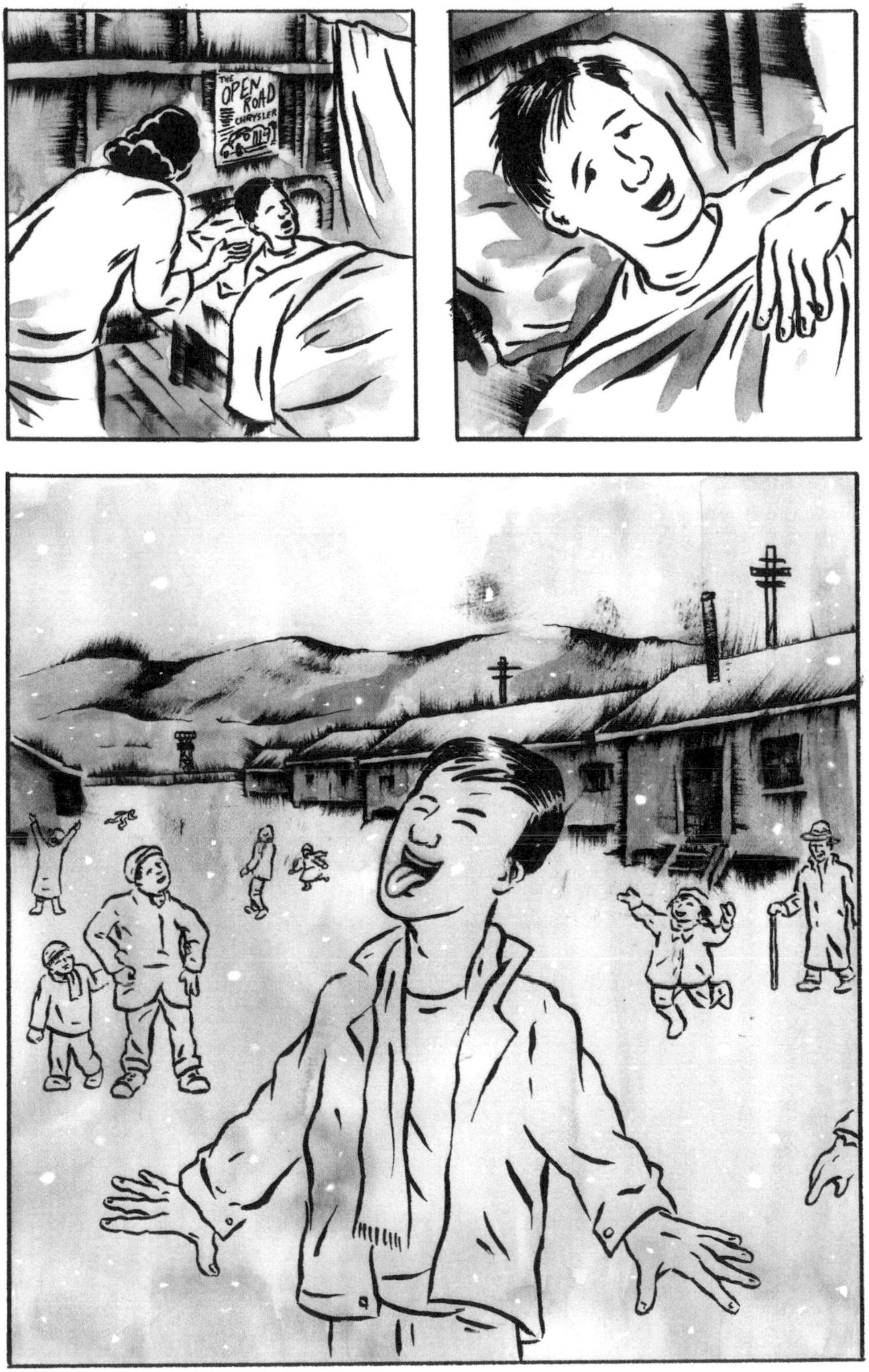
THE
OPEN
ROAD
CHRYSLER

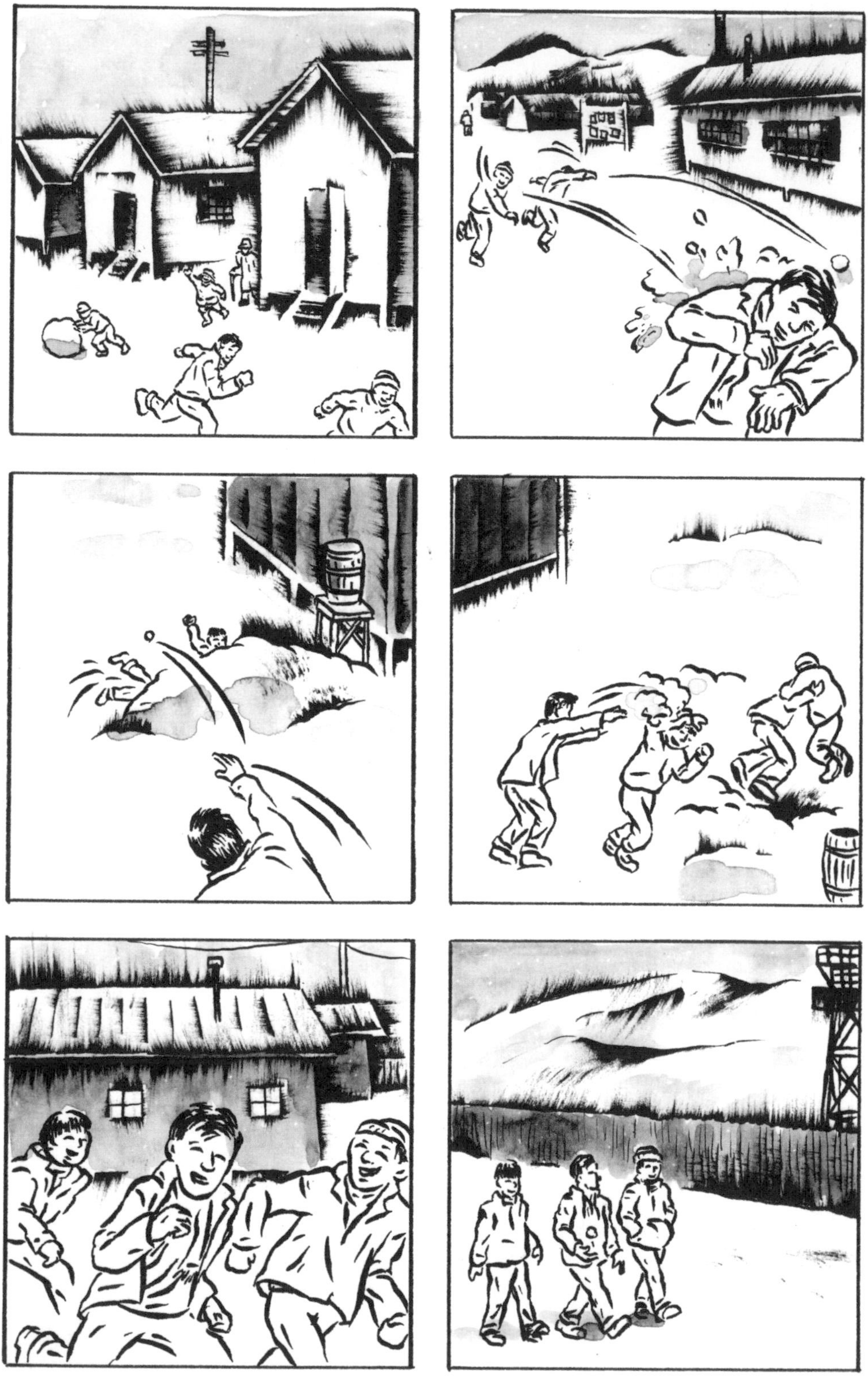

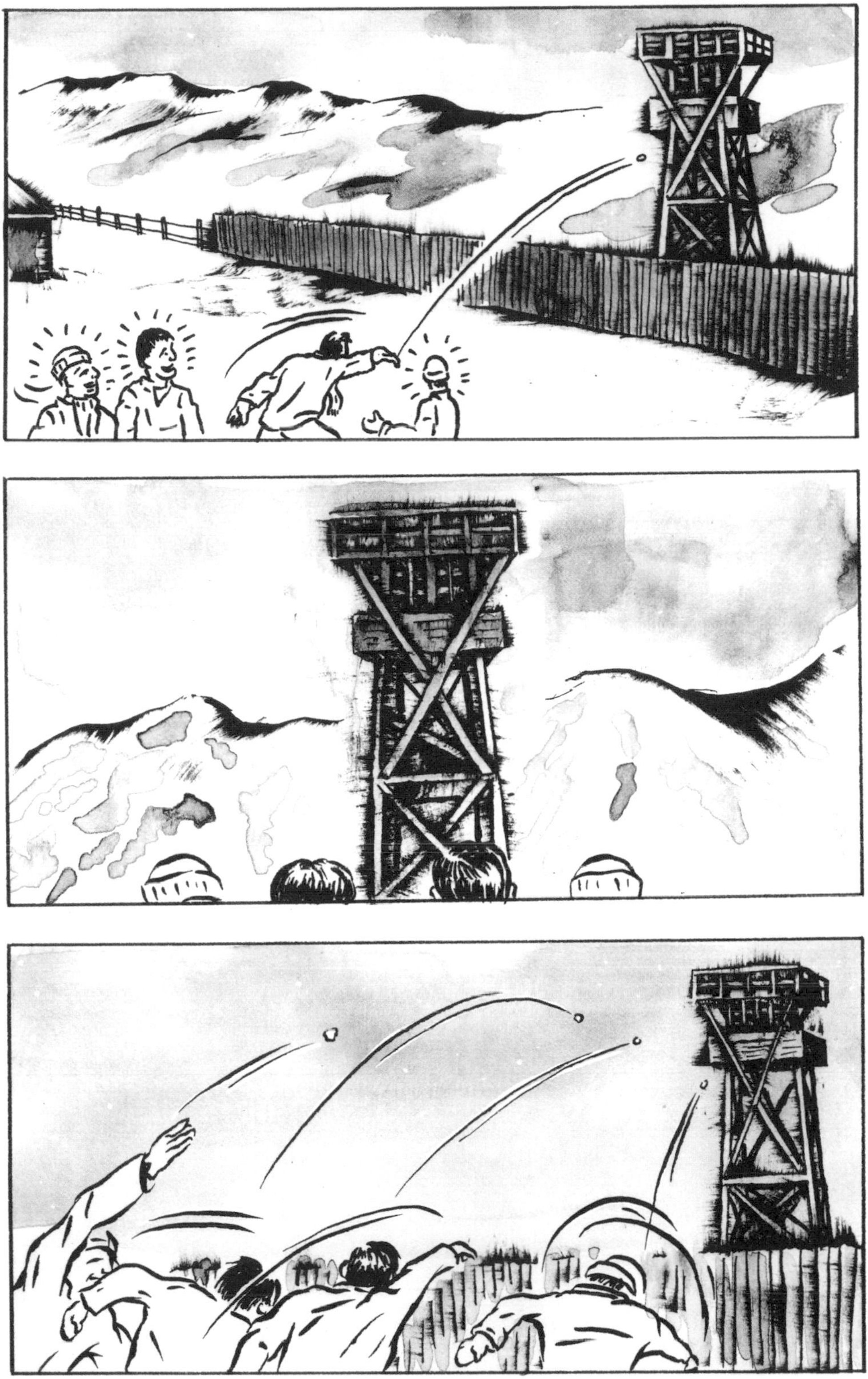

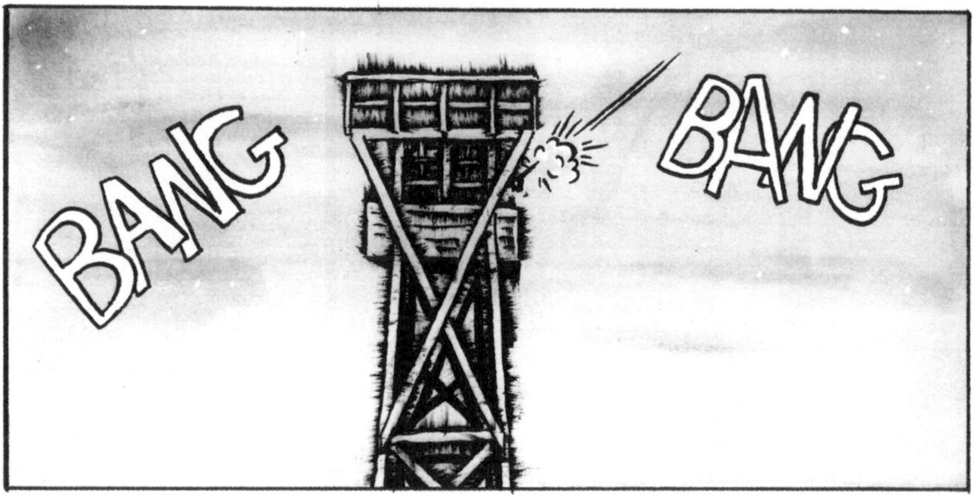
BANG
BANG
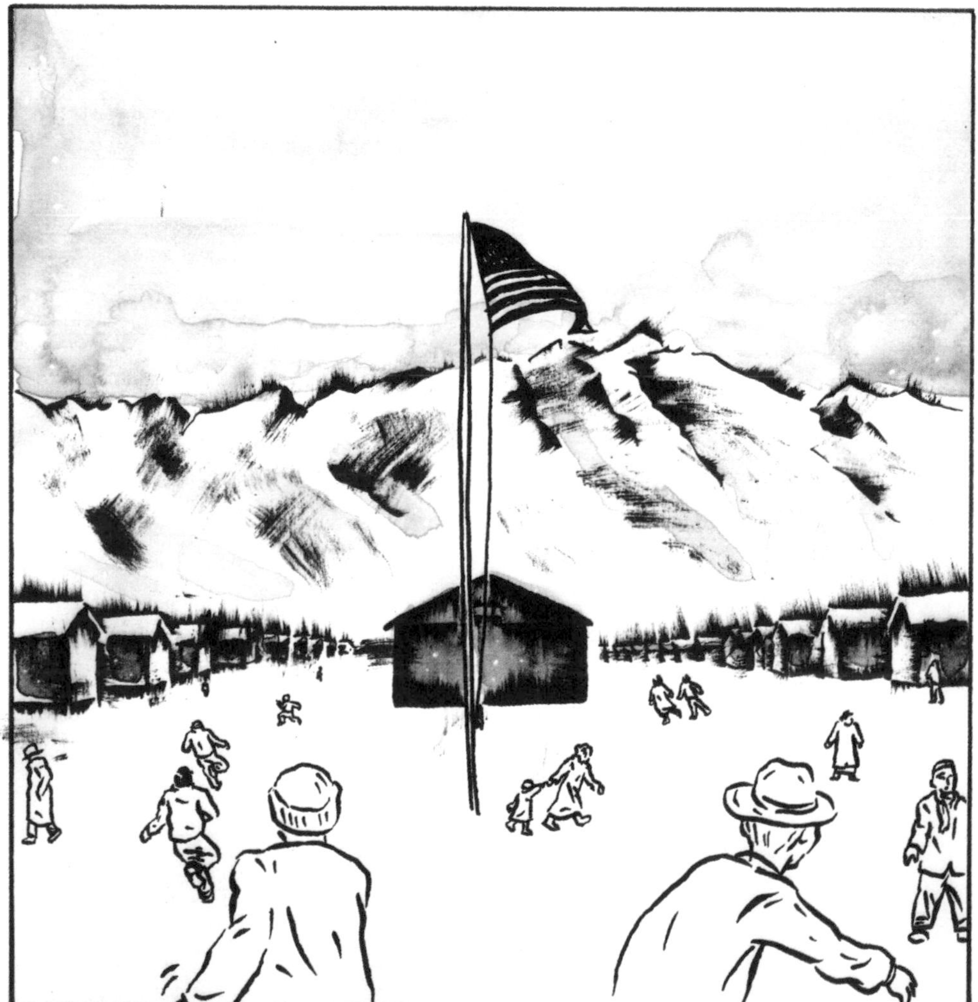

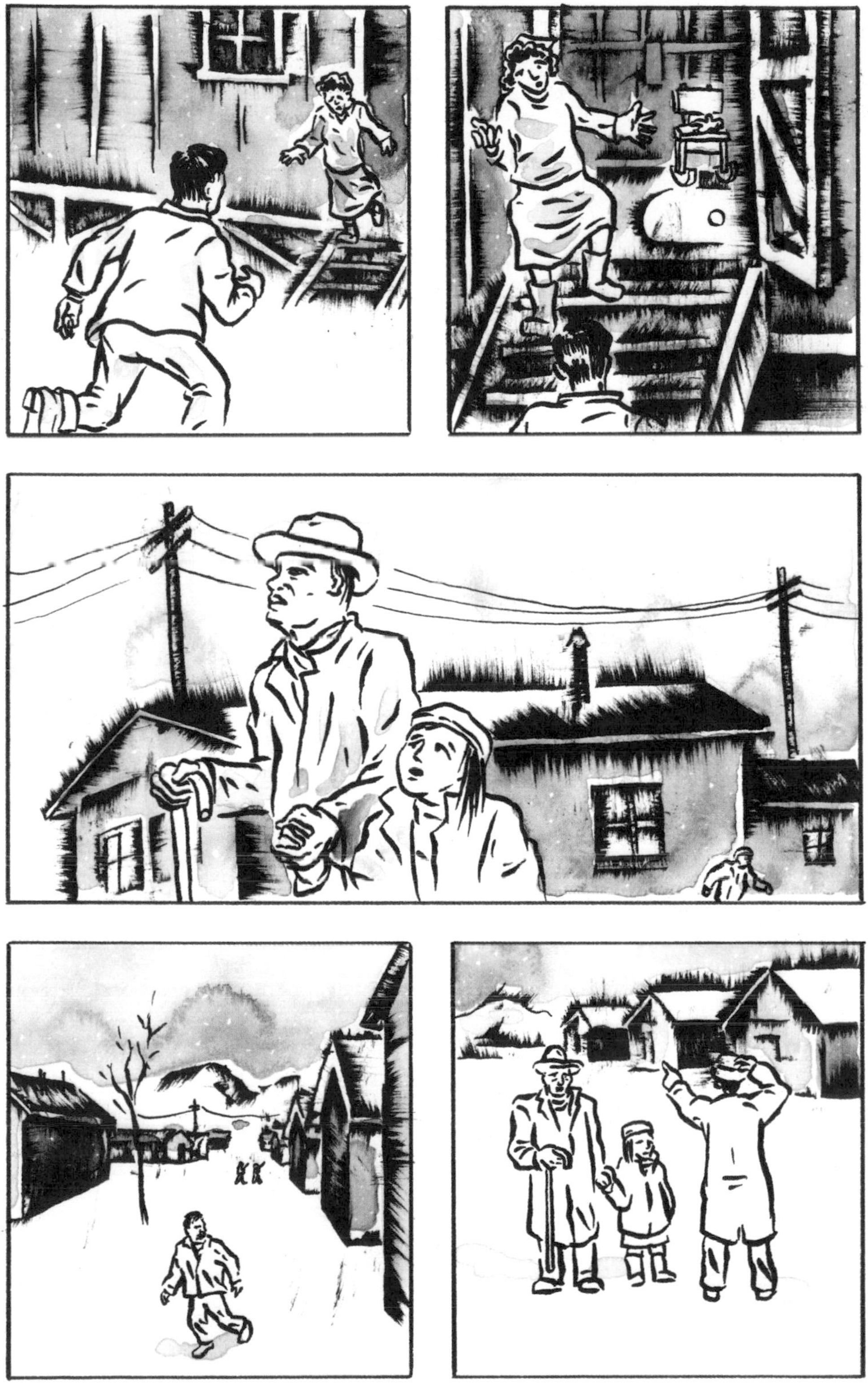

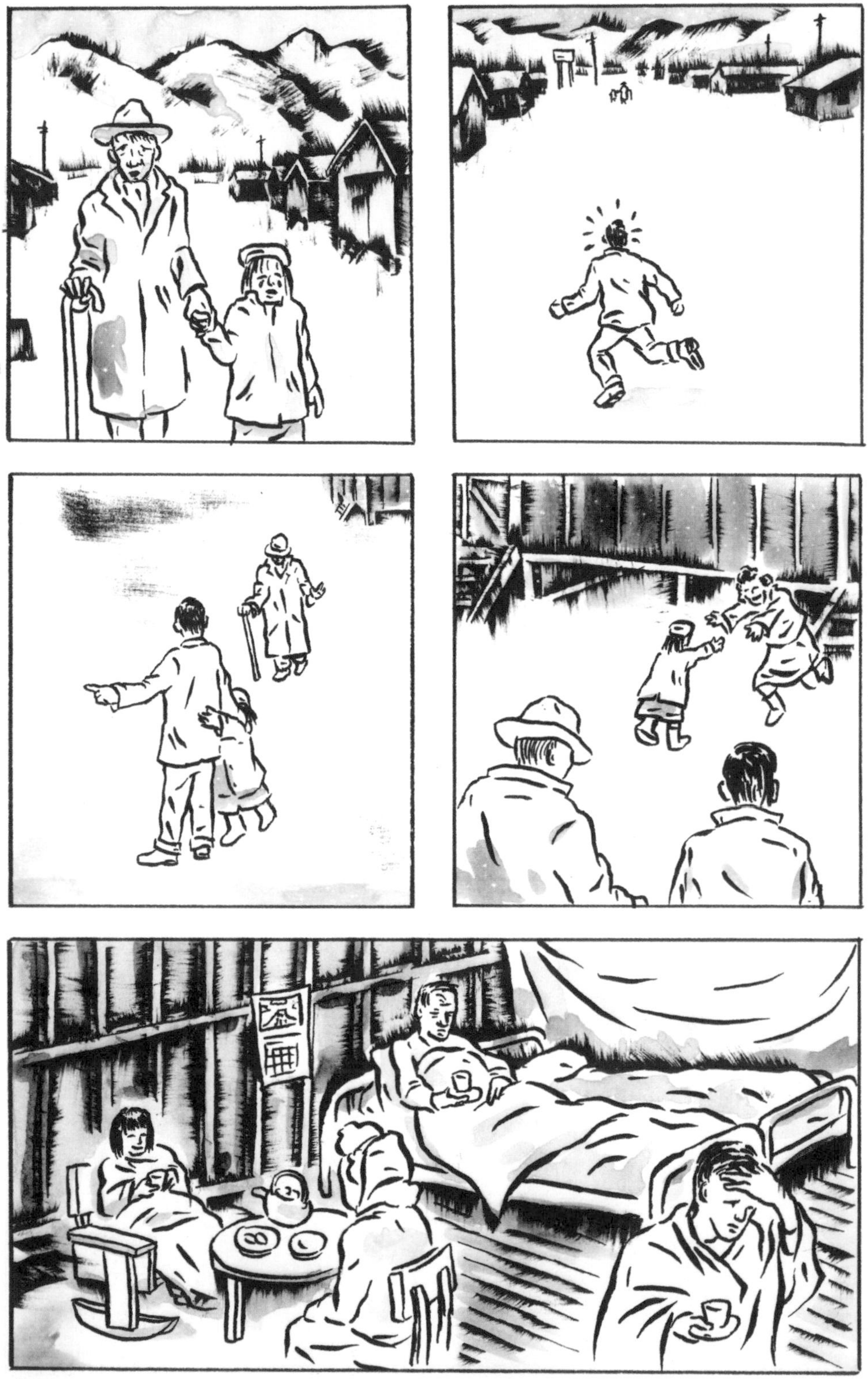

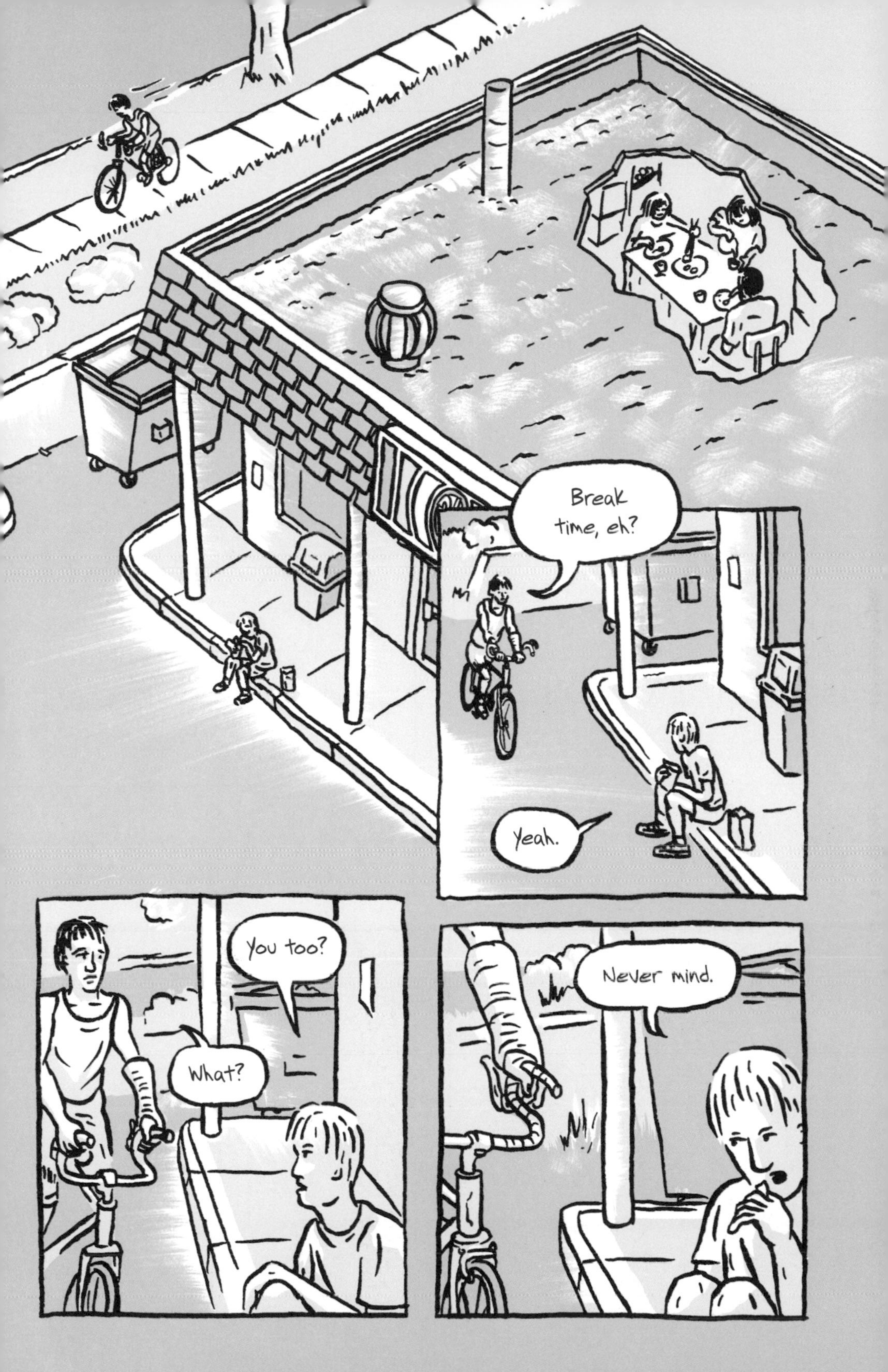
Break time, eh?
Yeah.
You too?
What?
Never mind.

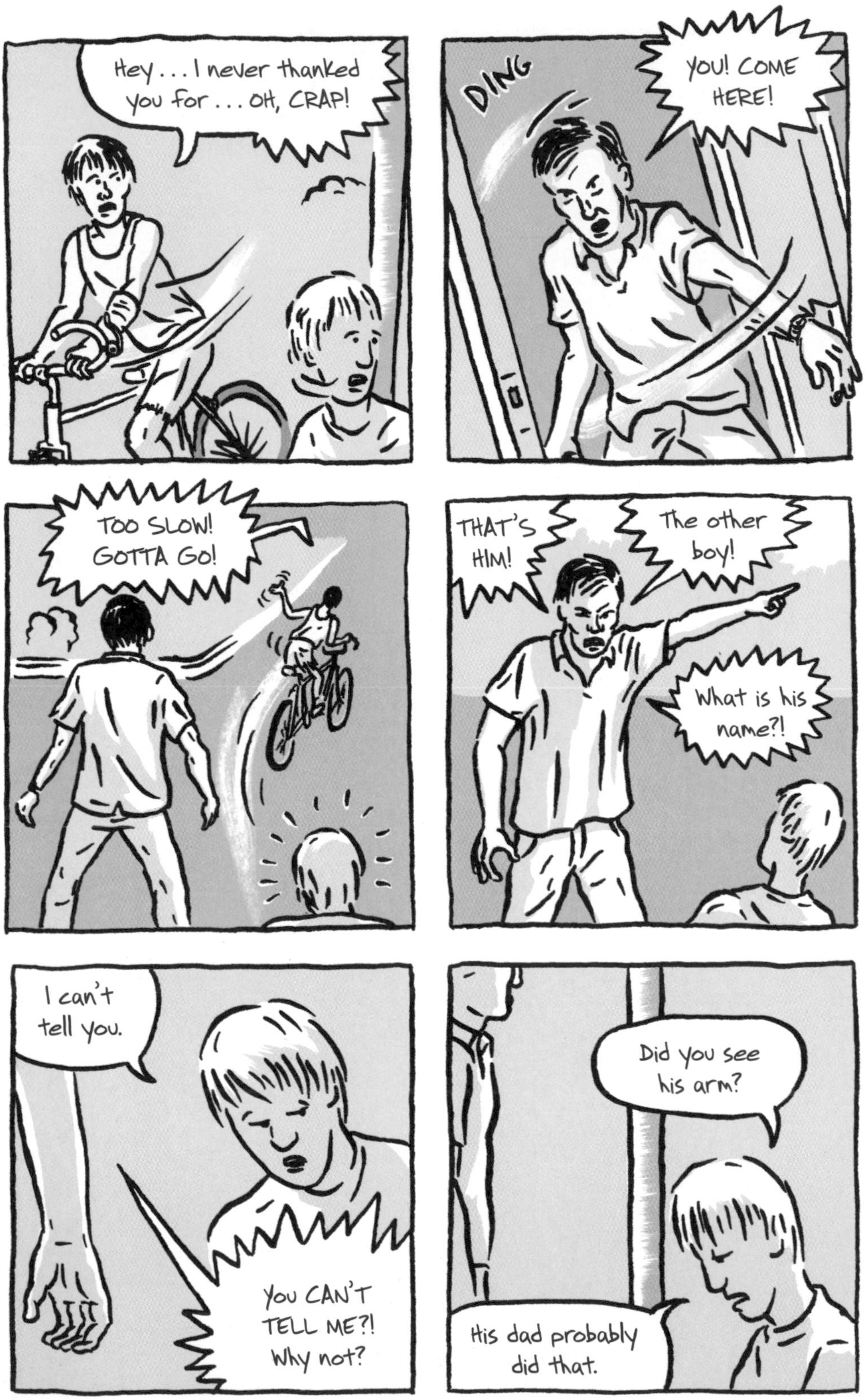
Hey . . . I never thanked you for . . . OH, CRAP!
DING
YOU! COME HERE!
TOO SLOW! GOTTA GO!
THAT'S HIM!
The other boy!
What is his name?!
I can't tell you.
You CAN'T TELL ME?! Why not?
Did you see his arm?
His dad probably did that.

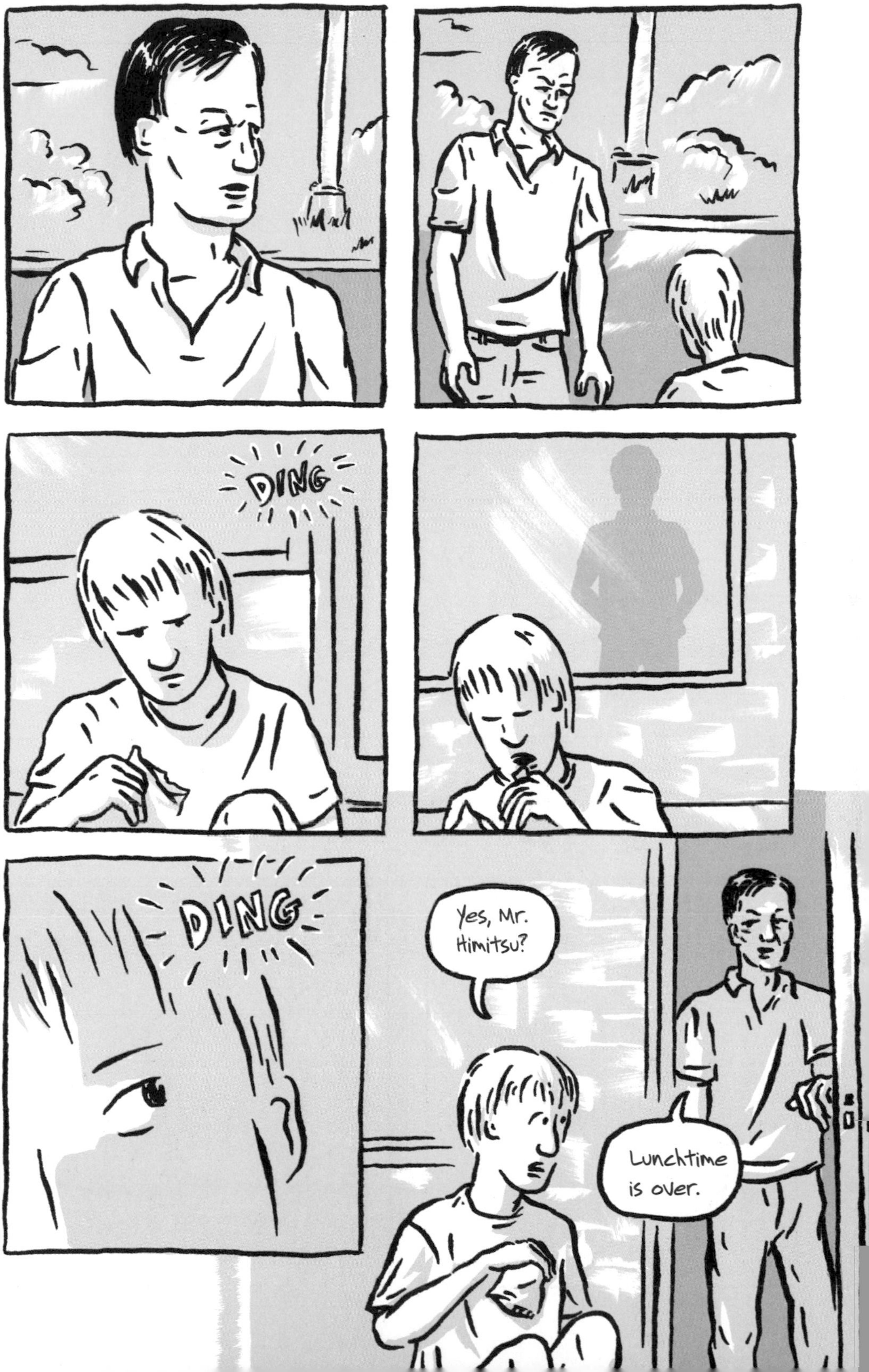
DING
DING
Yes, Mr. Himitsu?
Lunchtime is over.

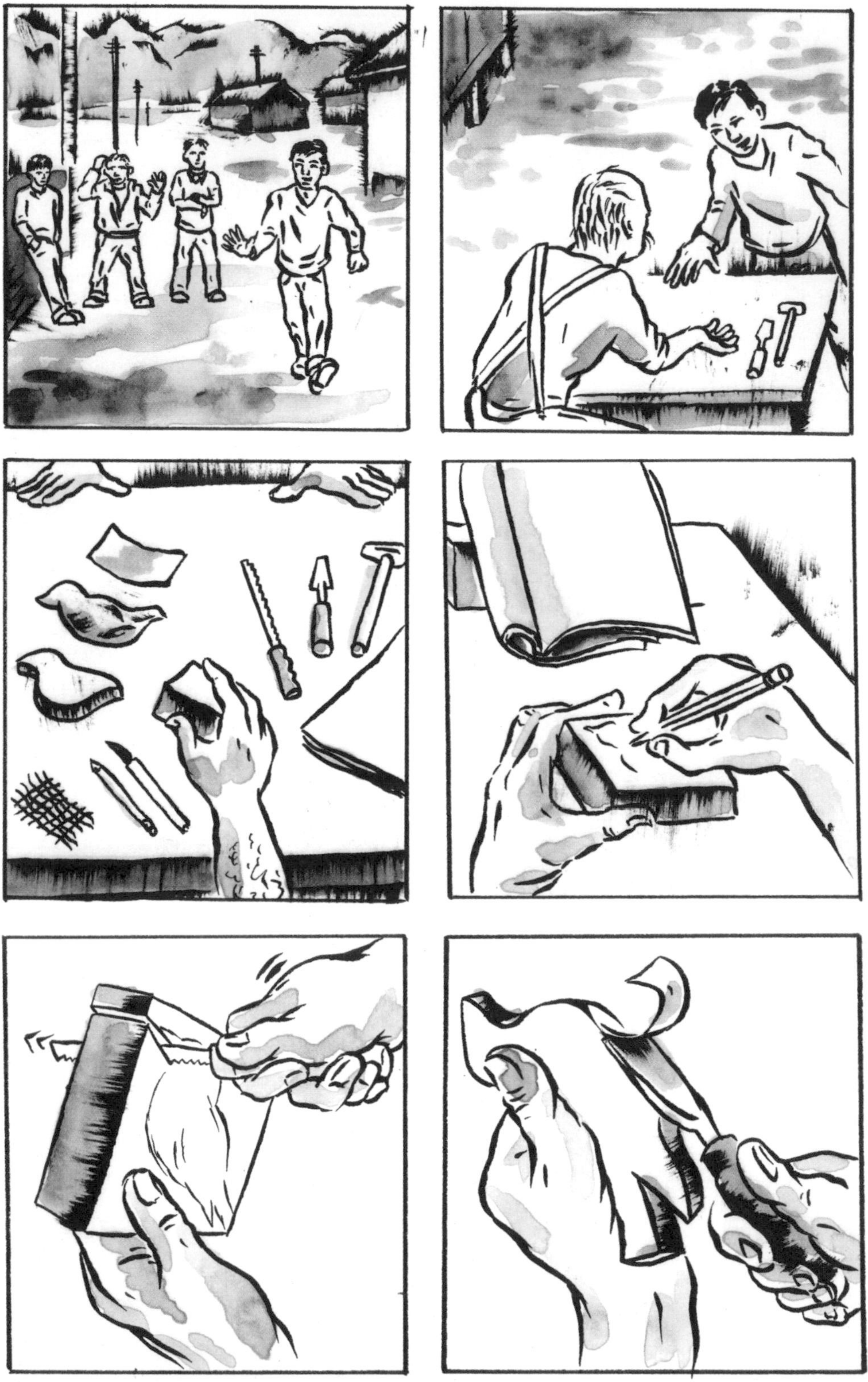

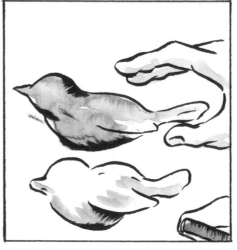

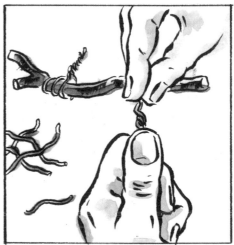

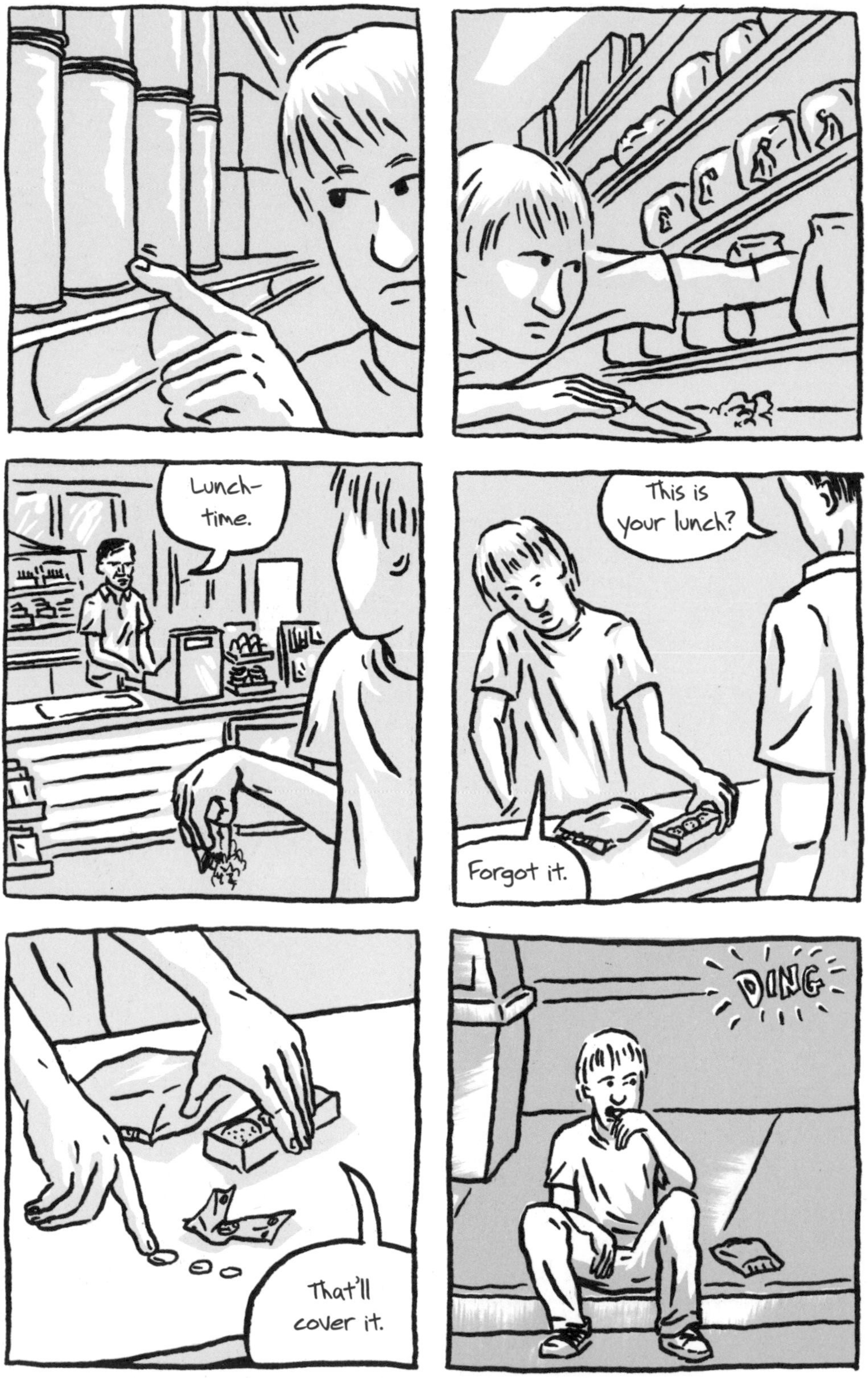
Lunch-
time.
This is
your lunch?
Forgot it.
That'll
cover it.
DING

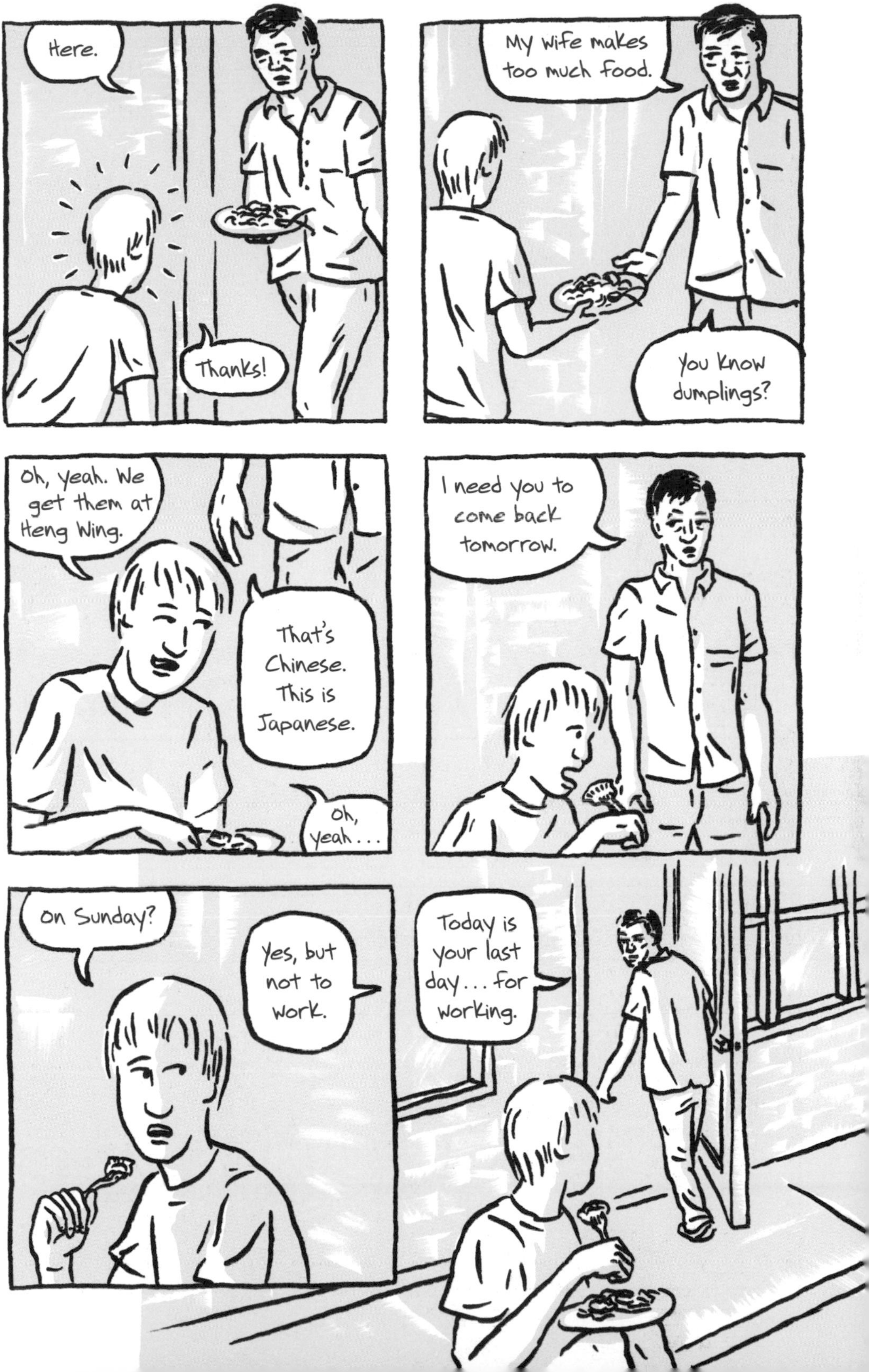
Here.
Thanks!
My wife makes too much food.
You know dumplings?
Oh, yeah. We get them at Heng Wing.
That's Chinese. This is Japanese.
Oh, yeah...
I need you to come back tomorrow.
On Sunday?
Yes, but not to work.
Today is your last day... for working.

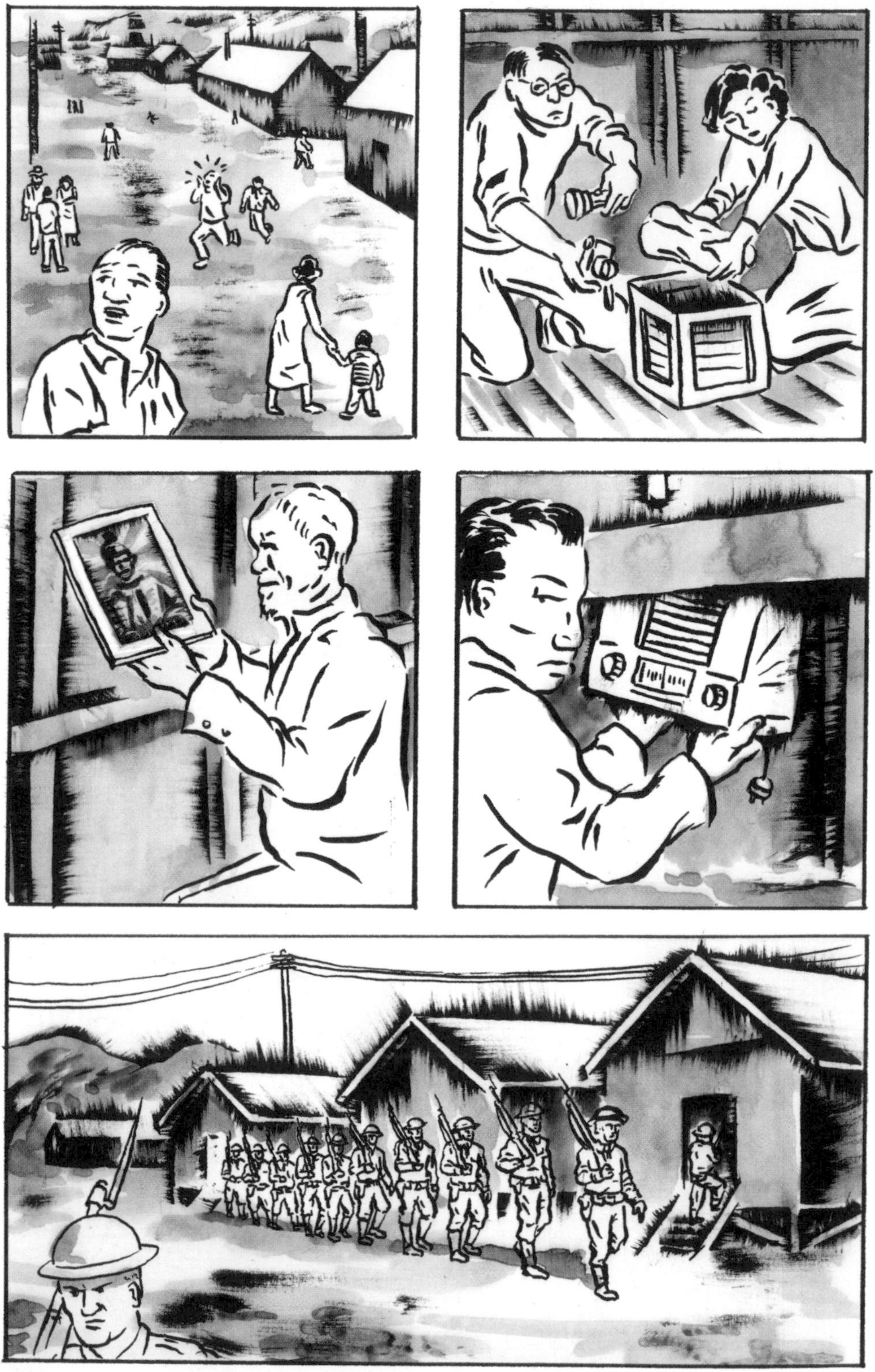

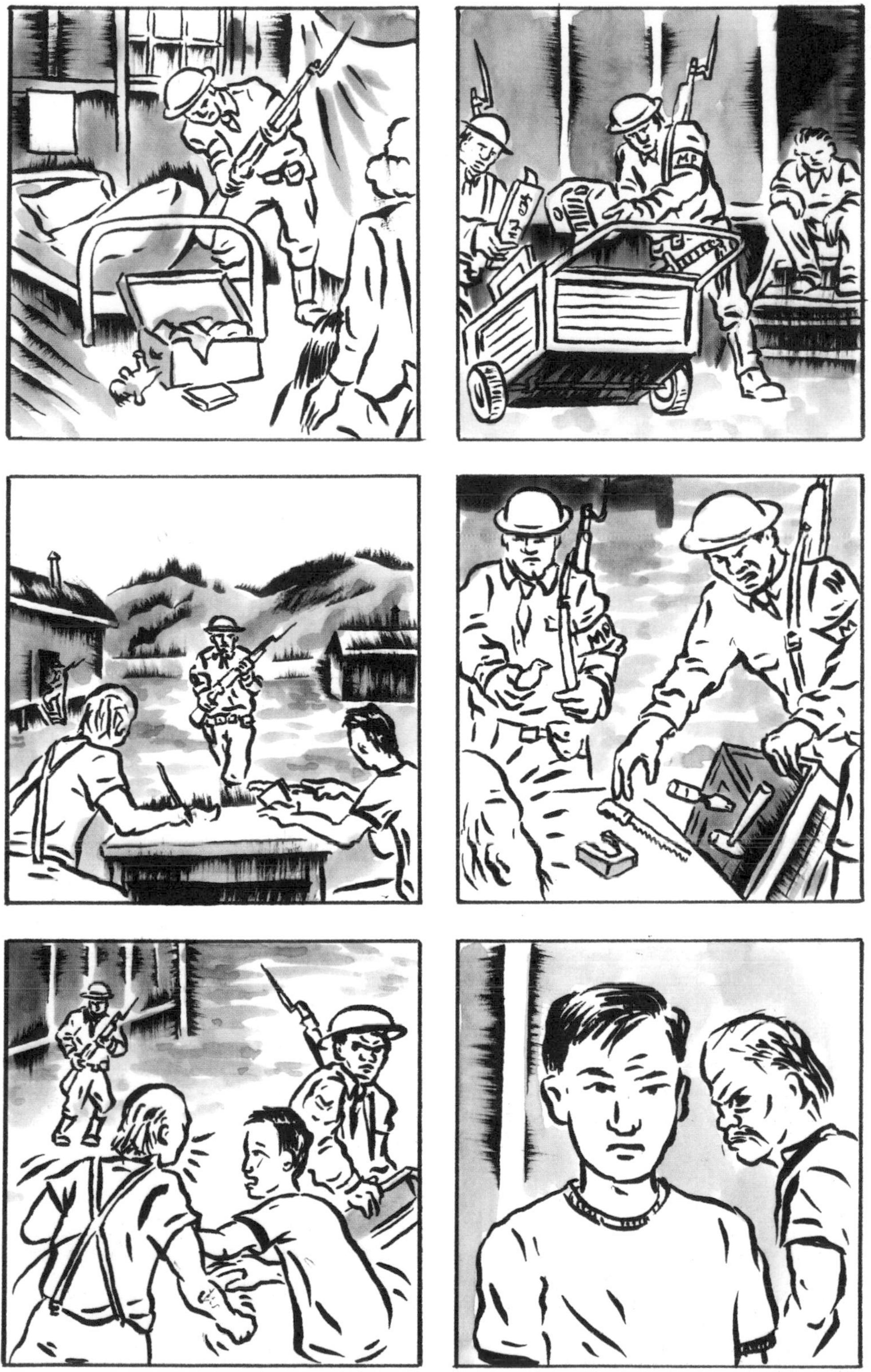
MP
MP

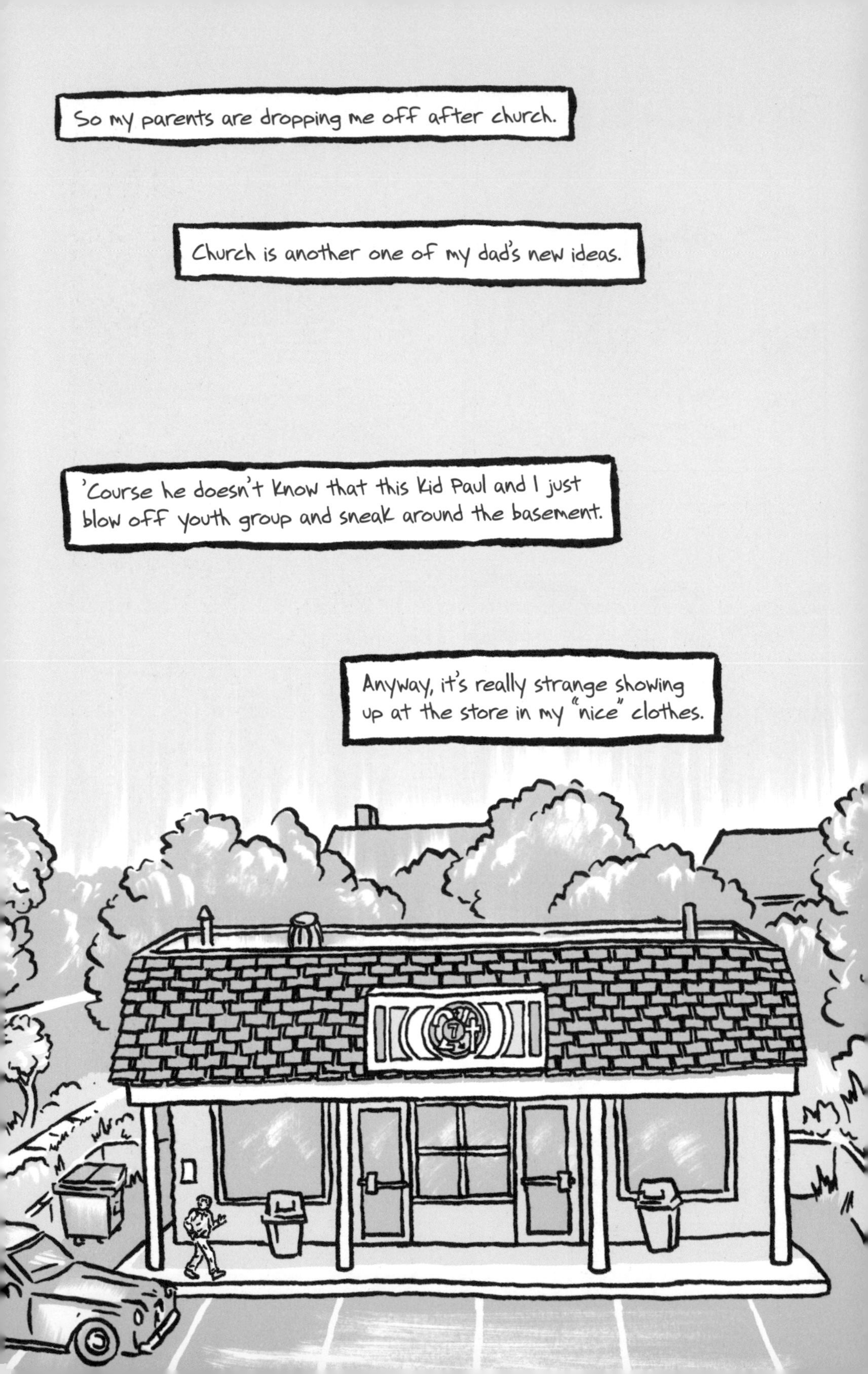
So my parents are dropping me off after church.
Church is another one of my dad's new ideas.
'Course he doesn't know that this kid Paul and I just blow off youth group and sneak around the basement.
Anyway, it's really strange showing up at the store in my "nice" clothes.

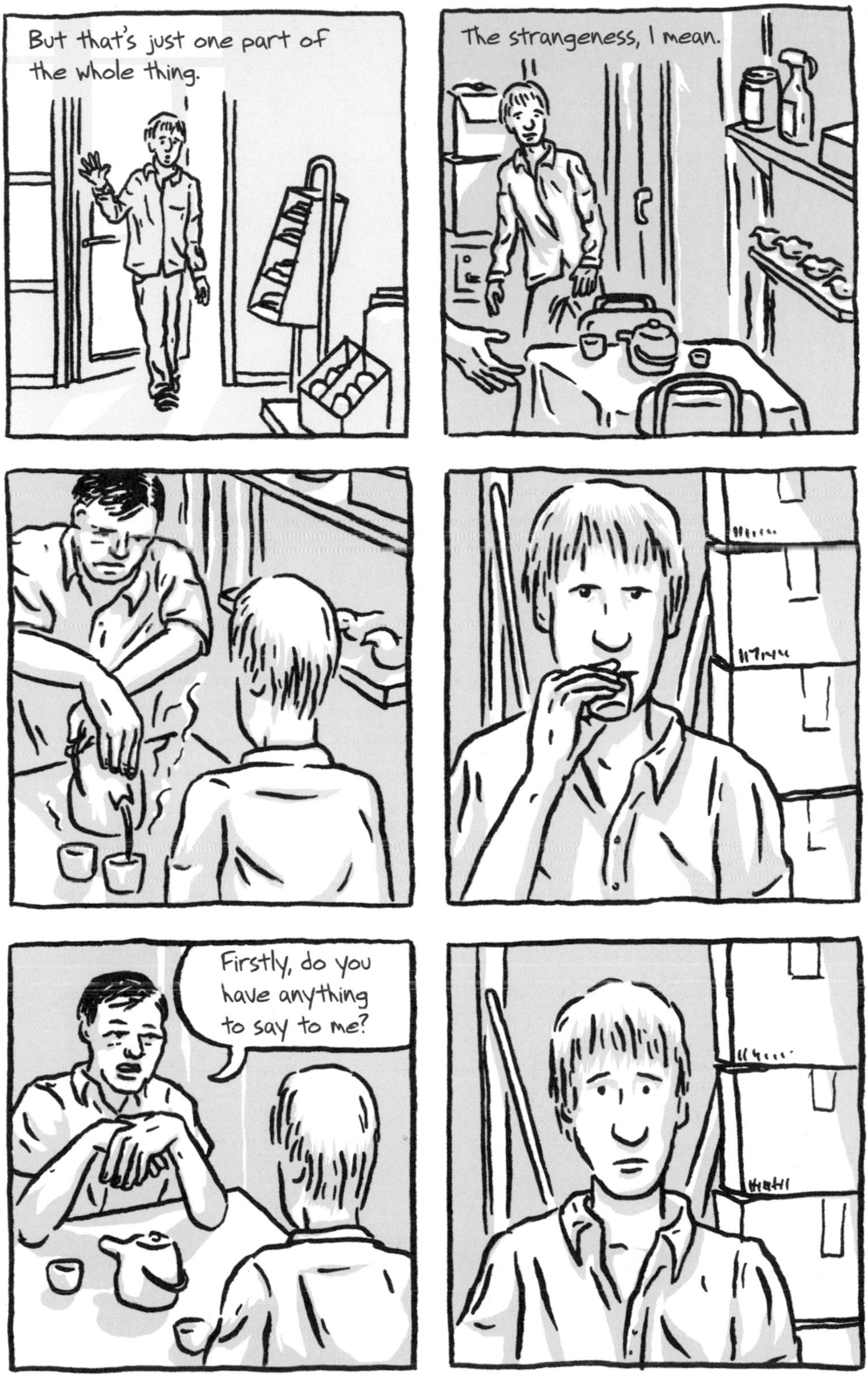
But that's just one part of the whole thing.
The strangeness, I mean.
Firstly, do you have anything to say to me?

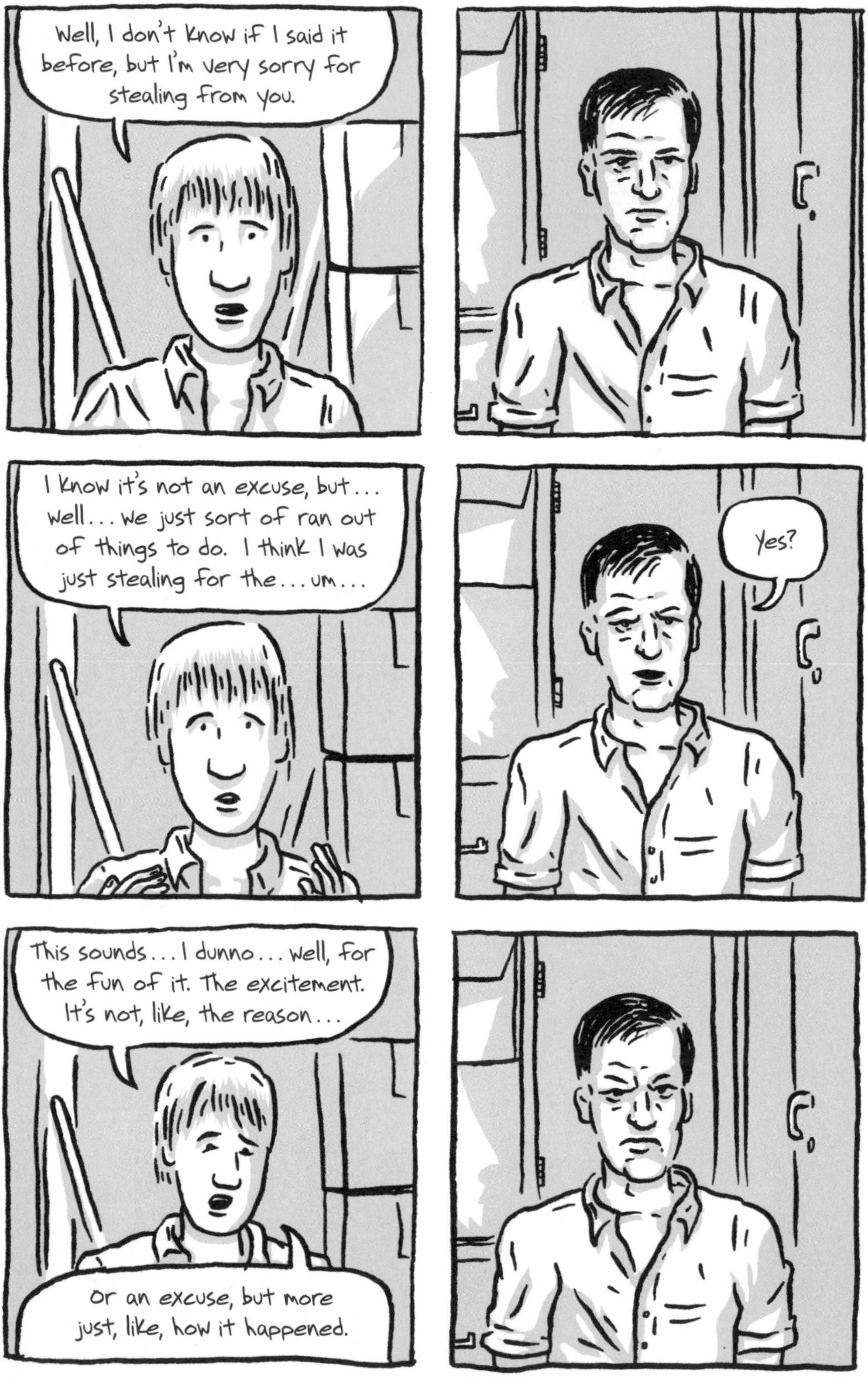
Well, I don't know if I said it before, but I'm very sorry for stealing from you.
I know it's not an excuse, but... well... we just sort of ran out of things to do. I think I was just stealing for the... um...
Yes?
This sounds... I dunno... well, for the fun of it. The excitement. It's not, like, the reason...
Or an excuse, but more just, like, how it happened.

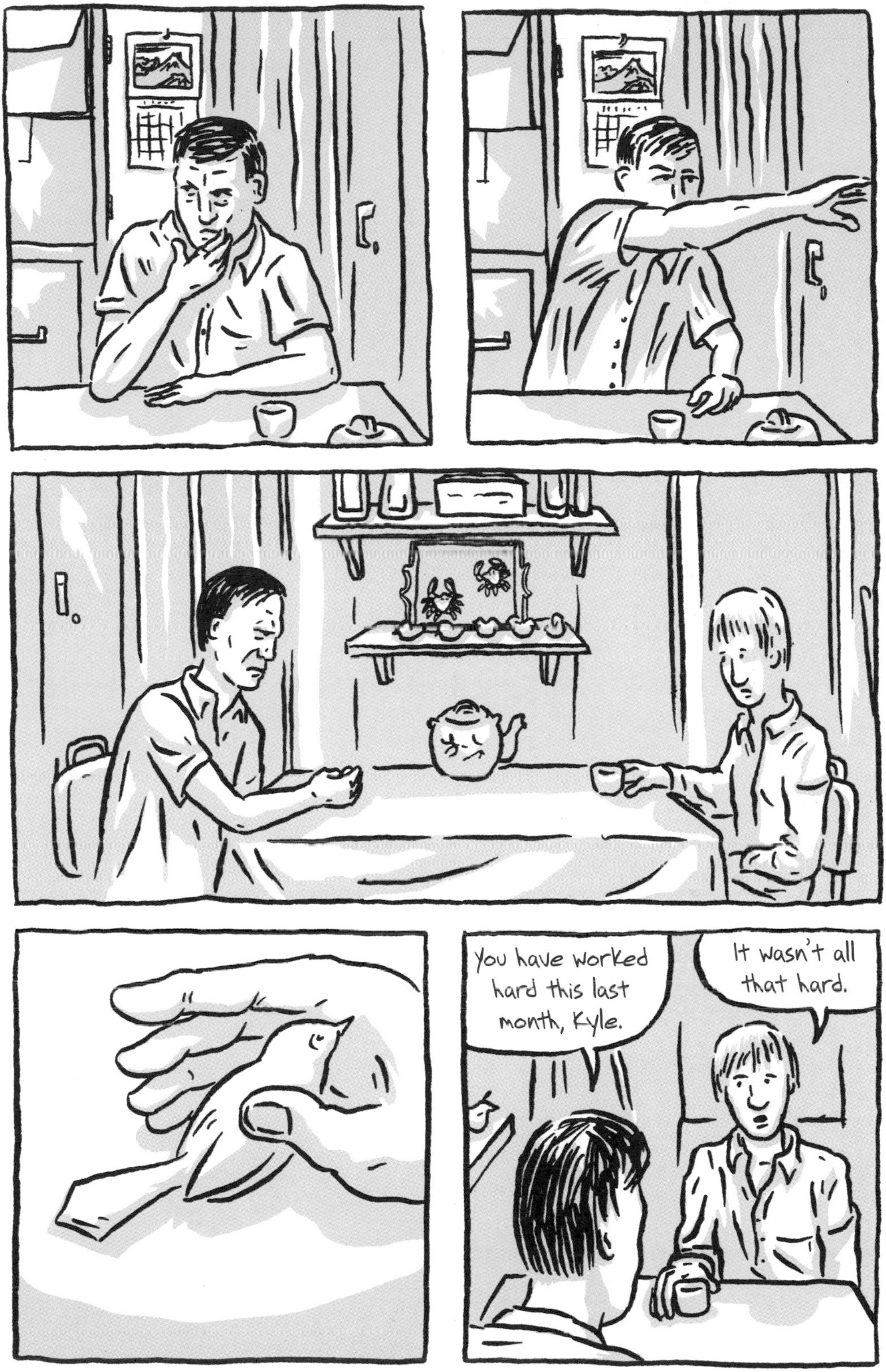
You have worked hard this last month, Kyle.
It wasn't all that hard.

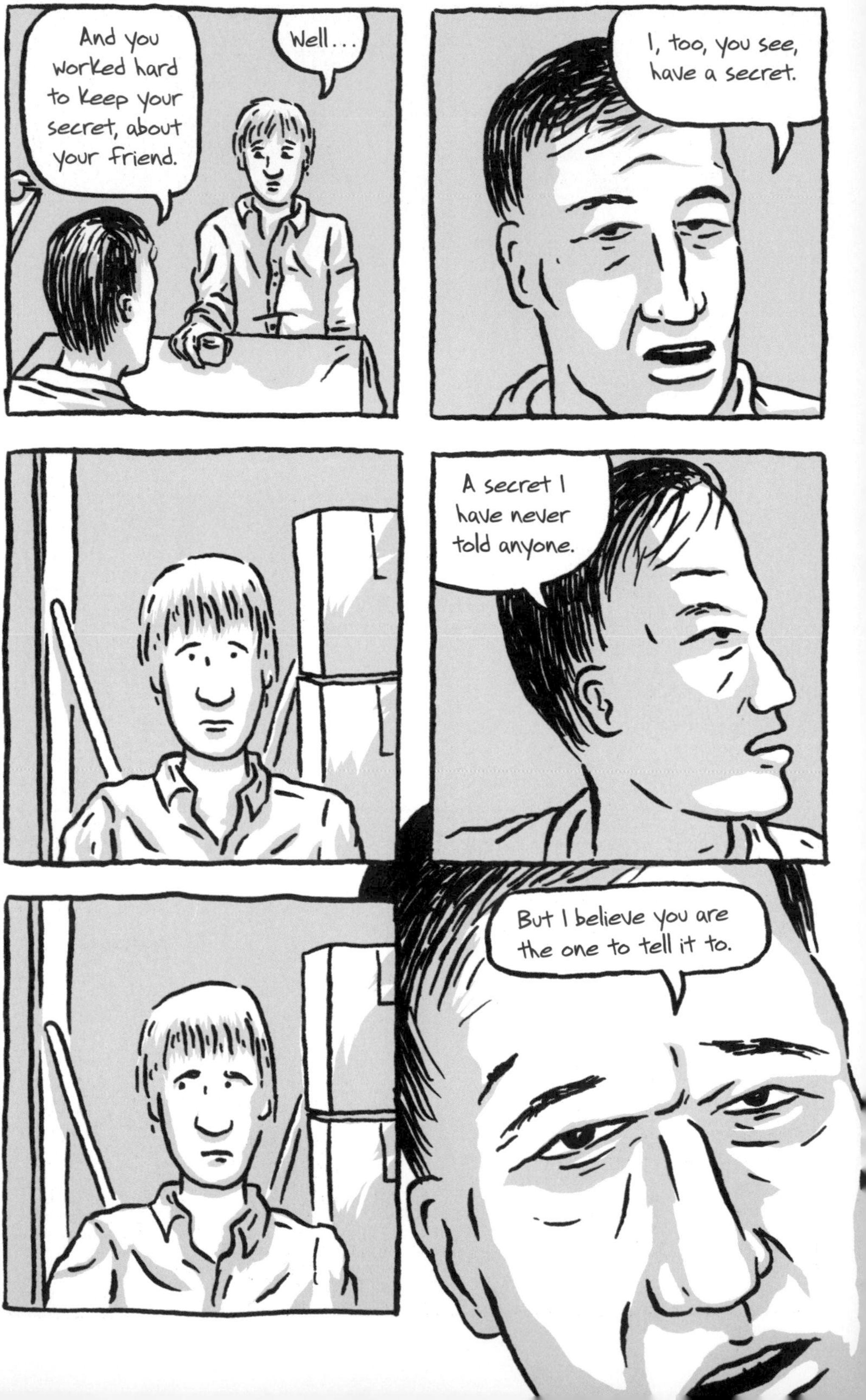
And you worked hard to keep your secret, about your friend.
Well...
I, too, you see, have a secret.
A secret I have never told anyone.
But I believe you are the one to tell it to.

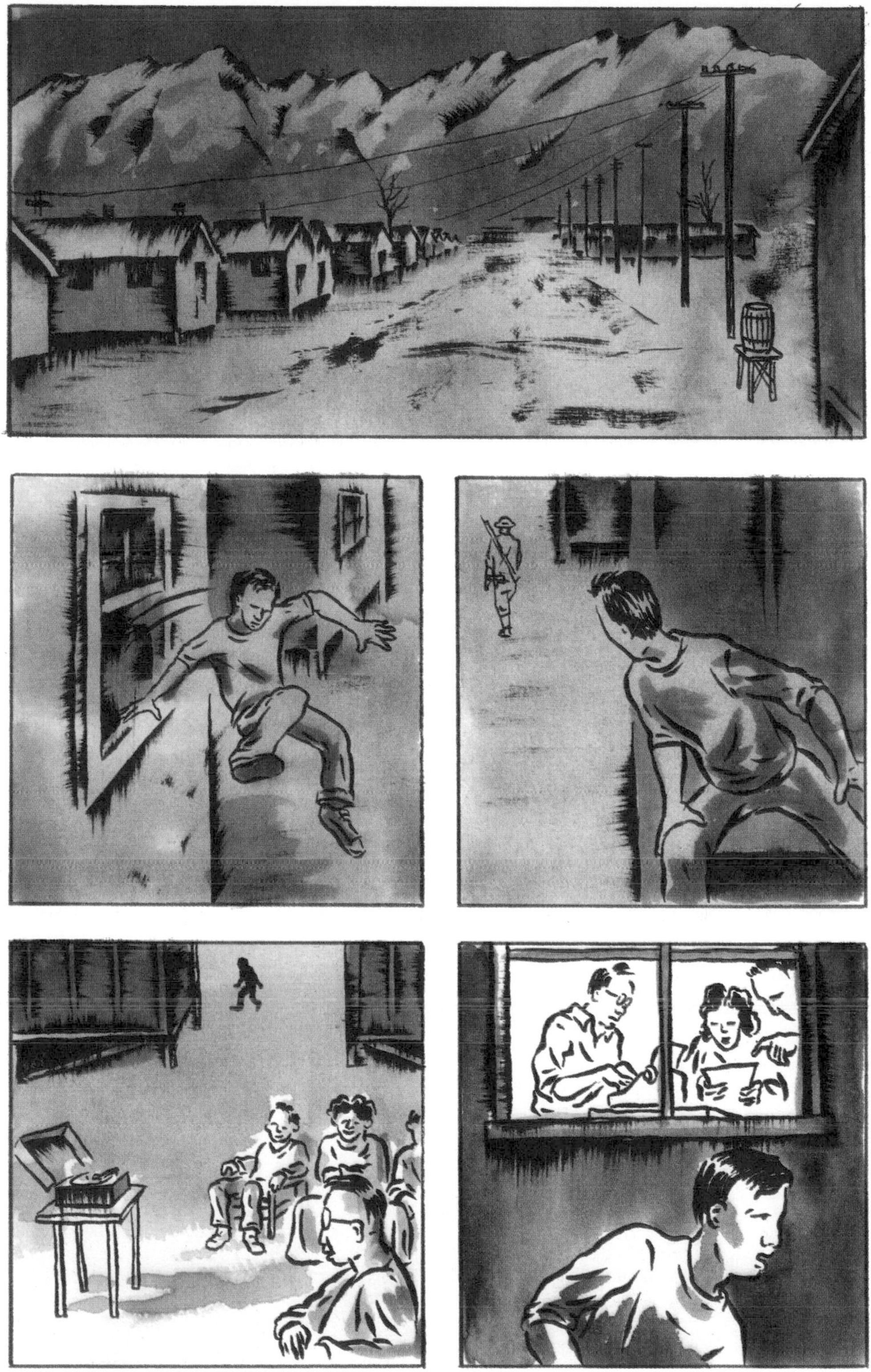

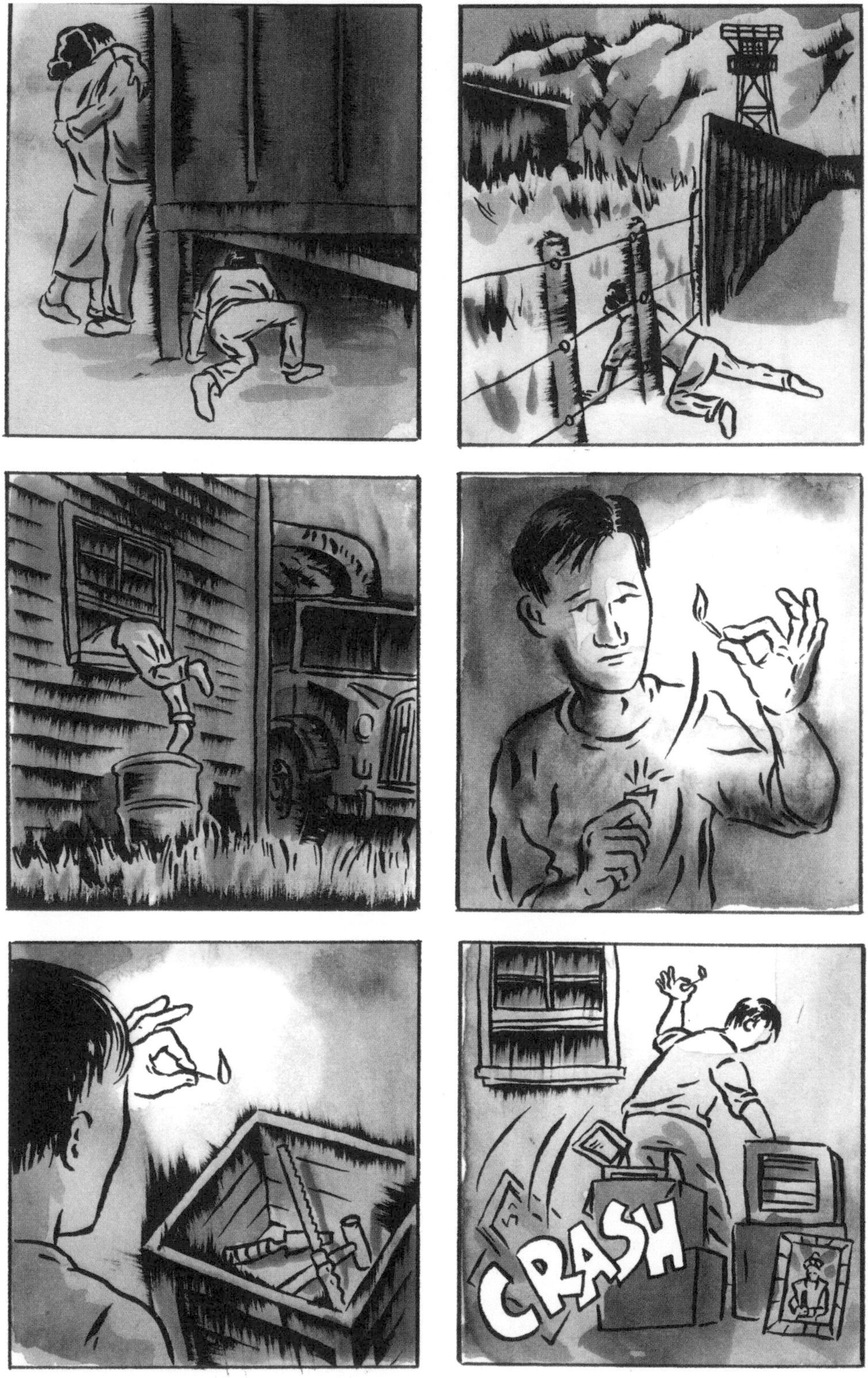
CRASH

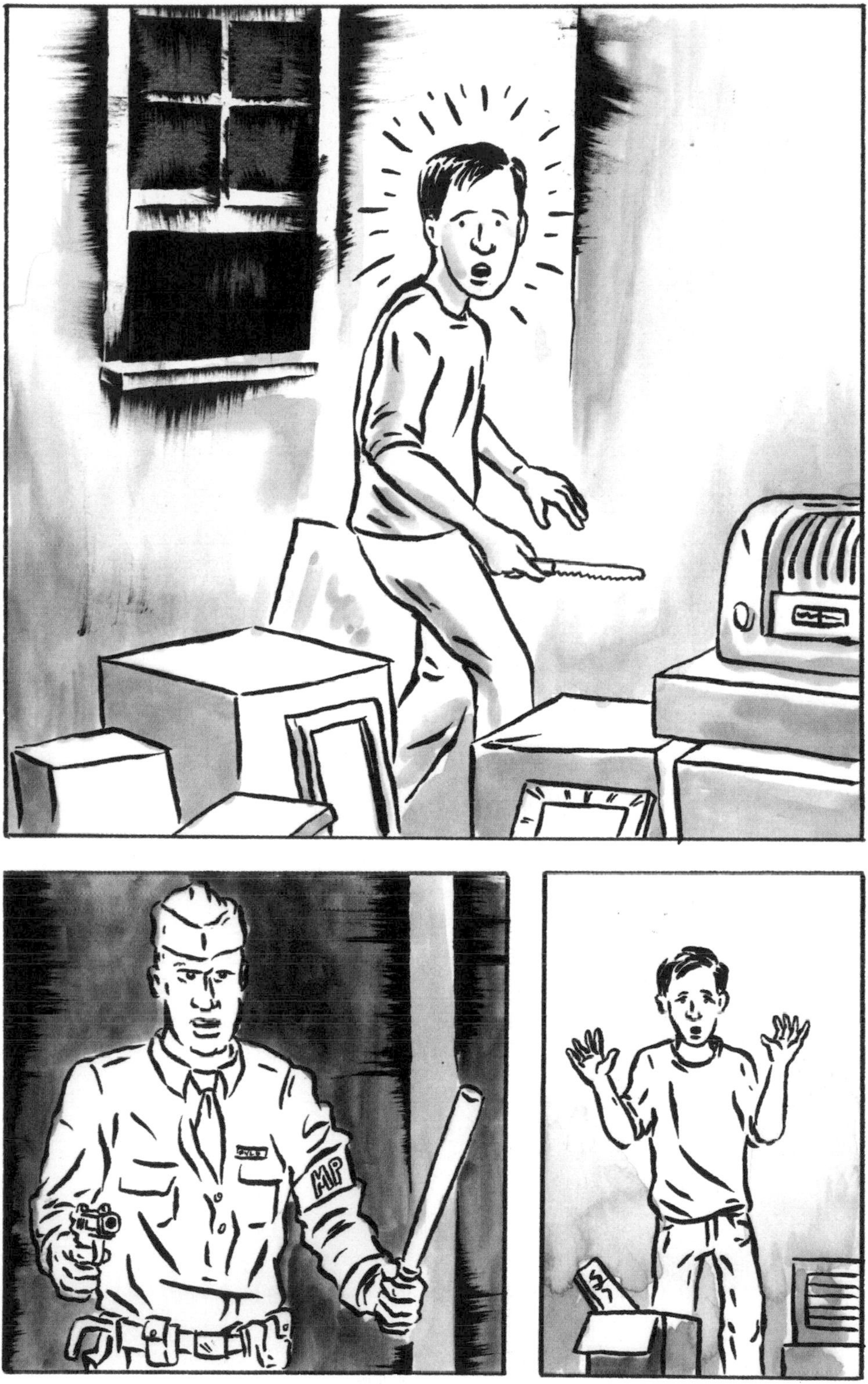
MP

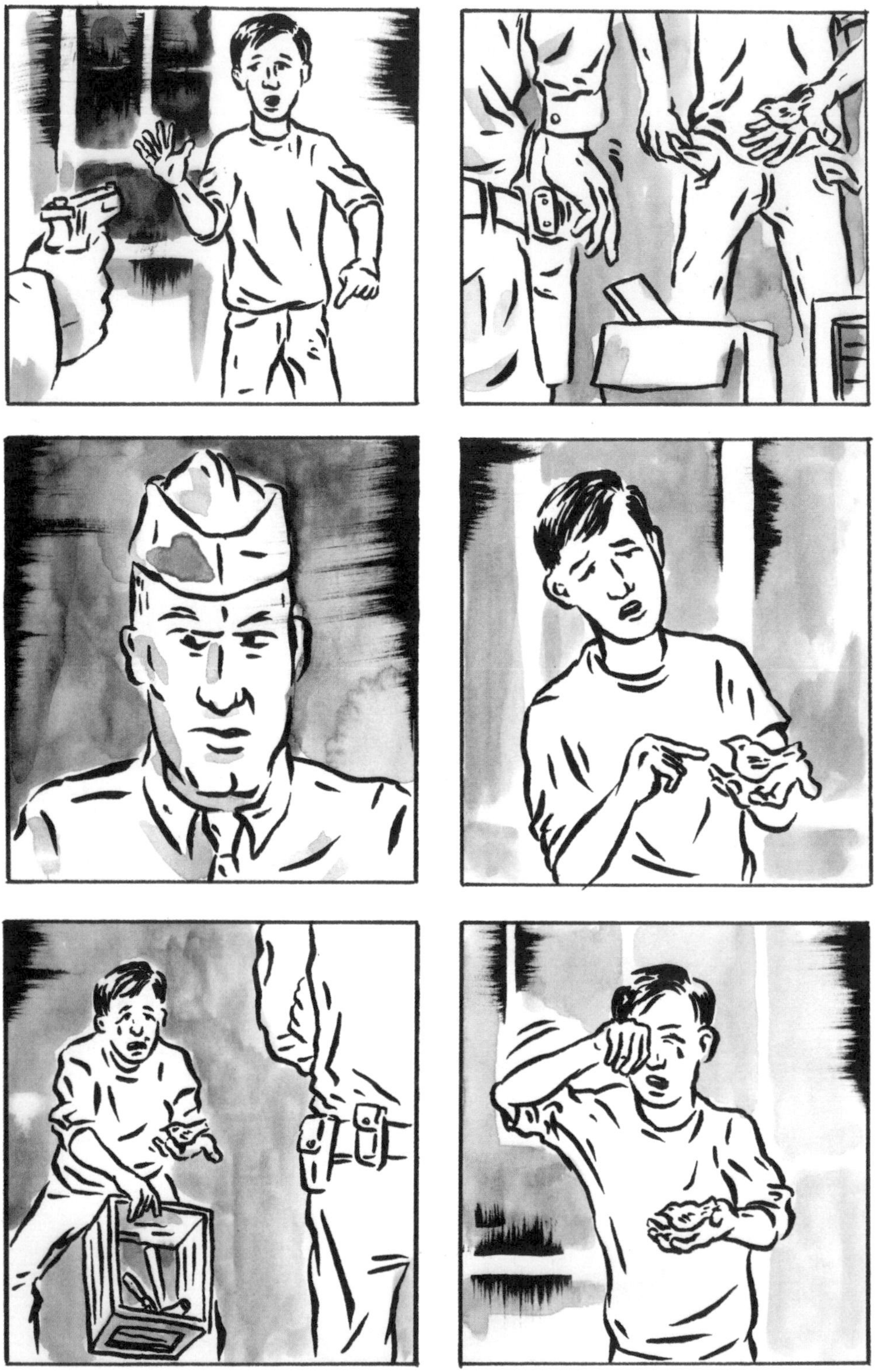

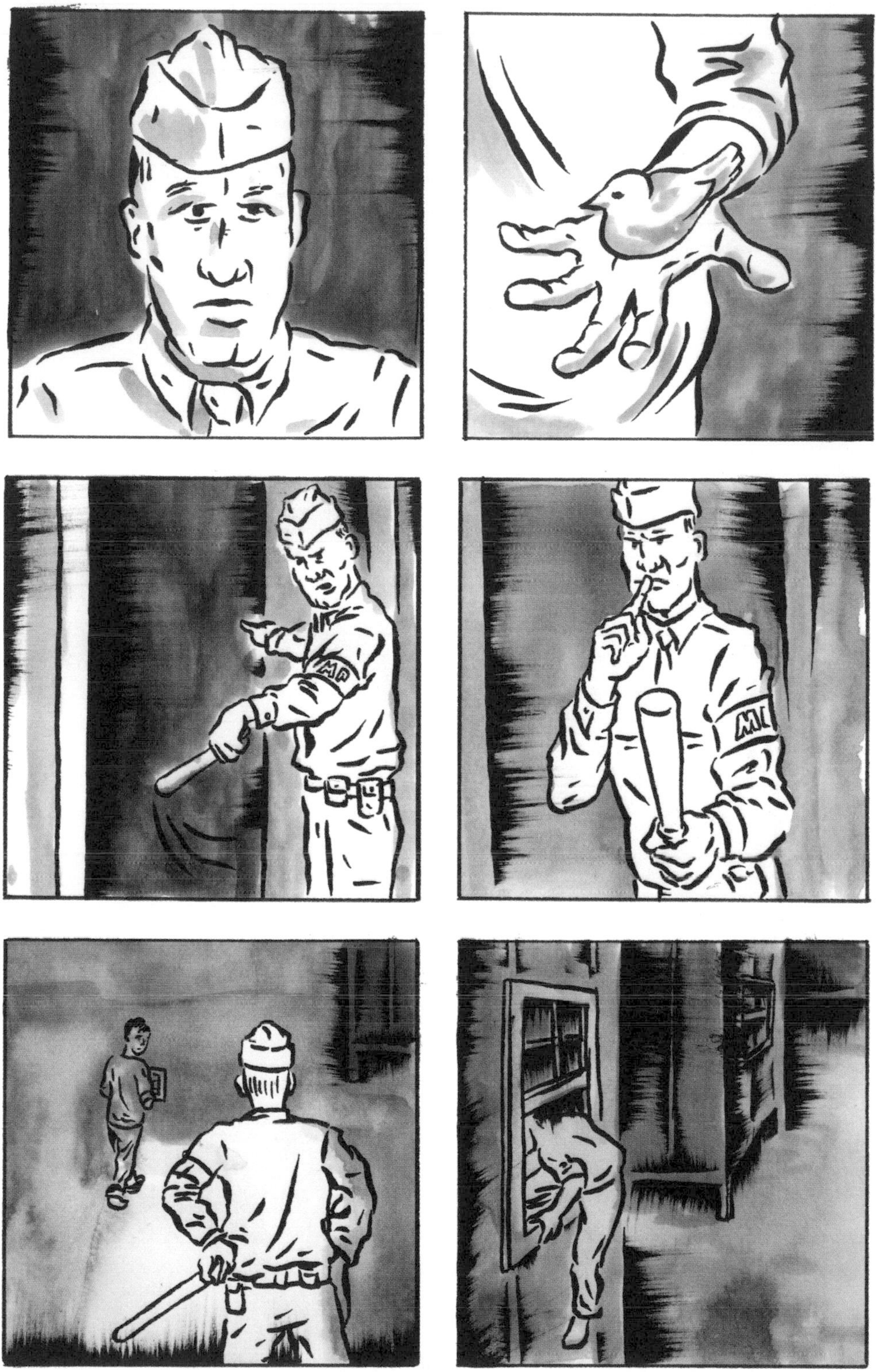
MP

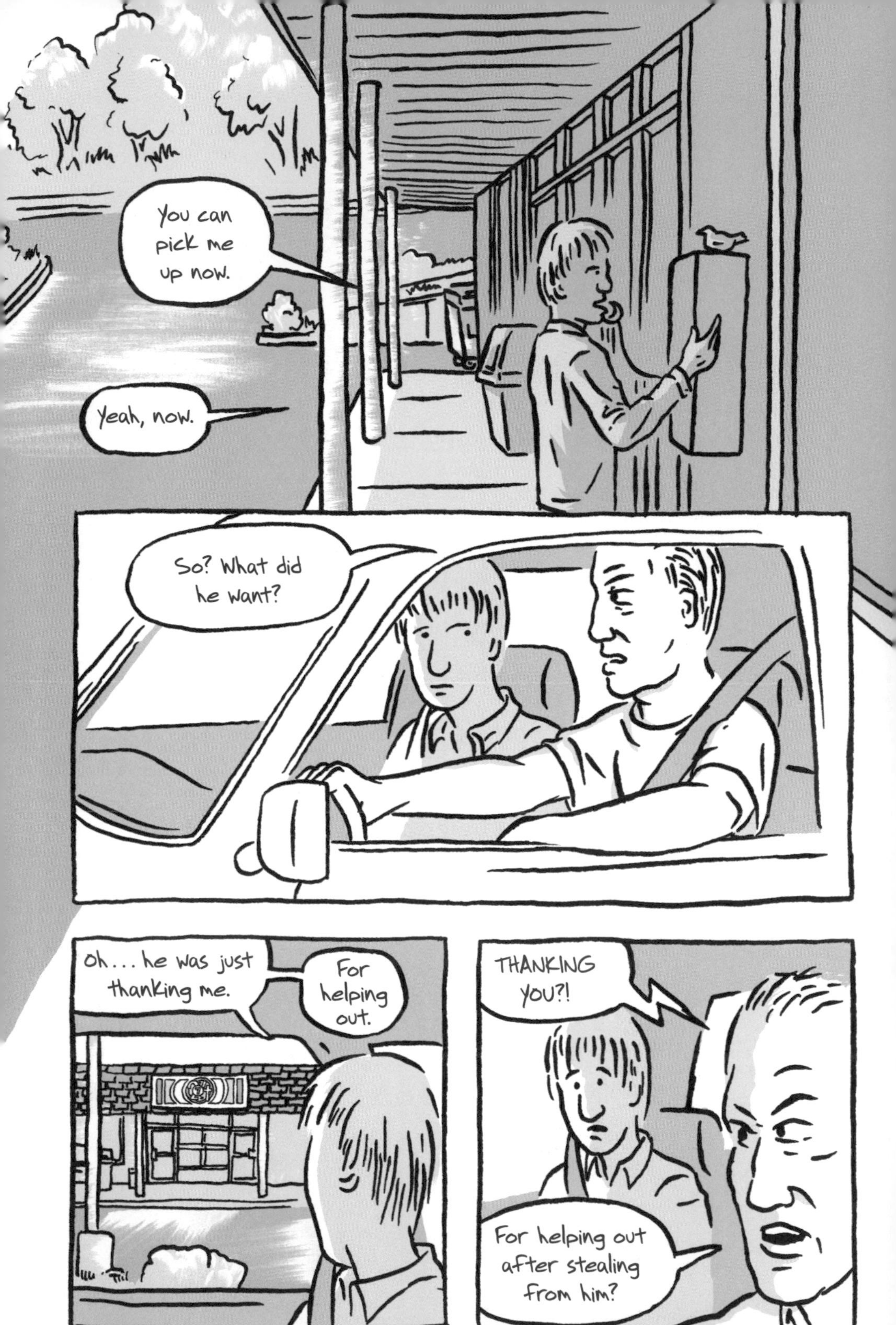
You can pick me up now.
Yeah, now.
So? What did he want?
Oh... he was just thanking me.
For helping out.
THANKING YOU?!
For helping out after stealing from him?

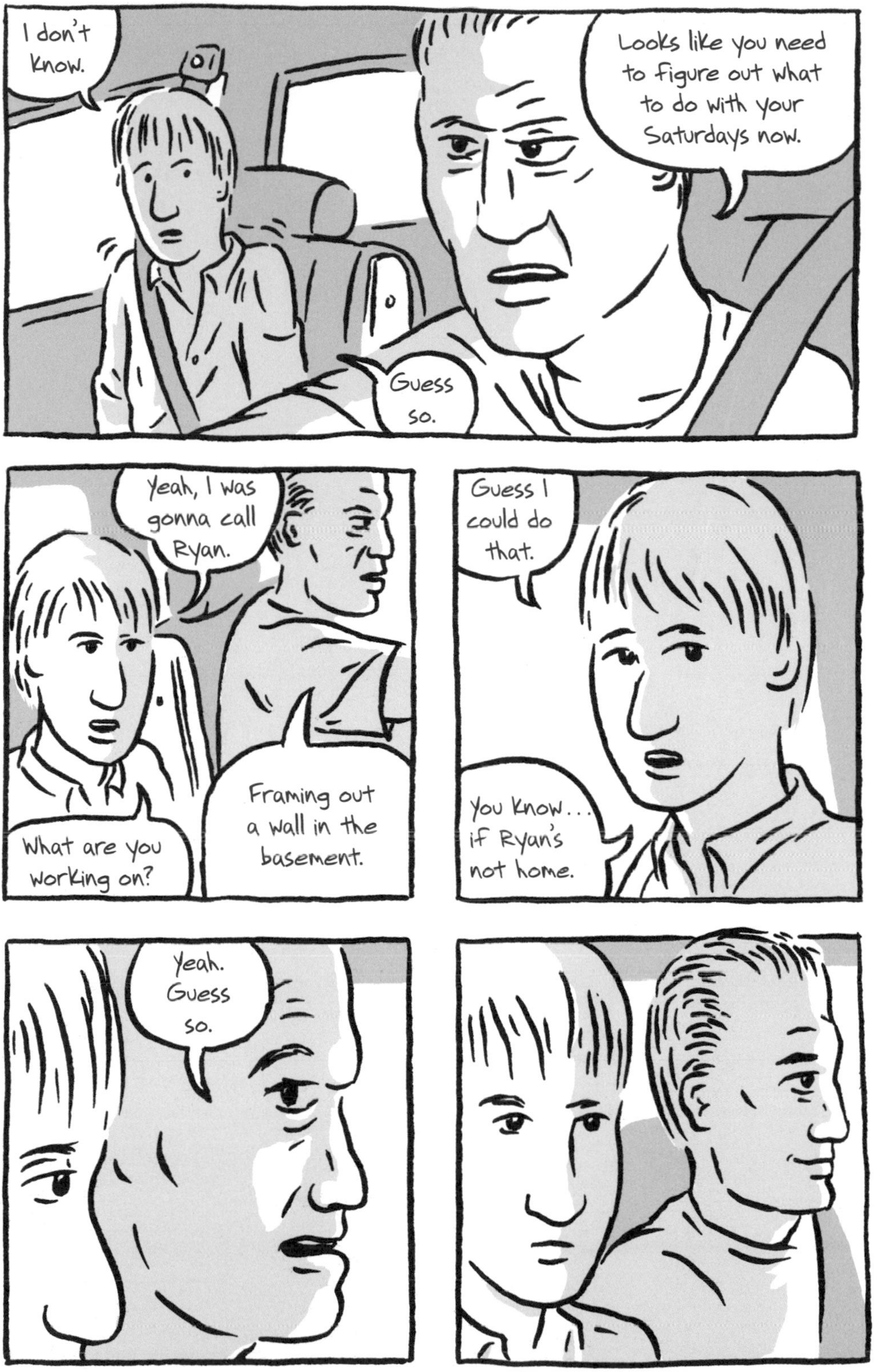
I don't know.
Looks like you need to figure out what to do with your Saturdays now.
Guess so.
Yeah, I was gonna call Ryan.
What are you working on?
Framing out a wall in the basement.
Guess I could do that.
You know... if Ryan's not home.
Yeah. Guess so.

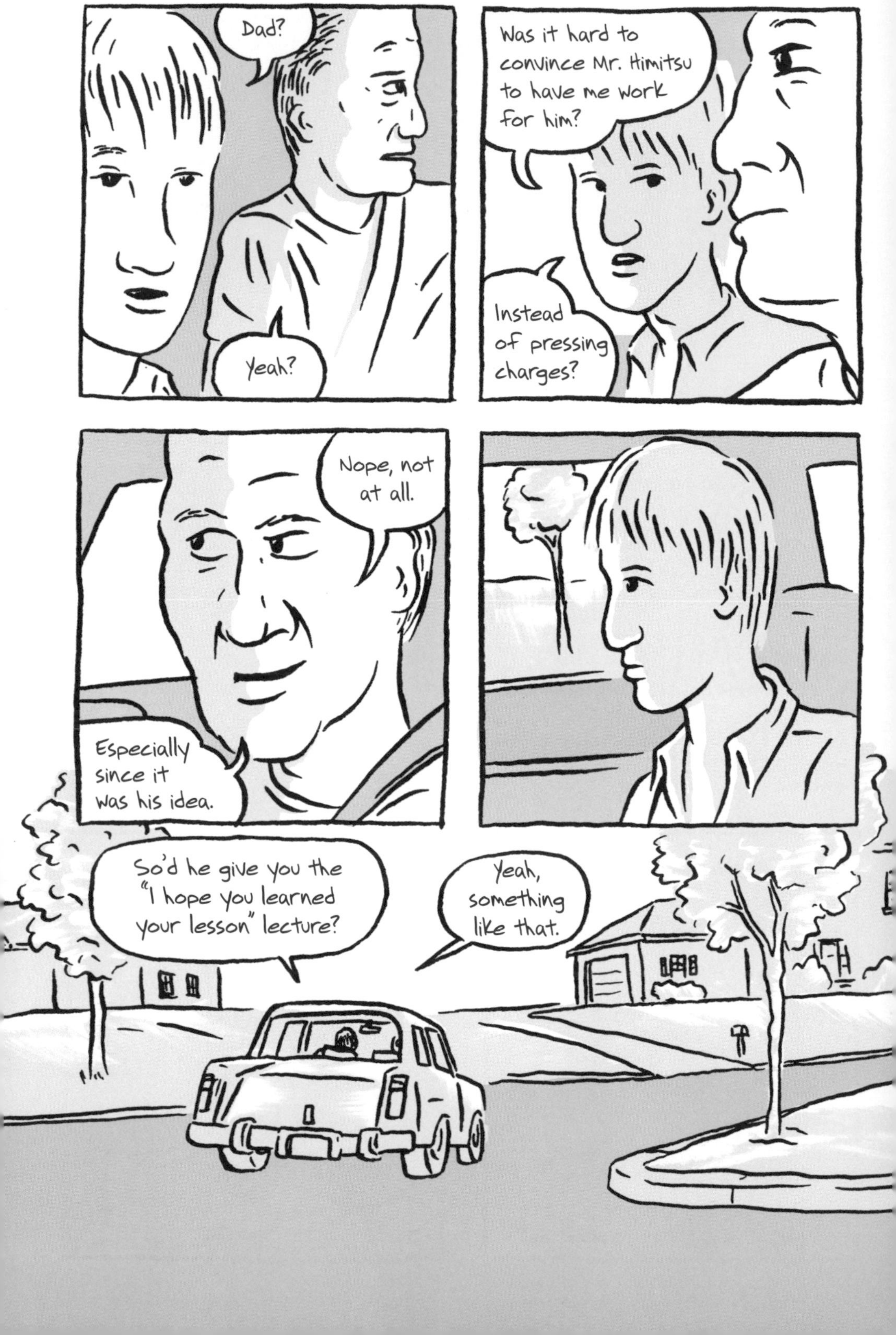
Dad?
Yeah?
Was it hard to convince Mr. Himitsu to have me work for him?
Instead of pressing charges?
Nope, not at all.
Especially since it was his idea.
So'd he give you the "I hope you learned your lesson" lecture?
Yeah, something like that.

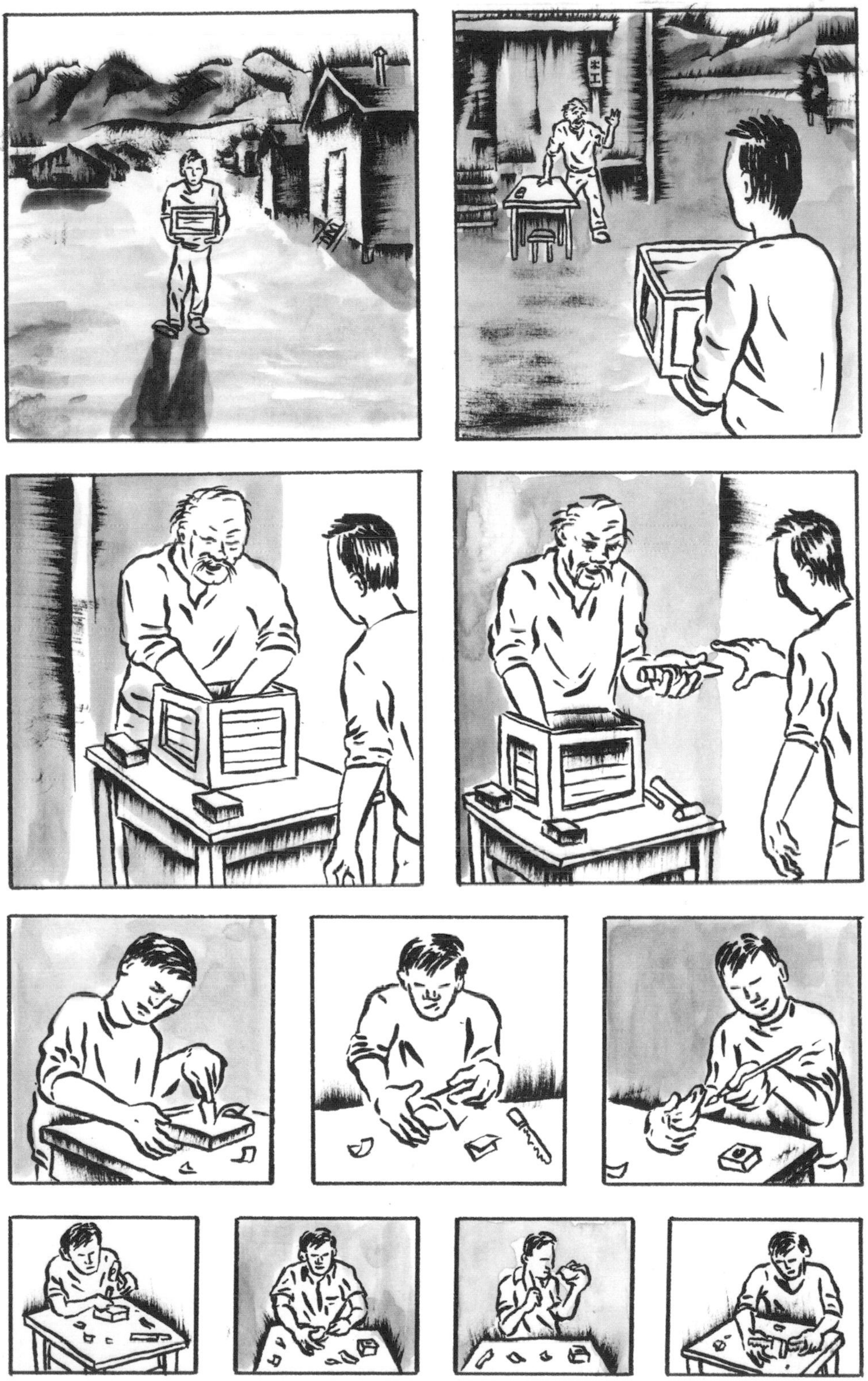

木工

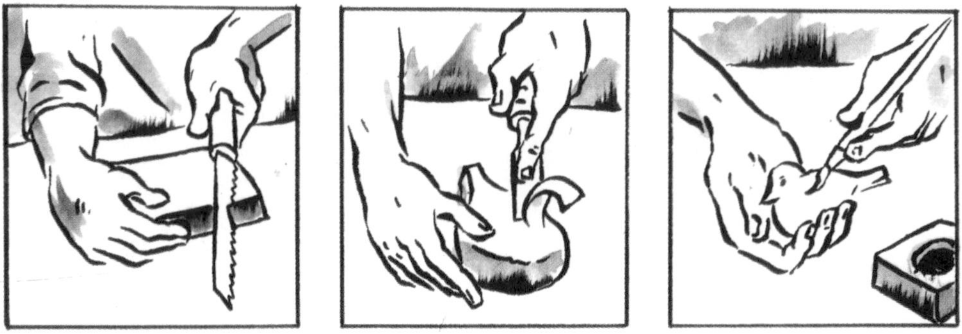

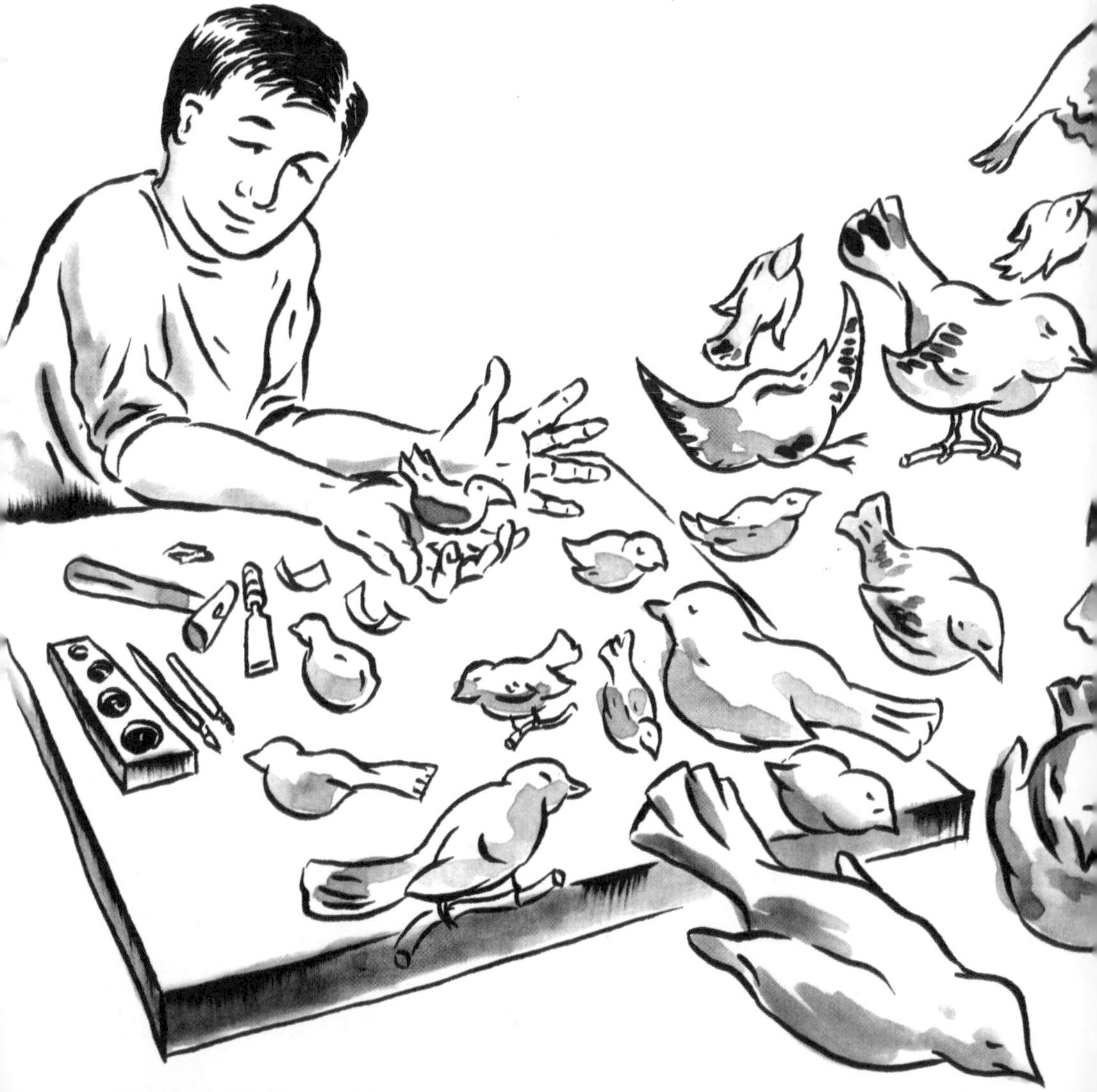

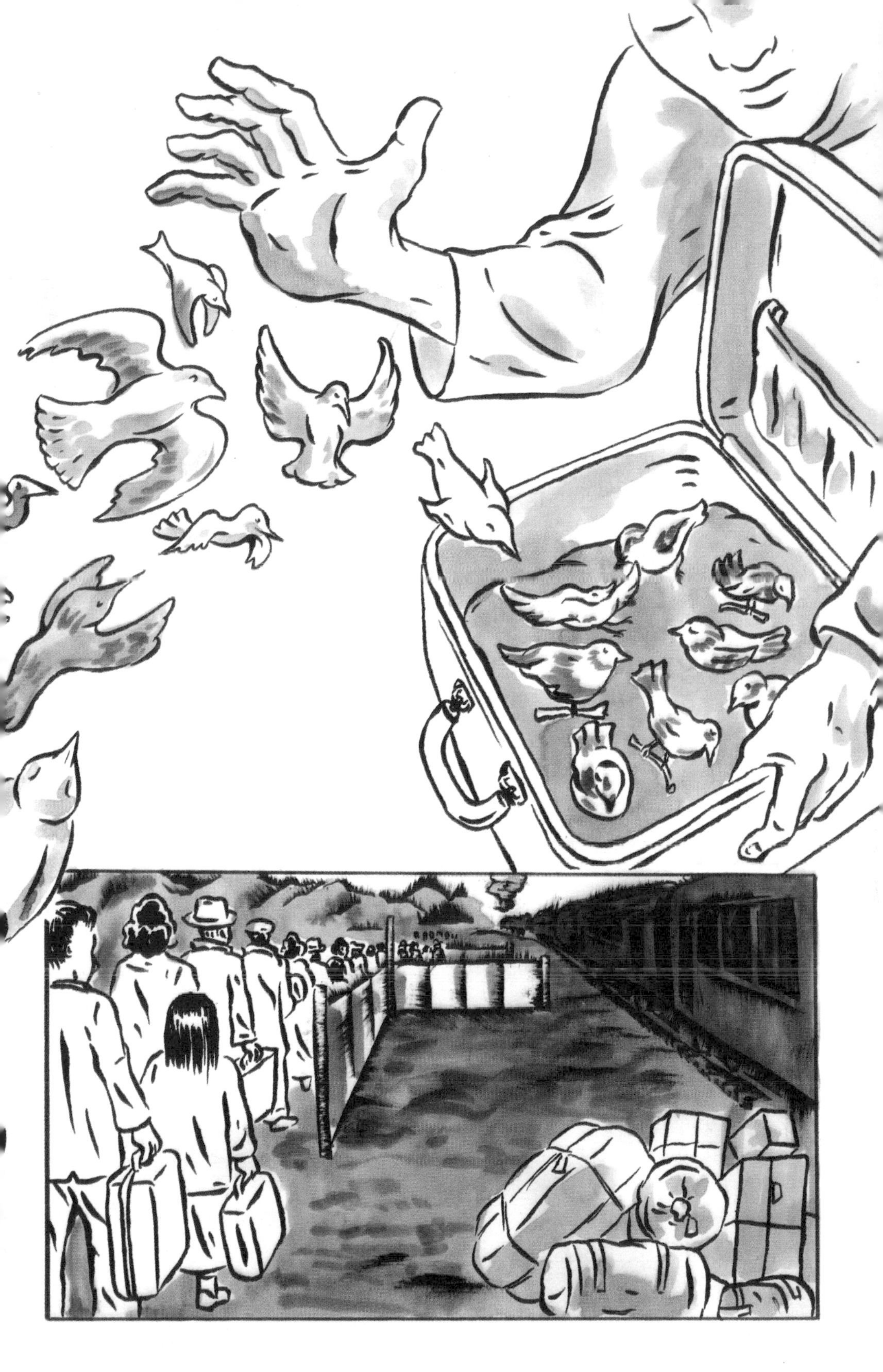

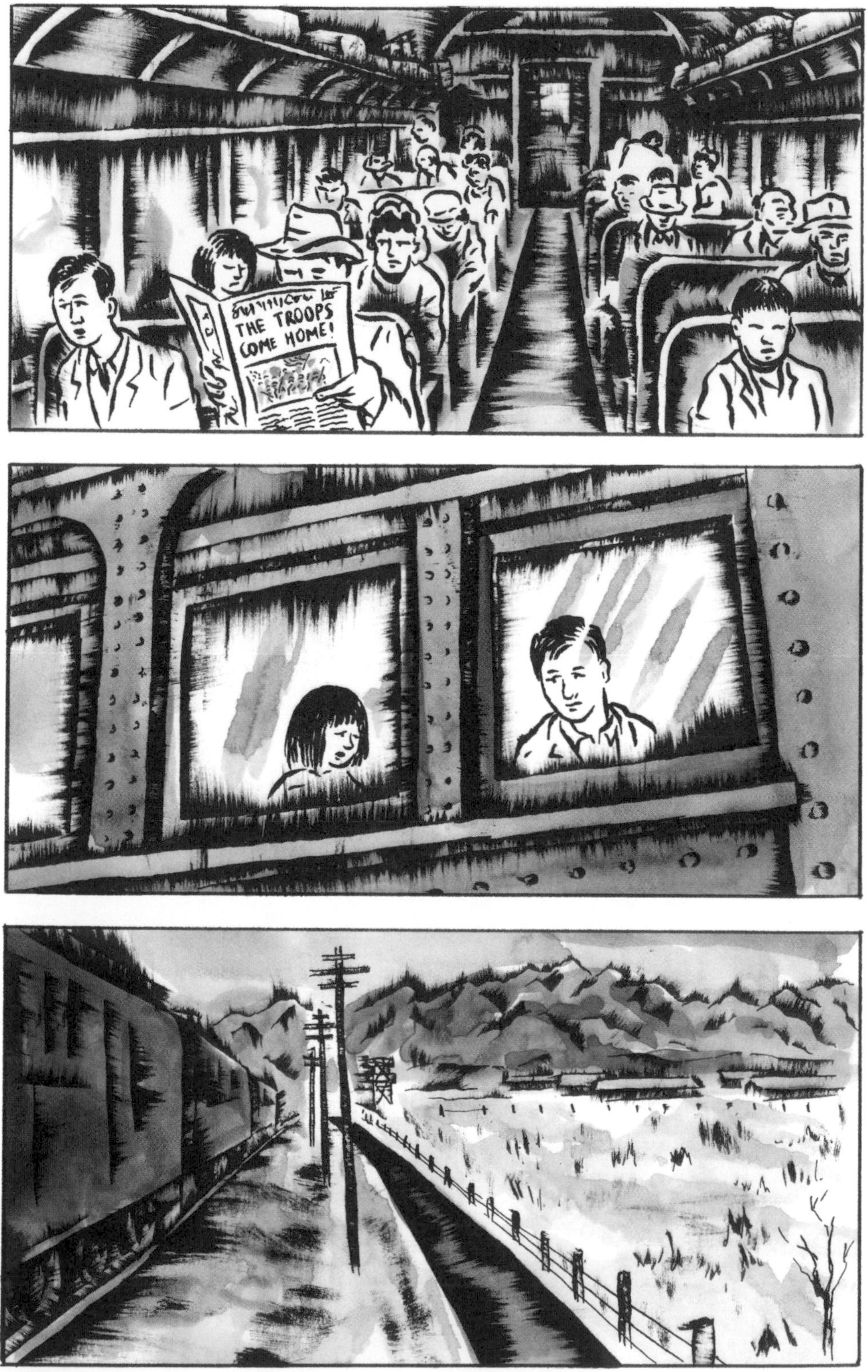
THE TROOPS
COME HOME!

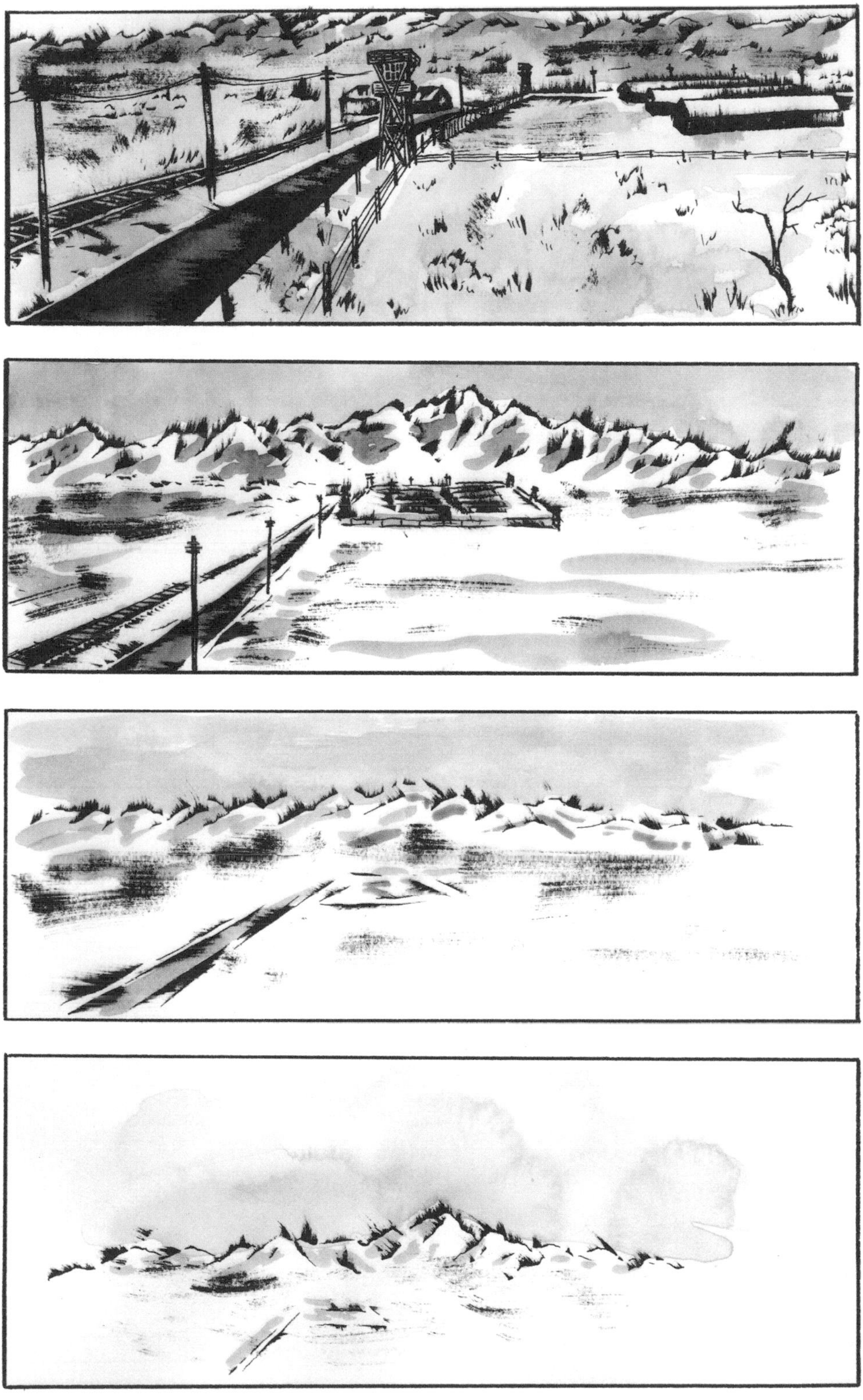

HISTORICAL NOTES

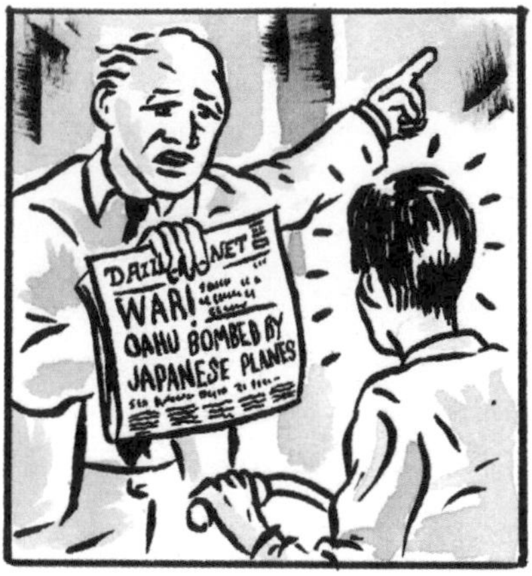
WAR!
OAHU BOMBED BY JAPANESE PLANES

ON THE MORNING of December 7, 1941, the Japanese air force bombed the United States naval base at Pearl Harbor, Hawaii. This act brought the United States into World War II. The FBI immediately began arresting Japanese-American community leaders such as priests, Japanese-language teachers, newspaper publishers, and heads of organizations. Thousands of Japanese-American homes on the West Coast were searched.

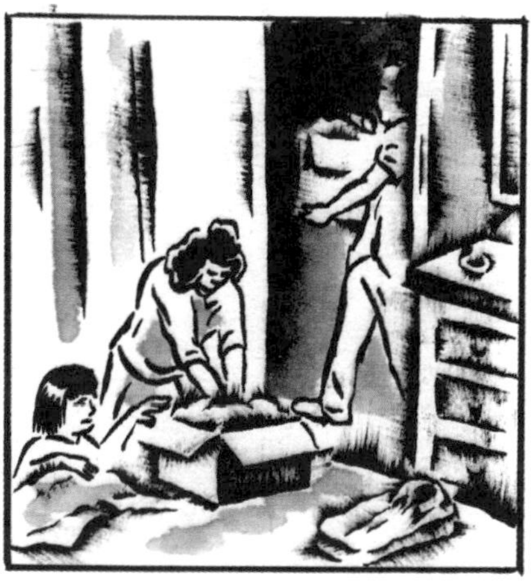

A little over two months after Pearl Harbor, on February 19, 1942, then president Franklin Delano Roosevelt (FDR) signed Executive Order 9066 authorizing military authorities to exclude civilians from any area without trial or hearing. This order paved the way for the internment of approximately 110,000 Japanese-American citizens and Japanese living along the Pacific Coast of the United States. Some families were forced to leave with as little as forty-eight hours' notice, resulting in a tremendous loss of property.

The internment happened in two stages. Initially, the evacuees were moved to assembly centers near major cities, where they were held until long-term internment camps could be built in more remote areas. The temporary assembly centers were located in such places as fairgrounds, racetracks, and migrant worker camps. People slept in converted offices, warehouses, pavilions, horse stables, or quickly constructed barracks. In late May 1942, the U.S. government began transferring the evacuees to specially built camps.

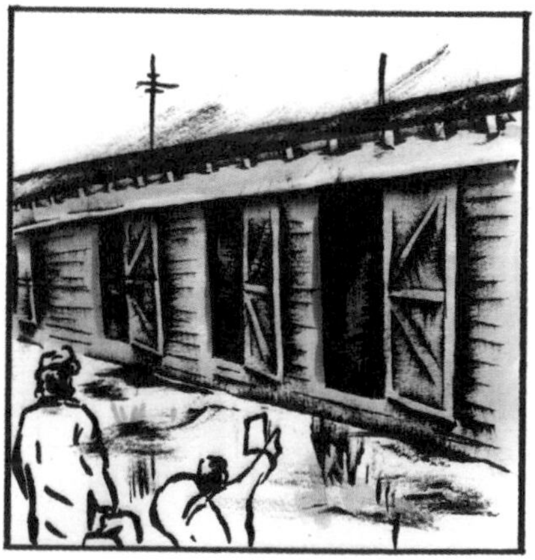

The internment camps, also known as relocation centers, were established in desolate, remote areas. Internees were housed in what was described in a 1943 War Relocation report as "tar-paper-covered barracks of simple frame construction without plumbing or cooking facilities of any kind." Mess halls and bathrooms were in separate buildings. Some locations were in areas where dust storms and extreme temperatures were common. Having been relocated from the West Coast, many people did not have appropriate clothing for the harsh winters.

Due to the camps' desolate and isolated locations, high-security fences were often not necessary. Armed guards were posted in guard towers, and there were some incidents of guards shooting internees who went beyond the fence. There were periodic inspections of internees' belongings, and potentially dangerous tools—chisels, knitting needles, saws—were confiscated, along with other contraband like radios, cameras, flashlights, and books written in Japanese.

Petty crime, previously little known among Japanese Americans, increased in the camps. Most of this crime concerned the stealing of scrap lumber, confiscated items, and food like fresh produce and meat from the camp authority's storerooms. "Everyone was hungry during the first months. Children filched potatoes from the warehouse whenever they got the chance. They would pack them in mud and then bake them in the desert," recounted Gene Oishi, who was a child in one of the camps. "Adults made nightly raids on government lumber supplies, with which they made furniture, shelves, and closets."

Many aspects of life in the camps led to a breakdown of the traditional family structures. Family mealtime, an important aspect of Japanese-American family life, ceased to exist in the relocation camps as children went off to eat meals with their friends. Many parents were first-generation immigrants (Issei) and had to rely on their American-born children (Nisei) to negotiate the English-only environment mandated at the camps. The lack of space in the barracks forced parents to have their children play outside.

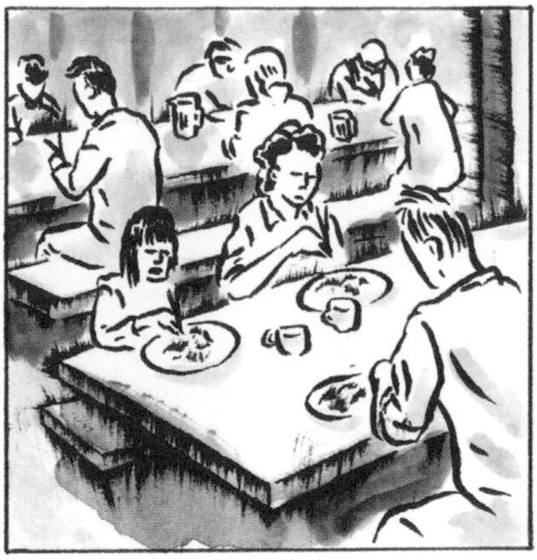

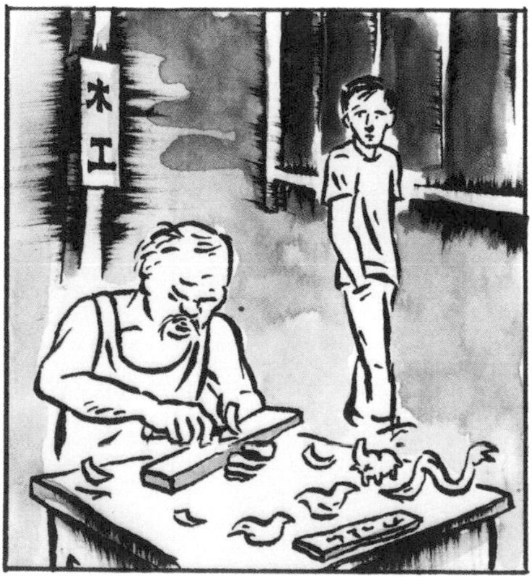
木工

Most available work in the camps went to younger adults, further isolating the older Issei. Unable to have any control over their situation and with hours of idleness on their hands, many of them turned to arts and crafts such as calligraphy, wood working, weaving, pottery, painting, stone carving, and artificial flower making. They used scavenged materials such as unraveled gunnysacks to make rugs, and they carved tiny animals out of peach pits or scrap lumber.

Author Delphine Hirasuna, a third-generation Japanese American (Sansei) and daughter of internees, has called this the art of *gaman,* a Japanese word that means "enduring the seemingly unbearable with patience and dignity."

As the war progressed, it became increasingly obvious that Japanese-American citizens posed no threat to the war effort. In fact, thousands of Nisei men and women, despite their internment, volunteered and served in the U.S. military.

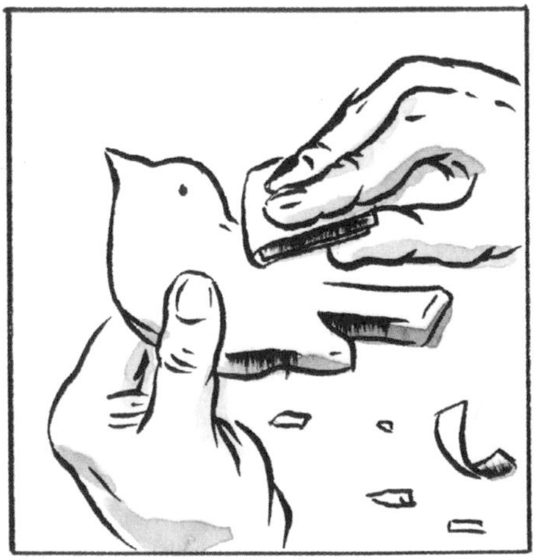

In December 1944, the U.S. Supreme Court ruled that no American citizen, regardless of cultural descent, could be detained without cause, thus ending the internment. Each internee was given twenty-five dollars and a train ticket home. Many returned to find their homes and farms in  disrepair and their stored possessions stolen. Forty-four years later, in 1988, the U.S. government issued a formal apology and provided for redress payments of twenty thousand dollars for each of the Japanese-American citizens detained, during World War II, in violation of the U.S. Constitution.

BIBLIOGRAPHY

Girdner, Audrie, and Anne Loftis. *The Great Betrayal: The Evacuation of the Japanese-Americans During World War II.* London: Macmillan, 1969.

Gordan, Linda, and Gary Y. Okihiro, editors. *Impounded: Dorothea Lange and the Censored Images of the Japanese American Internment.* New York: W.W. Norton, 2006.

Hirasuna, Delphine. *The Art of Gaman: Arts and Crafts from the Japanese American Internment Camps.* Berkeley, CA: Ten Speed Press, 2005.

Houston, Jeanne Wakatsuki, and James D. Houston, *Farewell to Manzanar.* Boston: Houghton Mifflin, 1973.

Kikuchi, Charles. *The Kikuchi Diary: Chronicle from an American Concentration Camp.* John Modell, editor. Urbana: University of Illinois Press, 1973.

Okubo, Miné. *Citizen 13660.* Seattle: University of Washington Press, 1983.

Wehrey, Jane. *Images of America: Manzanar.* Charleston, SC: Arcadia Publishing, 2008.

Much information is available online as well; see especially the Japanese American Legacy Project (densho.org).

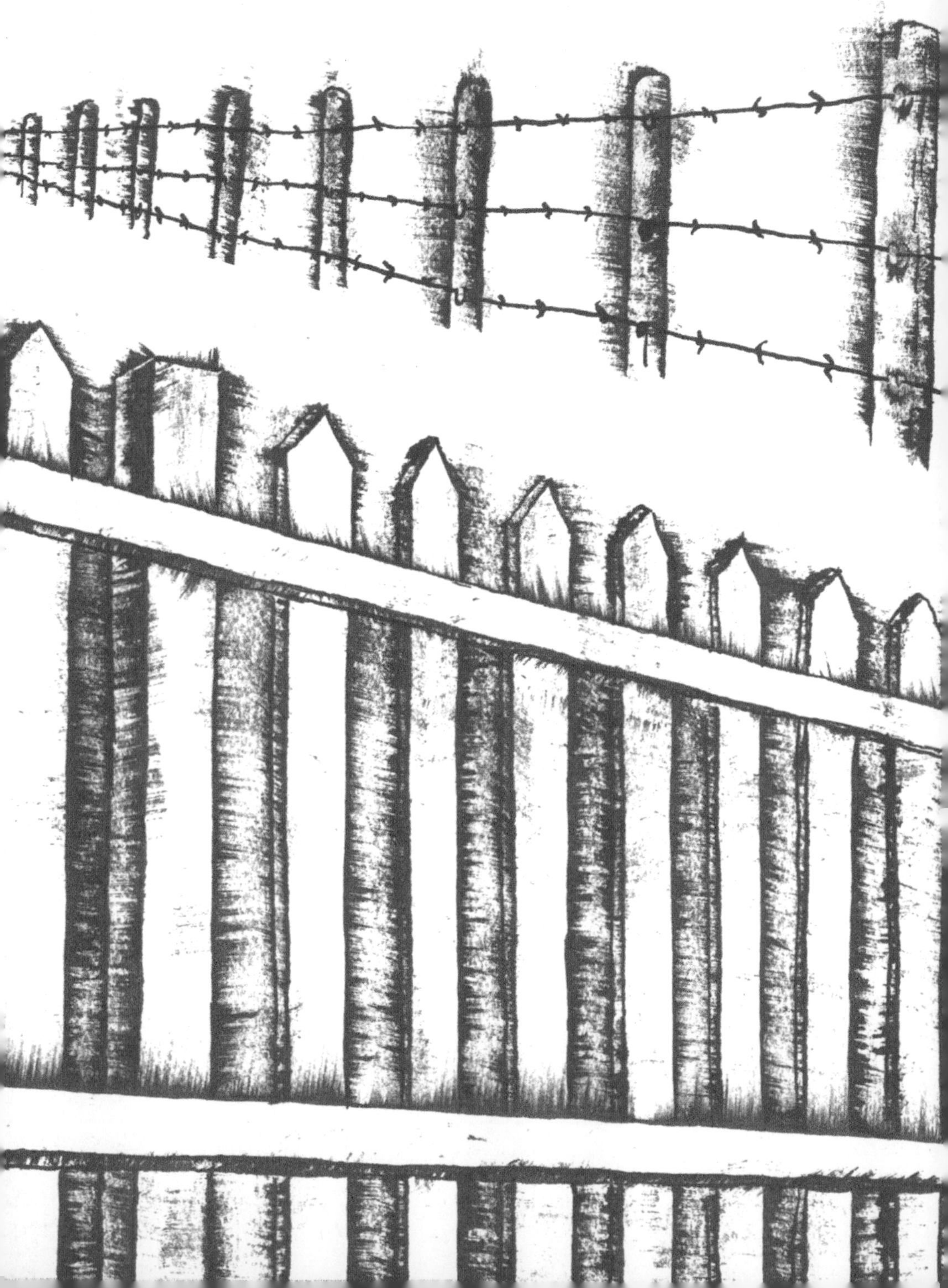